DATE DUE

SEP 27 2019	

The
KING'S
MERCY

Center Point
Large Print

Also by Lori Benton and available from
Center Point Large Print:

Many Sparrows

**This Large Print Book carries the
Seal of Approval of N.A.V.H.**

The KING'S MERCY

A NOVEL

LORI BENTON

CENTER POINT LARGE PRINT
THORNDIKE, MAINE

This Center Point Large Print edition
is published in the year 2019 by arrangement with
WaterBrook, an imprint of Random House, a division
of Penguin Random House LLC, New York.

All Scripture quotations are taken from the
King James Version.

The characters and events in this book are fictional,
and any resemblance to actual persons
or events is coincidental.

The text of this Large Print edition is unabridged.
In other aspects, this book may vary
from the original edition.
Printed in the United States of America
on permanent paper.
Set in 16-point Times New Roman type.

ISBN: 978-1-64358-291-7

Library of Congress Cataloging-in-Publication Data

Names: Benton, Lori, author.
Title: The king's mercy / Lori Benton.
Description: Center Point Large Print edition. | Thorndike, Maine :
    Center Point Large Print, 2019.
Identifiers: LCCN 2019020864 | ISBN 9781643582917 (hardcover :
    alk. paper)
Subjects: LCSH: Large type books.
Classification: LCC PS3602.E6974 K56 2019b | DDC 813/.6—dc23
LC record available at https://lccn.loc.gov/2019020864

Moreover it is required in stewards,
that a man be found faithful.
—1 CORINTHIANS 4:2

*This book is dedicated to my pastor,
Jon Courson, who for decades has taught
God's Word, chapter by chapter, book by book,
in a manner consistently practical and
profound—along the way inspiring more
than a few lines of dialogue that appear in
this story and in every story I've written.*

There will come a time when you believe everything is finished. That will be the beginning.

—LOUIS L'AMOUR

The
KING'S
MERCY

The EXILE

Summer 1747 — Spring 1748

Let every man seek his own safety
the best way he can.
—PRINCE CHARLES EDWARD STUART
to his defeated Jacobite army

1

July 1747
Cape Fear River, Colony of North Carolina

Alex MacKinnon roused to the press of wood beneath his cheek and an ominous churning in his gut. He tried to rise, but his hands were bound behind him. Without their aid he made it to his knees and, as the world spun in a blur of sunlit green, lost the contents of his stomach into mud-black water rushing past below. A powerful grip dragged him back onto rough planks. He felt solidness behind his back—curving barrel staves, hotly fragrant in the sweltering heat.

"Catch yo' breath," said a voice deep enough to have issued from a well's nethermost reaches. "Don't do no stupid."

Alex drew up his knees and dropped his head, then jerked as a lance of pain split his skull. Moving must be the *stupid* the well-bottom voice warned against.

"Still yo'self," it cautioned now.

Alex complied. The pain in his head receded to a pounding. Sweat stung what must be a gash at his temple. Dried blood stiffened his face. Arms, legs, torso all ached with the bruises left by blows. He'd been attacked.

"Ah, Demas," said another voice. "He's awake? Excellent. I was about to be concerned."

The speaker hadn't sounded concerned. He'd sounded downright blithe. And *English.*

The surface beneath Alex dipped. Nausea surged with the motion. This time he forced it back, eyes shut against the sun-glare.

"And here at last we've the tide to speed us along," the English voice added.

The scrape of wood on wood. Water splashing. Feet thumping boards. Men's voices rising and relaxing as at the end of prolonged exertion. All familiar. All wrong.

Alex opened his eyes. Though not yet high in the sky, the Carolina sun burned fierce. Bearing its assault, he took in what he made for the aft deck of a flatboat. Within his view a man, shirtless back a glistening blue-black, had hauled in a dripping pole and was stowing it along the deck rail, over which Alex had been sick. The vessel surged, picking up speed though none poled it now that he could see.

Alarmed, he looked out over silty water, expecting to see the merchant ship, *Charlotte-Ann*, riding at anchor beyond the smaller craft lining Wilmington's quay. He didn't see the quay. A tree-lined bank slid past, edged in mudflats dotted with quarreling seabirds.

They were on the river.

A throat's clearing curtailed his observations.

Squinting, Alex made out the Englishman seated on a crate shaded by a cabin in the craft's center. He wore no coat or hat, but his breeches and waistcoat were cut of good cloth and fit his trim person well. With dark hair smoothly tailed, he bore no trace of sweat on his brow, as if the neckcloth knotted below his chin didn't smother him. He looked not yet thirty.

The man bared good teeth in a smile, an expression that took his unremarkable features—longish nose, thin lips, hazel eyes overshadowed by strong brows—and rearranged them into a mask of disarming appeal.

He'd seen the man before. Alex closed his eyes, searching his memory for that face, and found it.

His eyes flew open. "Ye've made a mistake! I'd an agreement with the ship's master. Captain Bingham will tell ye . . ." But Bingham wouldn't. The *Charlotte-Ann*'s captain was complicit in this. Minding that now, too, Alex strained against his bindings. Could he pitch himself overboard, hope to reach the bank?

"I wouldn't try it," the Englishman advised. "Alligators infest these waters. You missed the last sighting. Quite the sizeable specimen."

Alligators. Alex had yet to see one of the fearsome beasts since they'd begun their piloted journey into Wilmington's sandbar-riddled harbor, but the *Charlotte-Ann*'s crew had encountered them on voyages past. His sweating scalp

15

crawled at the thought of jagged teeth closing over him, powerful jaws dragging him under the river's dark surface. Still, he'd rather face that battle than what awaited him at this riverine journey's end.

He made it halfway to his feet before the massive hand that had steadied him before clutched his neck from behind. Alex bucked and thrashed, in the process glimpsing the African who had hold of him. He sucked in air, or tried to. Thick fingers squeezed. Just as he felt himself sliding into darkness, the grip on his neck eased.

The Englishman in the shade had watched, unperturbed. "Demas once snapped a man's neck one-handed—so I've heard. Promise to cease thrashing about and I'll bid him release you. Then we'll discuss your situation like civilized men."

Glaring, Alex jerked his chin against the gripping fingers.

At a glance from the Englishman, his throat was released. The African hunkered within arm's reach, powerful hands loose between thighs like tree trunks.

Alex concentrated on breathing, forcing swallows past what felt like rocks lodged in his throat.

The Englishman raised a brow. "*Are* you a civilized man? I know you for a Jacobite, one of those Stuart rebels King George defeated . . . When was it? A year since?"

16

Alex might have told him to the day.

"Alastair Seamus MacKinnon by name, according to your papers," the Englishman went on. "Well, MacKinnon, I'm Phineas Reeves, and this craft we occupy belongs to Severn, the plantation for which we're bound. The journey will take the day long. Perhaps into the night. Time enough for us to become acquainted."

"It wasna meant to be *me,*" Alex ground out. "Take me back."

"To Wilmington? We're miles upriver, moving with the tide. Even were we not, Captain Bingham has no further claim on you. You're indentured to a new master."

The gut-churn threatened. "D'ye not mean yourself? Ye're the owner of the *Charlotte-Ann.*"

"Me? I'm but his overseer. A hired man, as is Captain Bingham. As for the prisoners brought over from London—including yourself—it was from their number the *Charlotte-Ann*'s owner was to have first pick. Surely Bingham informed you of the arrangement."

"He gave me to think otherwise."

"That would explain the difficulty we had in extricating you." Something akin to contrition crossed Phineas Reeves's face. "I was sent downriver to meet the *Charlotte-Ann* and bring back a likely man for Severn. You seemed exceedingly so to me, and Captain Bingham was agreeable to the choice. He'd sold the rest of his indentures before we started upriver, and I must return with someone. You can appreciate my position."

The shock of it was stunning. Reeves's voice cut through it like the jabs of a blade.

"I regret the headache you must be enduring. I'm afraid Demas doesn't know his strength."

Recalling the careful clenching of that massive hand at his throat, Alex took leave to disagree.

"This should help." Reeves held out a canteen. Too thirsty to refuse, Alex took it and drank while the man nattered on. "It occurs to me I haven't named your master. Edmund Philip Carey, Captain of His Majesty's Royal Navy, retired. His last command was the frigate *Severn*, for which his plantation is named."

Ceasing to listen, Alex looked round him again with aching eyes. The men piloting the barge were a motley lot: black, white, somewhere between, one possibly a red Indian. He knew little of the natives of this New World. Purportedly fierce, warlike, prone to taking a man's scalp off his head—if his fellow seamen were to be credited. Reckoning himself safe enough from scalping at present, he cast a bleary gaze across the wide river at the shoreline passing in a green tangle, raised the canteen to his lips, and drained it as dry as his plummeting hope.

Why had he trusted Bingham—an Englishman—after everything?

". . . and that's where I first met Captain Carey.

I was a cabin boy aboard the *Severn* . . . in another lifetime." Reeves, still chattering away, smiled again as Alex flicked him a glance. "Doubtless you're wondering what Captain Carey means to do with *you* for the next seven years."

He hadn't entertained the faintest curiosity. Until now.

"Plantations on the river tend toward the sprawling, thousands of acres, and so require to be self-supporting. Severn has its coopers, millers, carpenters. It *had* a blacksmith, until six months ago when an unfortunate accident rendered the fellow unfit for the work. That's where you come into it, MacKinnon. You're to be trained in the smith's art. I chose you for your size. You're the first man I've seen who comes close to matching Demas's physique. Perhaps with another stone or two of meat on those long bones, you shall."

Reeves grinned as though he'd delivered the best possible news.

Seven years. His strength spent at an Englishman's pleasure, without even the freedom of the sea. Demas seemed to sense the impulse to escape that again swept through him. The African tensed, but when Alex made no move, he settled again, hands loosening from the fists he'd made of them. Fists like hammers.

That was meant to be his lot. Hammers and fire and glowing iron. *Seven years.*

19

On his side again with the sun beating down like a forge's fire, grief and rage flowed over him. He was well and truly a prisoner in that godforsaken place, though why should that surprise? God had forsaken him months ago on a moor near Inverness.

16 April 1746
Culloden Moor, Scotland

From the first cannon's thundering, then the screaming charge that carried the Highland army into the Duke of Cumberland's scarlet lines, the battle had been bloody bedlam. Alex MacKinnon had slain too many men to count, with never attention to spare beyond the reach of his broadsword; just now a redcoat had his blade tip caught in its woven guard. Giving the sword a violent twist, Alex snapped the snagged blade clean. Wrenched nearly off his feet, the redcoat left his throat exposed above a muddied stock. Alex had only his sword arm free. The other gripped his uncle. Wounded by the redcoat before Alex could intervene, Rory MacNeill sagged against him, a gash opened deep in his thigh.

Raging against exhaustion as much as his foe, Alex roared with the effort needed to swing his blade across that exposed English neck. The redcoat slumped, dead before he hit the ground.

With the shout that carried him through the deed dying on his lips, Alex had space to look about. It was chaos on the moor, curtained in the gray of powder smoke and sleet. Icy needles flayed his cheeks as he squinted to see men reeling, locked in combat with sword and dirk, halberd and bayonet. Their screams mingled with the keening wind that cut through soaked linen, leather, even wool. Somewhere an officer shouted, gathering men—to fight or flee there was no telling. Around him lay the slain.

When no more redcoats loomed from the mist to challenge him, Alex thought of refuge, a place to lay his uncle, tend that gaping wound. At once he saw it, a dip in the moorland where the fighting had passed. He made out a blur of green farther along: pines, scrawny and wind-stunted. Shelter enough.

Strands of his uncle's hair whipped Alex's face as he grappled for a better hold. Pain tightened Rory MacNeill's voice as his hand clamped his thigh. "I'll manage, lad—dinna slow yourself on my account."

Alex drove his heels into the muddy turf to stay upright. "*Wheest*, Uncle. Let me help ye."

Rain had collected at the depression's base, along with bodies. Red-stained water gushed icy through Alex's cracked shoes as they wove their way, Rory cursing Charles Stuart with every step. As he ought to have been cursing Alex.

Surrounded by the fallen, plaids blending with moor grass and heather, he kent his uncle had been right to abide by the MacNeill's will. Their chief had dithered away the months of the Stuart campaign to retake the English throne for the exiled King James, neither lending the Jacobite cause support nor openly censuring it. Thinking himself wiser at twenty-two than Rory at nine-and-forty, Alex had crossed to Skye, joined his father's MacKinnon clan, and marched away to restore King James to the throne. Without the blessing of uncle, chief, or any saint he'd ever prayed to.

At Inverness, days ago, Rory had found him, tried again to persuade him from his course, knowing the ill turn the campaign had taken. Alex had given his oath to the House of Stuart. Men depended upon him. Did his uncle expect him to do other than hold to his word, having raised him to count it his bond?

Rory had thinned his lips, said no more, and stayed to fight beside him, but devil take him now if Alex meant to let the man *die* beside him too.

They made it to the pine thicket before Rory's knees buckled.

With his towering frame a throwback to the raiding Norseman who had been his several-times great-grandfather, Alex MacKinnon was no wee man, but Rory MacNeill shared his blood and the older man was a deal heavier. He slipped from Alex's hold and landed hard. The blood snaking through the fingers clutching his thigh thinned in a spate of freezing rain.

From the pines a corbie's cry erupted like a pistol's crack, a warning Alex was too slow to heed.

Needled boughs swept aside as a wall of scarlet coats burst from the thicket. He'd no time to raise his sword before pain burst at the back of his skull. There came an instant of blinding light, then darkness closed like a tunnel, at its end his uncle's face, twisted in pain and helpless fury, blood on the hands reaching for him.

2

July 1747
Cape Fear River

Alex jerked awake aboard the flatboat, poled upriver now against an ebbing tide. The sun hung above the towering trees through which the river snaked, its light falling aslant. He still smelled the salt marsh of the river's mouth, but stronger now on the humid air hung the tang of pine resin. Iridescent dragonflies darted at the river's edge. Mosquitoes clouded its surface. Some had landed on his sweating flesh and stuck there, sprinkled in the blond hairs of his forearms.

"Awake again?" the Englishman, Reeves, asked, stepping into view between a row of crates and the flatboat's cabin. "May I trust to your docility?"

Alex's hands had been freed while he slept, but the African hovered near, dark face gleaming. Rubbing at his wrists, Alex jerked a nod. Reeves held out another canteen. Alex took it and drank, getting his bearings. Along the craft's side two men drove poles into the river and pushed against the current. Voices issued from the cabin, sounding as men did when gaming. Reeves, the former seaman, had them on watches. The bell for Alex's own would soon be sounding aboard the *Charlotte-Ann*, if he was any judge of time.

Accepting the canteen once Alex drank his fill, Reeves took a seat on the bench beside the cabin. "It's a fine forge where you'll be trained, a well-appointed smithy," he began, continuing their earlier conversation as if there'd been no pause. "Though the work is limited to Severn's needs, that's plenty to be getting on with."

Alex stared at the riverbank sliding by. They were passing a plantation now. A break in the trees revealed a stretch of land planted in what must be Indian corn, leaves like sword blades waving. Nearer was a dock intended for craft smaller than their laden vessel. Against his will, curiosity kindled.

"What manner of plantation is—Severn, did ye call it? Rice? Indigo?" He'd heard those crops were grown in the Carolinas.

Reeves flashed a gratified smile. "Neither. Captain Carey manufactures naval stores—tar, pitch. Lumber too. Most of Severn's acreage is long-leaf pine, but close by the Big House, corn is grown, tobacco, flax for Miss Carey's weavers."

"Miss Carey?"

Reeves's smile twitched. "She's the captain's eldest daughter. Stepdaughter, to be precise. Though Miss Carey is mistress of Severn, Charlotte is the captain's true daughter."

"Charlotte? Has she yellow hair?"

Surprise brightened Reeves's eyes. "How could you—ah, of course. The *Charlotte-Ann*'s figurehead bears her likeness. A pretty girl, Charlotte. Everyone adores . . ." Reeves shifted a glance at Demas, then picked up smoothly, "Severn isn't the largest plantation on the Cape Fear, but it is of respectable acreage. Three slave gangs work the forest. A smaller gang runs the lumber mill— have I mentioned the mill? There are carpenters and coopers, a groom and some stable lads. Between the house, kitchen, and the weaving sheds, Miss Carey oversees twenty or so, women and girls, those too old to work elsewhere. I'm kept occupied overseeing the captain's business interests."

"What, then, does he do?" Alex interjected.

"Captain Carey? I suppose he oversees me." Reeves hesitated, then waved an apologetic hand. "An egregious oversimplification. There's much for a man of Captain Carey's station to manage. He cannot daily run hither and yon across the breadth of occupation Severn encompasses."

Alex raised a brow. "It's ye does the running hither?"

Reeves's mouth curved, as though the question amused. "It is. And I'd do more than that for the man. I owe Captain Carey everything. He took me in a year ago when I had next to nothing, treated me better than I merited . . ."

"Oh, aye?" Alex asked, catching another shift of those hazel eyes.

Reeves hesitated. "It's only . . . He isn't the man I knew aboard the *Severn*. He's also recently retired as a justice of the peace for the New Hanover court. It may be his years in that capacity showed him too much of human nature's less desirable aspects. Such is bound to leave a man jaded."

Never mind this Captain Carey, generous *and* jaded; Alex was having trouble enough taking Reeves's measure. The man talked too much. Was it fear motivating this chatter, fear that Reeves would feel the brunt if the new indenture he'd chosen failed to fall agreeably in line with his master's designs?

Perhaps so; Reeves chose that moment to produce a document from inside the coat he'd laid on the bench. The indenture.

May 1746
Inverness, Scotland

The surface beneath him heaved. His belly echoed the motion, spewing forth the oat gruel they fed those condemned to hell—and hell it must be. He'd spent his life on the sea in boats and never felt such a ruckus in his innards. *God have mercy.*

Memories surfaced. The shivering torment of naked stone—was that a kirk, where they put them after the battle? The dark and dank of a ship at anchor. Crowded flesh unwashed and festering. His uncle's face swam through the fractured images. Like Alex, Rory MacNeill had been stripped to his shirt—plaid, belt, shoes, sporran, anything of value confiscated. His uncle's wound was never stitched, the gash held closed by a strip of soiled shirting. He could lend Alex no support, struggling himself to remain standing when forced to it.

"Come, lad. They'll have us on our feet again. Let's show these Lobsters they canna best a Barra man." His uncle's voice lapped across his mind like waves on a shingle. "A minute more on your feet. Feel the sea air. Breathe it in. Clear the cobwebs, does it?" It hadn't. Still, he'd clung to the voice like a drowning man and shuffled forward. Light as bright as blades. Gulls screeching fit to pierce his skull. The shove of strangers' hands. Groans of suffering. The roiling. The thirst. "Rest ye now. I'm here with ye, Alex . . ."

Alex MacKinnon. His name. His father's clan, though he'd lived all but his first years among the MacNeills of Barra, harvesting the fish, pasturing the cattle, riding with his uncle to collect the quit-rents for their chief. He was twenty-two . . . no, it must be three-and-twenty now, an unworthy nephew to the man who took him to hearth and heart, orphaned at three.

"Uncle?"

A clink of metal beside him. "Aye, lad. They've kept us together."

Together in the stench and chill of a ship's hold. He could barely see the contours of his uncle's face, high in the cheek and brow as his own, beard grizzled with an old man's gray though he was now but fifty.

"We're alive, then?"

A low dry chuckle, familiar as sight. "Looks to be we are. Though I'll not argue if ye wish to call this hell."

Guilt weighed like a cairn. "I'm sorry."

His uncle's hand, rough and cold, closed over his arm. "Ye did as your conscience bid ye, lad. Ye've always had that about ye, a need for a purpose beyond yourself. 'Tis the Almighty knit ye so. Besides, 'twas I chose to stand with ye at the end."

A groan rose somewhere near. The wheeze of labored breathing. They weren't alone. Alex moved his legs, felt the pull of chain; his ankles were manacled to the timbers enclosing them in near darkness. "How long since the battle?"

"Tomorrow marks Beltane. We lie at anchor, still at Inverness."

A fortnight. He absorbed that as Rory bridged the gap for him. After the redcoats came boiling from the pines and bashed his head, they'd been trussed and tossed into a cart bound for part of the field where the measured crack of gunfire bespoke execution. Then, for no reason Rory could fathom, the driver had taken a turn in the track. They'd left the moor to jostle over miles to Inverness. There, forced inside a kirk crowded with shivering, wounded Jacobites, they'd languished for two days lacking food and water, another eight without doctoring.

"Why did they not shoot us on the field? Some soldier's notion of mercy?"

"Nay," croaked a stranger's voice. "None but a blackhearted cur would have spared ye a quick death to rot in this hold."

If it was a jest, no one laughed.

"Ye've been in and out of the mist all this while," Rory told Alex in lower tones. "I've been that afraid ye'd never come full out."

Hip and shoulder as well as head throbbing, Alex sat up. His own stench overpowered. Humiliation washed him in a foul wave. He flinched when Rory touched him again. "What mean they to do with us?"

"Hang and quarter us," someone from the shadows replied. "Bring us to trial first, o' course. They mean to take us to London."

Bones aching, Alex drew up his knees as far as the chains allowed, put his back to dank timbers, tried to make out the men around him, their sufferings marked by shuffles, clanks, groans. "How many are we? What is our number?"

A suspended moment passed, then out of the dimness came a response. "We numbered twenty-six together when put aboard. We're one-and-twenty now. Elsewhere on this ship are more."

Alex searched the dim forms huddled in the hold but could make out no man distinct. "Who speaks?"

"Archibald MacKenzie, of Inverness."

"MacKenzie," Alex echoed, putting name and voice to memory. "Tell your names, all. And d'ye wish, that of brother, father, or son that fell beside ye. Let us name our dead."

"My name ye ken," said MacKenzie. "I saw three cousins fall. Dougal, James, Duncan. Sons of my mother's sister."

"Duncan *I* am," said another. "Duncan Ross of Cromarty. My auld da—Hector Mor—fell to the cannons in the first rush."

"Ross," Alex said. "Who else?"

"Adam Cluny," a creaky voice answered. "An elder brother I lost. He was seventy-six winters, still hale."

"Aye, Cluny. And how old are ye?"

"Only seventy-three!"

A murmur—not quite laughter—rippled through the dark.

Out of the shadows, one by one, men made themselves known. Alex echoed back their names, putting all he could into them of respect, until it came round at last to Rory.

"Me ye well ken, but for any who cares, I'm Rory MacNeill, tacksman to my chief, the MacNeill of Barra, and this beside me is my sister's son, Alastair MacKinnon. Alex, he's called."

"MacKinnon," said MacKenzie, who'd spoken first. "A right wee giant ye are. I havena yet seen an English guard with gall enough to devil ye. We've vied for the honor of hauling your carcass about at muster."

"I'm gratified to have afforded ye the service." Alex waited, but there was no more. "Besides my uncle I counted only eighteen. Who's yet to speak?"

"That would be me," a voice said, younger and haler than Alex expected. "Hugh Cameron of Glendessary. Beside me fell my father, Alexander Cameron, and my brothers, Iain and Archie. I've but the one wee half-brother left, too much a bairn to take up arms for the Stuarts."

"Cameron. May your wee brother live in whatever freedom we've left him." A few weak *amens* arose, but Alex didn't add his own. His head was throbbing again. "I'll rest a bit, Uncle, I think."

"Aye, lad. Ye've earnt a wee lie-down."

"Earnt it, have I?"

"Listen."

Alex cast the net of his hearing past the

drumbeat in his skull. The men around him were speaking to one another. Talk of battles, aye, but more of home, of kin.

"Ye gave them back a bit of their dignity. 'Tis more than I've managed in a fortnight."

Alex slipped away and left them to it.

June 1746–May 1747
London, England

The river was the Thames, the fortress on its shore, Tilbury Fort. The prison ships that had plied the passage from Inverness anchored there. The Jacobites were transferred to new quarters, crammed within the fort. More ships lay at anchor, ready to receive the overflow into yet another foul pit. For Rory MacNeill and Alex MacKinnon, the name of the pit was the *James & Mary*.

June was waning. Those who would die of wounds taken at Culloden had likely done so. The rest had made it to London, where surely the waiting would be swift. But summer passed into autumn without word of the promised trial. Bowels griped. Skin broke open in sores. Flesh fell away to gauntness. Rage was a hot knife in the brain.

Alex clung to sanity, casting his mind like a greedy net back to his life before, to clean wind rippling over machair pastures where his uncle's cattle grazed; to open seas beyond their ketch's bow, at his shoulder the white sands and scattered islets hemming Barra's coastline like a tattered cloak; to clouds lying low on the rounded head of Ben Tangaval; seals barking their eerie chorus in the mist; burns rushing through sheltering glens. Sometimes it was hearth and home his mind caressed—the croft built in the shelter and with some of the stones of an ancient crumbling broch; a fire of peat turfs filling it with their smoked-earth smell; a table laden with the simple fare of men without wives to do for them; thick walls snug against a lashing sea-wind.

He talked of it all to the men in the hold and listened while they spoke of their places and people, guarding his mind against rumors that reached them through their taunting guards— of Highland farms razed, widows and orphans turned out to starve, weapons surrendered, glens trodden under English boots.

Five months after Culloden, old Adam Cluny ceased his suffering, having marked his seventy-fourth year in darkness. English hands hauled him from the hold, a sack of bones wrapped in oil-cloth, as Cluny's fellow prisoners stood in his honor and Alex besought their guards for better rations. The current half-pound of meal per day would see them all follow Cluny soon enough. Hugh Cameron stood beside him. Together they petitioned for clothing, some manner of bedding against the river's deepening chill. They were told to be grateful it wasn't yet winter.

God . . . someone . . . have mercy.

It was a black day when Rory MacNeill woke drenched in fever-sweat. The gash to his thigh hadn't healed as he'd feigned. In the weeks past, some foulness had reopened it and it had festered. "Why didna ye tell me, Uncle?"

"The way ye try so hard to lift these men . . . I didna have the heart."

They half-carried his uncle up to the deck when they were marshaled out, as once they'd half-carried Alex. It was at that time they heard of the lottery. "We'll not all be tried," he told Rory when the man was lucid enough to comprehend. "One in twenty will stand trial, chosen by lot. The rest will be granted the king's mercy."

"King's mercy, is it?" Rory said dryly. "And which will be the lucky ones, those of us who hang or those who dinna?"

His uncle did neither.

Two days after Rory MacNeill's body was taken to be buried in English soil, Alex learnt his own fate: not death but exile and transportation to the American Colonies, there to serve out a seven-year indenture. The news gutted him less than had his last words with his uncle.

"I wish ye hadna come after me, Uncle. I wish ye'd loved me less."

"Never wish it. I couldna be prouder of the braw man ye've made. I shall tell my sister so when I see her." Taking weak hold of his hand, Rory MacNeill added, "If Almighty God grants His grace, ye'll survive King Geordie's mercy."

Not until his uncle expelled his final breath had Alex dared whisper what he'd come to believe since Culloden. *Mercy.* "It's but a word, Uncle. There isna mercy to be granted, by king or God."

He was all but certain no God existed who cared enough to grant it.

Along with those of five other Jacobites sentenced to transportation, Alex's indenture was purchased by Roger Bingham, master of a merchant ship anchored in the Thames. The *Charlotte-Ann* and her cargo belonged to an Englishman in the Colony of North Carolina. One of their number, Bingham informed them, would owe his next seven years to that Englishman. The rest were Bingham's to sell once they reached port in Wilmington.

On a morning in May, over a year since his capture, Alex was rowed out to the *Charlotte-Ann*. He was just turned four-and-twenty, nearly three stone underweight, with a rattle in his chest that had plagued him since the winter. The tar-laden air of the Thames was thick with the clamor of seamen and customs officials haggling and hallooing one another from shore and deck, raucous as the gulls wheeling about the forested masts. Alex eyed the lines of the vessel set to carry him across the sea. She was straight and blunt of stern, three masted, square rigged like the frigates he'd seen off Barra's coast, the figurehead at her prow a lassie with yellow-painted hair.

Last of the indentures to board, Alex climbed the ladder to stand before the master and mate awaiting them on deck. Captain Bingham, hair clubbed back from a weathered face, had seen their bills of sale signed and locked away. Head and shoulders above the other prisoners, Alex drew stares from the crew busy about the rigging or stowing casks and crates. He made a lance of his spine, refusing to give an inch, as Bingham looked him over.

"Remind me—which are you?" Bingham's speech was flat and faintly nasal. He'd been born, another of the Jacobites had said, in a place called Boston.

"Alastair MacKinnon," Alex replied, with all the lilt of Barra he could infuse into the syllables.

Bingham lofted a measuring brow. "What are you, then, six inches shy of seven feet?"

"Seven inches shy, I'm told . . . sir." Wind through the rigging made a riffling whine. The deck heaved under his feet. Alex closed his eyes and was back aboard his uncle's ketch, off the coast of home. The pang of loss nearly doubled him. He opened his eyes.

Bingham stepped back, nodding to his mate. "See to their berths. Get them rations, water—and for pity's sake, some decent clothing."

Down into the hold they went. Not in chains or filth—or not barbaric filth. It was still a ship, cramped and dank. They'd hammocks, food enough, a ration of the rum. Whenever the seas were calm, they were permitted to walk under the sun, no more bound than was any man by prow and stern. Alex sometimes thought of the prisoners who survived the *James & Mary*—an outbreak of typhus after midwinter had again thinned their ranks. Of that original group that shared quarters with him and his uncle and hadn't gone to trial, he knew of two survivors: Hugh Cameron and Archibald MacKenzie. Neither man was aboard the *Charlotte-Ann*.

One week out to sea, he felt strength returning. Two weeks out, four of the crew lay dying of the bloody flux, leaving Captain Bingham applying to his indentures to replace them. The chief mate, learning Alex had some acquaintance with sea-going vessels, sweetened the offer with the promise of more generous rations and a berth with the crew.

"I'll take that offer," Alex said. Moments later his hands were on the rigging.

It went hard those first days, rising with the

watches to unaccustomed labor, but as the *Charlotte-Ann* cleaved the dark Atlantic, Alex found the rhythm of the work. He was hungry day and night; full sea rations weren't enough to restore the weight he'd lost, but as his frame gradually hardened to whipcord, the rage in his soul was banked. Work filled his days, the salt air his lungs, and there were moments—watching the sun sink westward in a beribboned blaze, or the stars netting the black of night—when he recalled how freedom felt.

3

Cape Fear River

A gain restrained, Alex watched the passing riverbank. Moss-draped oaks and swampy lowland had blended with sandier soils studded with pines of a height he'd never imagined. Herons stalked the occasional mudflat in a river bend. Turtles sunned on half-submerged logs, sliding into the water as the barge passed. Once a snake, patterned in irregular bands of brown and black, came undulating through the water nearly under his nose.

Demas, lounging nearby, saw it glide beneath the brushy bank. "Evil," he muttered, at which Phineas Reeves emerged from the cabin.

"A water viper, was it? They're quite venomous. You may tell them from the harmless varieties by their head. Like so." With forefingers and thumbs he shaped a triangle. "Though if you're close enough to distinguish that, you're likely to be struck. Or chased."

"Chased?" Sheened with sweat though they were, Alex felt the hairs on his arms lift. "They do that?"

"Oh yes. The males along this river can be aggressively territorial."

Reeves flashed him a grin, making Alex wonder if he'd imagined another implication in the words.

"We've made excellent time with the tide. With luck we'll reach Severn before nightfall. You'll have a proper look at the place."

Alex shifted his gaze to the bank, wondering less about their destination than about how long it would take to acquaint himself with the perils of that alien landscape. He'd no intention of spending seven years sweltering in a smithy. Whether he signed his name in his own life's blood mattered not. He was done keeping his word to Englishmen, or trusting a single promise out of their lying mouths.

June 1747
Atlantic Ocean

The sixth week out, after the *Charlotte-Ann* had weathered precarious seas for a night and day, Alex was on deck splicing lines in a rare moment of solitude when he grew aware of Captain Bingham come to stand near him at the rail.

"I've watched you, MacKinnon," Bingham said after a silence. "You've sailed before—as you said."

Alex cast aside several less gracious responses

before replying, "I've been on the sea in boats since I can mind."

"I cannot say the same for the other indentures."

"Highland crofters, the lot." Or they had been.

"Indeed," Bingham said wryly. "Which means I'll soon be needing crewmen. Wilmington hasn't a port the like of Philadelphia, or even Boston. Pickings will be slim."

Alex waited. Bingham cleared his throat. "It would seem life at sea suits you."

"Well enough."

"Over a life ashore?"

Alex ran a line through callused fingers as he measured his reply. "I begin to think so."

The captain's face creased with satisfaction. "As I'd thought. Of course the choice rests—"

The helmsman called out, pulling the captain away with the statement unfinished, leaving Alex shaking with relief. Bingham wanted him for the *Charlotte-Ann*. That must be what the man had meant to say. Crisscrossing the Atlantic, he would hear tidings of Scotland. Perhaps at the end of seven years he could even return to Barra. The croft by the crumble-down broch. The boat. The cows. Or whatever was left of it all.

Hope attached itself like a barnacle to his heart. Hope that he mightn't, after all, perish in some remote corner of the world, clanless and forgotten.

He should have known better.

July 1747
Wilmington, North Carolina

A pilot boat guided the *Charlotte-Ann* through the shifting sand bars guarding the Cape Fear River's mouth before they anchored at Wilmington, thirty miles from the open sea. Alex didn't accompany the small boats ferrying their cargo of British goods across the shallows to the quay, though he did his share of gawping. And streaming sweat. An enervating swelter blanketed the Carolina coast. Biting pests swarmed the air, thick as the forest rising behind the town. The timber structures comprising it looked vulnerable to Alex's eyes, as though any moment the forest might rise and swallow it whole. He hailed from a world of open skies and far horizons, and he didn't like the look of the place. As often as his work above deck allowed, he put his back to that hemming wall of green, thankful he need never set foot therein.

The day passed, crewmen mingling with merchants coming and going from the commission houses. Toward evening a man boarded the *Charlotte-Ann*, little distinguished from those seen throughout the day. Alex was about to dismiss him when a second figure ascended the ladder behind him. A few enslaved Africans had come aboard the *Charlotte-Ann* during the day. After the first, Alex had ceased to gawk, but he couldn't help doing so now. The man was a giant, as tall as Alex but easily two stone heavier than he'd weighed before Culloden, not an ounce of it spare. The African stood aloof while the rest of the indentured Jacobites were assembled for the white man's inspection. Assuming him the ship's owner, Alex turned back to his work, reassured when Bingham didn't call him into line. He didn't see the incongruous pair leave, nor which of his fellow Scots he took with him. By the morrow's close the hold would be filled with tar, shingles, hides, corn—the trade stuffs of the Carolinas. The following day they would set sail again, bound for Kingston.

In lifting spirits as twilight settled, Alex allowed himself to be distracted by the appearance of tiny yellow-green lights winking like faeries cavorting on the riverbank. Hundreds of them.

"Fireflies," a seaman named them. It was the first thing about the place he'd found remotely charming.

He went to his berth at the end of his watch, prepared to endure another stifling, muggy night, but was barely asleep when he roused to voices. Rough hands gripped him in his hammock.

"You coming with us now," said a cavernous voice, deep as the darkness.

The hammock tipped. He landed with his feet on the deck but staggered. "What?"

"You sold, man," said the voice, disembodied

in the dark but belonging, Alex sensed, to the owner of the hands still gripping him. "Bound upriver."

He'd barely time to tense when a second set of hands took hold of him. Lashing out, he knocked them away. Others took their place. He was manhandled onto the deck, where the smell of salt marsh and rotting fish congested the soupy air. A lantern sprang to light. Before him was the man he'd taken for the ship's owner earlier in the day, thin-faced, dark-browed. One set of hands grasping him, he now saw, were the size of dinner plates, black against his flesh.

Bingham was there, resignation in his gaze. Sick with understanding, Alex leveled a glare that made the captain step back. Then it was an all-out fight for his freedom. Or he'd meant it to be. In truth he never tore himself free of the giant African's grip.

"Settle him, Demas," said a mild English voice, threaded with a ribbon of mirth. "No lasting damage."

A force like a hammer's blow slammed Alex's head. This time he never felt the deck that broke his fall.

Reeves called it the Big House. White and columned, two stories tall, Severn's main dwelling was large enough his uncle's croft might have fit within its walls five, maybe six times, with

45

as many stacked atop. It was set back from the river by a sloping lawn, down which a walkway descended to one of the more substantial docks Alex had seen. The boatmen poled the flatboat past it into the wide mouth of a full-flowing creek.

Moments later they emerged from crowding woods to another dock. They'd rounded the Big House and were behind it now, where spread a veritable village of smaller structures. Alex had barely time to cast his gaze across the sprawl before a shout arose and the place erupted like an anthill overturned. Men, women, and children converged on the bank, dark faces contrasting with unbleached cloth shirts and short gowns. As fast as the boatmen unloaded casks, crates, and sacks, the people shouldered them away, chattering in accents difficult to grasp. Smells of cookery hung on the hot, heavy air. At midday he'd been given something called *pone*, a crumbly cornmeal bread. The sun was low in the west now, his head ached, and he was ravenous.

Demas gave a push as he stood to disembark. Hands bound, Alex half-stumbled onto the dock, catching the attention of those nearby. Bruised, blood-stained, sunburnt, clad in ragged breeches, he ignored the stares and followed Reeves up the crushed shell lane from the dock.

Reeves's glance fell across the ogling slaves, alighting upon a young woman, slender and graceful as a deer. "Mari, bring enough supper to the smithy for two."

Though its cast was foreign to Alex's eyes, no man could mistake her face for anything but beautiful. She gaped at him, dark eyes wide with fear. "Yes, Mister Reeves."

She hurried down a path, leaving Alex wondering, did he look *that* terrifying? Or had the lass's gaze flicked away before it showed fear to the hulking slave who shadowed him?

They escorted him past gardens set well back from the Big House, past curious elders who paused their weeding to stare, knobby hands gripping hoes. Alex locked his gaze on the tail of Reeves's hair curling below his cornered hat.

The overseer led him to a brick building, high-roofed but single-storied. Inside, the air was stale with the charcoal smell of a smithy, though the forge with its massive brick chimney stood cold. From rafters and walls hung all manner of worked iron, at least near the doorway where light spilled. Shadows crowded thick beyond. As Alex sidestepped a massive blocked stump topped with a broad anvil, the earthen floor heaved, or seemed to. He found his balance while Reeves strode confidently into the murky shop. As his eyes adjusted, across the space Alex saw an interior wall, rough-timbered, containing a doorway. Reeves halted before it.

"We've the new indenture, Moon. Come see to

him. I'm off to fetch Captain Carey." Movement in the shadows to the left, in the main shop, made Reeves pivot. "There you are." He inhaled deeply, as one testing the air. "And sober? Excellent."

At first the movement in the dimness held no form, as if the shadow itself had shifted. The shadow took a man's shape, not tall but strongly built through the shoulders and chest. As the figure emerged into light cast by the doorway, shock coursed along Alex's spine. Pity skittered in its wake.

"What good does sitting in the dark? You cannot hide forever." Reeves found flint and striker and soon had a candle lit. He dipped it to a second, both in pewter dishes. "Elijah Moon, I present Alex MacKinnon, late of His Majesty's custody. He's a Scotsman but he speaks the king's English—after a fashion."

Reeves moved toward the door, pausing to address Alex. "Supper will be along. Don't eat Moon meantime, if you can help it. You're going to need him."

Demas departed on the overseer's heels, leaving Alex alone with, he presumed, Severn's former blacksmith. Elijah Moon might have had thirty years on him, no more. He'd a full head of hair, light brown, untailed and tangled. His face had probably been well made in a rough-cut way. Difficult to judge with the livid scars of recently healed burns rippling down the right side of it.

They didn't mar his nose or mouth, and his eye appeared undamaged, but the reddened twists of flesh continued downward to vanish beneath the open neck of his shirt, the right sleeve of which ended in a knot where a hand ought to have been.

Alex looked up from that gaping loss. Beneath level brows pulled tight, the man's eyes were a piercing blue, staring back with resentment, and raw despair.

"He called ye MacKenzie?" Moon's voice was gruff, an accent less refined than Reeves's. A Cornishman, perhaps.

"No. MacKinnon."

Moon grunted acknowledgment, then circled behind Alex. A tug, then his bonds fell away. The relief was immense. So was his puzzlement.

"D'ye not fear I'll abscond with myself before this Captain Carey gets a look at me?"

Moon stepped away, a knife tucked under his maimed arm. "Reeves will have set his watchdog on the door." He gestured with a bristled chin at a smaller block stump by the forge.

Alex folded himself onto the crude seat. His head throbbed from Demas's *settling* of the night before, compounded by a day of battering sun. The skin across his shoulders prickled. His bruises ached. The dirt floor lifted and fell like a ship at anchor.

Moon crossed to a bank of shuttered windows, below which ran a workbench hung with tools.

"I was heating a bar," he said, answering the question Alex hadn't dared to ask—brusquely, as if desiring to have done with it. "I pumped the bellows hard and the forge just . . . exploded."

Wondering under what circumstances a forge might explode, Alex examined the chimney rising to the roof, the hearth and long bricked counter. Evidence of repair met his gaze.

The forge had been easier to mend than the man. Silence weighed heavier than the iron strewn about. Though banked, Moon's grief and rage weighed heavier still. His might have been one of the suffering faces Alex had carried with him from the *James & Mary*. Faces of men who, in a way that galled him still with failure, had been his to keep, his to protect, though not a one had asked it of him.

They weren't his now. Neither was this man.

At the crush of footsteps in the yard, he gathered himself to rise with what dignity his present state allowed to meet the man intending to be his master.

Only it was a woman who entered the smithy, and not the slave called Mari. She was white, barely more than a lass, dressed in a gown of buttery gold. An apron fronted it, fancifully embroidered for a servant, he thought. But he'd no notion of the actual wealth of Edmund Carey or what manner of servants the man possessed, aside from the slaves he'd seen. Her light brown hair appeared abundant, though a prim cap covered most of it. The color of her eyes was lost in the candlelight, but she'd a pretty mouth, gracefully bowed. And she bore a tray. Gripping it, she halted in the doorway as though surprised by the sight of him. She swung a look at Moon, who scowled at the tray.

"Joanna—ye didn't have to bring that. Where's Mari?"

The lass, Joanna, came into the shop, set the tray atop the forge counter, and replied mildly, "I was on my way so I saved her the walk."

"Ye might have sent Azuba."

"You know I like to take the initial measurements. Anyway, here's supper. Try to eat some of it." Though she sounded English, there was something of that flatness to the lass's speech Alex had heard from Captain Bingham. She fished in a housewife tied at her waist and brought out what looked to be a doll-sized wooden barrel. Turning to Alex she said, "Please stand, if you will, so I may take your measure."

Acutely aware of his unwashed, half-naked state, Alex kept his seat. "My measure?"

"You'll need shirts." Her gaze glanced along his length. "Breeches too. Unless you have them already supplied, Mister . . . ?"

"MacKinnon," Moon said. "And he doesn't, apparently."

"Mister MacKinnon," she continued smoothly.

"In that case, the sooner you stand and let me take your measure, the sooner you may sit again—to your supper."

Alex stood, relieved when he didn't lurch to catch his balance despite the ground's shifting. Even so, she took a step back, sweeping a look up the height of him, at the end of which their gazes clashed.

"My goodness," she breathed. "I'll need to stand on that block to reach your shoulders and . . . But you're wounded? Let me light a few more candles so I may see you better."

Her efforts doubled the light. She came back around to scrutinize him, clearly displeased. "You're bruised as well, and Mister Reeves left you overlong in the sun." Over her shoulder she asked, "Have you water in your room, Elijah?"

Moon grunted affirmation.

"It's just through that doorway, Mister MacKinnon. Take a candle, wash that wound to your brow or . . . I could tend it if you'd rather."

She'd made the offer sincerely, he thought, but on its heels her bottom lip slipped between her teeth, as if on second thought she'd rather he said no.

"I'll do it." He took a candle and ducked through the inner door, finding a small room furnished with two cots, a sea chest at the foot of one, a washstand between. Spare shirts, a coat, and breeches dangled from pegs. A looking glass hung beside a basin and pitcher on the stand. Alex set the candle beside them. While the ground's heaving went on, he poured water, slaked his thirst, splashed his face, then stooped to peer into the glass set to Moon's height. He probed the welt at his hairline where a bruise was coming up beneath broken skin.

Not for over a year had he seen his face, save piecemeal in a cracked glass shared with several sailors aboard the *Charlotte-Ann*. For a moment he didn't recognize the features framed by sun-bleached hair straggling in ropes grown past his shoulders. Though no longer the full-bearded wraith that had staggered off the *James & Mary*, he was still too much bone, too little flesh. And too much hair; he needed a shave. Best let the lass do what she'd come for. He needed clothing, too, but he was half-crazed with wanting whatever was on that tray.

She was quick about her business once he returned, pulling from her wooden bauble a ribbon marked at intervals, bending to stretch it from his waist to his knee. Murmuring a figure, she circled behind him. He felt the ribbon span his waist, there and gone in a flash. Reaching high, she took his measure from his nape to the small of his back.

He swayed slightly. She touched his side. "Are you all right?"

"I've been aboard ship a long while."

"Dizzy? I've never been long aboard ship, but I've heard it takes some time to pass." She removed her hand from his person. "Have you vermin, Mister MacKinnon?"

"Lice, d'ye mean? No." He'd been crawling with them when he left the *James & Mary* but had been deloused the day they boarded the *Charlotte-Ann*. When his scalp prickled—force of suggestion, surely—he refused to raise a hand to scratch the itch.

Behind him, the lass had climbed on the block chair to span his shoulders with her measure, then the circumference of his neck. "Raise your arms, please. Straight out to the sides."

The novelty of a woman's voice issuing from that height vanished with the acute regret that he hadn't washed beneath those arms. Hers came around him, the brush of linen sleeves tickling. She smelled of soap and lavender and, more temptingly, of the kitchen.

Dismounting the block, she came around him again, the top of her capped head bobbing beneath his chin. She was neat and trim in her person, her manner polite but not servile. A servant of high station, then. Head sempstress? Head house-maid? He was trying to guess her age—twenty maybe—when she slipped her measuring bauble back into her housewife.

"What else do you require, Mister MacKinnon? Have you any personal effects?"

What meager kit he'd had was left aboard the *Charlotte-Ann*. He shrugged. "What ye see."

"Nothing at all?" A crease formed between her slender brows. "We shall remedy that, but shirt and breeches are most urgent. Those you'll have by this time tomorrow."

He started to thank her, but she'd turned to speak to Moon, stepping close and lowering her voice. Her hand came up to clasp the man's undamaged arm. He stiffened, muttering, "All right, Joanna."

She turned away, not quick enough to hide a flash of pain. At the door she paused and looked at Alex. The gilded light from the yard traced a fraying vulnerability in her gaze, though he thought she meant to hide it. "Mister MacKinnon, may I know your given name?"

The question surprised him. "It's Alastair, but I'm called Alex."

Joanna nodded. "Welcome to Severn, Alex MacKinnon," she said, and took her leave.

Moon's gaze lingered after her until, sensing Alex's scrutiny, he jerked his chin at their supper. "I can hear your innards clamoring. Have ye at it. Only save me a crumb so I needn't lie to her later."

4

In the shelter of the hedged walkway, Joanna Carey paused to compose herself. Across the creek the sun had set. Its radiant wake couldn't displace memory of the man just encountered by candlelight. Alex MacKinnon was emblazoned upon her mind as though she'd looked into the midday sun.

"He's here!" Charlotte had exclaimed not an hour past, bounding into the sewing room where Joanna and Azuba, Severn's housemaid, stitched shirts for the mill hands.

"Who's here?" Joanna asked.

Her sister clutched one of her dolls—*the Annas,* Azuba called them, for Charlotte had given them rhyming names, Hanna, Georgianna, and Susanna. Hanna, the current favorite, had a painted wooden face, dark horsehair ringlets, and a striped gown Joanna had made to match her sister's.

"Phineas has the new indentured man!" Charlotte rushed to the window. "I don't see him now, though."

At nearly ten, Charlotte was past the age for dashing about, but Joanna didn't scold. Her sister could never remember such admonitions. *Mental*

56

deficiency was all the physicians who had visited in the past few years could deduce. Joanna had resigned herself to the likelihood of her sister always being thus: sweet-tempered and loving but with the inclinations of a very young child. Pausing her needle, she gave one of Charlotte's golden curls a tug. "Spying from the windows, were you?"

Unlike Joanna's eyes, which altered color with the light or even the gown she wore, Charlotte's eyes were a changeless blue. "I went round to all the windows trying to spot Jemma, and there was the flatboat—and the new man with his hands tied. He's very tall and hasn't a shirt, and he looks like a pirate!"

Joanna shared a glance with Azuba. They'd known what sort of men Captain Bingham was bringing: Jacobites imprisoned during the Duke of Cumberland's campaign in Scotland last year. But the man couldn't have journeyed all that way bound. Why was he now?

"Miss Charlotte." Azuba raised an eyebrow. "When have you ever laid eyes on a pirate?"

"Never," Charlotte said. "Elijah told me about them."

Elijah. The ache that had lived beneath Joanna's ribs for a six-month had pierced afresh. "At least we can remedy the man's state of clothing," she said, and had risen to see it done.

Memory of her sister's words now mingled

with that blazing image; barefoot, bare-chested, hair unbound, he'd looked every inch the pirate. He'd peered down his narrow nose at her with such caged intensity that she'd forgiven Mister Reeves's restraining him until he was safely delivered. The man had so unnerved her she was amazed she'd been able to take his measure, or commit it to memory.

Best get it penned before it fled. She forced her feet to move, into the house, up the stairs to the sewing room, where once she'd recorded the measurements, Azuba asked, "Well? He warrant all the carrying on?"

"And then some. He's a match for Demas— in height. But I could practically count his ribs." There'd been another difference, though. Touching Alex MacKinnon hadn't left her feeling the faint chill that had stroked her neck when she'd taken the measurements of the slave come to them in the service of Phineas Reeves.

"One pair of breeches to start, with seam enough to let out," Azuba said. "Two shirts?"

"Yes. I'll begin one now. Go if you need to." Joanna noticed the quiet as Azuba rose to see the supper table set. "Where's Charlotte?"

"Still hunting Jemma."

Joanna knit her brow, reminded of yet another concern. An orphaned slave, not yet thirteen, Jemma had recently faded to a shadow of her former lively self, skulking about the house and yard as if she'd cause to fear them all.

Azuba shook her kerchiefed head. "She Miss Charlotte's companion and we make allowance for that, but she meant to be helping in the kitchen too. Mari has a time keeping her on task."

Joanna smoothed over this worrisome ripple in their domestic routine. "I'll speak to Jemma."

"If you can find her." Well into her middle years, tall and spare, Azuba spread work-worn hands across the apron covering her gown. "You see Elijah at the smithy?"

"I did." Joanna turned, pretending to choose among the bolts of shirting. "This is hard for him."

"Master Carey needs a smith."

"I know." Fear for Elijah had weighed on her through the weeks after his accident, when even laudanum couldn't ease his pain. Or save his hand. She hadn't broken through his wall of despair since. It was hard to retain her equanimity when privately she herself went weeping, petitioning God to undo the terrible thing He'd let happen—still asking *why.*

"I know you know." Azuba came behind her and laid both hands on her shoulders, the nearest an embrace Joanna would allow, though she often longed to be the girl who'd melted into those strong arms and cried the day her mother died. An indulgence she'd allowed herself only once. Azuba gave her shoulders a squeeze. "It's hard seeing him hurt. He been like a brother to you."

And like a son to Edmund Carey, Joanna once thought.

Along with Phineas Reeves, Elijah had been a cabin boy aboard her stepfather's last command. The captain's personal servant, Elijah had accompanied him into retirement. He'd been part of Joanna's life since Captain Carey married her widowed mother. Mister Reeves had come into his former captain's employ little more than a year past and had quickly worked—and charmed—his way into her stepfather's confidence. And his heart.

If either man held Joanna's heart, it was Elijah, though not in the way he'd wanted. Days before the forge exploded, Elijah had asked Papa for her hand in marriage and was refused. Not by Joanna. She'd never had the chance. Shortly before Elijah approached her stepfather, Phineas Reeves beat him to it. Papa decided his overseer, not his blacksmith, was the preferable match. Duly proposed to with her stepfather's blessing, Joanna had been caught off-guard; Mister Reeves had never showed more particular attention to her than he had to Charlotte. She'd pleaded for time to consider the arrangement.

Six months on she was no nearer knowing her mind. All that made the present situation bearable was Mister Reeves's patience. He hadn't pressed her, despite knowing Papa meant to make his heir whomever Joanna married.

Azuba didn't know about Elijah's shattered hope. Not even Mister Reeves was privy to the fact he'd had a rival for her hand, if briefly.

"You be sure and thank the Almighty for this new man."

Her mother's personal maid from childhood, Azuba had been Joanna's rock since she was thrust into the role of mistress, at twelve. She was used to Azuba nudging her to lean on the Almighty for the strength to navigate the endless domestic concerns of Severn—waters often deep enough to drown—but this admonition took her aback. Thank the Almighty for the man come to take Elijah's place? Make the best of it. Hope it wasn't the final blow that drove Elijah to despair. But gratitude?

Azuba caught her disbelieving look. "We all see the bitterness Elijah's let captivate his soul. It ain't pretty. But you go on questioning in your heart like I expect you been doing, Miss Joanna, that's going to be *you*. So yes. Thank God for this new man—no matter he look the pirate—then wait and see what comes."

"Azuba? Miss Joanna?" They turned as one of the kitchen slaves, Marigold, appeared in the doorway. "Supper's nigh ready, but that Jemma ain't turned up."

Azuba stirred into action. "I've the table to set. Go on back, Mari. Make ready to serve."

"Maybe no hurry now," Joanna heard Marigold say as the two headed for the stairs. "Coming by the study I hear Master Carey say he going to see the new indenture afore supper. Still, that Jemma . . ."

Joanna stroked a folded length of homespun, her mind clamoring with needs. She ought to find Jemma—and Charlotte. She ought to start on Mister MacKinnon's shirt. She ought to whisper that prayer Azuba told her to pray.

She reached for the scissors.

Alex fell upon the food the sempstress had left with single-minded intent—a bowl of stewed greens, another of flat beans flavored with meat, two slabs of pone, honey-drizzled, and a fermented cider he gulped like air. On the verge of finishing what was meant for two, memory jarred him from the mindless need for nourishment. Seated on the block chair, tray balanced on his knee, he looked at Moon's back. "D'ye mean to let me eat it all? Come have what's left."

Moon swiveled, eyeing the remains. "Finish it."

Opening his mouth to argue, Alex caught a spark of light in the dooryard, beneath a great spreading oak, gray in the gloaming. The spark winked again, a yellow burst floating languid on the air, now just beyond the threshold.

"Ye see that?" He set aside the tray and rose. Moon grunted protest but settled as Alex crouched in the doorway and cupped his hands, capturing the creature. When it neither buzzed against him nor stung, he opened his hands. The insect, a sort of beetle, marched up the length of a finger, pulsed bright, and with a whirr of tiny wings took flight.

"It's their wee bums that glow." The laughter in his throat surprised him—and someone else. He heard a muffled giggle and the rustle of movement along the smithy wall, where light enough remained to spy the dirty brown toes not quite concealed around the corner. A child's, he thought. Laughter lingered in his voice as he said, "I see ye there."

The toes withdrew, followed by a scuffle of retreat.

He watched the fireflies until a whining about his ears bespoke the presence of less charming insects, then retreated into the shop. Moon hadn't budged from his stool. Alex nodded at the tray. "The lass who brought that—Joanna? She meant ye to eat it."

With the look of a man primed for battle, Moon bolted off his perch. "Ye'll call her *Miss* Joanna. Better yet, *Mistress*."

Though startled, Alex held his ground. "A bit grand for a serving lass, no?"

Beneath formidable brows, Moon's eyes

snapped. "Joanna—Miss Carey—is Captain Carey's stepdaughter, mistress of this plantation."

Miss Carey. The name rang in his memory. "Why, then, did she bring our vittles and take my measure like a common sempstress?"

Moon didn't answer as voices sounded from the yard. Alex recognized Reeves's as it drew within hearing. ". . . see the size of him. He'll make a blacksmith worthy of Hephaestus, given time." The overseer appeared in the doorway, a satchel slung at his shoulder, but stood aside for an older man to precede him. "Sir, here is Alex MacKinnon, one of Captain Bingham's six. The pick of the litter, by my estimation."

Alex leveled him a glare, then met the older man's scrutiny. Unlike most Englishmen of the upper sort, Severn's master wore no wig. Fashionably white with age, his natural hair was thick enough to arrange into proper side-curls, the rest clubbed at the base of his neck. He was of a height with Reeves, just under six feet. Though he'd seen at least sixty winters, he'd but the slightest paunch beneath a coat well-fitted, pleated tails falling nearly to the knee. With command in his bearing, he stood with feet braced like a seaman on a listing deck while Reeves set the satchel on the forge counter and completed the introduction. "MacKinnon, I present Captain Edmund Philip Carey, late of His Majesty's Royal Navy, master of Severn Plantation."

"You are of the Isles, MacKinnon?" Edmund Carey asked. "Skye, I believe, is the place from which that clan hails."

"Aye, I was born on Skye, but fostered among the MacNeills. Barra of the outer isles is . . . *was* my home." Surprise, in part, had prompted him to make claim upon his identity. Alex hoped surprise was all the man heard. Like skin over heated cream, it was the barest covering for defiance.

Carey gave no indication of what he'd heard besides the words themselves. "Perhaps it shall be home again, one day."

Hope stirred like a wind gusting through the smithy. Alex turned his face from it. They spoke their pretty words, the English, made their promises, then did as they wished.

From the satchel Reeves removed a corked inkwell, a quill, and the sheet of foolscap upon which the terms of his indenture were writ.

Captain Carey hadn't taken his gaze from Alex. "I'm told you didn't come peaceably after you were informed of your purchase."

"*Informed?* I was hauled from my berth, told I was sold, manhandled onto deck, then gi'en a *loundering* by that—" Alex broke off, realizing two things: his speech was doubtless growing impenetrable to English ears and the big African who'd been his guard upriver hadn't accompanied Reeves and Carey to the smithy. "Demas," he finished curtly.

Carey grasped a candle and held it high, gaze going to the knot on Alex's brow, the bruises over his torso and neck, the residue of dried blood his hasty ablution had missed. He swung toward Reeves. "Does he speak truth? This is Demas's work?"

Reeves grimaced. "I cannot say he lies, sir. But someone has."

This didn't please Severn's master. "You gave me to understand all was in order."

"I'd hoped MacKinnon had resigned himself and it would be of no matter. I'll tell you the whole of it, if you wish."

"I do wish," Carey said.

Reeves launched into his narrative readily. "I boarded the *Charlotte-Ann* to choose among the indentures, as per your instructions. When I counted but five, MacKinnon was pointed out. Bingham was of a mind to retain him as crew, but he being my choice, I was assured MacKinnon would be prepared to disembark upon my return that evening. I was later than anticipated coming to collect him. It isn't often I'm in town . . ."

"All right," Carey said. "You've your society in Wilmington. I don't fault you availing yourself of it once you'd seen to my concerns."

Reeves's face brightened in that disarming smile. "When I sent Demas and a couple of the ship's crew to fetch MacKinnon from his berth, he came up protesting—so vehemently as to

66

prevent conversation. I bid Demas settle him, an action carried out with more force than necessary, alas. Still, he's here and in one piece and . . . Shall he do, sir?"

Carey wouldn't be rushed, weighing all he'd heard. "So Captain Bingham failed to inform you of Phineas's choice?" he asked and, before Alex could reply, added, "What would you have done, MacKinnon, had you been so informed?"

The question startled Alex into honesty. "I'd have begged him to reconsider. Failing that, jumped ship and swam for it."

Surprise, and wariness, flashed in Carey's blue-gray eyes. "Have you plans to abscond with yourself now?"

A question fortuitously worded. "This isna where I want to be, but I've no such plans." *For now,* he added silently.

"One might call that generous," Carey said, "were you free to choose in the matter. You aren't—the price of rebellion against His Majesty. His mercy spared you a hangman's rope. Mister Reeves's choice granted you a future better than you deserve. Content yourself with both."

Alex opened his mouth to say something he likely would have regretted, when the forge inexplicably drew his gaze. He envisioned it fiery, himself before it, hammer in hand, glowing iron under his power, its secrets opening to him. With visceral memory he recalled the weight of his broadsword that icy April morning it was last knocked from his grasp.

A forge could allow for the creation of all manner of useful things.

Carey turned to Moon, silent since his master's arrival. "Well, Elijah. You've had a chance to look him over. Has he the makings of an Hephaestus?"

Moon had been standing in shadow. He shifted now, bringing his disfigurement into candlelight. "If ye can keep him fed, sir, I'll see he earns his bread."

Edmund Carey glanced at the tray atop the anvil; Alex had the impression the man knew who had, and hadn't, consumed the fare from his kitchen. "I'll say it again, Elijah. You're needed here. What's more, Severn is your home, as long as you wish it to be."

Moon's lips clamped tight as he nodded.

Alex grudgingly approved Carey's show of concern, but he knew it hadn't reached that yawning pit within that told a man all he'd known was lost, who he'd once been shattered beyond repair, whatever he might yet make of himself obscured in the rubble of present ruination.

All gazes shifted to Alex, keen with expectation. Reeves's lips parted in an eager smile, as if the man was confident of this coil he'd set in motion aboard the *Charlotte-Ann* ending satisfactorily, yet his eyes burned Alex with such intensity it seemed he meant to make it so by force of will alone. He held out the quill, but it wasn't for Reeves that Alex at last stepped forward and took it.

5

"Might I have a word, Miss Carey?"

Joanna grimaced before turning toward her stepfather's study, down the passage at the back of the house. *Miss Carey.* She loathed the address or at least how it sounded on Phineas Reeves's lips: *miscarry.*

"Yes, Mister Reeves?"

He stood in the doorway, dressed in a suit of brown linen she'd never seen. Purchased while in Wilmington, no doubt. His gaze fell to her burden—folded homespun, scuffed shoes. "For MacKinnon?"

Apparently he'd paid no heed when she mentioned needing to finish the man's clothing that evening, though he and Papa both took note during last night's supper when she'd inquired why the man had arrived like a runaway towed home. "He behaved himself civil enough in my presence. Why was he bound?"

Papa looked up from their course of pork cutlets. "You've seen him?"

"Me too," Charlotte piped, engendering a parental frown.

"You took your sister to the smithy before I could inspect the man?"

"No, Papa. Charlotte saw him from a window as he came off the boat."

"He looked like a pirate," Charlotte added, blue eyes sprung wide.

Papa's frown melted.

Mister Reeves threw back his head and laughed. "He does, at that."

"*Is* there cause for concern?" Joanna persisted.

"There was some misunderstanding about the arrangement on MacKinnon's part. But he's signed the indenture. Elijah says he'll do."

"The man ought to take a knee in gratitude." Mister Reeves raised his glass, meeting Joanna's gaze. "But I dare say a year on a prison ship has curbed his rebellious tendencies."

A year on a prison ship. In her estimation, such punishment might well cement such tendencies. But Mister MacKinnon's indenture was a *fait accompli*. She must do her part to see the man blended into the rhythm of Severn with as few discordant notes as possible.

"I thought you'd wish to know," Mister Reeves said now as she approached the study. "Our Jacobite in the smithy isn't the only item of interest I brought upriver. There's a letter from that clergyman with whom you're acquainted. I just remembered to pass it along."

"Reverend Pauling?" Joanna hurried to the study. In the center of the room, which held their library of some three dozen books, Papa sat at his enormous desk. Cluttering its surface were ledgers, documents, and nautical mementos— including a singularly large and perfect conch shell she'd found during the only trip she'd ever taken to the barrier islands lining the colony's coast.

Papa looked up at her entering, the letter spread before him. "David writes we may expect him in less than a fortnight. He would spend some days with us before venturing into the backcountry to preach. He mentions Elijah."

That meant the reverend had received her letters sent to his sister's home in Pennsylvania— the nearest he had to a permanent residence, for which Joanna was selfishly glad; being far upriver from Wilmington, isolated by miles of pine barrens from neighbors, they were forced to rely on itinerate preachers for their spiritual sustenance. Preachers like Reverend David Pauling, unwelcome in half the homes of New Hanover County for his radical New Light views, though the exhortations Joanna had heard from his lips were but Holy Scripture, clearly taught.

Already in the back of her mind she was planning for the visit. Like-minded neighbors who could spare the time would travel to hear the reverend preach, needing accommodation. "I'm so glad, Papa. I'll read the letter when I return to the house."

She felt Mister Reeves's gaze on her as she left

the room. "You're glad of this preacher's coming, or that he takes an interest in Moon?"

"Both, of course," she said, pausing at the back door, but when he made no further remark she hurried out.

It was nearing sunset as she reached the oak-shaded smithy, the very hour she'd approached it yesterday, yet how different it felt. She'd heard the occasional ring of hammering since midday; Mister MacKinnon's training had already begun.

Before she reached the doorway, Marigold stepped from the smithy with a tray. She crossed the yard to Joanna, who noted with a glance that every dish was picked clean. "You've served supper, I see."

"Yes ma'am. They finished it off quick."

Joanna lowered her voice. "Elijah?"

"Ate his share," Marigold whispered back.

Male voices rumbled from the smithy, then a sound she hadn't heard in months. Elijah's laughter, low and subdued, but it was his, no mistaking it. It rooted Joanna where she stood.

Marigold misread her hesitation. "That new man look fierce enough to scare a bear up a tree, but I see kindness in him. He . . . Well, maybe you'll see too."

"Papa wouldn't have approved a man we need fear," Joanna said, more sternly than intended.

Marigold's expression dimmed. "No ma'am. I best get these to the wash kettle."

They parted, though Joanna paused to glance back, regretful. Marigold hadn't lingered, but Joanna did, catching the conversation from within.

"Aye," came the Scotsman's voice, a deep rumble with the swell of sea waves in it. "Ye've worked me so hard, I may actually sleep tonight."

"Something wrong with the bed?" Elijah replied.

"Besides its ending at my knees? No. It's the sounds of this place. They're all wrong to my ears."

"Ye cannot hear the sea," Elijah said.

"Aye. Now ye say it, that's it. Ye canna even smell it here."

"Ye'll grow used to it. I did."

"Ye were at sea, then, a blacksmith?"

"Not a smith. A cabin boy aboard Captain Carey's last command."

"Reeves mentioned serving with Carey. He didna say ye were with him."

"No surprise."

An ache swelled in Joanna's chest. Here was Elijah talking freely with a man come among them only yesterday, as she hadn't heard him do since his injury, despite the months of patient coaxing, praying . . .

She closed her eyes, wincing at the resentment springing up in her soul. Was she so small of spirit as to feel slighted by Mister MacKinnon's effortless success, rather than rejoicing at it?

"Thank you," she whispered, finally heeding Azuba's admonition.

Elijah spoke again. "What made ye do it? Not that ye'd a choice . . . yet I think ye did choose."

Joanna frowned at the change of subject, awaiting enlightenment.

"I'd meant to serve my indenture aboard the *Charlotte-Ann*," came the reply. "But I can make my living at sea already. I didna need seven years to learn. The forge, though, that's a skill to stand me good wherever I fetch up next."

"So the mind of a man may plan. Perhaps ye ought to say *if God wills,* it shall be so. He may have other notions."

Joanna hoped Mister MacKinnon knew what to say to douse the bitterness that smoldered beneath Elijah's words.

"D'ye still believe there's a God?"

"Do ye?"

Stung by the bleak—nigh blasphemous—turn of their talk, Joanna marshaled herself and stepped into the smithy. The shop was high-ceilinged and commodious, yet Alex MacKinnon, on his feet, seemed to fill the space.

"I've brought your clothing, Mister MacKinnon." Though she kept her gaze on the Scotsman, she was aware of Elijah moving off to shutter the windows that had been open throughout the day. The place smelled like a smithy again, earth and fire rolled together, nose-stingingly acrid and sweet.

Mister MacKinnon stepped forward to accept her offering, dressed in those ragged trousers cut off mid-calf. His hair was tailed back, bare feet dirty, the day's sweat still a gleam across his chest. "I thank ye, Mistress," he said with a slight bow.

Struck by the formality of his manner, in contrast to yesterday's, she put the garments and shoes into his hands, feeling the warm brush of his fingers across the backs of hers. "Some items are folded in. A razor and strop, soap and the like. Would you care to try the clothes?"

The lofty blue eyes sharpened. "Now?"

"I'd like to judge their fit. Especially the shoes. They're the best I could find."

"Aye, Mistress. I'll be but a moment."

As Alex MacKinnon ducked into the back room, Elijah closed the last shutter, plunging the smithy into shadow save for the dimming light from the yard. "How did it go today?" she asked, with a nod toward the door through which Mister MacKinnon had disappeared.

"Well enough," Elijah said.

She waited for him to say more, until the silence grew unbearable. "Papa has a letter from Reverend Pauling. He's coming to visit soon."

Elijah grunted. Silence stretched again, aching and awkward, until Alex MacKinnon stepped from the sleeping quarters. He wore the new breeches and shirt, tails tucked, neckcloth tied, shoes on his feet. He'd washed his face and retied his hair. Though he was still bearded, it made for a startling transformation.

"Shall they do?" he asked.

"Very well. And the shoes fit?"

"Aye, *tapadh leibh.*" When she blinked, uncomprehending, he added, "I thank ye."

His long calves were bare. She snatched her gaze up, pinning it to his face. "Were the stockings unsuitable?"

"They're fine, Mistress. But I didna wash my feet." He started to smile, but she flinched. "Did I speak amiss? I was told to address ye so."

"Mistress is fine." At least it wasn't *miscarry.*

"But ye'd rather I called ye different?"

"I'd prefer Miss Joanna."

The man did smile, then, a singularly crooked smile, one corner curving up, the other down. "Aye, Miss Joanna. I can do that." He rubbed a hand across his bristling beard. "I ken ye're glad to see me covered decent, but *I* thank ye most especial for the razor."

Unexpectedly disarmed, she returned his smile, then glanced at Elijah, trying to think of something, anything, to say to engage him as Mister MacKinnon had done before she entered.

Elijah wouldn't meet her gaze. To her mortification, Joanna felt tears threatening.

"You're welcome, Mister MacKinnon," she said, and took her leave with what was surely betraying haste. She wanted to run back to the house, throw herself across her bed, and weep— for the loss of Elijah's friendship, his hand, his future, his hope.

She forced herself to smile through the day's remains, until the last candle was snuffed and Charlotte slept beside her, and she could let the darkness see her heart.

Even under the thinnest sheeting, he was too miserably hot to sleep, yet the mosquitoes were too relentless to lie uncovered. Alex slapped away a sting on his neck. Across from him, Moon rustled the cornhusk ticking as he heaved over on his cot. "Get used to it, will I?" Alex muttered.

Moon's voice issued gruff in the inky dark. "Sounds of ye stewing in your juices are no sweet lullaby."

Alex glowered. "Aye. Sorry."

"I'd not be sleeping anyway."

Moon's disposition had lightened over the day as he'd set about familiarizing Alex with the lay of the shop, the tools and their usage, the heating of the forge. While Moon manned the bellows, he'd set Alex to practice with hammer, tongs, and iron bar, past the point his back and shoulders screamed in protest. They'd finished for the day as the kitchen lass, Marigold, brought supper.

Moon had so far unwound as to speak to her without being coaxed. Then Joanna Carey had arrived with Alex's clothing and the man had drawn the shutters across his soul.

"Does she trouble ye so that ye canna sleep?"

"Who?"

"Miss Joanna. Ye go away inside yourself when she's nigh. What is it about her puts ye off?"

He sensed Moon's bristling before he sputtered, "She—I never said—Joanna Carey is the kindest, truest soul the length of the Cape Fear River."

Alex hadn't expected such fervent defense of the woman. "Ye've an odd way of showing her how ye feel."

"She knows how I feel."

"Oh, aye? I've seen the look of her both times she's come here. The look of a woman whose heart's being broke."

The bedtick across from him crackled. Alex sat up, braced, but Moon merely sat on the edge of his cot.

"Ye know nothing of her. Of us."

The raggedness of the words almost put Alex off, but if he was to survive in this place with its web of humanity stretched in sticky intricacy across race and station—and hearts, apparently— he needed to grasp its pattern before putting another foot wrong.

"Fair enough. But listen. I've been taken from everything and everyone I do ken, put ashore in this place to learn a trade I never thought to need, among a people I canna begin to fathom. Will ye help me, man? Help me get my feet under me?"

Moon's breathing was the only sound besides the chirring of night insects, the distant croak of frogs. Then, "There's nothing between Joanna and me. There can never be."

Alex waited, thinking Moon meant to leave it there. Perhaps it was the dark, no starlight beyond the small window to show a man's face, or perhaps it was Alex's turning the tables, presenting himself the one in need, that made Moon expand upon his reply.

"I wanted to marry her. So does Reeves. Captain Carey accepted *his* suit."

"They're betrothed?" Coming upriver Reeves had mentioned Carey's stepdaughter, but not as one spoke of his beloved.

"She hasn't given him answer." The hoarse words hung in the darkness. "It wasn't until Reeves asked that I summoned courage to do it myself."

"D'ye love her?"

Silence. The buzz of insects. Then, "I care for her."

Not exactly a declaration of passion. A breeze had arisen beyond the window, wafting in to dry the sweat on Alex's skin. He lay back and drew the linen to his waist, scratching idly at a bite on his shoulder. Even in the dark he could sense the room still heaving as it had since he stepped off the flatboat. "Ye and Reeves ken each other from long since?"

"Aye. And he's of no better birth than me, though he's picked up a polish of manner—along with his giant."

Alex fingered the healing welt on his temple. "So ye thought if Reeves had the gall to ask for the captain's stepdaughter, ye'd naught to lose in the asking?"

"Happen it was something like that. But then the forge . . ."

"An explosion, ye said. What caused it?"

"I've no answer to that. By the time I was able to examine the forge, it had been repaired." Moon's voice was a dead-calm sea. "Even had Captain Carey given his blessing, I'd never have held Joanna to it. Marrying a useless cripple?"

Alex couldn't let that pass. "Ye mind what Reeves said when he first marched me into this shop? He was right. I need ye. So does Carey." When Moon said nothing, he let the subject go. "Ye've said how ye came to be serving Carey on land. How does Reeves come to be doing the same?"

"He didn't tell ye?"

"Not in any detail."

Moon sighed. "As Reeves tells it, he was still in His Majesty's service when he got himself abducted off a quay by pirates, was forced to serve with them, then at some point escaped. Afterward came a deal of traveling through the colonies, positions obtained and lost, a few years as a merchant's apprentice. Nothing lasted. Early last summer he wound up in Wilmington to cross paths with Captain Carey. Not long after, our overseer left, and before ye could shout *hard-a-lee,* Reeves had the position. And here we are."

It was the longest speech Alex had yet coaxed from Moon. The words themselves were indifferent, but under them something deeper seethed. "D'ye hold it against Carey, choosing Reeves's suit over yours?"

"No," Moon was quick to say, slower to add, "Happen at first I did, but ye don't know Captain Carey. Aboard ship he was a father to us lads. Later he saw me apprenticed to a blacksmith in Wilmington, then hired me on when I was ready for the work. He's a good man. Ye've nothing to fear from him. Not if ye work honest—and hard."

The Englishman's suspect virtues aside, Alex was aware Moon had looked past himself to offer that encouragement. It surprised him, how much that felt like a victory.

6

The nail rod was three feet long, the charcoal fire built as Moon, manning the bellows, had instructed.

"Keep the rod down deep," Severn's former smith said. "Off the fire's top. Right . . . now check it."

Getting a feel for the iron after five days at the forge, Alex was already pulling the rod from the fire with the tongs. Several inches glowed orange-red, the tip almost white.

"Over the anvil," Moon said.

Alex turned from the forge's heat, took up a hammer, and positioned the bar with the glowing tip near the anvil's far edge. He delivered blows at an angle, drawing out the iron, fashioning a four-sided point, squaring off several inches above it.

"Hardie," Moon said.

Across the blade of the hardie, a device fitted at the anvil's heel, Alex positioned the rod at the length of a finished nail and struck so the hardie's blade half-severed it. A flip, another blow, then he stuck the heated tip into the anvil's pritchel hole and broke it at the nearly severed joint. A final blow flattened the head. He thrust the remaining rod back into the fire and, with water dipped from the slack tub, quenched the iron he'd worked. The contracted nail dropped through the pritchel hole, striking the earthen floor.

Alex grinned at it.

"Well done," Moon said dryly, amused at his pleasure in this most basic of apprenticeship tasks. "Do it again."

Leaving the finished nail lying, Alex took up the tongs, grabbed the heating rod, and swung back to the anvil. As he did so, the ground beneath him pitched as it hadn't done for the past three days. He braced himself, took up the hammer, began drawing the rod into another point.

He finished the rod, started a second, a third. Heat shimmered the air. Sweat soaked his shirt and the kerchief tied round his head. The ache of his arm spread to his shoulder, neck, back. The hammer's clank pierced his skull.

Moon stopped him as he reached for the fourth rod.

"Rest while I tend the fire." Moon scrutinized him, brows pulled tight. "We'll raise that anvil. It's low for ye. Your back and shoulders will be telling ye as much."

"They are." And his legs. Hang it all, his *teeth* hurt. He slung the hammer into its rack, dipped water from the drinking barrel, drank and drank again.

He'd meant to go out under the oak in hopes

there'd be a breeze, but he paused to clutch the doorframe until another wave of dizziness passed. When his vision cleared he saw the lurker, owner of the toes he'd seen poking from behind the smithy that first day. This time he glimpsed a small, nut-brown face peering round the corner at him before it vanished.

He went back for more water. "Who is it skulking out there?"

"Trying to get a look at ye without returning the favor? That'll be Jemma." Moon's words hovered like a cloud of midges. "They're trying to make a kitchen girl of her."

Speaking of kitchens . . . he felt like an oven, as if the insufferable heat came from within, not without. All his joints ached. Moon's voice reached him through a shimmering veil.

"On your feet, MacKinnon. While the fire's hot."

Alex pushed up from the block chair. The smithy floor heaved like a deck in rough seas. He lurched sideways with the motion, falling toward the forge. Something caught his arm, yanking him back. Next he knew his face was in the dirt, cracked shoe-leather blurring in his vision. Then darkness swallowed all.

"I've sent word to the families, informing them of Reverend Pauling's expected arrival," Joanna told their cook, Phoebe, and the girls flanking her broad frame. Three sets of eyes in glistening faces widened as she instructed them in the planning of several days' meals sufficient in volume to feed a crowd that might swell to fifty. Joanna brushed at the sweat beading her temple. Open doors emitted more flies than breeze into the kitchen's stifling confines. There was no help for it in summer, not with a brick hearth broad enough to accommodate three iron cranes, two turn-spits, and a scattering of spider-legged griddles. An oven was set into the sooty wall beside the hearth, near a row of long-handled ladles, forks, and tongs. "Other kitchens will contribute to the victualing, but as there's no telling what they'll bring, we must be prepared."

"Yes ma'am," Phoebe was quick to say, while behind her back the younger women shared a glance of dismay, as if she'd announced Pharaoh's army was descending on Severn like locusts, expecting dinner. Phoebe's plump hands smoothed her voluminous, grease-spotted apron as she sniffed the air. "Dorcas, get that meat turning!" she snapped at the younger of the kitchen maids.

Dorcas pressed her lips together, but took a stool beside the spit's handle and commenced turning a ham spitted over a dripping pan, a task for an unskilled child.

"Where are Mari and—" Stopping as voices reached her, Joanna faced the door as Marigold entered, dragging a scowling Jemma across the threshold by a pinioned arm.

"I don't give a rat's whisker! You meant to help in the—" Seeing Joanna, Marigold halted and thrust Jemma forward. "Look who I found skulking round the smithy."

Jemma pouted her lip. "Don't be telling tales on me."

Joanna strove to appear unperturbed as she took in Jemma's appearance. Gone was the child of a few months past, Charlotte's beloved companion. Still on the puny side for twelve, she'd gained a little in height—the most insignificant change and the only one not self-inflicted.

Jemma had never been a pretty child. With skin, eyes, and hair the exact same hue, amber as pecans, she'd drawn second glances from visitors to Severn, some who'd made uncomplimentary quips about her looks. At least in those days, she'd never been mistaken for a boy. Now, instead of the tidy homespun frock she'd worn, Jemma was dressed in a pair of cast-off breeches, all holes and patches. A shapeless shirt in little better state hung halfway to her knees. But her hair was the biggest alteration. Until recently it had been the child's best feature, thick and curling to her waist. Jemma had hacked it off—with a blunt kitchen knife, apparently—rendering it a ragged mop that didn't reach her shoulders.

"Jemma," Joanna said. "Quite a few people

have been missing you of late. Charlotte most especially."

The girl kept her smudged face lowered, gazing at her filthy toes.

Marigold gave her a shake. "Miss Joanna talking to you!"

"Yes ma'am." The words were lifeless. Where was the spirited voice she'd once heard throughout the house as Jemma and Charlotte played together?

"You found her at the smithy?"

Marigold nodded. "Caught her lurking—again."

"This isn't the first time?"

"No ma'am," Phoebe assured her.

At the spit, Dorcas added, "Jemma ain't never where she needed. This her job, not mine."

The other girl, Sybil, planted floured hands on her hips. "And I'm left to do up the dishes most meals."

"All right," Joanna said, stemming the flood of complaint. She'd seen defiance on Jemma's face when she was towed through the door. It had vanished behind an unreadable mask, as if she'd retreated inside herself where none could reach her. Very like Elijah.

"Jemma, why are you hanging about the smithy? Are you worried about Elijah?"

"No ma'am. No more'n everybody do."

"Is it the new man, Mister MacKinnon? Are

you curious about him?" When Jemma hesitated, then shook her head, Joanna drew a steadying breath. "What's wrong, then, Jemma? Just because you're working in the kitchen—or meant to be—doesn't mean you and Charlotte cannot spend *some* time together."

Jemma flashed her a look so brief, Joanna wondered if she'd imagined its desperation. "Miss Joanna? Can I ask something?"

"Of course," Joanna said.

"Could I help in the smithy instead? I seen Mister 'Lijah trying to teach Mister Alex while yanking at the bellows with his one arm. I could handle that job—the yanking."

Joanna looked up in time to see every woman under the soot-blackened ceiling beams roll her eyes.

"'Lijah don't need you hanging about his forge," Marigold said. "How you mean to reach the bellows, scrawny as you are?"

Jemma glowered. "I could stand on something!"

"Jemma," Joanna cut in. "Do you truly want to work in the smithy? Or are you trying to avoid working at all?"

She wished she could bite back that last question even before she caught the sharp looks Phoebe and her girls couldn't suppress.

Stupid, Joanna. She knew what it felt like to be thrust into a world of responsibility and endless work and feel one hadn't a choice in the matter.

Trapped. Overwhelmed. Terrified of failure. For an instant she felt the weight of that burden full force; not just her own, but that of everyone whose name was penned in Papa's ledgers, who labored under yokes as heavy and more so. It was too crushing to face.

But she could give Jemma this small choice, couldn't she?

"No ma'am," the girl was saying. "I want to help Mister 'Lijah. And that Mister Alex don't scare me much."

Phoebe and her girls erupted in protest.

"You *want?*"

"You spoiled little—"

"Never heard such foolery—"

"You ain't a boy!"

Joanna held up a hand for silence, considering Jemma. "All right. Provided Elijah is agreeable, we'll give it a try."

Marigold's shapely mouth fell open. Phoebe looked too shocked for words. Jemma's expression flooded with relief, as if she'd been delivered from a fate worse than death. Was that what she thought of spending time with Charlotte?

Joanna opened her mouth to add that she'd be down to the smithy to take Jemma's measure again, to provide her with a proper petticoat and gown, when a voice called out beyond the kitchen door—one so out of place it took a moment to recognize.

"Mari!" Heavy footsteps crunched on the path, then Elijah appeared in the doorway, breathing hard as if he'd run from the smithy. "Someone needs to go—" Seeing her, he cut short his urgent words. "Joanna."

"Elijah, what is it?"

"MacKinnon—he's collapsed. I cannot move him." Humiliation rippled across his scarred face. "I need help."

7

August 1747

When Joanna entered the smithy, Jemma seemed to shrink into the ragged breeches and shirt she still wore. The girl dropped her gaze to the linen draping Joanna's arm, the basin cradled to her hip, the pocket at her waist bulging with a flask and the last of Severn's Jesuit bark. "Miss Joanna. All that for Mister Alex?"

At his workbench, Elijah turned. He'd tailed his hair for the first time since his accident, baring his right ear, half-burned away. "Mari isn't here, if ye meant that for her use."

"I know." Preparation for Revered Pauling's visit had dominated Joanna's waking hours the past days, yet Alex MacKinnon had been in her thoughts. It was too soon to know if he suffered one of the seasoning fevers newcomers to the Cape Fear often experienced, or worse, the intermittent ague for which there was no lasting cure, only the bark for treatment. "Mari cannot be spared from the kitchen, nor Azuba from her duties. Papa's set the first meeting for two days hence. You'll attend?"

At Elijah's shrug—no more than she'd

expected—Joanna nodded toward the back room. "How is he?"

"Pitiful weak," Jemma answered. "Come see."

The room behind the shop was overwarm, pungent with the bodily distresses of the form overflowing its cot, draped by threadbare linen. Alex MacKinnon had come to them lean as whipcord. Now his pallid face was gaunt, the bones of cheek and jaw sharp. "Has he taken any food today?"

"Broth," Jemma said. "And that nasty bark powder Mari mix up. Never seen a man screw up such a face."

With Jemma hovering, Joanna set the basin at her feet and tucked her petticoat to sit on a stool beside the cot. Mister MacKinnon's hair fell in sweaty tangles. She bent to soak a cloth in the water while it still held its coolness.

"Pull back the linen, Jemma, to his waist." Jemma did so, wrinkling her nose. Mister MacKinnon's ripeness crowded Joanna's senses. "Would you find a candle and light it?"

As Jemma went out, Joanna pressed the cloth to the man's brow, astonished afresh by the length of him. Arms that went on and on, ending in hands square and powerful, long-fingered, callused. The hands of a warrior. *Hands that had shed blood.*

Pushing the unnerving thought aside, she bathed his face and chest, wondering what, besides his freedom, had he lost for the sake of that doomed Jacobite cause that had ended in his imprisonment? A wife? Children? Even if he mourned none, surely he mourned a life—home, livelihood, the familiar and known.

Was that why Elijah seemed more at ease with a stranger than with her? Did he recognize his own staggering loss in Mister MacKinnon?

What would it be like to have one's life ripped away, to be forced to start fresh in a new place? Panic at thought of losing those she loved—Papa, Charlotte, Azuba, Elijah—didn't quite overwhelm the flame of eagerness that flared beneath it. She quickly snuffed it, unwilling to look at what its light revealed: the things she wouldn't grieve to lose. Or gain.

She dipped a fresh cloth and touched it to Mister MacKinnon's mouth. When his lips parted she squeezed, dribbling water. He swallowed and groaned.

Jemma returned with the candle and set it on the stand. "Ain't he big, Miss Joanna? Big as bear."

There was more of the panther about the man than lumbering bear, in Joanna's estimation. The chest she'd bathed was broad and muscled, but now she *could* count every rib. "Has he spoken?"

"Yes'm. Nonsense, mostly."

"He was probably speaking his native tongue."

"That mumbo jumbo them men in skirts upriver speak?"

"It's called Gaelic. And they're *kilts,* not skirts."

More than a few Scotch families had settled on the Cape Fear since the failed uprising in Scotland, welcomed in the colony by Governor Johnston, Papa's longtime acquaintance. A clannish folk, the Scots. Most had clustered upriver near the trading hamlet at Cross Creek.

"Sometime," Jemma said, "seem like he fighting in his dreams. Other times he call out names of men, like he looking for 'em."

Looking for men? Had he been an officer in the Stuart army, a high-ranking clansman? Joanna thought they called them *chiefs,* as the Indians did. Alex MacKinnon seemed young for that, but what did she know about the wilds of Scotland and its people? She sighed, wishing the world were a kinder place. Wishing her place in it was other than it was. At least Mister MacKinnon would be his own master again, should he live out his seven years. With a fervency that surprised her, she hoped he would.

She fetched a tin cup from the washstand and dipped it full, her mind crowding with other concerns. "Jemma, have you spoken to Charlotte since you started helping in the smithy?"

She knew the answer. Jemma had rebuffed Charlotte's attempts to speak to her. Her sister played alone with her dolls, with only the prospect of families with children soon to visit to enliven her.

Jemma's face shuttered. "No ma'am. Been busy."

"Speaking of busy," Joanna said, eyeing the girl's ratty breeches, "Azuba spared precious hours stitching that petticoat for you. Why aren't you wearing it?"

Jemma dodged her gaze. "Miss Joanna, don't get mad at me asking, but why can't a girl wear breeches?"

Joanna opened and shut her mouth, then said, "It isn't proper."

"I can get up on that block to reach the bellows lickety-split. Skirts get in the way of nigh everything, and I'm always on the move."

As if she'd planned it, Elijah called from the smithy, "Jemma, there's a horse to shoe. I need your help!"

She'd forgotten to tell Elijah the one guest already arrived, Mister Forelines, had mentioned his horse was on the verge of losing a shoe. The man had beat her to it.

She nodded Jemma off to the yard. "Go on. I'm fine here."

Mister MacKinnon had grown restless, flexing those big hands at his sides. Seconds after Jemma left, his body jerked in a spasm, long back arching.

Joanna's heart thumped. At first she thought it

some manner of feverish fit and was uncertain what to do. Administer the bark? She feared he would choke on it. Still, she'd reached for her pocket to withdraw the flask when Mister MacKinnon rasped out, "*Cobhair orm*! *Na gabh air falbh.* Uncle . . ."

Uncle. Comprehending but the one word, Joanna leaned over him, touching his brow. He blazed beneath her hand. "Mister MacKinnon, you're at Severn. No one means you harm. Please, wake up and be well."

We need you to wake up, she thought. The sentiment wasn't nearly as startling as Alex MacKinnon's eyes, which flew open and fixed upon her.

"Mari . . . ?"

Joanna hadn't realized he'd grasped her wrist until his fingers eased their hold. His eyes rolled, then closed. Tension spooled out of Joanna, leaving her limp and saturated as the bedding.

He'd thought she was Marigold.

Sounds from the smithy yard reached her. A ruckle from the horse being shod. The tap of hammer against shoe. Mister Forelines speaking to Elijah. She'd greeted the man but half an hour ago, having come to the study unaware he'd arrived, carrying the basin she meant to fill at the well, and overheard part of a conversation about one neighbor who wouldn't be at the gathering.

"There's been another quarrel with Simcoe's

slaves?" Mister Forelines had inquired of Papa.

Asahel Simcoe owned the plantation bordering Severn upriver. The Careys had had little but contention from him since the day they took possession of Severn because of a boundary dispute begun with the land's previous owner. It had finally been settled in court—in Papa's favor.

"Apparently so," her stepfather replied. "Word came about an altercation between my slaves and Simcoe's in the woods at the boundary line. Phineas rode out this morning. May it prove a molehill, not another mountain."

Joanna made a *tch* of disappointment, revealing her presence. "Mister Forelines, I hadn't realized you'd arrived," she said when he turned her way. "Have you need of anything?"

Henry Forelines, owner of a mill downriver, bowed in greeting. "I've deposited my kit in the bachelor's cabin." Others would be making use of the old cabin on the grounds, men who came without wives or who didn't mind roughing it while their families enjoyed the comforts—if crammed quarters—of the house. "I've issue with my horse, though. Old fellow has a shoe come loose."

Mister Forelines's wig, perpetually in need of curling, hung slightly askew on his bald head. Joanna suppressed a smile. "I'm sure Elijah can see to that."

"He's managing, then, your blacksmith?"

"We've a new man in training," Papa said. "A Scotsman serving out his indenture."

Mister Forelines's brows rose toward his crooked wig. "A Jacobite?"

"A fevered Jacobite at present," Papa replied, reminding Joanna of her need of haste if she wanted to check on the man.

"Before I forget," Mister Forelines said as she turned to go, "I'm bound with a message from the reverend. He stopped over with Clan McGinnis, upriver, but should be arriving today—as will they all. You are forewarned, my dear."

He was right to call the McGinnises a clan. With twelve children, an uncle, and two aging mothers in tow, Joanna hoped they'd bring a canvas shelter to raise in the yard, else they'd be like prized tobacco in a hogshead barrel when it came to sleeping.

From the smithy a new voice, clear and carrying, jolted Joanna from her reverie, flooding her with pleasure. Reverend Pauling had arrived. So, then, had the McGinnises. She'd need to change into something more appropriate for receiving guests than her plain muslin day gown.

She slid her hand behind Mister MacKinnon's head, placed the cup's rim to his lips, and managed to get a few swallows of water down him. Leaving the flask with the bark tincture on the stand, she went into the smithy and found

Reverend Pauling on his way to her. They met beside the forge.

"Joanna." The skin around his blue eyes crinkled as he grasped her hands. A friend to the Careys since before her mother's death, the reverend was nearing sixty. He wore his natural hair tailed, and the faded hat he never could keep cornered.

"I'm so glad you're here," she said, and to her mortification burst into tears. "I'm sorry, I don't know why . . ."

"It's been a difficult season for you." Still holding her hands, Reverend Pauling drew her near and spoke in confidence. "I've seen Elijah now, and I tell you, Joanna, all will be well. All things are working together for the good of those who love God, who are called to follow Him—as Elijah is called."

Joanna's breath shuddered. "How can this be good? He's in such pain."

"He is, and I don't mean to call his loss good, but we serve a God who uses even our most crushing trials to produce in us a fragrance of His grace, as His own dear Son has been for us an example. Remember how Christ prayed the cup of suffering would pass from Him? But it pleased the Father He should drink thereof. And yet what came of that bitter draught?"

"Redemption," she said. "He drank it for us."

"Exactly. And He will work good for Elijah

through this. In time." The reverend's sorrow over Elijah's maiming was visible in his eyes. As was his hope. He squeezed her hands before releasing her. "What of this new man Edmund has acquired? Fallen ill, I understand. Not my particular thorn in the flesh?"

Reverend Pauling suffered the intermittent ague, and the fevers didn't always oblige him by the timing of their visits. Traveling yearly, holding meetings in homes, barns, or forest clearings, more than once he'd been aided by strangers who happened by a solitary camp and found the itinerant minister shivering in his bedroll.

"I'd hoped you could tell. You knew of him already?"

"Only what Edmund has told me. An exiled Jacobite, sentenced to indenture. Shall I look in on him?"

Reverend Pauling was always quick to fold himself into life at Severn. "I left a bark tincture there, but I must go and greet the McGinnises. They did come with you?"

"Down to the newest babe born three weeks since."

"Thirteen?" Ann McGinnis had her hands full. "I must help Azuba see them settled." She drew a breath, then let it out and said again, "I'm glad you're here."

"As am I," Reverend Pauling said and, with

a lifting of beetling eyebrows, ducked into the back room.

The fever was a scarlet thing, the color of his enemy. Day and night. Past and present. Dream and waking. They rolled across each other like mist over the flanks of Ben Tangaval, clashed and splintered as a ship gale-driven onto rocks, an unholy *stramash* permitting no respite. His bones burned. His flesh cracked with heat. He couldn't find his clansmen. The English in their red coats rose up from the heath, and he fought them until his blade ran scarlet too. Still his men died, and he couldn't reach them, couldn't find them in the dark of the ship's hold. Cameron. MacKenzie. Rory MacNeill. He'd as good as killed the man who'd been to him a father. Only he hadn't, for Rory bent over him, alive and speaking. Joy blazed. "Uncle . . ." It wasn't Rory's face but a woman's, bonny and brown. She offered something bitter as gall to drink, then gave him water to chase it down, but he couldn't lose that taste. He was hacking with his sword again, making a slaughter of his enemies on the freezing moor as his teeth rattled in his head. Only it wasn't a moor. And it wasn't a sword in his hand but a hammer. Cold vanished in a blast of heat. It wasn't men he struck, but iron. He pounded it, forging something for himself . . .

"Mister Alex, you take a little broth?"

Marigold, that was her name. He swallowed what she spooned into him. It hurt. Everything hurt. Cold again. How could he be cold when he knew this place was hot as hades?

Moon's voice: "It cannot be like before, Mari."

"Haven't you grief enough? Why heap on more?

"Mari. Please."

"Did that fire blind you as well? You can't see when a body cares for you."

Was it Joanna Carey of whom they spoke? Of course Elijah saw she cared for him, but no man wanted a woman's pity.

As if their talk had summoned her, Joanna was there, touching him, cooling him. Her voice soothed. Strength wrapped in gentleness. He floated on its cadence, buoyed as on a loch. A touch on his lips. Water . . . or a kiss? It was cool and lush, and he took it in, a groan escaping him.

A heavier hand rested upon him. A man's voice spoke, the words beseeching . . . Alex opened his eyes, but there was too much light. He felt unanchored in his flesh, without firm sense of who and where he was, only that he no longer burned.

"Alex MacKinnon?"

The name jarred soul and flesh together, as abrupt as a hurtling dog halted at the limit of its rope. He turned his head. Seated beside his cot was a man he'd never seen before, smiling at him, a smile at once gentle and spirited, above it a pair of intelligent blue eyes hung with shadows that spoke of weariness or . . . illness? Craggy features and weathered skin belied the impression. A man equally acquainted with sun and sickbed?

He found his voice, or a rough approximation of it. "Ye ken my name. Might I have yours?"

"David Pauling." The man removed a shapeless hat to reveal graying hair pulled back from his brow. "A servant of our Lord Jesus Christ, by the grace of God made a minister of His peace."

The expected reverend. "How long . . . ?"

"Nearly five days, I'm told. I'm here at the wish of your mistress, who ministered to you in your illness. How are you feeling?"

Joanna. He hadn't dreamt her. She'd been there watching over him. Kissing him? *That* had been a dream, surely.

The reverend had asked a question. "Weak as a half-drowned kitten, if ye must ken." His belly tightened as he spoke, emitting a growl.

"A kitten wanting its milk." Reverend Pauling stood. He was somewhat below medium height yet managed to fill the small space. "I know where the kitchen is, and from what I smelled upon my arrival, I'd say you've timed your awakening well."

The man took a tin cup from the washstand and offered it to Alex, who pushed up on an elbow to take it, dismayed at the weakness of his grip.

"I'll be back directly with something more filling." Pauling was gone before Alex could speak.

Trembling, he'd lifted the cup to his lips when he minded something else he'd dreamt. Not the kiss. Not the fighting. Not his men or even his uncle. The glow of fire and metal, the showering of sparks. He set down the cup, then flexed his gaunt right hand, minding the hammer's weight, the strength of his arm as he struck the iron— forging himself a sword.

8

There seemed no end to Severn's need of nails, but Alex didn't mind. Just as well he'd a task to occupy him, requiring nothing but muscle memory to undertake, being but two days since he'd risen from his sickbed—and considering the swell of folk bursting the bounds of Severn's grounds with whom he'd no wish to mingle.

Neighbors. The word had broad meaning on the Cape Fear. Some who'd gathered for the preaching had traveled farther to do so than most Barra folk would venture in a lifetime. For himself, he hadn't set foot beyond the smithy yard save to use the necessary. Even so he hadn't escaped notice.

The previous afternoon a man had needed an axe blade mended, a task Alex undertook with Moon's supervision. Trailing the man were two lasses Joanna Carey's age, capped and pink-cheeked with the heat. Lingering at the doorway while he worked, they'd whispered behind their hands—about Moon, he'd assumed. He'd glanced their way with hammer raised, meaning to scowl them off, and caught the dark-eyed stare of the taller lass. Her raking gaze left him in no doubt as to the object of their interest.

"They talking about you," Jemma confirmed, waiting in the smithy when he and Moon emerged that morning.

"They?" he asked, not wanting to know.

"Folk not from here."

While Moon watched, he laid the fire. "How d'ye ken what anyone's saying?" Yesterday she'd manned the bellows while he hammered out nails. She'd hardly left his side.

"I was in the kitchen afore sunup, fetching your breakfast. The help come along to this shindy got ears—they hear their folk talk. Want to know what they saying?"

"I can guess," he muttered.

"They saying you seven foot tall, ain't got a lick of proper English, you killed half the king's army afore they caught you, and . . ."

Alex shut his ears. The smithy doorway faced east. The sun was rising, with it the temperature. *So be the iron. Bend with the heat.* Let exile hammer him as it would, he'd emerge reshaped, of use to himself on land as well as sea. He'd still much to learn, about the forge, about the land of his exile.

"And many a nail to make," he muttered as Moon deposited a bundle of rods on the forge's counter, then crossed to the bench beneath the open shutters to set out what Jemma brought from the kitchen. Pone drizzled in honey, cured pork, biting cider to wash it down. They made short work of it and settled into the day's labor.

Sometime after noon Moon went out, leaving Alex with Jemma manning the bellows. Countless finished nails later, he hadn't returned. When the last nail thudded on the packed earth, Alex went to the water barrel, dipped the ladle, drank, then poured the rest down his face. "Have ye winters in this place?"

Jemma, gulping water from her hands, spat droplets as she laughed. "Comes round every December. Lasts all of a week."

"Good to ken," he said wryly, and poured another ladle-full over his head. Dripping water off chin and hair, he removed his leather apron, hung it, and stepped into the yard, pulling the sweat-soaked shirt away from his chest. The sun beat down from a sky hazed with clouds too meager to shade. Beyond the smithy yard the lane dividing the slave cabins and the shops was unusually quiet. He'd met few slaves as yet and could match but a handful of names to faces, but he'd grown attuned to the rhythms of the place. It was all but deserted.

"Where's Moon got to?"

Jemma fetched up beside him, her head barely topping his waist. "Gone to the preaching most like. Up at the Big House."

Set back with the other shops well behind the kitchen gardens, the smithy was too far removed to catch any sound of voices, preaching or otherwise. Still, he'd doubted Moon would be found among those gathered for the religious meeting, judging by what he'd overheard during Pauling's last visit to the smithy.

After a day at the forge, he'd been drained as a squeezed sponge, unable to budge from the block chair outside the room he and Moon shared, where Moon and the reverend had retreated. He'd leaned his head against the wall, half dozing, only to jerk awake in time to hear Pauling quoting, *"Shall we receive good at the hand of God, and shall we not receive evil? In all this did not Job sin with his lips."*

To which Moon said, "I never fathomed why God let such calamity befall a man who pleased Him."

"That's hard to accept, that a loving God can be more concerned with our eternal good than our earthly comfort. But as the apostle Paul wrote . . ."

Not wanting to hear whatever the apostle said on the matter, Alex had staggered out to the yard and lowered himself against the brick wall to sit, knees drawn, head cradled on aching arms. When the scuff of shoes paused beside him, he pretended to sleep until the reverend departed.

Had something the man said made a difference to Moon? Drawn him to the gathering Alex had thought he meant to avoid?

He glanced down at Jemma. "Why are ye not away to the preaching yourself, then?"

She flashed her amber eyes at him. "On account of helping you."

"D'ye want to go?"

"Maybe . . ."

Joanna Carey would be among the listeners. Would she be glad to see him on his feet? The fire was dying down. He thought it would be all right to leave it so. "Show me to the meeting, *mo nighean*?"

Jemma peered up at him, furrowing her brow. "What's that you calling me?"

"It means *lass*."

"Little girl?" she asked warily, as if ready to take offense.

"Or young woman."

"That's fine, I guess. Call me that." Jemma peered out from the smithy as if checking for threat, then squared her shoulders. "I show you the way."

She led him past the sprawling gardens, along the hedged walk that gave the Big House and lawn a sweeping berth and separated it from the kitchen, shops, and slave quarters. It was the nearest Alex had come to the house since his arrival. He studied it with interest as they passed the occasional spot in the dense hedge low enough for him to see across. On the ground floor a back door opened onto a terrace lined with flowering borders, overhung by balconies on the upper story. Coming round to the front, he glimpsed the colonnaded portico he'd seen only from the river in passing before his attention was captured by Reverend Pauling, midstream in his sermonizing.

He'd expected shouting. The reverend's voice was lifted above casual speech, yet his cadence was more akin to a man conversating with friends. Impassioned but not fierce.

Jemma left the walk, which veered toward the front of the house where the hedge terminated. On the lawn between house and river, under a canopy to shield the gathering, the people sat on benches, stools, chairs brought from the house. As Jemma led him to a fringe of poplars at the yard's edge, a few on the periphery glanced their way. Mainly slaves, spilling out from the shelter, unshaded from the sun. At the back of their number, Moon stepped away to meet him, brow knotting. "What's amiss?"

"Nothing. I finished the rods. Thought I'd come find ye."

Moon crossed his arms, hiding his wrist-stump, and nodded.

Pauling's congregation was a tightly packed cluster of caps and wigs. He searched the caps for Joanna, finding her nearer the back of the gathering, gowned in blue, unaware of his arrival. The lasses who had ogled him at the smithy noticed. Seated two rows forward of Joanna, one nudged her companion, who craned her neck at him. That caught Joanna's attention. She followed their gazes only to pivot forward again, a flush rising up her neck.

"For in the Gospels," the preacher was saying, "does He comfort with these words, *'Come unto me, all ye that labour and are heavy laden, and I will give you rest. Take my yoke upon you, and learn of me; for I am meek and lowly in heart: and ye shall find rest unto your souls. For my yoke is easy, and my burden is light.'* What He gives us to bear is often the means to free us from clinging to the things of this life that needlessly weigh us down. For even our afflictions are, in light of eternity, that very thing . . . *light*."

The relentless sun was no match for the indignation burning Alex's chest. He was staggered by the gall of a man who could speak baldly of such things to a crowd half composed of slaves. Or such as Moon.

Would Pauling call *his* exile and forced indenture an easy yoke?

Wishing he'd kept to his place at the smithy, he was on the verge of retreating when he spotted Marigold coming along the walk. She reached the point where the hedge began its curve and hesitated. When she spotted them, he elbowed Moon, who turned, saw Marigold, then pretended he hadn't.

Looking both affronted and distressed, the lass hurried to the rear of the gathering and touched Joanna's arm, bending to whisper. Joanna rose, and the two drew off for a murmured consultation.

"But how then do we cast off those burdens that are not Christ's?" the reverend continued. "How do we cast off that yoke that rubs us raw and take on His yoke in its place?"

"There is no casting off," Moon muttered, turning to go.

Alex fell into step. At the same instant Joanna and Marigold started for the walk. He and Moon gave place to the women. As she passed, Joanna lifted her gaze to him.

He was struck by the color of her eyes, different in full daylight than they'd been by a candle's glow. He'd known they weren't dark, but he hadn't thought them so blue. Not the clear blue of an autumn sky. A stormier shade.

The color of the Hebridean sea before a gale.

Joanna emerged from the stifling kitchen with the conflict Marigold had brought to her attention sorted. A minor squabble between Sybil and a girl Ann McGinnis had brought to serve had escalated into an altercation, exacerbated by the heat, which had shortened tempers and loosened tongues. One of the McGinnis's brood had lately attached himself to their slave, his mother's attention being taken up with his youngest siblings, particularly the newest. The boy was underfoot in the kitchen, but Ann's girl hadn't the heart to shoo him away. Joanna had promised to send the eldest daughter straight to the kitchen to round up her brother.

She'd missed Reverend Pauling's finishing thoughts on casting off burdens not of the Almighty, leaving her with the pressing question—how did one define *light* when it came to burdens? She didn't fear hard work, but there was no denying a heaviness weighed on her, making the daily tasks she'd applied herself to since the age of twelve feel more onerous with each passing year, not less so. One couldn't simply cease living, nor abandon those who depended upon one. Surely that wasn't what Reverend Pauling meant.

Joanna paused on the path between the vegetable gardens, overtaken by a longing to hide herself among the twining pole-beans, even as a contrary longing for fellowship sought to pull her down the path. She'd found scant time to enjoy the company of Elizabeth Martin and Lucy Woodard, the two young women present near her age, nor any of the women, aside from sorting their issues and fulfilling their needs. Despite her best intentions she was playing the part of Martha again when she longed to be Mary, sitting at the preacher's feet.

"Martha, Martha . . . ," she murmured.

Laughter floated on the bee-buzzing air. Lucy Woodard's. She and Elizabeth had plied Joanna with questions about Mister MacKinnon when last they'd spoken. Joanna had hoped her sparse answers satisfied, but she'd caught their straying glances during meeting. She'd been glad to see Alex MacKinnon join the gathering, but more thrilled to spot Elijah at the back of the crowd, though she'd sensed his discomfort when she drew aside to speak with Marigold. Mister MacKinnon had seemed ill at ease as well, a glower carved into his lofty brow.

Was everyone out of sorts this day?

She drew a breath scented with garden earth and shook herself into action. Reaching the walkway as a cluster of slaves trudged by, returning to work, Joanna halted the last in the group, Severn's head carpenter. "Gideon, bide a moment."

The man raised a hand to doff his cap. "Miss Joanna?"

"I'd meant to speak to you of a need at the smithy. When I tended Mister MacKinnon, I noticed his bed is far too short."

Gideon smiled, tight-lipped to hide jumbled teeth. "I 'spect no bed frame on this plantation be fitting him. You want us to build a new bedstead?"

"Or add a few inches to the one he has."

"More'n a few." Gideon scratched his gleaming brow before settling his cap in place. "We get on it directly, ma'am."

Parting with the carpenter, Joanna reached the lawn where guests still clustered, some speaking to the reverend, others waiting to, still others directing slaves setting up tables soon to groan beneath another meal. Out of the bustle Azuba emerged, beelining for her, features set in a look Joanna recognized. Something broken needed mending. Something lost found.

Not another McGinnis child, she hoped.

9

Pauling's eyes betrayed fatigue after a week of preaching, praying, exhorting, baptizing, and whatever else his flock required of its shepherd. He nevertheless offered greeting to one and all before retreating into the smithy's back room for, Alex supposed, one last go at Moon. The Careys' neighbors had dispersed to their homes along the river. The reverend would depart tomorrow astride a mare from Severn's stable, hitched now to the rail upon which Jemma perched, while Alex shoed the mount. Though most of Severn's guests had arrived by river, those come by road or bridle path seemed to have had at least one horse in need of attention. He'd grown reasonably proficient at shoeing.

"This one comes near," he said, setting down the hoof he'd been matching to various finished shoes Moon kept on hand, giving the mare's shoulder a caress as he straightened. The oak shading the yard murmured in the breeze that had sprung up. The sun was dropping west in a cloud-feathered sky. Compared to the blanketing heat he'd endured since the *Charlotte-Ann* dropped anchor, it was downright pleasant.

"Bide ye here," he told Jemma. "Fire's hot enough."

At the forge he put the shoe to heat and waited, catching snatches of conversation from the back room. Pauling's voice, clear and carrying. Moon's gruff, indecipherable replies.

"It's true we're promised suffering," he heard the reverend say, "that our faith will be tested. But we're promised also that all things work together for good, because the Almighty Himself is good. All things, not just those which seem good."

Pauling's message never wavered. Present suffering didn't mean the Almighty's promises were void. He'd the best planned for His children, and that best would include trials. Affliction. But understanding His ways wasn't the path to peace. Peace was always with us, because He *is* peace.

Could such baffling verbal thrusts do anything but further wound?

Alex took the shoe from the fire and commenced hammering, drowning the reverend's voice. Sparks flew off glowing metal as his mind rankled over his and Pauling's last encounter. Two days ago the man had caught him during a break in his work and attempted to engage him in conversation about the state of his soul.

"Save your breath, Reverend. Ye're wasting it with me," he'd interrupted. "I shed the rags of my religion in the dark of a prison ship. I'm of no mind to don them again."

Pauling hadn't flinched. "You're right to label your former religion *rags*. All man's efforts at religion are as rags in the Almighty's sight. It's in His righteousness we must be clothed if we would enter His kingdom."

Alex slammed down the hammer, driving out the man's voice—past and present—then forced himself to stop and examine the shoe. Another blow and he'd have likely bent it too far. He plunged it into the cooling bucket, sending up a vaporous hiss.

As it faded, the silence in the back room swelled. Curious and disturbed, he stepped to the doorway, just as Pauling's voice rose again.

"We give You thanks and praise for the fellowship of suffering, for the consolation of Your Holy Spirit, the comfort of Your steadfast love." Seated on Alex's cot across from Moon, Pauling leaned close, a hand to Moon's shoulder. "Even as we tremble at the awesomeness of Your power and sovereign might."

A shudder went through Moon as a tear rolled down his scarred cheek. Anger swelled in Alex's throat. He would stop this, physically remove the man if need be. Summoning the nerve to do so, he looked closer at Pauling. Tears coursed down the reverend's face as well.

"Kindle another fire, Almighty God, a fire

of faith in the heart of my brother. Comfort his soul. Grant him patience while he awaits Your guidance. I ask this believing that nothing is impossible with You."

Alex made the sign of the cross before he could check the reflex, ingrained in him since childhood. Though Moon sat with eyes closed, Pauling had caught the gesture. He nodded, as if to include Alex in their intimacy. Face shot through with heat, Alex stepped back into the workshop, took up the shoe, and returned to the yard, to the clear air and the breeze he hoped would scour from his mind the words overheard.

He brushed the mare's shoulder, letting his hand travel down chest and foreleg before he lifted the hoof and secured it between his aproned thighs. He'd arranged the needed tools on a block within reach. While Jemma fondled the mare's nose, he drove in the first nail. Satisfied with the angle at which the point emerged, he clipped it and reached for the next. He was on the last nail, the light in the yard gone golden with the sun's setting, when Pauling emerged from the smithy.

"How do you find her, Mister MacKinnon? Sound enough for a trek through the back-country?"

"I dinna ken what hazards might present, nor the nature of the land past that creek yonder." Alex nodded westward, though the smithy blocked all view of Severn Creek, which flowed beyond the orchard and the slave cabins. "Are there roads ye'll be following?"

Fitting the nail, Alex glanced at the reverend. Maybe it was only the deepening shadows beneath the oak that underscored his haggard pallor, but just now he didn't seem the sort to go adventuring in remote places.

"There's a road of sorts upriver as far as Cross Creek. From thence various trade paths cut across the colony. Eventually one strikes the old Warrior Path running north."

"Warrior Path?" Alex tapped in the nail and clipped it, then reached for a file. "Indian warriors, d'ye mean?"

"He talkin' about the Cherokees," Jemma said from her perch on the rail. "You ever run across them, Reverend?"

A smile lit the man's eyes, pale in their shadowed settings. "I've met a few of that tribe, as well as Catawbas, and what I believe was a band of Tuscaroras, though they may have been Mohawks ranging south."

Alex's estimation of the man rose a notch, hearing him speak so matter-of-factly of people he'd been led to believe were warlike and savage.

Jemma wrinkled her nose. "Tuscaroras sold my grandma for a slave."

The reverend looked as surprised as Alex by the statement. The horse shifted. Alex took a firmer grip of the hoof, filing as he asked the preacher,

121

"Can that be true? Indians are in the slave trade?"

"Some are, I'm grieved to say. Those living nearest the colonies sell their captured enemies to the English—or the Spanish—in trade for guns and cloth and metal tools." Pauling studied Jemma, thoughtful and intent. "From what tribe was your grandmother taken?"

"My granny was Cherokee, called Looks-At-The-Sun. Tuscaroras took her in a raid, a girl." Jemma sat straighter, gazing into the horse's gentle eyes. "Cherokees is my people."

Maybe that explained the look of her, Alex thought. She'd African blood as well, though. Perhaps white. He felt around the hoof, making sure all was secure and smooth. "Do these Tuscaroras live near enough the white settlements to trade their captives? Somewhere along this river?"

"Once, but no longer. They and the Carolinians went to war thirty years ago, after which most of the Tuscaroras migrated north to join the Iroquois."

"Iroquois? That's another sort of Indian?"

"Several, actually." Pauling squeezed his eyes shut and seemed to sway, but recovered himself to add, "They live quite far to the north, a confederation of tribes. But some Tuscaroras lingered in this colony . . . isolated bands."

"The Iroquois live to the north, ye said? How far?"

"A long way," said Moon, who'd come to the smithy doorway, his face betraying no sign of the emotion that had beset him earlier. "The Warrior Path runs north along the mountains into Virginia and Pennsylvania. Iroquois lands stretch farther still, into New York."

"Mountains?" Alex set the mare's hoof to the ground and straightened, taking in these new place names. "So the whole of Carolina isna like this, swamp and mosquitoes?"

Jemma giggled, slipping off the rail to join them. "No, Mister Alex. Carolina rolls up higher 'til you come up against them mountains. That's Cherokee country."

Alex reached for a rag to wipe the file clean. "And there's folk settled between here and there?" he asked Pauling. "People ye mean to preach to?"

"Yes, though the farther west one travels, the smaller and more scattered grow the settlements. You might find Lawson's account of his travels through the colony—*A New Voyage to Carolina*—of interest. His description of the backcountry holds true. Perhaps Edmund has a copy he'll lend."

That likelihood seeming remote, Alex asked, "How far are the mountains from here? Has anyone settled them?"

Alex worried he'd asked one too many questions when Pauling's brow puckered. "Very few . . ."

"Why, then, d'ye not keep to settled places like Severn?"

"It's what the Almighty calls me to do," Pauling replied, throat convulsing. "And by the King's mercy, I will do it."

Though the reverend looked as if a stiff wind might knock him flat, Alex bristled, annoyance eclipsing concern. "Dinna speak to me of the king's mercy. What power has *he* to ease your path, an ocean away?"

The reverend started to shake his head but curtailed the motion with a wince. The look that crossed his face was eloquent of alarm, shifting swiftly through comprehension, distress, and lastly, resignation.

"I speak not of England's king . . ." With that, Pauling's eyes rolled back and he fainted in the yard.

10

For days Joanna had sought solitude to ponder what snatches of Reverend Pauling's teachings she'd heard, finding only the seconds between lying down each night and sleep claiming her. With Charlotte readying for bed, she'd wandered into the sewing room to catch up on her stitching before losing the light. If only her thoughts could be marshaled into neatly stitched rows instead of scattering like peas spilled from a shelling pan. Her parting with Lucy Woodard skittered across her mind as she bent over a petticoat's hem. Joanna had apologized for having found so little time to spend with her.

Lucy had seemed more puzzled than disappointed. "I cannot fathom," she remarked before boarding the flatboat that would convey her family downriver, "why you don't allow Azuba more charge over domestic matters. She's capable, yet you seem determined to have a hand in every little thing that must be done, letting your slaves and their concerns pull you hither and yon all day long. You'll wear yourself threadbare before you're twenty."

Joanna had laughed away the exaggeration. She'd *be* twenty in a six-month.

Lucy hadn't shared her mirth. "It's as though you care if your Negroes *like* you. They're slaves, Joanna."

She'd stood on the dock while boatmen poled the Woodards away, bewildered that Lucy could so easily dismiss those who served her. From the time their management had been taken from her mother's lifeless hands and thrust into hers, Joanna had striven for fairness in her dealings with Papa's slaves. If her domestic managing differed from that of her neighbors, she'd never had opportunity to learn.

Her next thoughts were no more welcome. In the morning Reverend Pauling would depart for the backcountry, where he would preach through the autumn, then bide the winter in Pennsylvania. It would be spring, at least, before they saw him again.

She let the petticoat fall to her lap. Why did she retreat into work for solace instead of following her soul to the green pasture where it longed to feed? Perhaps the reverend would afford her an hour of conversation before he sought his bed.

As she quit the room, a commotion of muffled shouts punctuating a rhythmic pounding shattered that hope. Joanna reached the foot of the stairs as Papa emerged from his study, lunged for the back door, and yanked it open. On the dusky threshold a shadowy figure loomed, huge and humped. Papa stepped back as the figure pushed into the house, resolving into Mister MacKinnon, carrying something across his shoulder that created the illusion of bulk. The something was Reverend Pauling.

"This way," Papa said, needing no explanation.

Though clad in the leather apron that covered him chest to knee, Mister MacKinnon's shirt-sleeves were rolled high. The muscles of his lean arms stood out like ropes as he maneuvered the reverend into the study.

Azuba met Joanna at the study doorway, quick to grasp what was transpiring. "The shaking started?"

"I couldn't tell. Mister MacKinnon had him slung over his shoulder."

"Coming up that lane like he carried a feather tick," Azuba said. "I seen it from a window upstairs. I'll fetch another quilt."

Joanna slipped into the study as Mister MacKinnon lowered Reverend Pauling to the bed he'd occupied during the gathering—those few hours he'd slept. The tall Scotsman and Papa worked over the reverend with barely a word spoken, removing shoes and coat, arranging bedding.

Joanna approached. "We haven't any bark left, Papa."

The reverend's eyelids fluttered. "My bags . . ."

Joanna edged past Mister MacKinnon and took

127

up the reverend's hand. He was shivering. She reached for the coverlet folded at the bed's foot. So did Mister MacKinnon. Their fingers tangled as she grasped its edge. He drew back, giving her place.

"Even in summer he gets chilled," she said. "Soon as we get some of the Jesuit bark into him, it will help."

"Aye. The taste alone should make him forget his aches."

Joanna looked up. "Is it so nasty?"

"Ye'll not be forgetting the taste. Though I hope ye never make its acquaintance," Mister MacKinnon added.

Joanna grew aware of Papa standing back from the bed, watching. As though he had as well, Mister MacKinnon drew off, leaving her to take charge. Reverend Pauling's belongings were packed, save what he'd have needed come morning. Joanna found his supply of powdered bark, glancing aside to see Mister MacKinnon gazing at a map on the wall.

She looked away when Papa addressed him. "What happened?"

"He'd come to the smithy with the mare needing a shoe." The rumble of that Scottish voice, its cadence giving lilt to each word, filled the room with a sense of calm that beat back Joanna's worry for the man shivering in the bed. "Whilst I saw to it, he went in and spoke to Moon.

I was still shoeing the mare in the yard when out he came. He stopped to converse, seeming well enough, if worn, but by the time I had the shoe nailed, he'd dropped where he was standing. Has it come upon him so sudden before?"

"It has," Joanna began, but Papa spoke over her.

"I assure you, MacKinnon, we're acquainted with the particulars of the reverend's condition. He'll be well tended. Thank you for your aid. Good night."

Joanna frowned at the dismissal as Mister MacKinnon bowed and left the room. As quickly as he left, Azuba arrived, arms laden. While the woman prepared a tincture, Joanna stood back watching, stifling a yawn.

Azuba spared her a glance. "Go on to bed, Miss Joanna. I'll tend him."

As much dispirited as fatigued, Joanna said, "Charlotte must have been halfway through her bath not to have come downstairs. I best see her to bed." She bade her stepfather good night and went out into the passage, where she found her sister perched near the top of the stairs, peering through the balustrade with one of the housemaids clutching her shift to keep her there, gazing down at the one person Joanna hadn't expected to find in the passage—Alex MacKinnon, standing with his back to the stairs, watching the study door.

"You're still here," Joanna said.

He nodded. "Begging your pardon, Mistress. I'll leave ye now."

"I wasn't protesting. Would you bide a moment?" He checked, an eyebrow arched in question, but she first strode past him to the stairs. "Please see Charlotte to bed," she told the maid. "I won't be long behind."

The woman tugged on her sister's shift, but Charlotte didn't budge. "Azuba says the reverend's ill."

"To bed," Joanna said. "If you're still awake when I come up, I'll tell you everything then." Which guaranteed her sister would be wide awake. She faced Mister MacKinnon, feeling the strangeness of his presence in the house. "You look as though you're feeling better."

"I am." He regarded her before adding, "Was it ye, Mistress, sent the carpenters?"

"I saw the bed was far too short for you when . . . I came to see you, before."

He bent his head in acknowledgment. "I thank ye, Mistress."

"Gideon and his carpenters did the work."

Candles in their wall sconces threw shadows across Mister MacKinnon's face, accentuating high cheekbones, the orbits of his eye, the line of his jaw. "Oh aye. I meant just now to thank ye for coming to me when I lay sick. It was kind of ye, busy as ye've been."

Joanna thought of him lying in that too-short

bed, of touching the wet rag to his lips. Though he still looked much too thin, his skin was golden in the candlelight, his color good. "I didn't think you would remember."

"I dinna, exactly. I'd some verra odd dreams. But it's a relief to stretch out full in a bed to sleep." He drew in his bottom lip, studying her, then released it. "I expect ye're wishing me there now."

She blinked. "I beg your pardon?"

He took a step nearer. "It's only that ye look tired, Mistress. But then ye would do, after all the fizz and *thrangity*."

Doubtless it was her fatigue, but she found herself on the verge of giggling. "Fizz and . . . what?"

He did laugh, softly. "Sorry. I meant ye've had a great bother keeping up with your many guests, aye? Ye'll be plumb *wearit*."

That crooked smile. Joanna felt the pull of it go deep. Strangely, she no longer felt the weight of her fatigue. Impulse overtook her.

"Mister MacKinnon, if you'd bide yet a moment more, there's something I want to show you." She returned to the study before she could change her mind. Papa was intent on the reverend, talking with his back to her. Azuba, busy mixing the bark powder, glanced her way as she took the big conch shell off Papa's desk, but she hurried out without explaining.

Back in the dimly lit passage, she held out the shell, large enough it needed two hands, to Mister MacKinnon. It was bleached a creamy hue, though faint stripes could be seen spiraling around its broad end where thick spikes protruded, while the inner shell, visible along its flared opening, was a glossy pearlescent pink.

"I found this at the ocean when I was a girl," she said, feeling more than a little childish now.

"Aye. It's a braw conch. Biggest I've seen." He sounded uncertain what she meant by the offering.

"Put it to your ear."

He hesitated briefly, then did so. She watched his features, studying his expression. That crooked smile came softly, and his eyes grew abstracted, his voice taking on a husky note as he said, "I'd forgot ye could hear the sea's roaring like that."

"I thought you might miss it," she said, hoping he didn't ask why she'd thought so.

Still holding the shell, fingering its spikey protrusions, he took a step toward her, searching her gaze as a slave wouldn't dare. Possibly as an indentured man oughtn't. "Ye'll have enjoyed it, then? All the stir and bustle, people about the place, the preaching?"

"Not as I'd hoped." She'd spoken out of pure startlement. No one else had asked her if she'd enjoyed the gathering, but best she say no more on that subject. "And you, Mister MacKinnon? Did you enjoy it?"

"I didna care for yon man's preaching," he said bluntly, nodding toward the study. "This fever, though, it's a thing ye've seen him through before? I think ye started to say as much."

"The last time was in autumn."

"Aye, well. In that at least he kens of suffering." Before Joanna could respond to the statement, Alex MacKinnon held out the shell. "I thank ye, Mistress, for this. But I should go. G'night to ye."

Miss Joanna, she wanted to remind him, but he was already making for the door, leaving her holding the shell.

The usual creaks of the house settling on a summer night surrounded her, as did the trill of crickets, the throaty chorus of frogs. Absent were the noises of guests packed into her room. No tired whispers of mothers helping offspring to chamber pots. No infant cries muffled by a breast. Joanna yet lay wakeful, her mind teeming.

Charlotte was a sound sleeper; still, Joanna took care extricating herself from between the linens. She took up a shawl as she left the room, hair in a braid. If Azuba kept vigil over the reverend, she'd send her to bed. No need for them both to be awake.

Downstairs the candles were snuffed, but the pungent scent of her stepfather's pipe met her before his voice reached her ears.

"Sometimes, David, I think it shall hound me to my grave." Joanna halted at the study door. Papa had sounded more dispirited than she'd heard since her mother's death. "Now this new disturbance. I suspect it's proven of substance since Phineas hasn't returned."

He wasn't speaking of her mother, but of that interminable aggravation they'd inherited. In the early years she'd been too young to understand the many disputes that erupted between Asahel Simcoe and her stepfather—court battles over water rights, timber rights, boundary lines—stemmed from imprecise surveying of the original patents, an all too common occurrence in the colony. The last court ruling had settled the boundary and forced Mister Simcoe to pay remunerations for timber he'd cleared on Severn land.

"I'd been minded to ride out myself," Papa said, indecision in his tone.

"Go. I'm well looked after." Though the reverend's reply was thready, clearly his fever had broken. In the silence following, Joanna started to creep away, but Reverend Pauling's next query stopped her. "Is that all that troubles you, this neighborly strife?"

"Yes," her stepfather said. "And no. The weight

of it and more has been heavy on me of late—Severn, and what shall become of it. And Elijah. Charlotte. Joanna."

"I've spoken to Elijah," Reverend Pauling said. "His road is steep, but the Almighty will see him through."

"He's been the nearest thing to a son to me. Aside from Phineas, of course."

"This young Mister Reeves I've yet to lay eyes upon. Another of your former cabin boys, and the one you favor for Joanna."

"She hasn't accepted his suit."

"Nor rejected it?"

The night was humid enough that Joanna's shift clung beneath the shawl. She ought to leave them to their privacy, but she wanted—needed—to know her stepfather's mind on this matter.

"There's no love between them. I hope in time there might be friendship. Joanna is strong, bright, bred to the life, but this estate will need a man when I'm gone. The right man. Phineas has proven his devotion to Severn. He has a head for the business that, for all his admirable qualities, Elijah lacked even before his loss."

Reverend Pauling was slow to speak. "What of Joanna? What of the right man for her?"

Papa made no answer.

"Edmund, we are friends, you and I?"

"Of course," Papa replied gruffly. "And you know as well all that I owe you—my very life."

It was true. Had it not been for the reverend, none of them would have survived the year following her mother's death in childbirth. The baby, a much longed for son, died with her, plunging Papa into a grief so miring he'd been barely aware of his daughters—the stunned twelve-year-old struggling to step into her mother's shoes, the three-year-old bewildered by her mother's absence. In the midst of it, Joanna had penned a desperate letter. Though it reached Reverend Pauling at his sister's home, that troublesome ague had delayed his coming. His return letters, overflowing with encouragement, had sustained Joanna until the man himself had come, in time to pull Papa back from the brink of ultimate despair.

"Then for the sake of our friendship, hear me in this." The reverend's voice had grown hoarse. Joanna strained to hear, leaning closer to the open door. "You are weary under the burden of this life you've built on the backs of souls your ledgers claim—quite erroneously—that you own. Can you not see it? The greater the material comfort you accrue, the greater the burden of it will weigh. Joanna isn't exempt. At Grace's passing she took up her mother's yoke with a courage few her age could have showed, though it wasn't without struggle. By the time you were able to look about you, by sheer dint of will she was bearing it. I dare say she's borne it so long now,

136

uncomplaining, even she has lost sight of what it stole from her."

"Stole from her?" Papa echoed.

"Joanna lost more than a mother. She lost her childhood, or what remained of it. I won't compare her lot to that of the souls in your kitchen, shops, and fields, forced to work their lives away for bare subsistence, but can you not see the yoke your stepdaughter has borne . . . so ill fitted . . ."

Joanna leaned into the wall, one hand muffling her mouth. *"The greater the material comfort you accrue, the greater the burden of it will weigh."* The words pierced her with their truth.

Concern tightened her stepfather's voice. "I was wrong to let you speak of these matters. You need rest."

The reverend ignored that. "You keep men in chains, Edmund. But what of . . . your own?"

"There are no chains here, David. And Severn cannot exist without slaves."

If her stepfather's reply constricted Joanna's heart, the reverend's next words threatened to tear it free of her chest with yearning.

"Must it exist? What does a man truly need? A roof over his head, land to grow his food, or a place to work for it. You have these blessings many times over, yet maintaining them demands you do the opposite of what the Almighty requires of a man."

"And what is that?"

"To do justly, to love mercy, to walk humbly with your God. To simplify it, Edmund . . . love God and love your neighbor."

Joanna's mind cleaved to the words. What did a man truly need? What did she, Joanna, *need?*

The answer unfolded with astonishing clarity. A vision of a life that included no vast acres of pine forest needing to be exploited. No crops so abundant they required gangs of slaves to sow and reap them. No great house needing many hands to maintain it. No dirt-floored cabins filled with souls bound to them in servitude. Instead there was a tidy log house, far from that river that bound them to ships, that bound them to trade, that bound them back again to this place. And there was a man—an honest, hard-working, God-fearing man who loved her. Who would love their children. A man she tried to imagine as Elijah. But he wouldn't stay brown-haired and stocky of build in her mind. He transformed into a man outlandishly tall, lean-muscled, fair and blue-eyed as a Viking.

"Miss Joanna? The reverend taken worse?"

Thrusting the vision from her mind, Joanna turned to see Azuba coming along the passage, candle in hand. "He's better, actually, but needs rest. Papa should go to bed."

Before Azuba could say another word, Joanna brushed past her and headed for the stairs, but when she was again abed, the vision persisted.

That last part had been mere folly, imagining Alex MacKinnon in the role of husband. But what of the rest? She couldn't tear down the house around their ears and put up a log home in its place. She couldn't set at liberty every slave Papa owned. She couldn't force him to simplify their lives. Severn owned Papa's heart, but could she find a way to meet him in the middle, somewhere between her vision for her future and his?

11

Phineas Reeves came to the smithy the next morning, trailing Demas, who halted at the door while Reeves strode in, brightening at sight of Alex at the forge. "I feared to find you taken up residence in the burial ground, given the state in which I saw you last. But here you are, hale and hard at work."

Caught in a rare moment of solitude—he'd sent Jemma to beg a cider jug from Marigold as a playful trade for the kitchen poker she'd asked him to make—he spared the overseer a nod before striking the nearly finished poker, turning it across the anvil, striking again, until it grew apparent Reeves meant to linger until he paused for conversation. Thrusting the poker into the fire, he stared at the man in his clean suit and riding boots, leather satchel slung at his side—in neat order for one having spent the past week living rough in a pinewood shanty camp. "There's a burial ground?"

"What? Oh yes. Out beyond the orchard." Reeves gazed about the shop. "Speaking of . . . Is Moon still above ground?"

"Verra much so, but presently indisposed."

Reeves smirked. "Before the wind with sails out, you mean?"

"I do not," Alex said, though in fact he'd returned from toting the reverend up to the house the previous evening to find Moon nursing a flask. Severn's former smith had yet to rise from his cot despite the hammering. So much for Pauling's admonishments.

"Whatever you say, MacKinnon," Reeves said with a knowing gaze. "I'm just returned from dealing with our troublesome neighbor upstream. Are you yet aware of Simcoe and his machinations on our boundary?"

Alex shrugged. "I dinna ken a thing about it."

"Count yourself fortunate. I'll admit, this time circumstances didn't present themselves as straightforwardly as Captain Carey might wish them to seem."

"What d'ye mean by that?"

"That I'm unconvinced Carey's slaves haven't trespassed this time." Reeves raised an inquiring brow. "You'll know about tar-burning? It's a thing we do in autumn after the hog-killing, requiring kilns to be built. What burns in those kilns to create the tar is lightwood—heartwood from the long-leaf pine."

"I expect ye'd need a deal of woodland to keep such an operation going long-term."

"Exactly the crux of the matter with Simcoe. He's attempted to pilfer ours in the past, but this time it may need Captain Carey himself to sort it out . . . if he will."

Alex studied the man, suspicious of this unsolicited confidence—and the implication of Carey's unwillingness to oversee the matter. Or indifference. "Seems ye'd do best to discuss it with him, aye?"

Reeves produced an agreeable smile. "Right you are. I needn't have troubled you." His gaze shot past Alex. "Moon—feeling poorly, I hear."

Alex turned to see Moon in the doorway, squinting against the late-morning glare from the yard. "What evidence have ye," he asked, voice a growl, "that our people trespassed into Simcoe's wood?"

A muscle in the overseer's jaw twitched. "I never mentioned evidence—and MacKinnon's right. It's Captain Carey I must speak to of these matters. Besides, we cannot expect you to grasp what passes beyond the smithy yard."

Alex searched Reeves's expression for the disdain such words implied, but found no hint, unlike the unconcealed dislike on Moon's face as he returned to their room.

"Before I take my leave," Reeves said, as though Moon had never entered the conversation. "I presume Miss Carey has seen to your needs— she is diligent in her limited sphere—but do you find any lack in your present arrangement? Something I might provide?"

An unexpected offer from the man who'd

ordered him beaten and dragged off the *Charlotte-Ann* into the present arrangement.

"I've all a man could need."

Reeves made a deprecating gesture. "I meant to inquire sooner, but first your illness, then the issue with Simcoe . . . Still, I'm back now, if not in time for the grand gathering. I've yet to meet this reverend with whom the Careys are so enamored. Missed him again, it seems."

"Ye havena missed him at all. He took fever last night. He's abed in that room full of books."

"Is he?" Reeves's expression flitted from mild displeasure to surprise. "Room full of . . . You mean Captain Carey's study? You've seen it?"

"I have." For a moment Alex was back in that room with its reek of tobacco, its cluttered desk and map-covered walls—one map of the Cape Fear River, another of the entire colony. And Joanna Carey in the passage, coming toward him with that huge conch shell, face turned up in the candlelight. He'd swear the lass's eyes were a different shade each time he saw them. Last night they'd been a peaty brown.

Reeves was studying him. "Speaking of books . . ." He reached for the satchel at his side. "Do they interest you, MacKinnon?"

"D'ye mean can I read?"

"I'm aware that you can," Reeves said while he rooted in the satchel. "I saw you do so when you signed the indenture. I meant do you enjoy the pastime?"

"I've read a book or two in my day." Rory MacNeill, as tacksman to their chief, had been allowed access to the library at Kisimul Castle. Alex had made his way through most of the MacNeill's books—history, natural philosophy, half the works of Shakespeare—before he'd marched away to fight in Charles Stuart's army.

Reeves had found what he sought, a thick volume bound in tooled leather, which he proffered. "I had this from Captain Carey's shelves. I never leave Severn without a book on my person."

Mindful of his sooty hands, Alex nodded toward the block chair by the doorway. "Set it there, aye? Till I've washed."

"Proving yourself a man who rightly esteems the written word. It's Defoe's *The Life and Strange Surprising Adventures of Robinson Crusoe*, about a castaway who spends years on a remote island in the tropics before being rescued quite improbably by . . . But I'll say no more lest the ending be spoilt."

Alex was torn. He'd heard of *Robinson Crusoe* but never had opportunity to get his hands, sooty or otherwise, on a copy of the narrative. "Captain Carey kens ye're doing this?"

"He won't mind, but I'll speak to him. Return it when you've finished. Choose another, if you will."

Alex hadn't made up his mind whether to accept this reassurance before he was distracted by Jemma's voice in the yard.

"You oughtn't to follow me here. I told you I got to work."

Demas, who'd stepped inside the smithy to sit on a block chair out of the sun, propelled himself to his feet.

"You'd rather work than play with me?" It was the little miss, Charlotte, whose voice he'd heard from the stairs last evening, though he hadn't glimpsed more than the hem of her nightshift.

A scowling Jemma stepped into the doorway, cradling the cider jug he'd sent her to fetch. She stiffened, seeing Reeves, but when she caught sight of Demas looming an arm's length from her nose, she nigh jumped out of her skin. The jug hit the earth and broke, sloshing its contents over her dusty feet.

"Some chits ought to listen to they betters," Demas muttered.

Jemma bolted—away from the smithy.

"Jemma, come back!" The owner of the pleading voice stepped into the doorway, stopping short of the broken jug to stare after Jemma.

Alex stared too. He couldn't help it. It was the figurehead from the *Charlotte-Ann* come to life in the form of a lassie in a pale frock, golden hair ringleted about her shoulders, blue eyes tearful in a face of both stunning beauty and winsome innocence.

Reeves strode to the distraught girl and bent a knee. "Charlotte, you shouldn't be down here on your own."

"Jemma left me." The girl looked pleadingly at the overseer, who tilted his head in sympathy.

"I'm headed up to the house." Rising to his feet, Reeves held out a hand. "Come. We'll find your sister."

The child took the proffered hand as Demas separated from the shadows and stepped across his master's path. Reeves jerked his head back, leveling Demas a look. The big slave fell in submissively behind the pair as they passed from view.

An odd man, Reeves. For all the cordial insensitivity he showed the rest of them, he'd seemed genuinely compassionate toward Charlotte Carey. But what was he playing at, coming a hair's breadth from talking down Edmund Carey, who'd been so good to him, then all but forcing upon Alex the loan of the man's book? Ought he to return it to the man unread? Or do as Reeves suggested: read it and return it to Carey's study . . . where hung those maps he wanted very much to see again?

Halfway down the stairs Joanna heard her sister's sobs coming from the parlor. In the doorway of the green-paneled room, she halted. Just within stood Demas, arms laced across his massive chest. On the settee Charlotte sat. Before her knelt Mister Reeves, murmuring words Joanna couldn't catch. "Charlotte—whatever is the matter?"

Abandoning the settee, Charlotte rushed to Joanna to throw slender arms around her waist. "Why doesn't Jemma like me?"

With their guests' departure, Joanna had half-expected this. She held her sister as Mister Reeves stood, tugged his coat straight, and tucked his hat beneath an arm.

"I've only just returned, Miss Carey. I stopped by the smithy to check on MacKinnon, where I encountered Charlotte—and that girl who has distressed her."

Charlotte raised tearful blue eyes. "She ran off and left me."

Joanna swallowed back a sigh. Was she being too soft? Ought she to *force* Jemma to go on being Charlotte's playmate?

"They're slaves, Joanna . . ."

She would not do it. Not to Jemma. Or to Charlotte.

She met Mister Reeves's pained gaze. "It was kind of you to accompany my sister, and you just returned." The reason for his absence recalled itself. "Did you meet with difficulty?"

"I did, though it needn't trouble you. Is Captain Carey in his study?"

"Last I knew. With Reverend Pauling."

"Ah, yes. I hear he's fallen ill." Mister Reeves let out a sigh. "Miss Carey, I'd intended to return for the last day of meeting, knowing its importance to you. I regret I was prevented. Am I forgiven?"

It flashed across her mind that Mister Reeves had been called away by some urgent need during Reverend Pauling's last visit. Strange that it should happen again, but the man couldn't be blamed for trouble with a neighbor stretching back before his arrival, and with the slaves involved it had been his responsibility to see it sorted. "There's nothing to forgive, Mister Reeves. I do comprehend it couldn't be helped."

While she was still speaking, the man made her a bow. "You are all grace and kindness, Miss Carey."

Joanna responded with a curtsy made awkward with Charlotte's clinging. With a neat turn upon a heel, Mister Reeves left the room. Demas lingered long enough to cast her an inscrutable look before he followed his master in silence.

"Jemma's not a little girl anymore," Joanna said, having guided her sister to the settee and supplied her with a kerchief. "I know she's scarcely bigger than you, but she's nearly . . ." It struck Joanna that Jemma had reached the age when her own childhood had ended. The girl was twelve at least.

"It may simply be that now she's getting older, Jemma has come to understand how things are."

Her sister's brows knit above puzzled eyes. "What things?"

"Jemma is a slave, and there are certain . . ." She'd been going to say *lines that mustn't be crossed,* but in her sister's gaze, yearning for the hurt of rejection to ease, she saw herself reflected, seven years past.

"Why, Azuba?" Joanna hated the whine in her voice. She was twelve. Old enough to possess herself. "I know I have to step into Mama's place now, but it doesn't mean Mari has to go work in the kitchen. She could learn to run the plantation with me, like you helped Mama. Couldn't you teach us together?"

Face shadowed with grief, Azuba looked for a moment as if she might reach out and embrace her. Joanna stiffened, knowing she couldn't allow it or she'd plunge into a sea of tears and drown. Again. She must be strong for Papa. For Charlotte. For Severn.

"Miss Joanna. Lots done changed with your mama's passing. We all got to do things we don't want to do. Hard things." Her mother's dearest friend, after Papa, focused her brown eyes on something far away. They seemed to harden, to flash, then they shifted back to Joanna, softening. "It's the way things are, Miss Joanna. By and by you'll understand."

Joanna understood, but the chasm between what was and what she wished could be had left its wounds. "Charlotte, I think it would be well if you and *I* spent more time together. Would you care to learn what I do with my days? Maybe help?"

Charlotte's pale brows rose. "You're so busy."

Joanna's chest tightened. Pressing upon her now was the need to check on the reverend, settle the time for dinner, inform Azuba, discuss a menu with Phoebe, make sure the cook knew Mister Reeves would be joining them . . .

She wiped a stray tear from Charlotte's cheek. "And so your help would be most welcome. Even more your company."

Charlotte sniffled. "All right," she said, but when she started for the parlor door, Joanna stopped her.

"Charlotte? What was Mister Reeves saying to you when I entered the parlor?"

The child's face brightened. "He promised to bring me another doll, next time he goes to Wilmington."

Joanna hoped the man would keep his word. But their attempts at consolation felt like ribbons tied round a bleeding gash. She'd failed to speak to the heart of her sister's pain, and the reason was no mystery. The pain was her own, unassuaged after years.

The sudden rise of voices from the study jarred her attention. Though she couldn't make out

Mister Reeves's words, Papa's voice was strong enough to penetrate a gale: "And you've waited until now to speak of it? Show me, Phineas—this instant!"

Joanna reached the passage to see her stepfather fling open the back door, on his heels Mister Reeves, clapping on his hat.

"What is going on?"

Mister Reeves halted, features pinched, impatient. "Miss Carey, do not concern—"

"Phineas!" Papa bellowed from the yard.

Joanna motioned him on, hurrying down the passage. A glance into the study gave her pause. Reverend Pauling looked as if he meant to rise from bed. "Reverend, don't. We'll see to whatever this is." She took a step into the room, relieved when he sat back, looking up with shadows beneath his eyes. "What's upset Papa?"

The reverend's expression was grave. "It seems one of Edmund's slaves has met with tragedy. Mister Reeves returned with his body."

Joanna sucked in breath. "Who?"

"Edmund left before a name was uttered."

Joanna whirled toward the door and fled. She passed through the hedge, spotting Mister Reeves hurrying after Papa, headed toward the stables, where a cart stood, still harnessed to a horse. The knot of slaves gathered around it drew back at Papa's approach, revealing something canvas-wrapped in the bed.

The smell hit her. The stench of decay slowed her steps, but she came on, taking shallow breaths. All eyes were on the cart as Papa ordered Moses, his head groom, to unwrap what lay enshrouded in canvas. Broad features set in a rigid mask, Moses climbed into the bed. Around him rose a shifting cloud, black and buzzing on the air. Flies. One landed with a smack on Joanna's cap. She brushed it away with a shudder, stopping near the horse's head, daring to come no closer.

Slaves came from shop and garden. Carpenters and coopers. Gardeners and stable boys. Laundry maids and weavers. Children pinched their noses or pressed them into worn skirts. The faces of the adults around her were facades that hid emotion, as the canvas folds were drawn aside. She saw Elijah approach without the wariness of the slaves, right up to the cart's bed, saw his look of shock. Moses scrambled out of the cart. He staggered into the growing crowd, and Joanna knew a name was passing mouth to ear. Low moans went up.

Bothered by the smell of death, the flies, the rising tension, the horse took a nervous step in her direction. The cart rolled. Papa stepped back and saw Joanna. Alarm came into his face as the horse tossed its head.

A hand latched onto its headgear. Another stroked a broad, quivering cheek. *"Air do shocair . . . ,"* a voice soothed. *"Sin thu, a laochain."*

Alex MacKinnon appeared as she'd last seen him, sweaty and disheveled from his work, but he wasn't looking at her. Still soothing the horse in soft murmurings, he nodded at Papa, as though in answer to a question. At last he acknowledged her with a glance. "Mistress."

Flies buzzed above their heads.

A wail went up from the direction of the kitchen.

Mister MacKinnon stepped nearer. Strong fingers curved around her arm. "He'd have ye away from this, your stepfather. Will ye let me walk ye back to the house?"

Joanna stared blankly as the wailing came on, growing louder.

The slaves parted. Down the aisle that formed, Azuba walked, but Azuba wasn't the wailer. Behind her came Phoebe and Sybil. Supported between them, weeping so violently she could barely walk, was Marigold.

153

12

It was Marigold's brother, Micah, whom Reverend Pauling would lay to rest with words of consolation. Joanna wondered what those words would be as she made her way down the lane between the workshops. She'd no idea what she would say once she reached Marigold's cabin, where the reverend had gone an hour past. Neither fever nor chills had returned, but if he didn't rest for the time remaining until the burial, he mightn't make it through.

As she reached the smithy, which rang with evidence of Alex MacKinnon's growing proficiency, Elijah stepped from within and beckoned. As she neared, Joanna searched his face for any hint of warmth, detecting only grief, anger.

Inside the smithy the hammering ceased, but Elijah blocked her view within. "I'm hearing all manner of rumor about Micah. Happen ye know the truth of it?"

"I'm not certain." She knew only what Mister Reeves had told them, once Papa directed the grave dug and they were gathered in the study.

Elijah scowled. "Were ye there when Captain Carey had the tale from Reeves?"

"I was."

"What mean ye, then? That your intended's telling lies?"

"He's not my . . . Elijah, why would Mister Reeves lie?"

If Elijah had an answer in mind, he didn't share it. "Tell me what he said."

She clenched her teeth to stave off a return of the tears shed while listening to the overseer's account. "Micah was gathering lightwood for the tar-burning with two others from the work gang, out near Mister Simcoe's boundary line. Or that's what he was meant to be doing. The other two returned without him, claiming they'd no idea where he'd gone since they'd ranged widely. Mister Reeves had the whole gang stop work to search for Micah. It took them two days scouring the woods. By then . . ."

"I saw," Elijah said, face grim.

She hadn't seen the body and didn't want to imagine. "He was found on Mister Simcoe's land. Mister Reeves has no notion whether Micah knew he'd crossed the line, though I'd think by now they'd be well acquainted with it. Do you know why he might have done so?"

"No. Nor does Mari, in case ye mean to question her."

The words stung. "I'd never be so unfeeling."

"Joanna . . ." Elijah's gaze softened. He started to reach for her but aborted the gesture, looking away from the tears she couldn't stem.

"Mister Reeves sent the slaves back to camp with Micah's body," she went on, wiping at her cheeks, "while he and Demas had a look round. They found boxing on the trees at the edge of Mister Simcoe's land and met some of his slaves, who maintained they hadn't done it. Papa will ride out to investigate. And he means to go downriver to Wilmington and speak with his solicitor before things get out of hand."

Elijah's gaze narrowed. "All right. I expect the truth will out eventually." He turned on his heel and went back into the smithy. She heard him speak brusquely to Mister MacKinnon.

The hammer's clang started again.

Neither Papa nor Mister Reeves thought she should attend the burial. "It's their time to grieve," her stepfather said. "Let them be. If David isn't back within the hour, I'll go myself and fetch him."

"They won't want you there," Mister Reeves said.

Joanna didn't heed them. She waited for a chance to slip away unnoticed, through the back hedge, past the gardens, and into the bordering peach orchard where the air was clammy on her neck, cooling from the day's heat. Twilight had fallen by the time she reached the orchard's far edge, bordering the burial ground. Lanterns had been lit and set between crudely marked graves, splashing light on bare feet and worn hems. The slaves had gathered round a narrow gaping in the earth into which Micah's body had been placed. At its head stood Reverend Pauling, beside him Marigold, leaning on Azuba. Joanna remained rooted beneath the boughs, where shadows thickened.

"They won't want you there."

"They're slaves, Joanna."

As she watched, Reverend Pauling stepped back from the open grave and moved to Marigold's side to speak. Men came forward with shovels while women stood back, children clinging.

A wail went up, unleashing a flood. The sound of abandoned grief sent shivers along Joanna's arms. At first it was cacophonous, but after a time a rhythm formed as voices transitioned into song, the words lost to distance. The slaves milled about as they sang, filling the grave, comforting one another, swaying as they mourned. Joanna lost sight of the reverend, found him again, only it wasn't the reverend. The shape was wrong, too thickly set. The man moved into the knot of bodies gathered around Marigold. *Elijah.*

Uncertainty carved a moat around Joanna's feet. Dared she cross it? What if she did so and Mister Reeves was proved right?

The reverend would be her excuse. She would say she'd come for him. Grasping this thread of nerve, she left the orchard's shelter. A few paces off to the right, another figure separated from the trees—a looming figure in a pale shirt with a stride so long it carried him swiftly to her side.

She yelped in startlement.

"*Wheest,*" Alex MacKinnon said. "Dinna let them hear ye."

His hand was on her shoulder, the encompassing reach of it making her feel as diminutive as Charlotte. "Mister MacKinnon. What . . . what are you doing?"

"Keeping ye this side of the burying ground."

He stood so close she was forced to crane her neck to look into his face, what she could make of it in the dark. "Why should you?"

"Ye've no business among them now, aye?"

It was the third time she'd been told as much, and the third time was a charm—if the man's intent was to crumble her defenses and smash all barriers of decorum. "Who are you to tell me so? You overstep your bounds, Mister MacKinnon."

He made no immediate response. She could see his chest expand against his pale shirtfront. Before she could think what more to say, he stepped back, dropping his hand from her.

"Ye're right, Mistress. I beg your pardon. Ye'll do as ye wish."

Turning, he strode back into the orchard, leaving her at its edge.

Joanna glanced at the lantern-lit mourners, then bolted into the trees, arms raised to fend off branches springing back in Alex MacKinnon's wake. She sighted his broad shoulders catching starlight between the trees.

"Wait . . . Mister MacKinnon!"

He rounded on her so abruptly she nearly collided with him. Leafy boughs hemmed them in. His proximity, and their seclusion, set her heart to pounding.

"Why don't you want me to go to Mari?"

"*I* wouldna want ye there, were it me laying my kin to rest not knowing by whose hand he met his death."

That took her aback. "Are you saying Mari blames us—Papa or Mister Reeves—for this?"

"I canna say, Mistress."

He thought it, though. She heard it in his voice. Was that what Elijah thought?

"You meant to shield me from them?"

"Aye—and them from ye. I dinna fault ye pitying the lass, but mind who she is to ye. If ye draw lines between yourself and folk, the least ye can do is keep to your side of them."

Joanna flinched against the jab at that old bruise. "You've been here how long, Mister MacKinnon? A month? What do you know of the lines between us—Mari and me? You're not a slave."

He stood silent, looking down at her, then asked, "Am I not?"

"Indenture isn't slavery," Joanna maintained,

hardly knowing why she argued. From within rose that vision of a life without the distinction of slave and free. Where did a man like Alex MacKinnon, not slave but not free, fall into that vision?

"What would ye call it, then?" he asked.

"Opportunity." She'd snatched the first word that came to her. "I realize in your case it's also punishment, but it's a merciful one, isn't it?"

She felt his stiffening. The night's humidity drenched her in clamminess even before Mister MacKinnon spoke again.

"Is that what ye think?" His voice pelted like rain in the dark, though it was hardly louder than the breeze in the boughs, or the mournful singing of the slaves. "I was taken forcibly from my country, sent half a world away, and told never to return—even after I serve my sentence. Whether I manage to return despite all—and I mean to try—what I was, the life I had, is gone forever."

Joanna desired him to speak of that life, but couldn't bring herself to ask, not with the loss of it thick in his voice. "Mister MacKinnon," she began, but he didn't seem to hear her.

"After Culloden I was put wounded aboard ship and sent to London. There I rotted for a year with some twenty other men in another ship's hold. I watched those men die of their wounds, of disease, hunger, despair—including the uncle who raised me. We suffered in more ways than I care to say, Mistress, so believe me when I tell ye that I *do* grasp what those slaves yonder feel—a helplessness and rage the like of which ye dinna ken. Never mind they've full bellies, clothes to wear, cabins to sleep in. None of it is by their choosing. *Listen* to them."

With her own heart aching, Joanna did so. The singing reached them through the trees, unadorned, uninhibited. Not even in singing her favorite hymns that week past had she lifted her voice with such fervor. That didn't mean she hadn't the need. Was that what had drawn her to the burial, her own need? Not to comfort Marigold but to *be* comforted.

She blessed the darkness that hid her tears, until she sniffled, giving herself away.

Mister MacKinnon's fingers curled round her arm. His touch seared, as though he'd come straight from the forge and hadn't been lurking on the edge of the burying ground as she had been. "I heard ye and Moon talking earlier. I ken ye care for Mari, that ye weep for her. I heard it in your voice."

"Mari was my companion. As Jemma was Charlotte's."

"Did it end for ye and Mari as it has for those two?"

The man was too discerning by half. "My mother died—I was twelve. I took over the running of the house and kitchen. That's when Mari . . ." She couldn't continue.

She feared Papa would dismiss her longings for a different life without consideration, tell her she was foolish to think it possible. Would Mister MacKinnon agree, or might he know how to bring it to pass? Had his life in Scotland resembled the one she longed to live?

His grip on her tightened. "Mistress? Are ye all right?"

It was said so gently she'd the startling sense he was about to do what Elijah hadn't outside the smithy—draw her into his arms. Until Reverend Pauling's voice spoke from the darkness, practically beside her.

"Joanna? Is that you?"

Mister MacKinnon released her. Mortified at their discovery, she raised a hand and sought the reverend instead. "Yes, Reverend, I—Are you well?"

Leaves rustled. A pale face emerged in the space where she and Mister MacKinnon stood embowered. Reverend Pauling grasped her reaching hand. "Forgive my interrupting. I heard your voices . . ."

Joanna felt the sag in his grip, but Mister MacKinnon was faster to react, getting an arm around the reverend before he buckled. Reverend Pauling stayed on his feet but leaned into the blacksmith's strength.

"I believe you needn't carry me . . . this time," he said, a smile threading the exhaustion in his voice. "But an arm to lean on as we go would be welcome."

Despite his words, Reverend Pauling seemed near collapse, but Mister MacKinnon proved able to judge between the man's need and dignity, finding a path between the two. He let the reverend make it to his bed on his own feet. Joanna saw him settled, aware of their blacksmith lingering in the room, gazing at the maps on the walls. The reverend lay back upon the pillow, drained as Joanna feared he would be by the evening's exertions. He let out a long breath, closed his eyes, and drifted into needful sleep.

Sitting on the side of the feather tick, Joanna looked up to see Alex MacKinnon gazing now at the reverend, a frown pinching his brows.

"Thank you for your help, again." Seeming to take her words as dismissal, he dipped his head and stepped back. Joanna stood. "I'd like to continue our conversation."

"Aye, Mistress. I'll await ye in yon passage." He bowed and left the room.

When she turned back to the reverend, she found he wasn't sleeping after all but regarding her through slitted eyes. "Joanna . . . what were you doing in the orchard with that man?"

As she groped for answer, voices reached her from the passage. One of them was Papa's.

"Having my motives called into doubt," she said, then hurried out to find Alex MacKinnon standing by the study door, Papa coming toward him wearing an expression not best pleased.

"He's here by my leave, Papa. He was helping . . ." Her words died as she registered the second man in the candlelit passage. Not Mister Reeves, as she'd assumed, but a slightly older man with a seaman's weathered face, his dark hair touched with silver. Thom Kelly, former first lieutenant of her stepfather's last command, now master of his second merchant ship, the one that bore her name, the *Joanna*.

"Captain Kelly." She came forward to greet him with a hand outstretched. "When did you put into port?"

Thom Kelly took her hand as she curtsied. "We anchored at Wilmington three days ago, a fortnight ahead of schedule. Might I say you're looking in good health, Miss Joanna. Spritely as a woodland elf with leaves in her hair."

"Leaves?" Reaching up to touch the portion of her hair not covered by her cap, her fingers came away not only with a leaf, but the twig to which it was attached. Blushing, she recalled the man left waiting by the study door. "Forgive me, this is Papa's . . ."

But when she turned to introduce Alex MacKinnon, the passage behind her was empty, his departure so soft-footed she hadn't heard the door.

13

Then the preacher said his piece and up start the singing, dirt rattling down, and I couldn't bear to see poor Mari . . ." With the sun barely up, Jemma was nattering on about the burial, in lurid detail. Preoccupied with his own memories of the previous evening, Alex checked the forge fire.

"Less air out of ye, *mo nighean*, more through the bellows, aye?"

Perched on a block, Jemma pulled the lever, gusting air through the forge's inner workings that flared the charcoal with a muted roar. "Then I tell Azuba, 'Lookit—Mari gone wobble-legged!' But afore she slumped Mister 'Lijah come out the shadows to prop her up . . ."

Alex raked the charcoal, judging its heat by glow and hue. Not as expertly as Moon would have done, but Moon wasn't in the shop. If his tidy cot was any indication, he hadn't lain in it the night long.

They'd gone together to the burial, but upon seeing Pauling at the grave, such bitterness had filled Alex as to render him no fit company for those who sought the reverend's comfort. If four-and-twenty years had provided human carnage enough to glut him for a lifetime, how did a God who purportedly saw everything, for all ages, sit enthroned in heaven while men created in His image butchered one another continually? Even were Micah's death by mischance, the man had been enslaved lifelong. How could any reasoning soul come to this place and preach of God's goodness yet do nothing about the festering stink these planters perpetuated for their own ease and wealth?

"Mister 'Lijah!" Jemma exclaimed. "You was up and gone afore I got here. Mister Alex ain't said where."

Alex turned to see Moon striding into the smithy, clutching a bulging linen towel. He set it on the bench beneath the shutters, which Alex had opened for the day, then turned with a glare forbidding further mention of his absence. "Breakfast," he said. "I'll check that fire."

Throughout the morning, as he tackled the mending or dressing of every axe, draw knife, plane, and adze routinely used in the cooperage, Joanna Carey troubled Alex's thoughts. He'd been unfair, the things he'd said in the orchard. Not about the slaves spurning her presence at the burial, hard as that might be for her to swallow. But the rest. He'd taken out his anger on her when nothing about his exile, Micah's death, or the institution her stepfather embraced

166

were of her doing. Worse, he'd battered down the door barring her own private pain; the loss of her friendship with Marigold—an illusion of friendship to his thinking, but real to her.

As he gripped the hammer and felt the forge's heat, the burn of hard-worked muscles, his fingers recalled the slenderness of her arm . . . and he nearly missed a stroke when a voice spoke at the smithy door.

"Elijah Moon. Have you time to greet an old comrade?"

Startlement flared in Moon's gaze. His features stiffened, but he went to greet the man Alex had glimpsed last night by candlelight, up at the house. While Jemma manned the bellows, he finished hammering a chipped adze. By the time the lass climbed down and went to the water bucket, Moon and the man were deep in conversation.

Alex took the drinking gourd from Jemma, who trotted out to the yard where it was cooler. While he drank, Alex assessed the newcomer. A man nearing forty, not tall but straight of bearing. To judge by his gaze, he was coming to grips with Moon's disfigurement, landing between tacit sympathy and acknowledgment that the man he'd known—and valued, Alex sensed—wasn't to be dismissed as lost.

Moon's posture eased. "What brings ye upriver?"

"Aside from wanting to see you?" Beneath one arm, clamped to his side, the man carried a long bundle wrapped in canvas. This he laid on the bench, unrolling it to reveal objects Alex recognized. Marlinspikes, slightly curved in mimicry of a dagger's blade though none so sharp, used for working heavy lines aboard ship. These were over a foot in length from tapered tip to looped handle.

Moon leaned in to finger one. "Happen they need repair, or be ye looking to supply the *Joanna*?"

"The latter, if your apprentice is up to the task."

Moon made introductions, after which the man, Captain Kelly, gestured at the spikes. "I'm told you're acquainted with the use of these, MacKinnon. I'm in need of several dozen."

"How soon?" Alex asked.

"With the Spaniards lurking I mustn't let the *Joanna* anchor overlong. I leave tomorrow, early."

"Spaniards?" Alex asked.

"Indeed," Captain Kelly said. "They'd the temerity to sail into the mouth of the Cape Fear, just after the *Charlotte-Ann*'s departure in July. The militia held them in check, and they turned tail, but I doubt we've seen the last. So. The spikes. Think yourself equal to the task?"

As Alex took up the nearest, weighed it in his hand, fingers curling round the looped handle, the dream that had visited him on his fever's trailing edge blazed across his mind.

He might have been brandishing a sword.

"Aye, I do." He met Captain Kelly's gaze, canting his head toward Moon. "Mind, it'll take us both—his brain, my hands—but I expect we'll manage."

Alex stepped back, letting the pair sort the details. When Captain Kelly left the smithy, Moon called Jemma in and joined them at the forge. "We'll finish the blades tomorrow. Let's sort through our scrap, see what's serviceable for spikes." A wry twitch touched the corner of his mouth as he caught Alex's gaze. "Your hands and my brain?"

"As it'll be for a while yet. Or d'ye think your life's work a thing I'd master in a month?"

Snorting at that, Severn's former smith made for the scrap iron leaning against the wall, leaving Alex wondering if he'd imagined that twitch had nearly folded into a smile.

Supper preparations were underway in the kitchen. As Joanna strode the bricked walk to the house, details of the meal flew her mind, replaced by words from the previous night that wouldn't cease pestering: *"If ye draw lines between yourself and folk, the least ye can do is keep to your side of them."* Twice she'd come near to telling Alex MacKinnon what she wished to do with those lines, and twice they'd been interrupted.

On impulse, she turned down the lane to the workshops.

Mister MacKinnon was at the forge, Elijah close by, absorbed in what they were crafting. It was Jemma, standing on a block to reach the bellows lever, who spotted her. "Miss Joanna!"

When both men snapped their heads her way, Joanna hesitated. She couldn't address the subject so much on her heart in front of Elijah. Or Jemma, else the entire plantation would know of it before the day was out.

"Mister MacKinnon, I'd like a word with you."

Elijah frowned. "Happen this can wait, Joanna? Kelly needs these spikes, and we've a long way yet to go."

"I'll wait. By the pasture fence. When Mister MacKinnon's through with that spike, send Jemma for your supper. I'll not keep him long." Not waiting for an answer, she crossed the yard and the short stretch beyond to the pasture fence.

Her stepfather didn't keep many horses, but those he did were of fine stock, graceful and long-limbed. One mare had a colt, not as gangly as it had been but full of romp and spirit. It trotted to her, making her wish she'd brought something from the kitchen. All she had were willing fingers to scratch the base of its bristly mane and fondle its thrusting nose.

Behind her the ring of hammering ceased. Moments later footsteps approached. Alex MacKinnon appeared beside her. He leaned his forearms atop the fence rail, bringing his gaze almost level with hers. He'd removed his leather apron. His shirt was damp with sweat, though he'd washed his face. When he reached for the colt, she gave place, drawing back as the animal shifted toward this new source of attention.

The afternoon air hung heavy and warm below a clouded sky.

"Ye've my ears, Mistress. What d'ye wish to say?"

He'd sounded wary despite his outward composure. Her heart was pounding. "I'm sorry to interrupt your work."

"I'm glad for the respite. I've hours of it ahead of me."

She moistened her lips, uncertain how to begin. Into her silence he asked, "Did the reverend pass an easy night?"

"The fever hasn't returned, but he's worn." Otherwise it would be to the reverend she spoke. But Reverend Pauling wouldn't be there in the coming weeks. She needed an ally at Severn, someone who would see the merit in her vision. Perhaps even advise her in it. She hoped Mister MacKinnon would be able and willing.

Trying to match his self-possession, she faced him. "What you said last night, about the lines between us, my family and the slaves—"

"*Wheest*," he interrupted gently, straightening but still gripping the fence rail. "I oughtn't to have said such things, Mistress."

"Miss Joanna," she reminded him. "And whether you spoke amiss or not, I've been thinking about it—even before last night. You're right. I do find it difficult to keep from crossing those lines."

He leaned toward her slightly. "Can ye imagine a life without them?"

The question rattled her with its perception. "I can. All of this . . ." She swept a hand toward the smithy and beyond. "It's so much more than any three people need, isn't it? I could live very well without most of it. The problem is I don't know how to do that." Alex MacKinnon gazed at her with an intensity that disconcerted. "Why do you stare so?"

"Oh . . . it's your eyes. They're green in this light."

"Are they?" she asked, off-footed by the change of subject. "I suppose they are green."

"Not always. They're as changeable as the sea. Green one day, gray the next, then blue as a rising storm. Just now I see flecks of brown in the green, like wee selkies—seals—gliding in and out of waves."

Joanna felt her jaw drop open, but she had no words. It was the most attentive, poetic—dared

172

she think *romantic*—thing a man had ever said to her.

The warmth in her face must have been apparent, for Mister MacKinnon laughed softly, seeming embarrassed in his turn. "They make me think of home."

A subject upon which she gratefully pounced. "Would you tell me about it?"

He looked at her blankly. "What? Barra, d'ye mean?"

She nodded. "Is that a town in Scotland?"

"No. It's the western isle where I was raised—by my uncle."

"Not your parents?"

Something like a shutter slammed down across his face, stiffening his jaw. Though clearly reluctant to say more, at last he relented. "Both my da and mam died whilst I was yet a bairn. My uncle took me in, raised me."

"The uncle you lost, after the rising?"

"Aye. My nearest kin."

"I'm sorry," she said. "May I know his name?"

"Rory MacNeill," he said. "I thought it was Severn ye wished to speak of?"

"It is." She drew breath and plunged in. "A few nights back I had an idea—a vision, I suppose—for Severn, for changes I'd like to see. But I don't know how to go about it. I don't know if it would work."

"All right," he said cautiously, as though

feeling his way through her words. "And ye want to tell *me* about it?"

"I do."

Though clearly wary of the conversation, he said, "Go on, then."

When it came down to it, there really wasn't much to say. "I want to live a less complicated life here."

"In what way?"

"Every way. I want to manumit our slaves, but only after we've found them a way to live, to support themselves—unless they wish to remain with us. Many are skilled enough to find work elsewhere, paying work." She'd meant to say much more, but paused. Mister MacKinnon was staring at her as if she'd sprouted horns. She couldn't gauge whether he found anything she'd said commendable, or was merely surprised.

"Have ye told your stepfather any of this?" he asked.

"No."

His brows danced high at that. "Why not?"

"Papa has poured his heart into Severn, made it what it is, and all his plans have to do with maintaining the status quo, or building more. I don't know what he'd say to my wanting . . . well, *less.*"

"But why are ye telling me? I'm a traitor. A rebel. Why would anything I have to say matter to ye?"

Though she couldn't decipher his expression, he'd asked the questions with apparent sincerity.

"Mister MacKinnon, I understand what you did and the punishment you've endured, but I don't think it right or true that you be defined by a single choice. Your life began long before the Rising." Warmth crept into her face. "I only meant to ask whether the life you had on Barra, before all that, might possibly have resembled . . . well, what I have in mind for Severn."

His mouth twitched as he asked, "Are ye trying to ask was I a poor man compared to your stepfather?"

"That's putting it bluntly," she said, the warmth intensifying. "Perhaps *modest* is the word I'm looking for."

"Again I'm asking, why?"

"I thought—depending on the manner of living you had, of course—perhaps you'd know what could be done, what steps taken, to create a simpler life here at Severn. That you'd be willing to help me present a reasonable and workable plan to Papa."

One he mightn't shoot down half-fledged.

Alex MacKinnon studied her for an uncomfortably long moment, then said, "Would ye care to hear my first impression of Severn, as I was being brought upriver on the boat?"

"I would," she said, hoping it meant he was willing to help her.

"I saw the house first, ken, standing tall and white above the river, and I thought as how the thatched croft I was raised in might have fit inside it about a dozen times over. So I need to ask ye, all this . . ." He echoed her earlier gesture. "It's all ye've ever kent?"

"I remember my home with my mother, before she married Papa. It wasn't as large as Severn . . ."

"But not a one-room croft with a goat in the corner and nothing but a peat fire to warm ye or cook your food? Speaking of which, d'ye ken how to get along without a bevy of slaves in the kitchen to do for ye?"

She opened her mouth to say of course she did—it was marginally true—but hesitated a split second too long as her mind scrambled for how to bring the exchange back on track to her purpose.

"MacKinnon!" Elijah called from the smithy door. "Jemma's brought supper. And Joanna, your presence is requested in the house for your own."

Joanna hoped she only imagined the relief that flashed across Mister MacKinnon's face at the interruption, before he made her a slight bow.

"Pardon me, Mistress. I must eat a bite, then return to my work. Good day to ye."

Disappointment held her mute, but when he was a few strides away she noticed something stuck into the waistband of his breeches. "Mister MacKinnon?" she called, even as his hand snaked behind him and felt the thing.

Turning to stride back to her, his mouth curved faintly. "I almost forgot this," he said, and held out to her what she saw was a corn-husk doll. "I thought maybe the wee lass might like it."

"Charlotte? Well . . . yes, she loves dolls," Joanna said, forbearing to add that her sister's dolls were of a very different sort. She took the corn-husk creation in her hands and examined it closely. It was one of the better such specimens she'd seen. Far more than a crude stick figure, it was shaped like a properly gowned young woman, well-proportioned and graceful. It even sported a head of hair gathered into thick braids, the exact brown of her own. "Is this horsehair?"

"Aye. It was the only thing I could think to use."

"*You* made this?"

His smile broadened at her surprise. "With help from Mari, who found me one to use for a pattern, glue from the carpenters, a bit of twine. I'd seen a few bairns about with such dolls and thought . . . well, that day your sister was so upset at the smithy . . . I just wanted to do her a kindness." His gaze, which had been on the doll, rose to meet hers. "I thought, if ye fancy the notion, ye could make a wee gown and cap for her?"

She'd never seen such a look on the man's

usually stern face, self-consciously proud of his creation, hopeful it would please not only Charlotte, but her as well. She was unexpectedly moved.

"Mister MacKinnon . . . this is very thoughtful. Thank you. Yes, I'll make her a gown. Perhaps one to match something of Charlotte's. I know she'll like this doll. Very much."

Even if she didn't, Joanna was thoroughly taken with it.

"Aye, then, Mistress," he said, pleased, and bowed to her again. A few strides away he paused, turning back. "Miss Joanna, I mean to say. And ye dinna need to go on calling me Mister MacKinnon. Alex will do, if it please ye."

Seated on Joanna's left, Captain Kelly cut into the braised beef on his plate, then paused his knife when there came a lull in the discussion Mister Reeves had been having with her stepfather, about the latter's impending trip downriver.

"Mister Reeves," Captain Kelly began, "might I make a particular inquiry into the events that brought about your . . . disappearance from the *Severn*?"

Mister Reeves had been reaching for his wine glass. He took a sip then, eyes dark in the candle-light, curled his lip to smile at the man seated across the table. "What do you wish to know, particularly?"

Despite the cordiality of his tone, Joanna sensed he'd bristled at the question. Because of the captain's hesitation before the word *disappearance?*

"I've acquainted Thom with the broad strokes of your history, Phineas," her stepfather explained. "But left the specifics for you to share, should you so desire."

"Thank you, sir," Mister Reeves replied, never taking his gaze from the *Joanna*'s captain. "I'm happy to acquaint Mister Kelly with whatever he wishes to know of me since our parting."

Captain Kelly stirred in his chair. "One of those broad strokes being that you were actually taken off the Kingston quay by pirates. Captain Carey will not know, having already left His Majesty's service—I cannot recall how long before—but as first lieutenant I led the crew in an exhaustive search throughout Kingston, cursing you the while for a deserter."

"Two years and a six-month," Mister Reeves said. At Captain Kelly's quizzical look he added, "From the time Captain Carey left the *Severn* in the hands of Captain Potts to that day in Kingston of which we speak."

"You make it sound like a prison sentence," Captain Kelly said, then with a grudging note of concurrence addressed Joanna's stepfather. "I'll admit, sir, Captain Potts didn't run the tight ship you ran."

"Potts was a scoundrel," Mister Reeves said. "No better than the pirates who abducted me."

Joanna's eyes widened as she stared across the table. Mister Reeves appeared to be clenching his teeth. His face had whitened, bloodless skin pulling taut across the bones of his cheeks.

"Here now," Captain Kelly said. "That's taking it too far. The man wasn't completely derelict in his duties."

Mister Reeves clearly had something to say to that, but he gave a slight jerk of his head and asked, "Was there a question in your original observation, Mister Kelly?"

"As noted," the captain replied, "we made a thorough search of the Kingston waterfront. There were no pirates rumored to be in the vicinity. What was the name of the ship that took you aboard?"

"The *Isis*." Mister Reeves said the name with more than a tinge of bitterness. "I was taken off the quay as I was returning to the *Severn* with the crate of limes I'd been sent to procure, manhandled into a boat and rowed some distance—with a sack over my head and my mouth gagged so I couldn't call out. And no, I cannot prove my claim."

Papa raised a placating hand. "No one is doubting your word, Phineas. Are they, Thom?"

"Of course not. I was merely curious as to

the unfolding of Mister Reeves's life since our parting in Kingston."

Joanna was thankful Charlotte had taken her supper earlier, and that Reverend Pauling was resting, not bearing witness to this strained exchange. "Mister Reeves, perhaps you could tell Captain Kelly the manner in which you acquired Demas. That is an interesting tale."

"The hulking slave who shadows you?" Captain Kelly glanced toward the door as if expecting to see Demas, though the taking of meals was one of the few times Mister Reeves didn't keep him close.

"I met him, a slave, aboard the *Isis*," Mister Reeves said. "We found common cause in our desire to escape. He couldn't have done so without me. Afterward he chose to serve me over life as a fugitive."

Frustration tightened Joanna's brow. Mister Reeves had omitted every exciting detail of his and Demas's escape. He'd made it sound a grand adventure when telling her and Charlotte. Uncertain how to redirect the fraying conversation, she reached for her glass, only to find it empty. In seconds Sybil was there to refill it.

Sybil, she recalled, had complained of a stomachache that morning. Joanna caught her gaze. "Are you feeling better?"

"Yes ma'am." Sybil made a curtsy before moving away to fill her stepfather's glass.

Joanna caught Mister Reeves eyeing her, mildly disapproving. He thought slaves should serve at table unacknowledged, but she could never disregard the presence of another human being in the room. What would Mister MacKinnon have thought of the small solicitude? Perhaps he'd have condemned it too. It seemed he'd been about to oppose her notions of change, out by the pasture fence, yet he mustn't be completely put off by the ideas she'd raised, or by her. He'd bid her call him Alex, and had somehow found the time to make a doll for Charlotte. She hadn't showed it to her sister yet. She'd gown it first. Scraps remained from the last petticoat she'd made for Charlotte. A sprigged gown in green and pink—

"Joanna?" Papa's voice penetrated her reverie.

"Mister Kelly addressed you just now," Mister Reeves said, looking amused. "I don't think you heard him at all."

Joanna flushed. "Forgive my woolgathering, Captain."

Thom Kelly nodded. "I only wished to know the cause of your most charming smile."

"Was I smiling?"

"A Mona Lisa smile, if I might so boldly name it."

That banished the amusement in Mister Reeves's gaze.

"Nothing of consequence," she hurried to say.

182

She met Papa's gaze across the table. "I'll bid you good evening, Papa—Mister Reeves, Captain— and go check on Reverend Pauling before I help Charlotte to bed."

She rose before one of them could assist in her escape.

14

Alex counted on Jemma being too drowsy at the bellows to notice his deception. Still, he waited until he was nearly done with the marlinspikes before miss-striking the iron. At his curse of feigned frustration, Jemma's drooping eyelids widened. Before she could blink, he'd plunged the spike into the slack tub and tossed it with a clank onto the scrap pile.

Jemma yawned. "All done, Mister Alex?"

"Almost, *mo nighean*. Give it one good blast." Jemma pulled the bellows lever. Wood creaked. Air rushed. Embers glowed. Alex thrust the final rod into the heat. "Now get ye to bed, and dinna come back 'til ye've had your fill of sleep. I'll tell Moon I gave ye leave."

"Leave for what?" Moon inquired from the doorway. He crossed the shop and raised his hand to Jemma. She clasped it, nearly buckling when her feet hit the floor. He steadied her, then turned his attention to the finished spikes. He'd left the smithy at sundown and not returned until now. "One short?"

"He messed up that'n over on the hee . . . eap." Another yawn broke Jemma's last word as she slipped into the night.

Spotting the rejected spike, Moon turned a frown on him.

"I havena seen Mari since the burial," Alex said before he could question the easily mendable mistake. "Have ye?"

"Aye," was all Moon said before disappearing into their sleeping quarters. He emerged with a bundle tucked beneath his maimed arm. By then Alex was hammering the final spike. Moon left the smithy without challenging him over the scrapped one.

Alex forbore asking where he was bound.

It isna theft, he told himself, slipping the misshapen spike beneath his cot's ticking. Perhaps in the end it would make a crude sword. Time, and mastery of the art, would tell. But it wasn't theft. Yet.

He swept the shuttered smithy, mind slipping back to Joanna Carey.

He'd gone out to the pasture thinking she meant to scold him over their exchange in the orchard, not agree with him, much less broach the subject of freeing their slaves. But what had possessed him to blather on about her eyes? The lass had blushed as if she'd never had such a thing said of her. It wasn't his place to be saying it. It was a line he mustn't cross again—hypocrite that he was.

She intrigued him, and aroused in him a

tenderness he didn't want to feel. Not if he meant to leave this place and never look back. He'd sensed the unhappiness in her from their first encounter, had thought then it was to do with Moon.

He'd had time to know her better. Moon grieved her, aye, but it was her very life that vexed her, its burdens, its injustices. She wanted freedom as badly as he.

Or was it something more, that she wasn't seeking merely after her own peace of mind? She seemed genuinely to care about the likes of Marigold, Azuba, Jemma. Admirable, but naïve. Even on such short acquaintance, he doubted Carey would embrace her notion of turning Severn on its head, if she ever mustered the courage to voice it. He minded her by the pasture fence, struggling for words. She'd wanted to know about his life before the Rising, thought the knowledge might somehow help her. He'd said too much, unable to resist her appeal. Or those eyes.

Such were his thoughts as he took up the book Reeves lent him and went into the shop where candles burned, meaning to lay tomorrow's fire before he settled in to read awhile.

As he stepped into the shop, so did Edmund Carey, coming in from the yard. They halted, gazes riveted, until Carey cast his around the smithy, landing on the marlinspikes heaped on the forge's counter.

"You've had a long day," he observed, stepping into the candlelight. His white hair was undressed, swept back in a simple tail, lustrous and curling. He wore naught but a waistcoat over his shirtsleeves, as though he'd been in the act of undressing when the notion to visit the smithy overtook him.

As to the purpose, Alex waited to be enlightened.

"Where's Elijah?"

Uncertain if Moon's dalliance, or whatever it was, with Marigold was a thing Carey would frown upon, Alex said only, "He went out a bit ago. I was set to drop into bed, myself."

Not precisely true, as he'd meant to read a page or two by candlelight first. He gripped the book close to his thigh as Carey nodded. "I leave in the morn with Captain Kelly and cannot say how long I may be in Wilmington. You know of the trouble with our neighbor?"

"Aye, I've the broad strokes."

"Then I'll not repeat the tiresome business." Halting with the anvil between them, Carey planted his feet like a man once used to rolling decks. "I've come to see how you fare, MacKinnon, an inquiry overdue. With the gathering and David's illness, then this ugliness Phineas brought us . . ." A distracted furrow scored his brow, quickly banished. "Have you need of anything, or is there some way in which your situation might be improved—within reason?"

Alex felt his nape bristle. "There's naught ye can do in that regard, sir."

Carey waited, no doubt to be sure that was all he meant to say. "How do you find the work?"

"I expect Moon's kept ye informed of my progress."

"I'd hear it from you." There was interest in the man's gaze, and confidence he'd have his answer ere he left the smithy. However long retired, Edmund Carey was still a captain at heart. He likely viewed those who served him on land as he must have done his ship's crew, their welfare his responsibility, and benefit. The care was genuine but administered from behind a wall of dignity and distance cultivated from years at sea, which Alex supposed must do for slaves, but what of his daughters? Especially the one who wanted to change so much. He felt sorry for Joanna Carey, trapped in a life that didn't suit her, but he could do nothing to help the lass.

"I find it agreeable enough." He put all thought of the secreted marlinspike firmly from his mind.

"I'm glad to hear it." Carey's gaze fell upon the book clutched at his side. Recognition sharpened his gaze. "From my library?"

"Aye. Reeves took it—out to the pinewood, he said. He passed it on to me. A loan, is all. He didna speak of it to ye?"

"He did not." Alex proffered the book, but Carey made no move to take it. "*Robinson Crusoe*. You've a liking for fictional tales?"

"I do, though my tastes run broader."

Carey eyed him. "You've some learning, then?"

"Of my own initiative, mainly. I'd access to . . ." He stopped himself, but too late.

"Access to?" Carey prodded.

"The library at Castle Kisimul," he said, trying not to grind his teeth over the words, which he saw needed further explaining. "My uncle was tacksman to our chief, the MacNeill."

"I see. And did you aid in those duties?"

"I went round with him, collecting rents," Alex said. "Mostly I fished and minded cattle."

Carey waited. Alex said no more.

"I see no reason you shouldn't avail yourself of my meager collection, if you're so minded. When you've finished with *Crusoe*, return it to my shelves and choose another. Joanna will admit you if I'm not there."

"Do I hear my name taken in vain?" With a swish of buttery gold linen, Joanna stepped into the smithy. "Reverend Pauling said you were out here, Papa."

"Checking on MacKinnon. We fell to speaking of books."

Carey explained the lending arrangement. Joanna's gaze sought Alex's, holding more than the present subject could account for. Still hopeful he might help her with that other matter she'd apparently not yet discussed with her stepfather. Before she could speak further, her sister's childish voice rose, and the sound of Reeves's laughter in reply.

Was the entire household congregating in the smithy?

The pair arrived, Reeves smiling at whatever the lass had said. When Charlotte's gaze alighted on her father, she abandoned the overseer and ran to him. Big as she was, Carey scooped the girl into his arms. "Oughtn't you to be abed, miss?"

Charlotte giggled. "Yes, Papa!"

One soul, at least, had breached those barriers of command. Alex wasn't the only one who noticed; he caught Joanna's expression, a look blending love, loneliness, and longing. She caught his glance in turn and blinked such feelings away. "Come to the library for a book whenever you wish, Alex. You're most welcome."

Charlotte was swung to the ground. Joanna left the smithy with her sister, never noticing she'd snagged Reeves's attention. The man shot a look after her, then directed a searching one at Alex, who met it blandly, pretending he hadn't noticed she'd used his name familiarly for the first time.

Three mornings later, finished with *Robinson Crusoe*, Alex went to the Big House to return it, never expecting Pauling to answer his knock at the back terrace.

"Good morning." The reverend opened the door wide in welcome. "I've heard no ring of hammer. Were you up late reading?" He eyed the book.

Alex hadn't set eyes upon the reverend since the burial. How long the man had been risen from his sickbed he didn't know, but he looked improved in health. "Moon has himself a headache. There's no work pressing, so I'm giving him peace to sleep it off."

"I'll be down to see Elijah directly he wakes. Is it Joanna you've come to see? I believe she's abovestairs."

"No—I've the book to return. I'm permitted to choose another."

"Come in, then, and do so." Pauling admitted him. "I'm on my way upriver today. Packing now."

Alex entered the study to find the bed in the corner made, saddlebags nearby. "I'll be quick and leave ye to it."

"Take your time."

Putting his back to the reverend, Alex found an empty slot on a shelf, slid *Robinson Crusoe* into it, then pulled out books at random, hoping one would snag his interest and he could be away with it. He scanned for the title the man had mentioned in the smithy yard, the one by Lawson, but couldn't find it.

"I take it Joanna is acquainted with this lending arrangement?" Pauling asked.

"Aye, she is."

A clatter of something going into a saddlebag. "Have you had much chance to speak with her since your arrival?"

Though Pauling didn't reference the conversation in the orchard he'd interrupted, Alex felt heat rise from the neck of his shirt. "Not overmuch," he replied cautiously, wondering what the man was thinking. Did he know about the lass's unconventional ideas on slavery?

Not your concern, he reminded himself, focusing on book spines.

"About Joanna," the reverend pursued, "I'd ask a favor of you, Mister MacKinnon. It would much relieve my mind to know you're looking out for her in the weeks ahead."

Alex tensed, gripping a book half-pulled from the shelf, and glanced aside. "What d'ye mean?"

Pauling took a seat on the bed. "Edmund informs me you and he have spoken little as yet, though I believe he came to see you before heading downriver?"

"He asked how I was getting on. No more."

"Of course." The man paused briefly, then said, "Permit me to speak frankly of the Carey family, and a little of its history."

He didn't want this, whatever this was. He faced the man. "How is that *my* business?"

Pauling held his gaze. "One may argue it isn't, but will you bear with me?"

Alex breathed out a sigh, but nodded for the man to go on.

"Edmund is the only father Joanna recalls," Pauling began. "Grace, Joanna's mother, wasn't yet thirty when she married Edmund, though nearly seven years widowed. For Edmund it was a marriage late in a life mostly spent at sea."

"And ye think he stills sees the world thus," Alex cut in. "And those who serve him—as crew to be cared for, from a distance."

Pauling blinked. "You have his measure. Yes, that's an accurate way of describing Edmund. But it isn't just from him I feel Joanna needs protecting."

Alex raised a brow. "Who else?"

"I speak of Phineas Reeves."

"The man who's asked to marry her, with Carey's blessing?"

"True. Edmund has placed a great deal of trust in that young man. I've come to think he feels some guilt—misplaced, of course—for how Reeves's life unraveled after they parted ways. He desires to make up for it. Of course, there's genuine fondness on Edmund's part as well. And he feels relief to have found a younger man as devoted to Severn as I'm sure he once hoped for in a son, capable of one day taking its reins. But though he may well be the right man for Severn,

I doubt Phineas Reeves is the right man for Joanna. She loves the Lord deeply, and while I cannot see into a man's heart, I sense nothing of that devotion in Mister Reeves."

Alex agreed the pair were ill matched but remained baffled by the conversation. "Ye ken I'm no better in that regard, aye? I told ye as much."

"You did. Mister Reeves, however, seems to take pains to conceal whatever he believes—at least on any matter I attempted to address during our few encounters at table."

Alex averted his gaze to the bookshelf. "How does the man's lack of religion translate to Joanna's needing my protection?"

"A good question," Pauling said, a smile in his voice that quickly faded. "I doubt even Edmund has the Almighty's will and plans first in his heart when it concerns Joanna. I believe he's placed Severn's needs ahead of hers. Whatever we pour our treasure into will ultimately captivate our hearts. What captivates our hearts we worship. What we worship remakes us—into its image."

Alex turned back to face the reverend, trying to discern exactly what the man expected of him. "I'll bear what ye say in mind, but surely ye ken I've nothing to give her—or anyone."

"You've more than you know," Pauling countered. "The Almighty has you on a path,

Alex MacKinnon, with good plans for you. For those to whom you're linked."

Alex shook his head. "What d'ye ken of me? From what I can tell ye havena given Moon, whom ye *do* ken, any true comfort. He's taking that from—" He bit back Marigold's name before it passed his lips.

"I'm aware of the avenues of comfort Elijah has pursued," Pauling said. "Such will prove fleeting. Elijah will eventually recall that only in Christ is found healing and true deliverance."

"What deliverance is there? He canna grow another hand."

Sorrow crossed Pauling's features. "A man may grow in ways other than the physical. The Lord has yet to complete that work in Elijah, but it has begun."

"Begun how?"

"For one, the Almighty sent him you."

"I suspect a certain king might beg to differ," Alex said dryly. "But what use am I, hardly better than a slave? Speaking of which, Reverend, if there's a God in heaven with a purpose for men, it isna *this*." He spread his hands, sweeping them toward the back of the house, beyond which lay the community of slaves that populated Severn.

In that much, he and Joanna Carey were of one mind.

"That is one of the reasons I'm appealing to

you on Joanna's behalf. Unlike Mister Reeves and Edmund, your heart isn't invested in *this*." Pauling echoed his gesture. "Yet the Almighty has allowed you, by whatever series of events and decisions brought you to it, to be in this place—*for such a time as this,* one might venture to say. If you allow it, there will be good to come of it. For yourself. Perhaps for Joanna. And others."

"Ye dinna ken that. How can ye?"

"Because I know who sits upon the throne of heaven," Pauling said, "and He is both good and sovereign. A battle is being waged upon this earth, Mister MacKinnon, between the forces of our God and our enemy, Satan, who comes to steal freedom, kill hope, and destroy souls, and for a time he is permitted to do so. But who do you think is ultimately in control of the unfolding of this world's events? Of time, and nations, and your own yearning heart? It's a question you will one day need to answer for yourself."

Alex stood defiant before the man. "I can never believe as ye do."

"Why not?"

"I've said as much—because of what I've seen, and what I see when I look around me now."

"Then look up. Look to the Almighty in faith. Believe that He is who He says, then you will see beyond what meets your eyes."

"Ye speak in riddles, man."

Pauling's smile came swift. "It is a mystery, faith. But *I* have faith that one day you'll embrace it."

"I've seen what comes of blindly following another man's cause. I'll not follow yours."

"You speak of Charles Stuart?"

"I do."

"Then well I understand your bitterness. But I would never ask you to follow any man's cause—frail and flawed as we all are. Only the Almighty."

Alex could only stare at the man, lost for what more to say in the face of such stubborn belief. Whatever religion he'd claimed before the Rising, it hadn't resembled what this man possessed. Or what possessed him. *"What we worship remakes us—into its image."*

"Reverend Pauling?" Joanna's uncertain voice broke the tension.

Alex looked at her, hesitating in the study doorway, with her soft brown hair and change-able eyes and lovely mouth, and wondered how much she'd overheard. Any of it was too much.

Without another word he strode to the door, avoiding her gaze, which he sensed stuck fast upon him.

"Alex? Did you come to choose another book?"

Unable to ignore her, he halted, already half out of the room. The gown she wore today was a powdery blue. Her eyes were warm in contrast.

He dropped his gaze. *Protect her.* How was he meant to do that?

"I dinna have time for more reading, Miss Joanna. I've returned the one." Before she could detain him further, he made for the back door. As he turned to shut it, however, he heard her voice lifted.

"I was going to show him the doll we made together, for Charlotte."

He paused with the door nearly shut, wanting to hear more, though it was the reverend she addressed.

"I fitted her out in the sweetest gown. But when I suggested calling this one Marianna, Charlotte said no, that he'd made her hair the same shade as mine so she must be called Joanna . . ."

15

September 1747

During Edmund Carey's absence, August passed into September with little to mark the transition. The days remained insufferably hot. In the midst of a particularly stifling spell, Moon announced they wouldn't heat the forge. With Jemma sent grumbling to the kitchen, Moon and Alex saddled horses and headed for the sawmill upstream on Severn Creek. They rode past fields of corn and tobacco, Moon in the lead, his pace too languid to outdistance that nagging voice: *"Though he may well be the right man for Severn, I doubt Phineas Reeves is the right man for Joanna."*

The reverend's concerns had embedded themselves in Alex's brain, but there he meant to halt them. With effort, he focused on the sway of the beast beneath him, the thud of hooves on the sandy track that traced the rushing creek.

*"Yet the Almighty has allowed you, by whatever series of events and decisions brought you to it, to be in this place—*for such a time as this . . ."

His horse shook its head, ridding itself of a persistent fly, as Alex tried to shake away thoughts of the Careys. He'd made Pauling no promise, save he'd bear the request in mind. He hadn't even meant that.

"If you allow it, there will be good to come of it. For yourself. Perhaps for Joanna. And others."

"*Wheest*," he muttered as they followed the track upstream, angling through forest now.

He was still awed by such trees, thick and rough-barked, straight as ships' masts for several times the height of a man, where their needled boughs filtered spears of morning sunlight. He breathed in the scent of oozing sap, sharp on the air. Beneath the massive pines little by way of understory grew. With nothing obstructing his view save scattered saplings, industry taking place within the forest's edge was visible, slaves building structures of cut wood and grassy turves.

"Is that to do with the tar-burning?" he called ahead to Moon, who turned in the saddle to look. "I thought it a thing done in winter."

"That'll be the first of the kilns. It's early for it but that's Reeves's business. He'll answer, not I."

Moon sank back into silence. They rode on.

Alex heard the sawmill before he spied the millrace that flowed back into Severn Creek. Following the race upstream, they came in sight of the mill itself, with its waterwheel, creaking gears, and the rasping chunk of metal blades biting through timber. They dismounted in a yard where pinewood planks lay stacked, waiting to be rafted downstream.

The mill foreman, a wiry slave in his middle years, came out to meet them. "Mister 'Lijah. How you keeping?"

"Well enough, Jim. Thought it time I brought MacKinnon to see the mill."

Jim craned his neck to meet Alex's gaze. "You the one brought on for the smithy? Big enough for it, you don't mind my saying."

Alex returned a nod. "So they tell me."

"It's slow at the forge," Moon said. "Have ye any trouble here?"

Jim glanced at his crew—two at the blades, one at a sluice gate—before turning back to Moon. "Mister Reeves come yesterday, looking over things. He say there trouble?"

Moon clapped his hand to the foreman's shoulder. "No, Jim. We're here to see do ye need anything done at the forge, is all."

"Always needing nails." Jim gave Alex a measuring look. "Ever seen a sawmill?"

"I come from a place thinly treed, so no. I havena."

"Take your time. Look around," Moon said. "I'll take the horses into the shade."

The mill was a simple structure with its floor above for the sawing and below a long room crowded with stored lumber. A lean-to attached to the ground floor served as an office. For a time Alex watched the working of the sluice gate, the water pouring over the wheel, filling its buckets and turning it. He counted nine revolutions of the wheel in a minute's span, listened to the chunking of the blades as the slaves guided the lumber being cut, until Moon gave a whistle, ready to head back, no more garrulous than earlier.

Leaving Alex to stable the horses, Moon gave him leave to find a place out of the heat to rest. He took his time with the beasts. Voices rose and fell as slaves went about their work in the glare beyond the stable doors. He was brushing down the second horse in its stall when he heard Joanna's voice raised.

"Mister Reeves, I saw you. You and Demas had her cornered, frightened as a rabbit facing hawks. What could she have done to warrant such terrorizing?"

Alex maneuvered along the horse's side until he gained a view of the yard. Silhouetted against the sunlight's blazing, clutching a stack of shirts, Severn's mistress faced its overseer. Between them stood Jemma, barefoot in her ratty shirt and breeches. Reeves attempted to brush off Joanna's concern with a condescending smile.

"Come now, Miss Carey, is that not overstating matters? I've the right to question a girl I find holed up idle in the dairy shed."

"Questioning? Demas had his hand on her. I'll not abide—"

"Forgive me, Miss Carey, but these are your stepfather's slaves and I answer to *him.*"

"Allow me to finish, Mister Reeves." Joanna spoke as sharply as Alex had ever heard. "I understand the slaves in the fields, mill, and forest are your concern, but as I've reminded you, the rest are mine to manage. Should you have issue with one of them, bring it to me. And for heaven's sake, cease using Demas to intimidate children!"

Reeves stared, smile vanished. "You do realize, once we wed, you'll be required to submit to my judgments. Wouldn't it behoove you to accustom yourself to the process?"

Joanna seemed robbed of speech at such presumption. Or was it? Had she given the man the answer he sought?

"Why are you out in this heat at all?" Reeves pressed.

"I've the mending finished for the stable hands, but it's no concern of yours where my duties take me."

One thing Alex could say for Reverend Pauling, the man had the lay of this particular landscape.

"I'll take Jemma to the house." Joanna called the name of a stable lad but got no reply.

Alex eased out of the stall, secured it, and came forward into the light. "I'll see those get where they're intended." Not until he'd halted at the edge of the sunlit yard did he see Demas, standing back from the opposite door, a shadow within shade.

"How long have you been lurking?" Reeves asked, not at all pleased by the interruption.

"I shouldna call it lurking. I was tending the horses Moon and I had out to the mill this morn."

Joanna crossed to him and held out the garments. Her fingers slipped warm across his as he took them. Her gaze flashed up. In the stable's shade her eyes were deeply blue.

"Thank you, Alex." She looked away. "Come, Jemma."

The lass sidled up to him. "Mister Alex, you need me at the smithy? Something out at the mill you find to do?"

"The foreman asked for nails."

"I can help with nails!"

"Miss Carey," Reeves said, glowering at the lot of them. "You've accused me of being harsh with your stepfather's slaves. It's no wonder you should think so when you allow them to brazenly contradict you."

Joanna cast Alex a mute plea. "If she's needed in the smithy, that's where she belongs."

"Oh, aye," Alex said. "There's cleaning to be done. Sorting too. We left the place in disarray." It was a stretching of truth he didn't regret when relief flashed across Joanna's gaze.

"Thank you," she said again as footsteps scuffed the earth of the stable yard.

It was Marigold. "Miss Joanna—canoe put in. Man come up from Wilmington, asking for you."

Joanna's face softened; there was grief still in the lines of Marigold's face. "I'll come now, Mari." Without another word, she followed Marigold toward the outbuildings nearer the house, Reeves two strides behind.

Demas followed his master.

Jemma relaxed at Alex's side. "Don't you want to see who's come?"

"D'ye?"

"If you come with me."

Reeves had overtaken Joanna, who walked with shoulders stiff, facing forward.

Alex handed the garments she'd stitched to a lad who poked his head from the nearby box stall where he'd been hiding. "Ye ken what to do with these?"

When the lad nodded, Alex and Jemma headed out into the hot sunlight. Jemma trotted to keep up with his strides that ate the ground between them and Demas, last of the group ahead. The big slave shot a look over his shoulder at Jemma, then raised those flat eyes to Alex before turning to follow his master.

At his side Jemma faltered. He touched her shoulder, dropping them back a pace. "He threaten ye, did Demas?"

Jemma shook her head. "Never mind, Mister Alex. I'm all right."

Alex gave her shoulder a squeeze. "I'll be watching that one."

By the time they arrived, Joanna, in possession of a letter, was coming up from the dock, Reeves and the messenger trailing her to the kitchen. Seeing Alex, she paused. "I've a letter from Papa."

Outside the kitchen, Reeves took note of them and broke off conversation with the letter's bearer. "Miss Carey, I'd appreciate knowing the letter's contents, *if* you're minded to share."

Joanna seemed about to protest but then changed her mind. She broke the seal and unfolded the page. Others drew near from gardens and kitchen. Azuba, who must have seen the canoe's arrival from the house, fetched up at her side. Alex watched Joanna's face as she read silently. Her brow furrowed. The hand not holding the letter covered her mouth.

Even Reeves couldn't miss her distress. "What is it?"

Joanna's eyes glistened as she raised them. "Papa's detained in Wilmington," she began but seemed bereft for how to continue.

"How long detained?" Reeves asked.

Joanna ignored him. "It's very bad news. The *Joanna* . . ."

"Not sunk?" Azuba breathed.

"Captured, by pirates. Two crewmen escaped to tell of it." Joanna looked down at the letter as though she needed to read it again to believe its news. "The rest attempted to fight off the pirates. Their bodies were dumped overboard to wash up on shore. Some have been identified, including . . ." She gripped Azuba's arm. "Captain Kelly."

Alex would later wonder what drew his attention in that instant, for the man made no sound or gesture to warrant it, but it wasn't at Joanna he was looking when she related that final bit of news; it was Reeves.

16

The *Joanna*'s loss was a blow to Severn's economy, that of her crew a sorrow, but Captain Kelly's death struck deepest. Joanna sat with Azuba in the sewing room, half-suffocating in stays and gown, staring through the open window more than attending to the breeches she'd meant to piece. Through the branches of a shade oak, the stable yard was visible. The dreadful news had driven from her mind the unpleasant encounter there with Mister Reeves. It returned now, furrowing her brow as she recalled what she'd seen in the dairy shed—Mister Reeves and Demas looming over Jemma, who would have been curled up cowering had Demas not had hold of her arm. Mister Reeves hadn't said what she'd done amiss, aside from being idle. Had he come upon Demas menacing Jemma and was attempting to conceal it?

While she couldn't conduct a simple conversation with the man who wished to marry her without it ending in frustration, she'd communicated with Alex almost effortlessly. With nothing more than a look from her, he'd taken Jemma under his wing, exactly what she'd needed him to do. Turning that thought over in her mind brought to memory something Reverend Pauling said before his departure. "Should you have need of aid while Edmund is in Wilmington, I suggest you turn to Alex MacKinnon."

"Papa's indentured man? Why not Mister Reeves?" She'd nearly said *Elijah,* but that answer was plain. The reverend's trust in the Almighty hadn't wavered concerning Elijah, despite no outward evidence of change. He bid her continue in prayer, with patience. Then regarding her own need, Reverend Pauling gazed at her with shadowed eyes and asked, "Of the two, Reeves and MacKinnon, which would you expect to give the greater weight to your concerns?"

She had a ready answer even then but hadn't given it.

Though she'd begun to put into words to Alex her hopes for Severn's future and learned a little of what his life had been in Scotland, she wanted to know more, both of him and what he thought of her ideas.

"Azuba," she said into the stuffy silence, startling the woman half-dozing over her own stitching. "I'm going down to the smithy to check on Jemma."

She didn't notice Mister Reeves exiting her stepfather's study at the end of the downstairs passage and ran headlong into him.

"Miss Carey," he said, grasping her arm. "I didn't see you there." She made to pull away. Mister Reeves didn't release her. "Our exchange earlier has bothered me. Allow me to apologize for my short temper."

This was unexpected. The man had never before hinted he so much as noticed his rudeness. "I'll allow it," she said. When he looked at her blankly, she added, "You asked to apologize. That isn't the same as doing so."

His gaze cleared. "Of course. Therefore . . . I apologize for losing my patience with you and saying the things I did."

"To which things are you referring?"

This time his look of incomprehension cleared without her assistance. Amusement replaced it. "I see what you're doing, Miss Carey. You're testing me. Very well. Let us say I'm apologizing for all of it. Was that the answer you wanted?"

It wasn't even close. Joanna sought for a way to tell him so, but the house was too stifling, her thoughts too muddled—and the man apparently too dense—to know where to begin.

"I accept your apology, Mister Reeves."

She pulled from his grasp at last, but before she could make her escape he said, "Since the subject of marriage has been broached . . . I've wondered about your answer to my proposal."

She shouldn't have been surprised. It had been months since he'd asked her. Why was she no nearer to knowing her mind? Or was it that she knew, but feared her answer would disappoint her stepfather and complicate his planning for her and Charlotte's future? She must tell Papa of her vision for Severn, as soon as he returned. She sought for an excuse to put Mister Reeves off a little longer but hadn't gotten the first word past her lips before he stepped closer, his gaze earnest.

"Have you noticed, these days of Captain Carey's absence, how admirable a pairing we make? Case in point, how smoothly we've just overcome this small misunderstanding. Does it not bode well for a future together?"

Joanna stared, expecting the man's earnest countenance to dissolve into amusement again. It did not. "I've no answer for you yet, Mister Reeves. I'm sorry—I'm called to the kitchen."

She fled the house, hoping he wasn't watching which way she turned once she reached the path beyond the hedge.

"Alex, there you are." Joanna's voice had him straightening from the fence rail he'd been leaning on, watching Carey's mares at graze, tails swishing at flies in the afternoon heat. She joined him beneath the oak that spilled its shade over that corner of the pasture. "One might think you head groom at Severn rather than blacksmith, as often as I've seen you with the horses today."

"We'll not be heating the forge 'til morning. Until then I'm a man of leisure." He smiled over the word, but she didn't return it. She looked wilted with the heat, and with sorrow. Still, she mustered a smile in return. Given the day she'd had, the effort touched him. "I met Captain Kelly only the once. He seemed a good man."

"He was." She blinked, glancing at the line of clouds advancing from the west, on which he'd been keeping a hopeful eye.

Silence fell, thick and sticky as the air between them.

"I didna mean to overhear ye earlier, with Reeves. I couldna help it."

She huffed a little breath. "Reverend Pauling advised I seek your help while Papa's in Wilmington, if an issue arose that Mister Reeves and I cannot resolve."

"Did he?" It was one thing to suggest he keep an eye on the lass. What was Pauling thinking, putting similar notions in her head?

Yet he'd been standing in the exact spot Pauling would no doubt say he was *meant* to be standing when she shared the news from that letter. What had caused him to look at Reeves in that moment he couldn't say, but he'd seen a flash of something that wasn't sorrow or shock cross the overseer's eyes upon hearing the letter's tragic news. Something more akin to satisfaction. It had passed swiftly, and Reeves had evidenced sorrow, shock, solicitude, everything he ought to have demonstrated, leaving Alex wondering if he'd imagined anything else.

"I'm not sure what the reverend thinks I can do for ye, such as I am." Joanna dropped her gaze to the opening of his sweat-stained shirt. He'd removed his neckcloth, baring more than a little of his chest. He watched the color mount in her cheeks before she looked away. He edged back from her a very little. "What ye and Reeves quarreled about at the stable, it's not my business, is it? Save for Jemma."

A frown troubled the smooth spot between her brows. "Have you spoken to her?"

"She's clammed up tight about it." At her look of disappointment, he unbent enough to ask, "Is it Demas ye're worried about? Is that the quarrel between ye and Reeves?"

Joanna sighed. "Yes and no—to both questions."

He'd no idea what she meant. "Did ye resolve the matter?"

"Yes. And no." She gave him a wry look, then a hopeful one. "On the surface it would seem resolved but . . . may I be honest with you?"

A man could drown in those sea eyes. "Aye," he said warily. "Ye may."

Up rose that pretty flush as her lashes fluttered. Not playing the coquette—he doubted she knew how—but with shyness. Above the bodice of her gown her chest swelled as she breathed, the skin there smooth and white, dewed with the faintest sheen. He lifted his gaze to her eyes. Had they always been rimmed in a darker blue? Leaning closer, he saw the brown that flecked their centers; between the blue and brown, every shade of gray and green imaginable. He could stare at them as he once had the sea . . .

Only the sea never noticed his staring, as she clearly had. Hastily he straightened, putting a few more inches between them.

"Mister Reeves apologized," she said, "but I don't know whether to appease me for the sake of peace or if he really understands my perspective on . . . things," she concluded, with a lift of her hand toward the outbuildings busy with the labor of slaves.

"Have ye spoken to your stepfather yet?"

She shook her head. "I mean to once he's home."

He ran his bottom lip between his teeth, debating the wisdom of engaging her on the subject, but he was curious about a thing. "Should he consent to the notion, how would ye go about setting them all free? Are there laws to govern such things in this colony?"

It seemed a thing she hadn't yet given thought to. "I expect there must be. Papa will know."

"I'm sure he will." If Edmund Carey was unlikely to embrace her notions, Alex had no doubt what Reeves would say. The man evidenced not a shred of the fellow feeling Joanna showed those beneath her in station. Was there a way for her hopes to be realized?

He caught himself, too late. Something was shifting in his heart, making room for this woman and her concerns, as it had for Moon, for Jemma. What was it about her that had awakened this urge he longed to deny, more so than even Moon had done? *"Ye've always had that about ye, a need for a purpose beyond yourself. 'Tis the Almighty knit ye so."*

Rory MacNeill's words, spoken in the dark as death hovered.

He was still in the dark, but he'd seen in Joanna a light, a spark of that same defining quality. It made him want to shrink away from it—and rush to it to share in its warmth.

He knew stepping between her and Reeves would do him no good. Still, he asked, "How much control has Reeves over Demas?"

Another furrowing of her brow. "I wish I knew. I've wondered why Papa even allows—" Thunder broke like a whip's cracking, cutting off her words. On its heels a breeze gusted, drawing their gazes westward.

The distant line of clouds had altered most dramatically. Coming toward them swiftly now was the most ominous storm front Alex had ever seen—he who'd grown to manhood on

Barra, witness to countless storms advancing upon the isles. While they'd been speaking, the approaching clouds had thickened, forming a shelf that stretched as far as Alex could see, the leading edge turned a sinister gray, dangling tendrils like groping fingers, feeling its way forward. Beneath it swept a curtain of rain and wind that bent the lofty tops of the pines.

"Look at that, Joanna. Have ye seen its like?"

"I have," she said, voice small beside him. "The day after my mother died." A raindrop struck the earth beyond the oak's shelter. Thunder rolled, deep and deafening. In the pasture the horses were coming in briskly to the stable. "Alex, don't stay beneath this tree."

Joanna scurried away from it herself, leaving him with the hairs on his arms rising, the breeze drying the sweat on his skin. He followed her, half-thinking to call out, ask her to wait out the storm in the smithy so they might talk as she'd wanted.

She was already passing it, and there was Moon come to the doorway. Joanna didn't slow. Moon turned a glower on him as he ducked within, head and shoulders wet with rain. The smithy was empty, save for the two of them. "Where's Jemma?"

"Asleep on your cot." Rain drummed on the ground outside. Moon went to close the shutters. "What did ye say to vex Joanna?"

"Has she need of something more to vex her this day?"

Moon turned on him an unreadable look before the light in the smithy dimmed with the windows' shuttering. "A black day in more ways than one. At least it seems the heat will break."

The breeze from the dooryard was cooler than anything Alex had felt since his arrival on that shore.

Jemma slept through rising wind, drumming rain, even the thunder's booming. Moon was in a blacker mood. It occurred to Alex he'd known Kelly longer than anyone else at Severn, save perhaps Edmund Carey.

"Was Thom Kelly part of Carey's crew when ye joined the navy?"

"He hadn't been for long." Seated on his stool in the shadows, Moon drank from his flask, then offered it to Alex, who took a swallow before handing it back. The liquid burned its way down his throat as he watched the rain fall beyond the smithy door.

"What of Miss Joanna and Kelly? Were they friends?"

"Why do ye ask?"

"Because she's grieving and . . . who's to comfort her?"

Moon took a drink. "Joanna's used to dispensing the comfort."

Alex took a moment to compose his next

question. "D'ye think folk hereabouts see her as fully a person?"

Moon shot him a blank look. "What does that even mean?"

"She's unusual for a mistress, d'ye not think? One with the heart of a servant, always tending to the needs of everyone around her. *Dispensing the comfort.*"

"What's wrong with that?"

"Did I say was anything wrong?"

"No." Moon gazed at the flask, slump-shouldered. The fight drained from his voice. "All I ever wanted was to serve. To be of use."

"What d'ye think ye're doing with me?"

Moon's head lifted. "This won't last. One day ye'll know all ye need to. But if I'm to go on . . ." Before Alex could seek to clarify the unfinished statement, Moon's gaze shifted to the forge that had betrayed him. "Think ye that a man can remake himself?"

"It's what I'm forced to do."

"Ye're a whole man, with two hands to serve ye. Bend a little, bear the seven years with patience, ye'll be free to go or stay as ye will. But where can I go? What man would give me work?"

"I heard Carey tell ye there's no reason ye canna stay, if that's what ye want."

"And be of what use?" Moon crossed to the scrap heap, knelt, and fingered a piece of cast-off iron. He swiveled to look at Alex. "Ye know well enough by now how a thing broken can be remade. Iron from a splintered wagon wheel shaped, hardened into an axe blade, that blade when it's worn into something else. How many times, though, can that iron be pounded and reshaped before it grows brittle and crumbles to nothing?"

"That," Alex said, "ye'll ken better than I."

Moon stood, facing him with the rain battering the yard. "I cannot slip my chains, MacKinnon. I'm more surely bound by this"—he held up his mutilated wrist—"than ye with your king's mercy."

17

Reverend Pauling's letter reached them in October, carried downriver on a barge bound from Cross Creek, addressed from a backcountry plantation near a river called the Yadkin. The reverend wrote of the planter, Duncan Cameron, a reclusive Scotsman who permitted no language but Gaelic to be spoken in his presence.

"Everyone has to speak it?" Charlotte asked.

"Apparently, though it seems this Mister Cameron makes an exception for traveling clergy. He allowed Reverend Pauling to preach to his slaves, so they *can* speak English, just not in his hearing." Of more interest to Joanna was the mention of the overseer the eccentric planter had recently acquired, also surnamed Cameron:

> They met in Wilmington. Upon discovering the younger Cameron, Hugh by name, could speak Gaelic, the elder Cameron insisted Hugh accompany him to Mountain Laurel, his plantation. The Situation of the place is unique, nestled among wooded Ridges quite steep, though I should not call them Mountains being

many miles still from the high blue Peaks to the west.

The reverend described Mountain Laurel in some detail before returning to the subject of Joanna's interest:

> I have learned that Hugh Cameron is but recently arrived in the colony. While not admitting to taking part in the Jacobite Rising lately extinguished, much less to having been a Prisoner of the Crown, a certain light in his eyes at my mention of Alex MacKinnon leads me to surmise your Scotsman may be acquainted with this one.

Eager to inquire, Joanna chose a moment when the clanging from the smithy stopped to head in that direction under a sky of autumn blue, the reverend's letter in hand. Alex and Jemma were alone when she entered the smithy, having abandoned anvil and bellows for their dinner. Both looked up when she entered, Alex with a cup to his lips. He set it down and stood, surprise shifting to a look so quickly smothered Joanna would have thought she'd imagined it, but for her own stomach-dropping response.

He was glad, maybe even relieved, to see her.

She hadn't spoken to him since that September

day by the pasture fence, when the storm rolled in. In that time Papa had returned from Wilmington, grieved by Captain Kelly's death, disheartened by the *Joanna*'s loss, mired in a mood she'd known blacker only once. She'd yet to broach the subject she'd twice now spoken of with their blacksmith. While she longed for a life that didn't include such rigorous trade across oceans—and the need for slaves to facilitate it— she'd wanted the divesting of their ships to be by choice, carefully executed, so the proceeds could be used in other ways. Such as providing for the slaves she longed to see manumitted.

At least she might bear good news for one soul on that plantation. "I've a letter from Reverend Pauling."

Jemma swallowed a mouthful. "Where he writing from, Miss Joanna?"

"North Carolina still, a place in the back-country called Mountain Laurel." She swung her gaze back to Alex, who, though still appearing pleased to see her, seemed to regard the letter she bore with some misgiving. "He writes of a newly hired man there, a young Scotsman called Hugh Cameron. Might you know him?"

Misgiving yielding to startled interest, Alex said, "Aye, I kent a man by the name. Does Pauling say more of him?"

Joanna, flushed with gratification, read aloud the part pertaining to the Camerons, then glanced up to judge his expression. Pleased, intrigued, yet with a distance of memory in his gaze.

"It could verra well be him, though I'd thought he was indentured—most of us kept at Tilbury were."

"What's Tilbury?" Jemma asked, the very question in Joanna's mind.

"A place in London they put traitors to the Crown," he told her, glancing at Joanna as he did so, as if recalling their conversation out by the pasture fence. "How far is this Mountain Laurel? From here, I mean."

She shook her head. "I don't know. Cross Creek is maybe fifty, sixty miles upriver. Mountain Laurel is farther still—overland, it seems. Near the Yadkin River, the reverend wrote."

Alex's gaze sharpened. "Have ye a notion where that river may be?"

"No. Perhaps one of Papa's maps shows it. You should come for another book."

"Aye. Maybe. Thank ye for bringing me word."

He was smiling softly, the tilted curve of his mouth holding her gaze. "Shall I write to the reverend, in case he lingers at Mountain Laurel? Bid him tell the man of your connection?"

"If ye wouldna mind the trouble."

Those blue eyes pulled at her. "It's no trouble," she said, and had to look away again. Jemma was watching them. "I should let you return to your dinner."

She'd eaten hers with Charlotte, alone in their room save for the Annas. She, Charlotte, and Papa hadn't sat down to a formal meal together since his return from Wilmington. Each day she asked Mister Reeves, who was permitted into Papa's room of a morning to discuss business, whether to expect him at table that evening. Always the answer was a sad shake of head. "I doubt it, Miss Carey."

She was turning to leave when Alex said, "I havena seen your stepfather since his return. Have ye had opportunity to speak with him?"

Joanna turned back, reading the unspoken communication in his gaze, what he wouldn't say in front of Jemma. Had they spoken of her hopes for Severn's future?

"I've barely seen him. It's hard to know how much to intrude when he doesn't leave his room."

"I'd heard he'd taken the losses hard, but he hasna come out in a fortnight?"

"That ain't long, not for Master Carey," Jemma interjected but promptly clamped her lips shut as though remembering it was Joanna there with them.

"That's true," she said, and watched Jemma relax, realizing she wasn't to be scolded. "Jemma, how is it with you? Are you getting along all right here in the smithy?"

"Yes ma'am. Just fine. Better than fine. Right, Mister Alex?"

"Aye, *mo nighean*," Alex said. "Ye're doing a braw job."

"That's good?" the girl asked.

"Verra good."

To outward appearance, Jemma seemed to be thriving. Though she still wore her ragged boy's clothing, she was cleaner, that amber thicket atop her head pulled back into a stubby tail. *Mo nighean*, Alex called her. Joanna would have liked to inquire what it meant, but when she met his gaze again she simply mouthed, "Thank you."

His slanted smile as he glanced down at Jemma, stuffing her mouth with corn pone, was answer enough.

Joanna went straight from the smithy to pen a reply to Reverend Pauling, informing him of the *Joanna*'s loss and Alex's connection to Hugh Cameron. A day later it was borne upriver by a merchant headed for Cross Creek, with a prayer that it would find the reverend before he departed Mountain Laurel.

October passed with work to tend as the last of the field and garden produce was harvested. Papa joined them on occasion at table, where he appeared so grim and exhausted Joanna hadn't the heart to press him with her thoughts on Severn's management.

Winds and rain on the Carolina coast ushered in November but brought no reply from Reverend Pauling. Joanna sent a copy of the letter to his sister in Pennsylvania, where she trusted he would receive it eventually.

That letter was barely launched upon its journey when Azuba, who'd heard it from Marigold, related the news that Alex had injured himself at the forge.

"It's none so bad as burns go," Moon said, inspecting the palm of Alex's right hand, blistered and aflame as though he'd grasped a live ember and couldn't release it. What he *had* grasped was a heated rod left on the counter to cool. He'd known better than to touch it, had put the rod there himself. It had happened in an instant's distraction, his thoughts on Joanna Carey. That was all it had taken for the damage to be done.

"I'm surprised ye went this long," Moon said. "I cannot show ye, but my right hand was covered in burn scars."

"Still, best he don't wield a hammer for a bit," said Marigold, come to tend the burn. "Let this heal up some."

Alex did his best not to wince at the pain of what was, by comparison to Moon's healed burns, a minor injury. He sat by the anvil, injured palm upturned on his knee, as Marigold scooted another block chair close.

"Fetch me their basin," she told Jemma, who was hovering in concern. "See they got water on hand. If not, I use what's in that drink barrel."

Jemma emerged with the basin as a shadow darkened the smithy doorway.

"I see we'd similar notions, Mari."

Marigold dropped his injured hand as Joanna entered with their supper tray. "Oh, Miss Joanna. I ought to have brought that."

Setting the tray on the bench below the shutters, Joanna turned to survey them, holding a salve pot and a linen towel. "It's all right, Mari. Have you need of these? Azuba told me what happened. Is it bad?"

More than the present situation seemed to haunt her gaze, Alex thought, watching it flick to Moon. They were all thinking of his accident.

"You want to see to him, Miss Joanna?" Marigold nodded at the forge counter. "There be what I brought. I'll just go on back to the kitchen."

Joanna took in the other pot of salve and roll of bandaging. "You needn't . . . ," she began, but Marigold was already making for the smithy door.

Moon followed her out.

"Ye dinna need to," Alex said, awkwardness thick in the air. "I can manage."

"I want to," Joanna said. She gathered up the salve and bandages, instructed Jemma to set the basin nearby, and settled on the block chair Marigold had vacated. While Jemma went to examine the supper she'd brought, Joanna poured water into the basin, took up his right hand between hers, soaked a cloth, and began cleaning dirt and soot from around the burns on his palm and across the pads of his fingers.

Her lashes lay soft upon her cheeks as she tended him. "This looks painful," she said, head bent.

It was, but her touch was sure. Her hands were capable but smooth, those of a gentlewoman, the nails long and oval, neatly trimmed. She wore no cap, but a small lace pinner at the crown of her head. She'd a wee cowlick to one side of her hairline, a tiny peak where it parted to be swept back. He'd the urge to lean forward and kiss it, just there . . . until she touched a tender spot on his little finger.

He caught his breath, biting back a wince.

She glanced up. "I'm sorry."

"*Wheest*," he said, and saw the color rise faintly beneath her fine skin. While she began to wind the linen around his salved hand he asked, "Have ye spoken to your stepfather?"

She raised her lashes, revealing eyes more green than blue today. "Not about *that*. Mister Reeves says Papa's in no mood for conversation."

"Have ye told *him?*" he asked, but the scuff of booted steps in the yard drew their attention. *Speak of the devil,* Alex thought as Reeves entered the smithy and halted.

"Miss Carey, I'd wondered where you'd gone."

Joanna secured the linen bandage with a knot

at Alex's wrist, gathered up the salve and extra linen, and stood. "I was tending to—"

"I see plainly what you're doing." Reeves's glance settled on Alex, a look so scorching it compelled him to his feet. Jemma had turned, but like a startled wee mouse hoping to escape notice, she didn't move another muscle.

"How bad is it?" Reeves asked, with a nod at Alex's bandaged hand.

"He oughtn't to be at the forge for a few days," Joanna said.

"Is that so?" Reeves's gaze flicked between them, still searching but less heated. "Then I wonder, MacKinnon, would you be willing to lend a hand in building kilns for the tar-burning? We've a few more need constructing."

"I could. Though I dinna ken how it's done."

"Simple enough to watch and learn." Reeves blazed a grin, all its edges sharp. "Get Moon to show you. It'll make him feel useful." He fixed his gaze on Joanna. "If you're done here, Miss Carey, I'll see you back to the house."

She obliged the overseer, though if Reeves was as conscious as Alex of her displeasure in his brusque bidding as she glided out past him, the man hid it well.

18

A zuba? Miss Joanna! Best come quick!"
Bent over sewing, they both jerked erect at Marigold's frantic call.

"Angels help," Azuba said.

"What now?" Joanna asked, rising and hurrying out.

"A tar kiln's exploded," Marigold told them, halfway down the stairs. "One dead, others burned."

Dead. Joanna froze, gripping the banister. Alex had helped build the kilns at Mister Reeves's request. So had Elijah. She didn't think either was helping with the burning—she'd heard the clang of Alex's hammer that morning.

"Who?" she asked, searching Marigold's distraught face.

"Grandpa Jo!"

Azuba moaned. Grandpa Jo—Josiah—was Severn's oldest slave. He'd worked the fields as a younger man but had long since retired to lighter work, including overseeing the tar kilns.

A pit opened in Joanna's chest as she forced herself to focus on those who could be helped. "Are the others being brought in?"

"Already in the kitchen," Marigold said through tears.

Azuba hurried back up to fetch the needful supplies, passing Charlotte on the stairs. The child was pink-cheeked with excitement over something to break the monotony of her days without Jemma's company. "What's happened?"

"Some men were burned at a tar kiln, but I don't want you near them." Their suffering would frighten Charlotte.

"Joanna . . ." her sister whined.

"Stay in the house, Charlotte, please." Joanna followed Marigold to the back door, noting the door to her stepfather's bed chamber was shut fast.

"I tried," Marigold said, catching her glance. "He don't answer."

Joanna's thoughts flew to Alex, but swerved away as swiftly. She'd help Azuba do what they could to ease the injured men's pain. Afterward she would *not* go to the smithy with what was becoming a constant urge to seek out the only man on the plantation who seemed willing to listen to her. Papa was here. She would stand at her stepfather's door and bang it down if she must, but he was going to come forth and deal with this situation. They needed him.

Joanna understood the construction of tar kilns and their potential for exploding if not properly built or monitored throughout their burning, but not even the injured slaves, seared by flying debris during the explosion, could tell her the cause of the morning's tragic unfolding, save that old Josiah, standing close to the kiln at the critical moment, had been struck in the head by a chunk of burning lightwood, then covered in a rain of embers and pitch, his clothing set aflame. Those uninjured had put out the flames, but the old man had likely been dead before they ignited.

Joanna had no need of banging on her step-father's door to acquaint him with the tragedy. Mister Reeves beat her to it; the two were in the study when she returned to the house.

"I'm attempting to explain, sir," Mister Reeves was stating, "that I'm not convinced it *was* an accident."

Joanna halted at the half-open door.

"Do you imply Josiah brought about his own death—on purpose? Or another slave? Half of them were injured and none, to my reckoning, had a grudge against that old man. He was well loved."

Joanna had heard the wailing from the slave cabins as she left the kitchen.

"He was what, eighty?" Mister Reeves replied. "Mightn't he have overlooked something, failed to check on the work of others less skilled than himself?"

"All my slaves put to the tar-burning are skilled."

Neither man was looking Joanna's way. They stood at opposite ends of the desk, facing each other across its clutter.

"The slaves weren't the only ones involved in building the kilns," Mister Reeves admitted. "MacKinnon was put to the task, by me."

"MacKinnon? What on earth for?"

As abruptly as a tallow candle set before a hearth, Mister Reeves's expression melted with contrition. "MacKinnon burned his hand at the forge a few days ago. Badly enough he couldn't wield a hammer. I asked him to help with the building of the kilns—the laying of lightwood, nothing strenuous. I gave instruction for Moon to show him the way of it."

Papa stared at Mister Reeves. "Are you blaming MacKinnon for this mishap? Or Elijah?"

"Moon?" Mister Reeves appeared taken aback. "No sir. But do you think it mere coincidence a kiln explodes the one time MacKinnon has anything to do with them?"

"No, Papa. Alex mustn't be blamed for this." Both men fell silent at Joanna's entrance.

Mister Reeves recovered quickly but didn't conceal his annoyance at the interruption. "Miss Carey. Eavesdropping, were you?"

"I've a question for *you*," Joanna said, ignoring his. "Did you inspect the newest kilns prior to their firing?"

"I was busy elsewhere."

"So you'll blame a man who never until now has seen a tar kiln built, when you admit you failed to perform what is your reasonable duty? You are Papa's overseer. Whatever the cause, I consider it your oversight for not checking the kilns. Josiah's death is on your head, Mister Reeves."

"My head?" he challenged, features drawn into lines of wounded affront. "How do you figure—"

"Enough!" Papa halted the argument, fingertips pressed against his temples. He swung his gaze to Mister Reeves, then back to her. "This was meant to be a private conversation, Joanna."

Flinching at what amounted to a dismissal, she glanced at Mister Reeves, who wasn't quick enough to hide a flash of satisfaction. "Forgive my intrusion," she said, her tone still sharp. She made an effort to blunt it. "Papa, I'm relieved to see you out of your room. I only wish . . ."

"It hadn't taken another tragedy to bring it about?" he finished for her.

"Yes. But now that you are, might I broach a matter I've been wanting to discuss with you?" She hesitated to speak freely before Mister Reeves, but he would have to hear about it eventually.

"What is it?" her stepfather asked. "To do with Charlotte?"

"Yes, and everyone at Severn. Everyone

still alive." Knowing it was too late for Micah, Josiah, countless others who had lived and died there, bound to them in service, compelled her to ignore her better judgment, which was telling her to hold her peace and wait. "Papa, you've worked very hard over the years to make Severn and all your business endeavors prosperous, but I wonder if you've considered that what we have now is enough. More than enough."

"Enough for what?" Mister Reeves asked.

Ignoring him, Joanna fixed her gaze on her stepfather, who looked nearly as puzzled as Mister Reeves had sounded.

"What are you saying, Joanna?"

"I'm saying that I wish to manumit our slaves. All of them. Those who wish to remain and work here at Severn may do so, but we'll provide for them a reasonable living."

Utter silence filled the room. Mister Reeves's look of astonishment vanished in a bark of laughter. It unleashed a flood of mirth, nearly bringing the man to tears. "Oh, Miss Carey. You do amuse!"

She ground her teeth as her face grew hot— with anger as much as embarrassment. She held her tongue and gazed at her stepfather. "Papa? Have you nothing to say?"

He lowered himself into his chair, looking thinner than she'd noticed in a very long time.

"Sir, surely you aren't considering such nonsense?" Mister Reeves asked, mirth faltering at Papa's silence.

"Phineas," he said, quelling in his tone. He held Joanna's gaze. "Joanna, you have always had a tender heart and, as David recently reminded me, your role here hasn't been easy. But surely you realize the scenario you've just described is as impossible as a man flying to the moon?"

"Why should it be, if we were willing to live modestly?"

With a brow raised at Mister Reeves's snort, her stepfather said, "To clarify, it would be impossible with *these* slaves to live in such a manner *here*. There are laws governing the manumission of slaves in this colony."

Alex's question on the subject rang in her mind. "What is the law?"

A sigh escaped Papa's lips. "Shall I tell her, Phineas, or would you care to do so?"

"I'll do it, sir. Then I suggest we summon Moon and MacKinnon to account for themselves—for we've still that matter to resolve."

"So we do," said her stepfather, then waved him to continue.

Mister Reeves turned to her. "Miss Carey, would it surprise you to know the laws of North Carolina state quite clearly that any manumitted slave must leave the colony within a six-month, or risk being taken up and sold back into slavery? So you see, whatever notions you've been harboring about us living with the likes of Mari and Azuba—and whoever else has taken your fancy—are . . ." He'd grace enough to suppress what Joanna saw welling, the urge to laugh again. "Such notions are, as Captain Carey said, as likely as humanity ever visiting the stars."

No commotion had marked the kiln's exploding, so Alex and Moon remained none the wiser of it until Jemma raced in with the news.

"The turfs muffled it," Moon explained as he and Alex set to work with rake and shovel, along with the slaves who could be spared, clearing the remains of the ruined kiln near the edge of Severn's forest. "Had ye been nigh ye'd have heard it. Felt it too."

Under Moon's supervision and that of the old man they'd called Grandpa Jo, Alex had spent three days unloading lightwood from carts driven in from the forest, laying it to build the kilns. Over wood rich in pitch that would burn down to tar, cut turfs had been laid, with chimney holes left tunneled into the heart of the kilns to regulate airflow. Too little air and the fire wouldn't burn hot enough to produce the tar, which collected and ran from each kiln through a trough, down to a barrel set to catch it. Worse was too much air, too hot a fire.

Josiah's body had been wrapped and removed

to the burying ground. In the pit that had been the kiln and around it for yards, splintered, blackened wood and broken turf lay as though a cyclone had touched down. The air reeked of tar and burning, even through the kerchiefs tied across their noses. Alex went about setting order to the area with a heart heavy for those who grieved. Across the smoldering pit, Jemma drug a rake through a wafting of smoke, the cloth over her mouth and nose soaked with tears.

Other mounds rose yards away from the exploded kiln, their chimney holes smoking. Alex cast them a narrowed eye.

Hauling cooled debris single-handed, Moon caught such a look. "It's unlikely to happen again."

Alex met blue eyes above a faded kerchief. "Will there be looking into it? By Carey, I mean."

Moon was about to reply when Jemma fetched up and nodded toward the wagon track. "Here come Mari."

The kitchen lass made straight for them. "Master Carey," she said, out of breath after the brisk walk. "He asking for you, 'Lijah. You, too, Mister Alex. In his study." Marigold shot a look at Jemma. "*You* come to the kitchen, and I don't mean for eating."

They dipped their kerchiefs at the well to wash, but with garments stained and reeking, neither looked or smelled fit for an interview with Severn's master. They passed beneath a moss-draped yard oak, its leaves drifting down to lie brown upon the lawn. Despite the misgiving on Moon's set face, he went boldly into the house, pausing at the study to knock. Alex glanced along the passage but saw no indication of its female occupants before Carey bid them enter. He followed Moon within.

Reeves leaned a shoulder against the hearth mantel, where a fire burned. Carey, seated behind his desk, didn't rise. "Tell me what you can of the explosion, Elijah. I understand neither of you were present at the time?"

"No sir, we were not. I don't know what we can tell of it."

Alex stood near enough Moon to sense his thrumming tension, but he kept his gaze on Edmund Carey. The man looked tired, aged, unwell.

"You understand the building of kilns. You may well have heard the slaves talking. Think, Elijah. Was anything at fault in its construction rather than its managing? Phineas bid you show MacKinnon the way of their building."

Moon glanced from Alex to Reeves. "Never did he say such to me."

Before Carey could swing his frown to the over-seer, Reeves said lightly, "I asked MacKinnon to have Moon instruct him."

"Is that so?" Carey inquired, addressing Alex.

"Aye sir. It is."

"Did either of you build the kiln in question?" Carey asked.

"I helped with it," Alex said.

Reeves straightened from the mantel, his scrutiny intense. "And other kilns?"

"Two others."

"I oversaw MacKinnon's work, no matter no one asked it of me," Moon interjected, his tone heating. "Nothing was done amiss."

"We're only speaking to MacKinnon's inexperience," Reeves said, "not casting blame."

Moon's snort of disbelief begged to differ.

"I will own," Alex said, "it may have been my fault, though I ken no way to prove it, aye or nay. D'ye see fit to assign blame to me, so be it."

Moon stepped forward, shaking his head. "I'll not hear of that. MacKinnon did as I bid him. And sir, ye know I'm well able to judge the building of a kiln, as was Josiah."

"No need to take on in MacKinnon's defense. Miss Carey has already . . ." Reeves's words trailed off at Carey's pointedly cleared throat, but his gaze flashed to Alex, as if to gauge his reaction to his mention of Joanna.

Alex gave him nothing, leveling his gaze.

"Phineas, may I recall your attention?" Reeves jerked his gaze from Alex as Carey stood, his posture erect despite the weariness about his eyes. "One who leads must know when to accept responsibility and not shift it, fair or otherwise, be he master, overseer, or blacksmith. The blame for this regrettable occurrence lies not with MacKinnon or Elijah or Josiah. It lies with me."

Reeves stared. "You, sir? You weren't present at the kiln."

"I wasn't present in any sense of the word! Neither, for that matter, were you—as Joanna pointed out."

For such a mild dressing down, Reeves appeared inordinately off-balanced, as if the patterned hearth rug he stood upon had been yanked from beneath him. "Regrettably, sir."

"You may go, Elijah," Carey told Moon, who stirred with alacrity to obey. "And you, Phineas."

Alex turned on his heel to follow Moon.

"MacKinnon," Carey said, "I'd have you bide a moment."

Reeves hesitated, jaw clenching with displeasure, but when Carey merely awaited his departure, he made for the door, shooting Alex a look in passing that might have exploded a kiln unaided.

As the door shut behind the overseer, Carey said, "I hope you'll pardon Phineas. Not an hour past, Joanna championed you most fervently, practically on the spot you now stand. It seems to have rankled."

"Had I need of a champion?" Alex asked.

"Joanna thought so. But let the matter rest. And the Almighty rest the soul of a faithful old slave."

Alex's teeth ground over what he wished to say to that, for Carey was studying him closely.

"What rank did you hold in the Pretender's army, MacKinnon?"

The question jarred. *Pretender.* With his own feelings about Charles Stuart conflicted at best, Alex forced his jaw to relax. "I was a foot soldier. I didna hold a rank."

"Not even as captain?"

"No." He'd led his clansmen briefly at Culloden, after so many had been slain. "Never officially."

Carey looked surprised, and thoughtful. "I begin to think you've the makings of one." He moved nearer the hearth, stretching out his hands to the blaze, though Alex found the room over-warm. "How came you to be aboard the *Charlotte-Ann* when Phineas came downriver to find me a blacksmith?"

"Ye ken how, sir."

"In part. But I'd hear the tale from you. Taken prisoner in the final battle of the Jacobite uprising, as I understand it?"

"Culloden, aye." He didn't want to tell this tale, didn't want the words to pass his lips. But Carey was nodding, expecting him to continue. "We were put aboard ship at Inverness, hundreds of us, wounded, half-starved, and brought thus to London, some put into Tilbury Fort, the rest onto

242

ships moored on the Thames, chained in holds for a year before a lot was cast and some given the king's mercy, others taken to trial. Of course we were half of us dead by then, including my kinsman."

"A brother?" Carey asked. "Father?"

"An uncle, but father to me."

"Ah. Rory MacNeill, as I recall." The name hung on the room's warm air, until Carey prompted, "And after you were granted the king's mercy?"

"Upon our release from the ship I was carted away with the rest, my indenture bought and sold. Next I kent I was being rowed out to the *Charlotte-Ann*, which I boarded weak as a wobbly colt. Ye ken the rest."

"A wobbly colt?" Carey looked him up and down, seeming amused by the comparison. He'd filled out in the weeks spent at the forge. He was nearly back to the size he'd been before he joined Charles Stuart's army, though his muscles now were harder, more defined.

"Your physical strength is one thing you've regained," Carey said. "I hope in time the trade you're learning will give you purpose. A chance at another life. Should you choose to continue that life at Severn . . ." When Alex merely returned his gaze, struggling to hide his aversion to the notion, Carey gave a curt nod. "A discussion for another day."

The fire crackled. Somewhere the house settled with a creak. Or a footstep overhead?

Alex recalled a thing he'd meant to say. "I'm sorry for the loss of Josiah. All your losses of late, sir."

Carey bent for a poker to stir the embers in the hearth. He went about it, taking his time, then set the poker in its stand. "I'll be honest, MacKinnon. I've known a great weariness of spirit these past weeks, but looking at you now . . . I think if you are standing after all your losses, what right have I to fold under lesser blows? You encourage me."

It was the last thing Alex had thought to hear from the man, on this or any day. "How so?"

"By the very fact of your drawing breath." Carey set his mouth firm, then added as if to himself, "I am determined. I shall shed this shadow." Contrary to his dark words, a swift smile touched his lips. "I was thinking what David—Reverend Pauling—would say to us both were he here, that a battle is being waged between the Almighty and our enemy, and the prize is our very souls."

Alex felt the jolt of surprise as the faintest of currents running through his bones. "He said something of the sort to me."

"I've sensed that battle these weeks past." Carey held his gaze, searching, then looked away. *Why art thou cast down, O my soul? and why art thou disquieted within me? hope thou in God: for I shall yet praise him, who is the health of my countenance, and my God."* He made a fist and lifted it. "I know this."

Alex had presumed Edmund Carey a man of faith, having hosted the reverend and their worshipping neighbors weeks before. He'd gathered the man was subject to periodic bouts of melancholia but until now hadn't known the depth of the darkness Carey battled.

Dismissed from the house, he went out wondering if it was anything like the darkness that warred within his own soul.

19

February 1748

Jemma ran away from Severn late that winter, and Alex MacKinnon was among those who brought her back, looking for all the world like another captured fugitive. While Jemma was marched to the kitchen by Mister Reeves, Demas on their heels, Alex headed toward the smithy. Even through window glass Joanna saw his lip was cut and swollen, one eye bruised.

She'd been the one to suggest he join the search. "He recalled to me a conversation he and Jemma had with Reverend Pauling, about the Cherokees," she'd told her stepfather. "Jemma called them her people."

Her stepfather had nodded, thoughtful. "Her mother had Cherokee blood. And the grand-mother, here before I took ownership, what was her name?"

"She was called Maggie," Joanna had said. "But Jemma—and others—maintain she called herself Looks-At-The-Sun, or Sun-Gazer. Something of that sort."

"So MacKinnon thinks she's trying to reach the mountains?" Papa was looking more robust than in autumn. Time spent out of doors, the relative calm of the winter—no deaths, losses, or illnesses other than the usual agues and a few cases of worms that had little tummies bloated—had helped lift his spirits. "If the girl trusts him at all, it may do some good to have him along."

Perhaps it had, for they'd returned with Jemma. Joanna had been prepared to go straight to her, but perhaps it was Mister Reeves she'd best speak to first. Papa had warned him once against too freely using the whip when punishing a slave.

By the time she reached the passage below, Mister Reeves had entered the house. He stood outside her stepfather's study, blocking her path. "Where's Captain Carey?"

"Away to the mill. Why is Alex returned looking as though he wrestled an alligator? What happened to him?"

Mister Reeves barked a laugh, then studied her narrowly. "Such concern for your stepfather's indentured man."

Joanna willed herself to patience. Her inter-actions with Mister Reeves had been few since the day he and Papa derailed her hopes for Severn, save for meeting at table. In Papa's presence Mister Reeves was all politeness, but she couldn't bring herself to feel any warmth for the man. Not when he brushed aside so readily what was most important to her. As he seemed to be attempting to do now. "Was it Demas?"

"Ought I to take offense you haven't asked whether *I* am to blame?"

It hadn't crossed her mind that he could cause Alex such injury and come away unscathed. "I merely seek the particulars of the matter, which you are clearly reluctant to relate. I'll have the story from Alex."

It would take but a moment to visit the smithy. Then she'd go to Jemma, no doubt being washed and fed—and scolded—in the kitchen. She tried to move past Mister Reeves, but he took her arm in his cool grasp. The wrinkling of her nose was purely involuntary.

"Miss Carey, I don't wish to quarrel. I've been a week on the river and days in a swamp. I'm exhausted and, as you discern, in need of a bath. As for MacKinnon—yes, it was Demas caused his injuries."

"Why?" she asked, searching his impassive face.

"I cannot answer that. I wasn't near enough to see the start of their quarrel."

Joanna pulled her arm free. "You never inquired?"

"It didn't seem important. They ceased their brawling when I reached them." Mister Reeves at last stood aside. "Have one of the girls heat water for me and bring it to my room, if you'd be so kind. And mind you deal with Jemma, Miss Carey. You cannot let disobedience of this magnitude pass unpunished."

Suspicion gripped her. "Have you already seen to that?"

"You've made it clear she's your concern. But I shall make her mine if you neglect to curb her willfulness."

She found Alex alone in the smithy, pacing the shop, coat and breeches stained with filth. His stockings were ruined, his hair unkempt, but his face . . . The window's thick glass had done it a kindness.

"*What* happened upriver?" she asked at the doorway. It had begun to sprinkle, cold on her cap and shawl. She hurried inside where the forge was newly lit, a welcome warmth.

"Jemma isna pleased with me," he said, halting to face her. "Is she all right?"

"You'll know better than I. I've not seen her, but *you* . . . Have you water in your room?"

"I havena looked." He did so, coming out with the pitcher. "Moon's left it full. Why d'ye need it?"

"I mean to tend your face. You shouldn't leave those wounds unwashed, as I expect they have been for days."

Reluctance etched his injured countenance. "Ye dinna need to."

She ignored the half-hearted protest. "You'll need to sit. I'll never reach."

That brought a wincing half-smile to his broken mouth. "Ye managed it once."

She dropped her gaze, softening at the recollection of standing on a block chair to measure him.

"I didna ken ye for who ye were, at first," he said.

That was a thing he'd never told her. Not that they'd spent a great amount of time in conversation over the winter. She'd tried not to darken the smithy door more than was needful, though she'd been happy to do so whenever her duties required it. Yet something about the man, quite at odds with his imposing stature and sometimes daunting silence, reassured her now. What was it Marigold said of him, all those months ago? Something about seeing kindness in him. She'd seen it in how he treated Elijah and Jemma. Perhaps Reverend Pauling had seen it as well.

"Who did you think I was?"

"Ye willna be miffed if I'm honest?" She caught a teasing glint in the one blue eye not swollen nearly shut as he set the pitcher on the anvil and folded himself onto one of the block chairs near the forge.

"I won't be. Tell me."

"I thought ye were head seamstress maybe. Or a housemaid. An indenture, I suppose, like me."

She had to swallow when she caught his gaze, as powerful in his present state to rattle her as ever, only now it pulled at her and set her heart racing—with yearning. "What if I said I wish I had been?"

His uninjured eye flared at that. "What d'ye mean?"

They'd never spoken again of that vision she'd had of what Severn could be for her family, for Azuba, Mari, all their slaves. She hadn't told him how Papa and Mister Reeves had summarily dashed it.

"You were right, Alex."

He'd picked up on her change of mood. The teasing fled his gaze. "What about?"

"I'll never see our slaves freed and living here. A law prevents it." She broke their gaze when his became too searching. She touched his coat sleeve, which bore a tear—not to mention spatters of what looked like dried blood. "I'll take your coat for mending. For now, tell me how this happened."

"First tell me something," he said, catching her hand in his. "Ye've been carrying this knowledge around for weeks, have ye not? I've noticed a heaviness on ye, the times ye've been by here."

"You have?" To her knowledge, no one else had.

"Aye. Have ye spoken of it to anyone?"

She slipped her hand from his to fetch a towel

from his room, then soaked and wrung it. "I guess I didn't see the point."

He studied her through the slit of his wounded eye. "Why are ye here now? Ye might've sent Mari to do this. Or"—he laughed without humor—"taken no thought to me at all."

She'd been reaching for him, about to turn his face so his injured eye was better lit. "Don't you deem yourself worth the effort?"

Their gazes held again. It was he who looked away first. "I'll tell ye what ye asked to hear, while ye do what ye came to do."

Joanna cupped his face and tilted it. He hadn't shaved in a week at least. Beard stubble glinted dark gold in the light from the forge's fire, reminding her of his piratical appearance back in summer. His lips were set, his lashes lowered. His brows were full, darker than his hair. She wanted to stroke one, but contented herself with tracing the skin around his wounded eye, briefly brushing his temple, all of which bore bruising.

He was stone beneath her touch. Then he drew a breath, and she realized he'd been holding it, and holding himself utterly still. She pulled back, uncertain. He reached up, fingers encompassing her wrist.

"I'm not made of glass," he said gruffly. "Dinna go chary of me."

"I don't want to hurt you."

"Ye're doing quite the opposite."

Her belly fluttered at his words, the quirk of his mouth. "You said you'd tell me about Jemma. And Demas."

"Aye. I did."

She washed his brow and around his bruised eye, then down his cheek and jaw, while he spoke of their search upriver for Jemma, getting word of her along the way, finding her at last in Cross Creek.

Joanna drew back. "However did she get so far?"

"She willna say. I suspect more than one boat spirited her upriver. I doubt she'd have made that distance afoot."

"I've been as far as Cross Creek only once." Joanna stepped around him to reach the damage done the other side of his face, the cut to his cheekbone and the split in his lower lip. "She didn't come willingly once you found her, I'm guessing."

"She didna." Jemma had bolted at sight of them, he said, vanishing like a rabbit into a patch of swamp. Alex and Demas had given chase, and in the process ran right over the scaly back of an alligator, half submerged in a woody tangle. "I'd thought it another rotting log."

A shudder passed through the flesh beneath Joanna's fingertips. With her own breath caught in her throat, she cupped Alex MacKinnon's cheek and placed a kiss on his brow, the gesture pure reflex, born of her relief that he'd done such a thing and hadn't suffered lasting injury.

His head jerked slightly, and for an instant she froze, unable to meet his gaze. Her face wasn't warm; it was on fire. "S-so there *was* an alligator?"

"Oh, aye," Alex said after the briefest pause. "It about took off my leg when it writhed round and made for me. I staggered but stayed on my feet. I hadn't a weapon to hand, so I kicked it in the snout. Then I dodged away, darting through trees and muck. I heard Jemma's screeching and made for the sound. Guess the beast didna like the carryings-on. It didna chase me."

"Thank the Almighty for that," Joanna said, having regained her composure while he spoke.

"I dinna ken whether the Almighty had anything to do with it, but Reeves said it must have just eaten its fill to have been so sluggish."

"I'm sure of it—the Almighty, I mean—even if you aren't." She washed the cut on his lip, gently running the damp cloth around his mouth. "And this?"

She was close enough to hear the breath he drew. "When I caught them up, Demas had Jemma lifted off the ground, kicking and screaming. I suppose I was still worked up from the alligator. I didna think, just lit into him."

"An alligator *and* Demas?"

"The more fool I," he said ruefully. "I canna

254

say now he was doing the lass any real harm. But that's what I thought when I laid eyes on them. I ken that's what Jemma thought." Silence held them briefly before he said, "May I ask of ye a favor, lass?"

Lass. She liked the implication of the word, as though no inequality of station existed between them. "You don't want me to tell Papa, do you? The part about you and Demas."

"I'd rather we let it go." She still held the dirty towel. He reached for her other hand and held it. Again. "I doubt Reeves will speak of it."

Joanna wasn't thinking about the overseer. She glanced down at Alex's lap, thinking how easy it would be to fold herself onto it. When she raised her gaze, she saw invitation in his eyes, but warning too. As if he were bidding her do the reckless thing she was contemplating and cautioning her not to do it. She spread her fingers, entwining them with his, felt the deepening of his breath.

"I need a bath," he said.

She laughed, though her heart was banging crazily, her mind screaming every warning reason could produce. "Your face is clean."

Something shifted in his eyes. Wanting bloomed, banishing the warning. "Joanna . . . ," he said, an instant before Elijah appeared in the smithy doorway. Instead of pulling her to him, as she'd been sure he meant to do, Alex pushed her away. She'd dropped the towel. Sweeping aside her petticoat, she bent for it to hide her face, if only for a moment.

"Joanna, why are ye here?"

She straightened, certain Elijah had seen too much. "What do you mean? I'm only—"

"Why are ye *here*," Elijah repeated, and she heard the furious urgency in his voice, "instead of seeing to Jemma? Reeves is taking the whip to her—now!"

Joanna was still shaking an hour after all was said and done and she'd retreated to the sewing room to pace in agitation, leaving Charlotte distracted by Azuba and her dolls, none the wiser as to what had happened. There was that to be thankful for.

Shock at seeing Jemma tied to a post behind the kitchen, wailing in the falling rain as the whip landed across her bared shoulders, had boiled over into rage. In the midst of it, she'd all but assaulted Phineas Reeves and torn the whip from his hand, as Phoebe and her girls, Marigold, and Elijah stood back from them. And Alex, who'd followed her from the smithy.

"What do you think you're doing?" Mister Reeves had demanded, hazel eyes lit with an incongruous light, face glistening with rain.

"What are *you* doing? Not half an hour ago you told me Jemma was *my* concern!" Awaiting no answer, she'd called to Phoebe to untie Jemma, whose shirt hung bunched about her waist, revealing narrow shoulders crossed with livid stripes, blood running pink, mingled with rain. When Phoebe hesitated, darting frightened eyes at Mister Reeves, Alex and Elijah pushed forward through the ring of watchers.

Jemma had fallen into Alex's arms. He'd hoisted her against his chest and straightened, ready to carry her to the kitchen, when Papa arrived from the mill. Still in the saddle, he'd ridden into their midst, demanding an explanation as the cold rain grew steady, drenching them all.

"Sir," Mister Reeves said, "I'd spoken to Miss Carey, told her in no uncertain terms that she must deal with the girl—punish her—else I would do so, and I asked her to bid one of the kitchen girls heat water for me to bathe, presuming that was where she was bound. I waited. When none came I went to draw the water myself. I spied *her*," he said, pointing at Jemma in Alex's arms, "skulking away from the kitchen alone, bound for who knew where. I asked after you, Miss Carey," he said, turning on Joanna, dark hair plastered to his skull. "No one knew where you were. So I did as I'd warned you."

Mute with guilt, Joanna glanced at Alex, hunched over Jemma, sheltering her with his body. A few moments was all it had been, but had Elijah not found her . . .

Papa took Mister Reeves's side. "Phineas, I know in the past I've tempered your ideas of fitting punishments. In this case, while I regret it was needful, I judge that you weren't in excess."

"Only because I stopped him!" Joanna protested. "How far would he have taken it had I not?"

"It's done, Joanna," her stepfather said, then to Alex, "Take her to be looked after."

Joanna followed Alex out of the rain, Jemma small and stiff in his arms. He took gentle care of her, laying her on a pallet in the kitchen, clasping her hand while Phoebe and Marigold tended the wounds crisscrossing her shoulders. Seven stripes.

Jemma had cried herself to sleep. Instead of leaving her in the kitchen, Alex scooped her up, pallet and all, and took her to the smithy once the rain ceased.

"You'll let Mari or Phoebe know if the wounds look to be inflamed, come morning?" Joanna had asked.

"I will," he'd said, and she could tell that despite his self-possession, his anger was as seething as her own. And his concern. "Dinna worry—not about that."

"Alex," she whispered now, her hair still damp and straggled from the rain. Had she thanked him, for any of it? She would go to the smithy first thing tomorrow. She would—

"Miss Joanna?" Azuba's softened voice, the touch of hands on her shoulders, gave Joanna a start. She hadn't heard the housemaid enter the room.

She turned, stepping back from that almost-embrace, meeting the gaze of the woman who'd been the nearest thing to a mother she'd known for the past seven years. A brown-skinned woman in faded linen, graying hair covered in a cap. A woman her stepfather owned.

"I'm sorry," Joanna choked out.

Azuba's forehead wrinkled. "Why are you sorry? You didn't whip that child. Or are you thinking it was too harsh?"

"Of course it was."

"A slave run off like she done, it's what happens."

"Azuba, you cannot possibly think it was the right thing to do?" Though she'd seen red when she snatched that whip from Mister Reeves, and much of what had followed was a blur, she recalled snatches of words spoken around her as she and Alex hurried Jemma into kitchen. Had it been Marigold who'd muttered behind her, "Fool girl thinking she gonna be a wild Indian . . ."?

It was true, Jemma had set her hope on an impossible dream, thinking she could find refuge with a people who might share her blood but might as easily kill and scalp her as take her in.

She wanted freedom that badly. Didn't they all? Didn't Azuba, born into slavery like Jemma?

"Do it matter what I think is right?" Azuba asked, the sorrow beneath those words unimaginable.

"To me it does. This isn't how I want things to be." It tumbled out of her then, the vision she'd had the night Reverend Pauling, on his sickbed, had spoken of her to Papa, and all that her heart had woven into it since.

Azuba stared at her, no expression on her face.

"I want that life for you, too, Azuba. I don't want to live apart from you, or Mari, or so many others—not if you're willing to remain with us. But I want you to be free. Legally. Only it—"

She stopped, startled by a noise in the passage. A sniffle, poorly muffled. Azuba reached the door and pulled Marigold into the room. A crying, angry Marigold, wrapped in a bulky shawl, who didn't look at all contrite to have been caught eavesdropping.

"Mari," Joanna said. "You heard what I was saying?"

"Yes ma'am. I did."

Joanna had hated it when Marigold began calling her *Miss* Joanna. She hated even more to hear *ma'am* out of her mouth. "Will you keep it between us?"

Marigold's gaze dropped to the floor. She

hunched herself into her shawl. "You want it kept secret?"

Joanna took in Marigold's face more closely, noticing its puffy roundness. Had she been weeping over Jemma?

"Are you all right, Mari? It was a horrible thing to see."

Mari snorted. "Maybe it put some sense in her . . . *ma'am.*"

Joanna flinched.

"Mari," Azuba snapped. "You ain't helping matters."

"I'm sorry," Mari said with barely contained defiance. Fresh tears spilled down her cheeks. "I want to say one thing. Can I say one thing, Miss Joanna, afore I shut my mouth about what I heard you saying?"

Joanna felt her belly clench. "Yes, Mari. What is it?"

Marigold's nose ran freely with her tears. "If you was going to do like you said, set everyone free, I wish you'd done it afore Micah had to die!"

Hand muffling a wail, Marigold fled the room.

Joanna looked at Azuba, who quite uncharacteristically appeared at a loss for words.

"I wish it too," Joanna said dully. "But it isn't going to happen."

Azuba said, "I know."

"You knew about the manumission law?"

Azuba shook her head. "I know Master Carey. He a good man in many ways, Miss Joanna. But he ain't ever gonna choose to do a thing like what you want, even if he could."

Jemma was asleep on his cot. Since Moon had yet to return to the smithy, Alex had given up trying to sleep on the cold floor and laid himself out on Moon's cot. It was too short—the least of what was keeping him wakeful. He couldn't stop seeing Joanna marching up to Reeves, grabbing his wrist, snatching away the whip. The man had been too startled to stop her, standing with his mouth catching rain. Alex had been taken aback, and thrilled, by her fierceness as she stood up to the man, and to her stepfather once he arrived. After that it had all been about Jemma, poor mite. She'd be in a world of pain when she woke, likely sooner than either of them wanted, but she'd heal. In body at least.

He wanted to tear Reeves limb from limb. He wanted to do nigh the same to Edmund Carey. He wanted to find Joanna, pull her into his arms, do what they hadn't done there beside the forge. Was she lying awake worrying over Jemma, longing all the more for her life to be different? Had she room in her thoughts for him?

He oughtn't to be thinking of her. He'd managed not to do so all winter—half of the time, if he was honest, while the other half he'd merely been waiting for her to appear in the smithy doorway again. Today she had, and every touch on his face, every meeting of their eyes, had pushed him a little further past reason. And that swift, sweet kiss on his brow when he told her about the alligator . . . He could almost think he'd dreamt it again.

He hadn't, though. Not this time. And by the look in her eyes, she'd startled herself in the doing of it.

She'd the loveliest eyes, that changeable sea color, fringed by lashes darker than her hair. He longed to know what she looked like with all that brown hair spilling down . . .

He stifled a groan before it left his lips.

If he didn't put Joanna Carey from his mind, he'd never sleep. He latched on to the next image it presented, the winding river that flowed past Severn—just how far past he'd a keener notion now. This land was vast enough a man might easily lose himself in it, a thought that no longer intimidated. He was longing for escape, more than he had since the day he signed that wretched indenture.

But he'd left it too late. His heart was entangled. Not just with Joanna, but more and more she was filling his thoughts.

Could he leave her, knowing her unhappiness?

What would his staying help in that regard? He admired her for her kind heart and all its naïve yearnings for a life more like the one he'd known in Scotland than he'd let on. He wanted her. Maybe even loved her. But he was still what he was, a prisoner, indentured for rebellion. And in truth she barely knew him.

He could change that, let her break down the walls he'd kept intact.

Did he want her to know him?

Aye, he did. In every sense of the word. Even with no way he could see to make that lovely vision of hers ever come to pass, or play a part in it. Unless . . .

He'd still over six years to serve out his indenture. If he could manage to abide the place for such a length of time, would she wait for him? Refuse Reeves—a likelihood after that day—and any other man who sought her hand?

But if Carey had rejected Moon, what made Joanna think *he* was even remotely acceptable?

Did she think it?

Whatever she was thinking, he longed to run his fingers through that hair all fallen down to . . . Would it be her waist?

He turned over, groaning into his borrowed bed.

20

With a mended bridle delivered, Alex paused to fondle the questing nose of one of Carey's mares, taking the faint noises nearby for that of another horse—until a distinctly human sniffle drew him to the last box stall before the doors open to the yard beyond. Joanna, he was thinking, though it surprised him she'd give vent to her feelings in the stable.

It wasn't Joanna he found, wrapped in a shawl and crying her heart out in the empty horse box. "Mari?"

The shawl slipped off Marigold's shoulders as she turned, and he saw past the marks of weeping to the fullness in her face, the thickness of her waist for which her winter gown and petticoat couldn't account. When had he last seen her? She'd come to the smithy less frequently of late, and yesterday, during the fiasco of Jemma's whipping, he'd been distracted to say the least.

"How far along are ye?"

Marigold snatched up the shawl, but it was too late to hide the truth. "He tell you?" she all but wailed, bursting into fresh tears.

Alex hurried into the stall and grasped her

shoulders. "*Wheest*, lass. Ye dinna want to draw attention, aye?"

She melted against him, brow pressed to his chest. He stroked her back, then held her away. "Ye've told Elijah?"

"He knows."

Alex's gut clenched at her leaden tone. "Will he not claim the bairn?"

"It don't matter. Slave mama makes a slave baby. You ain't figured that yet?"

His mouth tightened. "Of course it matters. D'ye want him, Mari?"

"My baby? Of course!"

Alex touched her cheek, stroking away a tear. "Elijah, I meant."

"Reckon I'd take him as he is and be glad." She closed brimming eyes, heaving a breath. "But *he* think he ain't fit for nothing. Not smithing, farming, or fathering."

She was about to dissolve into weeping again. As Alex folded her against his chest, hoping to head it off, there came a faint noise behind him, a rustle like a mouse in the hay. When he looked up from Marigold's bent head, they were alone.

"I'll speak to Elijah, see what he has to say for himself." And what he thought Carey would do. "Does Joanna ken about the bairn?"

"No sir, she don't. Azuba suspects, but she ain't asked me outright yet. I don't like to think what Miss Joanna going to say."

That surprised him. "Ye were friends once, aye?"

"Things change."

Oh aye, they do. He held her away from him. "Come now. Wipe your face, and go back to whatever ye're meant to be doing. It'll be all right, one way or another."

If Marigold found the words as empty as they felt leaving his lips, she pretended otherwise.

Joanna was breathing hard as she settled on the stool beside Alex's cot, where Jemma lay moaning in restless sleep. She'd come meaning to check the girl's dressings. Catching sight of Alex on his way to the stable, she'd turned aside to follow, letting him reach the stable ahead of her, not wishing to draw attention from anyone nearby.

She'd lain awake last night, racked with guilt over those few sweet moments in the smithy and what they'd cost Jemma, helpless to stop imagining what might have happened had Elijah not interrupted and the day unraveled with its awfulness.

Something like what she'd just seen?

Lying facedown on the cot, Jemma stirred, stiffened, then whimpered. "Mister Alex? I'm thirsty."

"It's me, Jemma." Joanna rose and poured water from the pitcher into Alex's cup. "Can you sit up?"

"Miss Joanna?" Jemma turned her face to the side, one bleary amber eye blinking up at her. "I can drink like this. Hold it close?"

Jemma shifted to the cot's edge and hung her mouth over the side. Joanna held the cup rim to her waiting lips and tipped it. Jemma sucked in the water noisily, a little at a time, then laid her head down. "Thank you . . . ma'am."

"Oh, Jemma." Joanna stroked her curls, in need of washing though the rest of her had been bathed. Where did she begin to ask this child what was wrong? "I never meant this. I'm so sorry."

"Me too." Jemma's body shuddered. "Never been so scared."

"When Demas found you? Or yesterday?"

"Both. I just wanted to find my people."

Joanna wanted to tell her that they—everyone at Severn—were more her people than some Indians she'd never seen, but was that true? Was she wrong to want it to be true?

Jemma was quiet, her back rising and falling. "Jemma?"

She didn't reply. Joanna decided to let her sleep and check the dressings later. Or tell Alex to do it.

"Joanna?"

As if her thoughts had summoned him, she turned to see him standing there, looking at her with eyes and mouth and posture proclaiming welcome. Relief. Warmth.

Yearning filled her. Uncertainty rooted her, until he beckoned her into the shop.

She couldn't meet his gaze. Looking past him, she spied a length of metal on the forge's counter. A marlinspike, she thought, like the ones he'd made for Captain Kelly.

"Does the *Charlotte-Ann* require marlinspikes?" She hated the tinny sound of her voice.

Alex half-turned toward the spike. "A piece of scrap. It's nothing." He took a step nearer, studying her face. "Something's amiss with ye, lass. Is it Jemma?"

"She's sleeping."

"What, then?" Two strides closed the distance between them. Long fingers grasped her arm, anchoring her where she stood. "Ye're clearly upset. Is it yesterday? Or maybe . . . what happened between us before?"

She blinked, blurring her vision. "And what was that?"

"Ye ken the answer, lass."

She pulled free. "Perhaps you shouldn't address me so informally."

"Yesterday it pleased ye fine," he said, dropping his voice to a husky lilt that nearly undid her. "Is it that ye're blaming yourself—or us both—for what happened to the lassie?"

"I saw you in the stable. With Mari."

Understanding dawned on his face. "Did ye, then?"

That was all he had to say?

"And now I'm asking myself . . . what sort of man *are* you, that you would make me think you'd welcome me into your arms and yet I find Mari there the very next day."

She'd blurted it, the only way she could have gotten the words out without tears interfering. They came anyway. She wiped at them angrily.

More than one reply flashed across his eyes before he turned and strode toward the bench. He retraced his steps like a stalking panther, radiating the vitality that had so rattled her at their first meeting. If anything, it was more intense now, well fed and worked as he'd been the past months.

He stopped before her, forcing her to cant her head to meet his gaze.

"The sort of man to comfort a lass when he finds her crying in a box stall. There's nothing between Mari and me of the sort ye're thinking ye saw. The lass was in need of a friend. That's all I am, or ever will be, to her."

She held his gaze, saw nothing there but sincerity and felt ridiculous for entertaining such suspicion—and beset by that older ache. If only that friend Marigold needed could be *her.*

"Is Mari upset with me still? She was, yesterday."

Alex shook his head. "She didna say so."

"What, then?"

"That's for her to tell, if she wishes." He said no more of the matter. What he did say was, "Joanna, if I was to touch ye now, would ye allow it?"

The question was a yanked rug, tumbling her thoughts. She looked down, saw he already grasped her arm. She wrapped her fingers around his forearm, feeling the hard muscle beneath his shirt, all he wore though the day was chill. "You *are* touching me."

"Not the sort of touch I mean." His other hand cupped her face, big and warm. She leaned her cheek into it, resistance melting. "Mari's a comely lass. No man could think otherwise. But *I* dinna want to watch her eyes change with the light. I dinna want to touch her, or feel her touching me. I dinna want to ken the secrets of her soul."

He took her hand and placed it flat against his chest. His heart beat beneath it, as strongly as her own. "And you want those things of me?"

"Only if ye want them too."

Words abandoned her, but when he pulled her to him, she went willingly, going up on her toes to meet him as he lowered his head. An instant before their lips met, he stopped.

"Dinna do it unless ye mean it," he whispered against her mouth.

"I mean it," she breathed, past reason now.

It wasn't the brush of lips she'd imagined her

first kiss would be but deep and full, even before he picked her up and held her tight against him, their bodies molded until she lost track of her edges, felt herself bleeding into him. Then her feet felt earth, and though he'd set her down gently, it felt like crashing from a great height.

He was breathing hard, a look of urgency in his eyes. "Joanna, I need to hear ye say it—that ye'll wait for me to serve out my indenture. I didna think I could last seven years in this wretched place, but I'll do it for ye. I'll serve my time for Carey if I ken ye'll be mine at the end of it."

He'd brought reality down hard. "You mean . . . Are you asking me to marry you?"

"I'm asking, what is it ye want? Not for Severn, or your stepfather, your sister, or anyone ye've the looking after. For yourself."

Had anyone ever asked her such a question? She spread her hands across his chest, over his beating heart, and knew what she *didn't* want—to marry Mister Reeves or any other man who wasn't Alex MacKinnon. She wanted him with a hunger and a tenderness she'd never imagined. He was head and shoulders above all other men, in ways beyond the physical.

And he wanted *her.* He cared for her.

Joy swelled in her chest, even as dread bubbled beneath it. Papa had spurned Elijah's suit. What was she to say to convince him of Alex's suitability? *I'm in love with your indentured blacksmith, who rebelled against our king and got himself exiled. I mean to marry him, not the man you've chosen.* Was she brave enough to defy Papa's wishes so she might stake claim to Alex's love, and a life together?

"I want freedom," she said.

"Then come with me." His blue eyes were earnest as he grasped her hand again. "Take it."

"Come with you . . . where?"

"Wherever we will. Whenever ye're ready."

Joanna's heart gave a thump. "But it's not lawful for an indentured man to marry—I do know that. You're obliged to serve a full seven years. I'd wait for you, but we needn't *go* anywhere."

The curving of his mouth bordered on a wince. "Surely ye ken your stepfather wouldna permit us to marry, not were I free today. Even should he, I could never step into a planter's shoes, become an owner of other men. I willna remain at Severn a moment longer than I must. Neither will ye, if ye mean to be my wife."

Joanna grew aware of the chill seeping in from the open smithy door. The smell of iron and earth. The beating of her heart. "Go with you and leave Charlotte? Papa?"

Leave. Walk away from it all.

For a heady moment the bars of her cage flung wide. Standing outside it was a man she desired, beckoning her to walk out to him—or promise to do so—abandoning everyone she loved. Everyone but Alex, in whose eyes disappointment was welling.

"So your answer is no?"

"I'm not saying *no*. I need time to think about this. Pray about it." The words tumbled out, panic nipping at their heels, afraid she might lose him if she couldn't make him understand. "There's no hurry. We've time to find the right way. The best way."

They had years, didn't they?

He was quiet for too long before he asked, "It's a thing ye need pray about?"

"Of course."

She could see he put little credence in the need. It jarred her more than anything thus far. Was she truly contemplating marrying a man who didn't trust the Lord? Who wanted nothing to do with Him?

"Either ye havena decided what it is ye want," he said, "or ye lack the courage to grasp it. I'll not take from ye what ye canna give freely."

"Alex." Was he telling her he would give her time? Or telling her this was at an end? There was one way to know, though such brazenness brought a furious blush. "Will you kiss me again?"

"No."

She went from hot to cold. "I thought you wanted—"

"I want ye badly," he said. "But ye dinna ken what *ye* want."

"I want you. I think of you all the time."

He softened at that, and almost smiled. "I'm glad ye do, but that's not what I'm saying."

"What, then?"

"Listen to me. I can see this life doesna suit ye, that ye're playing a role cast for ye by circumstance—what ye thought was expected of ye with your mother gone and no one else to step into her shoes. Ye're longing for escape, but I willna let ye use me thus if all ye want is a moment snatched here and there. If ye truly want *me,* then ye must take me as I am."

Use him. Was that what he thought she was doing?

"That's not at all what I want, but tell me this: why do you want me?"

"Why?" he echoed. "Only that ye've a heart as wide as that river yonder. Ye're stronger than ye've any notion of. For years ye've borne a burden too heavy for ye, putting the needs of all around ye before your own, making the best of a life ye didna choose—one I canna fathom why anyone *would* choose. What man with half an eye in his head to see ye wouldna love ye, wouldna want to cover ye, protect and provide for ye—and set ye free of this prison?"

Joanna thought her heart would actually burst.

He *saw* her. More clearly than any man ever had. All but the one vital thing.

"Alex . . . I'm also a Christian."

He had her by the shoulders before she could take another breath. "If that's what's stopping ye, lass, I'd never ask ye not to be."

She searched his eyes. "But you won't be one yourself?"

"No." A sheen came over his gaze, unyielding. "*If* there is a God, I wouldna trust Him with anything of matter to me."

She stared, waiting for him to unsay those words. When he didn't, the weight of what she must say next fell upon her, crushing.

"Then I cannot be with you." No matter she loved him, wanted him, could imagine doing with no other man what they'd done moments ago. Wanted no other man's embrace. She could almost hear Reverend Pauling saying gently, firmly, *"Be ye not unequally yoked together with unbelievers."*

Was there more binding a yoke than marriage?

Alex dropped his hands from her. "There's still Reeves. I ken ye dinna love him, but maybe his views on the Almighty are more suited to ye."

Something inside her tore asunder. She thought it was her heart. "Mister Reeves isn't suited to me in any fashion, nor I to him."

Alex flinched. For an instant she thought he might soften, relent, but all he said was, "I'm sorry for that."

That seemed all there was to say.

He'd found Jemma awake after Joanna left the smithy, in too much pain to sleep. He helped her sit, checked her dressings, saw the lash marks were scabbing over, and asked did she mind if he worked. "I don't mind. Can't pull on that bellows yet, though."

"I ken that, *mo nighean.* I'll manage. D'ye want to go to the kitchen, be with the women for a while?"

"If you walk me over."

He'd done so. Moon still wasn't there when he returned. That spike was. In short time he had the forge aglow, a hammer in one hand, iron in the other, the end of it starting to resemble the sword he'd long envisioned. Starting to resemble the battered flatness of his heart.

Joanna. He'd won *her* heart, won it and tossed it back at her, broken. And hated himself for it.

But it was better this way. Better to excise her from his soul now. Not let this uncertainty stretch out for months, years. Otherwise she would hold him back, if the time came and he'd a chance to run as Jemma had done.

Not *if,* he amended, hardening his will. *When.*

He turned over the metal, brought the hammer down, and it struck him: what use was a sword in that land crowded with trees?

It was an axe he should be forging.

21

O n a balmy March day that presaged summer's heat, Azuba marched Marigold into
the sewing room, where Joanna was instructing
Charlotte in the stitching of a simple seam. For
what felt the hundredth time.

"Miss Joanna, Mari got something to confess."

The word brought Joanna's head up faster
than Azuba's clipped tone. Marigold's face
held the puffy distress of long weeping. Slim
fingers grasped the heavy shawl draping her
form, holding it close. A shawl, on such a warm
afternoon?

"Mari, are you ill?"

"Best we talk private, Miss Joanna." Azuba
nodded at Charlotte, who was no longer feigning
attentiveness to her sewing.

Joanna rose. "Charlotte, we'll stop for now."

Charlotte went with telling alacrity, beelining
for the company of her dolls. For the past fortnight her sister had trailed Joanna dutifully
around the house, gardens, and shops, but she
wasn't the least bit keen on sewing. Or perhaps
Joanna's company. Joanna had been admittedly
short of temper, as well as sleep and appetite,

since the day Alex kissed her and everything unraveled. She summoned the fortitude to meet whatever new crisis she was about to be presented as Azuba shut the door and turned on Marigold.

"Best just show her."

Marigold slipped the shawl off her shoulders and straightened her spine, thrusting out a belly that strained her gown and the stays beneath.

Worms. That was Joanna's first thought—and how odd someone Marigold's age would have such a severe case. No wonder she looked miserable. Then truth struck.

"How . . . how long?" she finally asked.

"She been hiding it half the winter under that shawl," Azuba said. "Nigh six months gone, she reckons."

"Six," Joanna echoed. "And the father?" There was a chance it wasn't whose name flamed across her mind.

Marigold stood mute, head lowered.

"I caught on nigh a month ago, told her to tell you then," Azuba said.

She ought to have caught on as well, Joanna realized. Even with all that had distracted her the past few months, the evidence had been there. Marigold's frequent visits to the smithy. Elijah comforting her at her brother's grave. His absences from the forge with no explanation. When had it begun? Surely not before Elijah's accident, for he'd sought Papa's blessing to marry *her*. After, Marigold had been the only one he let tend his wounds, once he'd been able to make the choice.

Had this been one of the reasons he'd pushed her away, so she wouldn't see what was going on under her nose?

Joanna's gaze dropped to that rounded belly, another possibility occurring. "Not Mister Reeves?"

That brought Marigold's head rearing up. "I'd not let that man touch me save with a whip."

Answer enough. Unless . . . "He never forced himself on you?"

"No ma'am. Never."

Joanna sighed. "What has Elijah to say on the matter?" she asked, weariness in her bones.

Marigold's chin quivered. "Reckon you best ask him, Miss Joanna, since I don't rightly know."

They waited in the study for Elijah to come. Marigold stood between Joanna and Azuba, gaze cast down. Papa, at his desk, appeared resigned. When Elijah entered and saw them gathered, he paused, glancing at each without meeting a single gaze. His hesitation lasted only a moment before he came deeper into the room, halting in its center where the window's light showed his scars no mercy. His back was to Marigold, who stood with fists clenched, full lips pressed tight.

"Elijah," Papa said, getting to his feet. "You see what's happening here. Marigold is with child and claims you are the father. Does she speak truth?"

Elijah crossed his arms, tucking away his maimed wrist. "I can say nothing on the matter."

Apparently he meant it. He stood there, stubbornly mute. Papa came from behind the desk so that they stood toe-to-toe. "You deny the child?"

"I can make no claim on it."

In the silence after the gruff reply, Marigold stifled a whimper.

"Mari," Papa said. "Come stand beside Elijah."

Visibly shaking, Marigold obeyed. They were nearly of a height, though Marigold seemed small beside Elijah's broader frame. She splayed her hands over her belly as if to shield her child from his apparent indifference.

Before Papa could speak, Mister Reeves appeared in the study doorway, gaze raking the room, coming to rest on Elijah and Marigold. As if she sensed him there, Marigold turned. His gaze fell to her belly with a look of swift comprehension.

"Sir," he said, addressing Papa, "I was coming to speak to you about a matter, but it can wait."

Papa beckoned. "Come in, Phineas. There's nothing secret here now."

Mister Reeves stepped into the room, his gaze

going to Joanna, who dodged it. She'd barely spoken to the man since the whipping. Jemma had resumed her work in the smithy, she'd been told. Joanna had stayed away. Not because she didn't want to speak to Alex, or see him. Because she wanted to, desperately.

"Elijah," Papa said, as Mister Reeves went to stand beside him, the two confronting the silent pair. "Are you saying Marigold has lied? Because if this is your child she's carrying, I'm prepared to let you purchase her. Choosing to manumit her would, of course, necessitate your leaving Severn, and the colony, but you'd have her and the child. They'd be yours."

Joanna's pulse leapt, hope and dismay clashing within her. Marigold free. Marigold gone. Elijah gone.

Marigold gasped and covered her mouth.

"What . . . what is your price?" Elijah asked hoarsely, as if his throat sought to close over the words.

Papa named the sum. Elijah was silent.

Joanna stepped forward. "Why not simply give Mari to him? Why make him purchase her freedom?"

"Miss Carey," Mister Reeves said, cutting in, "given the loss of the *Joanna,* we're in no position to be giving away slaves."

Papa cleared his throat. "I'll say no more on the matter until I have a straight answer from you,

Elijah. And I grow impatient. Did you father this child upon Mari?"

She could hear Elijah breathing, could see his face in profile now. The scarred side. She saw his shoulders slump.

"I'm no father," he said and, without a by-your-leave from anyone, turned and left the study.

Joanna hesitated, too stunned to move at first, but after meeting Marigold's pleading gaze hurried after Elijah. She pushed her way out the back door. "Elijah, wait!" she called, and nearly ran into Alex on the flagstone terrace. Beyond him, Elijah was disappearing around the hedge. "Alex? What . . . ?"

"What just . . . ?"

They'd spoken over each other. He reached for her, for she'd drawn up abruptly, but his fingers barely brushed the shoulder of her gown before he dropped them again. Though the sight of him gripped her heart unmercifully, she drank in that bittersweet draught until she thought she'd drown in it. He was beautiful, her fair-haired, blue-eyed, towering warrior, and as unreachable as the mossy boughs of the oak tree beginning to leaf above them.

"You knew about them, didn't you? This is what Mari told you that day in the stable."

He didn't answer that. "What happened in there? Did your stepfather threaten him?"

Stung, she said, "No. He offered to let Elijah

284

buy Mari's freedom, but Elijah never even admitted the child is his."

"It is," Alex said.

"Of course it is," she said, wishing he'd told her. Wishing she could talk with him now, hear his mind on the matter, wishing they could deal with the situation together. And wishing they could sweep it all aside and just be free.

Her resolve to stay away from him had nearly crumbled these past days in the face of her heart's desperate reasoning. Alex had asked her to wait for him while he served his seven years. What if she agreed to do so? Perhaps in that time he would change his thinking about the Almighty. Change his heart. If he loved her, and she loved the Lord, wouldn't that one day make a difference? It was what she prayed for every night before sleep claimed her. Every morning at its release.

"Why are you here?" she asked. "At the house, I mean."

His hands were fisted. "I didna ken if it would help at all, but I thought, if Moon wouldna claim the child . . ."

"That *you* would?" Their gazes met in a blaze of pain she was certain he felt, too, for his sharpened with question as though he were asking, *What matter if I had?*

"Would it help Marigold in any way?" he asked.

"Not unless *you* wish to buy her freedom."

285

"With what?" he asked.

The constraint between them sucked the very air away, robbing her lungs. She was dimly aware of Azuba and Marigold leaving the study on the other side of the door, going deeper into the house together. "If you want to help them, then talk to Elijah, try to change his mind."

"I mean to." He'd said it with determination, and certainty, as if he knew why Elijah refused to acknowledge his child, or accept Papa's offer.

"Thank you . . . Mister MacKinnon," she said.

His eyes flashed her a look that scored deep, before he bowed stiffly and left her.

Joanna didn't recall her feet carrying her back inside the house, only that she stood in the downstairs passage gulping air, vision tunneled to a blur, while someone nearby was repeating that hateful word, *miscarry . . . miscarry.*

A hand gripped her arm. "Miss Carey? You're positively a ghost. Do sit down."

Joanna resisted Mister Reeves's tug on her arm. She needed to keep moving, fast enough to escape this pain. This cage.

"Did MacKinnon upset you? I saw you speaking to him."

Her tunneled vision widened. She'd been on the verge of a faint, but it was passing. Feeling rushed into her limbs. Her heart. She looked into Mister Reeves's solicitous face and forced words to come. "About . . . Elijah."

"Was that all?"

"Of course." While their eyes had carried on another conversation entirely.

As if the trail of her thoughts were written across her face, Mister Reeves's mouth twisted. "Come now, Miss Carey. I know you find MacKinnon appealing, but if he's dallied with your heart in any way, I would blame myself. I brought him here, thinking he would make a fitting blacksmith—Hephaestus, god of the forge, I prophesied. Give him his due, he's done well in the smithy, but whatever he's contributed in that regard cannot outweigh his distracting *you* from the course you're meant to follow."

Belated alarm pierced her veil of heartache. "I don't know what you're saying. There's nothing—"

From the end of the hall came Charlotte's voice. "Joanna? Did Marigold do something bad?"

Her escape. Joanna hurried toward her sister, holding out her hand. "Come, Charlotte. I'll explain as best I can."

"I wish you would do exactly that."

Mister Reeves's voice had been soft behind her, yet his words sent unsettling ripples through her as she ascended the stairs with Charlotte.

22

March 1748

The forge had yet to dispel the morning's cool, but the banked tension coming off Elijah Moon fairly blistered the air. Alex raised the hammer to the nail rod he'd been working while Moon went on with what occupied him— randomly picking up tools from the bench and putting them down, with more than necessary force. He hadn't uttered a word since rising. Not to Alex. Not to Jemma on her bellows perch, casting looks from one to the other. Earlier, when Moon visited the necessary, she'd asked what ailed him.

"Ye havena tweezed it out of Mari yet?" he'd replied, surprised what transpired in Carey's study yesterday wasn't already common knowledge in the slave quarters.

"Mari got a baby coming, but she clammed up about it."

"Best mind your business, then."

He shot a glare at Moon's back. In that moment of inattention the hammer caught the bar a glancing blow. He fumbled and dropped it, narrowly missing his toes as it struck the earth.

Moon turned, eyeing him balefully. "Give attention to your work."

Alex didn't bend for the hammer. "As ye've given attention to yours?"

"What's that supposed . . . ?" Moon began, then dismissed the question. "I care not."

"Liar," Alex said. "Is that what this is about, then, walking out on her as ye did? Because ye do care, and it scares ye?"

Moon narrowed bloodshot eyes, hand fisted around the handle of a pair of tongs.

Jemma stared, having let the bellows go still. Alex jerked his head toward the door. She pretended not to understand the dismissal. He gave her a final warning with lifted brow, then set the nail rod on the counter and stepped from behind the anvil, halting several paces from Moon, who'd turned away.

"That's right, turn your back. On me, this smithy, and Mari. May as well go ahead and end yourself, as I ken ye mean to do."

Behind him Jemma gasped.

Moon faced him, his grip on the tongs tightened. Fury boiled in his eyes. "What do ye want from me, MacKinnon?"

"To stop playing the self-pitying fool who'd throw away every good thing he has like it was garbage. Is that what ye think of her? Of the bairn she's carrying for ye?"

Moon hurled the tongs. Alex ducked. They

slammed into the wall. With a squeak like a mouse, Jemma leapt from the block and bolted from the smithy.

Moon seemed not to notice. "What does everyone expect me to do?"

"Take up the offer made ye. Buy her freedom. Or was she nothing but a body to comfort ye, help ye forget for an hour what ye've lost?"

"What I've lost? I've a roof over me and food to eat for now, but I've no means of earning enough to buy her, or the child. Even should I manage it, where are we to go? How will I provide for myself, much less Mari and the babe?"

"There's always a way, if man but tries," Alex said, then in desperation added, "Have ye no faith in the God Pauling preaches, who's working all things for your good? I mind the man sitting in that back room, praying his heart out for ye, asking for patience while ye waited for guidance. D'ye not think Carey's offer is what he meant?"

Moon stubbornly glowered. "Heard all that, did ye? But ye don't even believe it."

"What I believe isna the issue." Alex loomed over him, sorely tempted to strike the wee fool.

It was Moon who struck. "Joanna might say otherwise."

"Leave her out of it."

Moon snorted. "Ye must think me blind, MacKinnon. I've seen how it's been between the two of ye. Or was. I don't know what happened, but I only have to look at her now to see her heart's been broken."

Moon was distracting him, throwing back his own words in his face like a smoke screen. But he couldn't stop himself. "Ye've made your choice. Joanna's no more concern to ye."

A throat's clearing had them both swinging toward the doorway where Reeves leaned, watching them with interest.

"You cannot keep the peace with anyone, can you, MacKinnon? Demas, Miss Carey, now Moon. Seems I've come in time to prevent one of you killing the other."

"What d'ye want?" Alex snapped, finding no patience for the man.

The overseer pushed off the doorframe to stand erect, dressed for traveling, satchel at his side. Smiling. "I've a message from the gang boss out at the mill. They've need of a smith."

"What need?" Moon asked.

"I didn't ask. I'm bound downriver with a mare Captain Carey means to sell and in a bit of a hurry."

Alex had heard from Moses, Severn's head groom, that Carey meant to sell some of his horses in an effort to recoup a portion of the losses the past year had dealt him. Severn's stock was well regarded along the Cape Fear.

"Aye," he said. "I'll go directly."

"Excellent. I'm obliged, MacKinnon." The

overseer raised a brow. "No doubt I'll see you again in a day or two, if Moon doesn't bash your head in first."

The mill was silent when Alex reached it—alone; Moon had been in no frame of mind to accompany him. There was no sign of the wiry mill boss, Jim, or anyone, but the murmur of voices, audible above the rush of water, led Alex to surmise they were down at the creek, where lumber was rafted downstream to the dock. Deciding to check inside the mill before heading down the path, Alex hitched his mount and approached the office. It opened to the yard below the elevated mill floor. When his knock got no answer, he opened the door. The place was empty save for its simple furnishings.

Around the rear of the mill was the room that ran the structure's length, where lumber set aside for Severn's needs was stored, the broad doors open, the dusty air within thick with the tang of milled wood.

"Jim? Ye sent word ye'd need of a smith. Ye've got one."

At first he thought that, aside from the stacked lumber creating a warren of aisles to either side, the storage room was also empty. Then a faint scuffing reached his ears, off to his left, back among the stacks.

"Are ye there, man?" When still no answer

came, he suspected it had been a rat, or one of those larger creatures, possums, that made the noise. They tended to crawl into places like this and could be the devil of a nuisance to extricate.

Voices in the yard reached him. He went out to find the mill slaves coming up from the creek. They saw him and halted at the head of the path. Jim wasn't with them, but Alex recalled another's name, a tall man with a sprinkling of white in his hair.

"Tom, I'd word you'd need of me. Where's himself to be found? Down at the creek still?"

Tom's scanty brows rose as he squinted through a slant of sunlight. "Jim be up here somewhere. You check the mill?"

"Office and storeroom." The mill floor was partially open. Jim would have heard him calling.

"He talk of fetching board from the storeroom. Sure he ain't there?"

"I'm sure." Unless the mill boss had hidden himself and ignored his call. Unlikely.

"You say he sent for you?" Tom scratched his bearded jaw. "To my knowing everything's—"

"What?" another slave cut in, gaze lifted past them to the mill across the yard. "Jim burning something?"

"Smoke coming up," someone said as Alex pivoted. A column, pale gray but darkening, was ascending from the structure. The acrid scent of it hit his nose.

"Fetch the pails!" At Tom's shout the slaves sprang into motion, hurtling toward the wooden pails stacked outside the mill office, ready to hand for such emergency. *Fire.*

As the slaves grabbed up the pails, Alex sprinted around the mill, thinking of that scuff he'd heard. He staggered as he made the turn and from the corner of his eye caught a figure darting behind a pile of uncut timber outside the doors. He'd no time to call out; smoke billowed from the storeroom. Inside, it was thick in the air. The crackle of flames came from his left where he'd heard the sound he'd put down to a varmint.

"Jim! Are ye here, man?"

Ducking low, he made his way through the stacked lumber. Fire lit that end of the long room. Its heat drove him back. He hurried toward the doors, grabbing up an armful of cut shingles on his way. Out in the yard he tossed them down, bellowing for the men to bring their pails. Even as he shouted they rounded the corner of the mill, water from the pails splashing.

"Left side!" He moved aside so they could pass, then hurried in, gathering up more shingles, out into sunlight to drop them, in again as the slaves came running out to refill their pails at the mill pond. He detected no lessening of heat or flames, spreading through the seasoned wood with alarming rapidity.

How long it went on—Alex rescuing wood, the slaves running in and out to douse the flames—he couldn't have said. Eventually Tom grabbed his arm. "Let this go. Fire done spread to the mill workings. We got to save those."

Eyes streaming, throat burning, Alex abandoned his attempt to save the lumber but made one more dash into the storeroom. Surely a fire at his mill should have brought Jim running. Could he have been inside after all?

"Jim!" Heat and smoke were thick. Flames lit the path through the stacks like the corridors of hell. Tom was right. Not just the lumber but the structure's walls were burning. The ceiling above, part of the mill floor, was in flames. Finding no sign of Jim, no answer to his shouts, Alex started back through the warren but was still a turn from the doors when a portion of the ceiling fell in ahead, cutting off his exit.

A spasm of coughing gripped him. Doubled with it, he found the air slightly more breathable at knee height. Crouched, he sought to clear the path, grasping a half-blackened timber from the fallen rubble to wrench it aside. His left hand closed over a smoldering portion, and he bellowed at the searing. He struggled out of his shirt and wrapped it around his right hand, a shield that would soon char to shreds. The fire's heat smote his back, blistering in its intensity. The flames made a roaring now. He gagged on smoke as he pulled aside another timber, head swimming, eyes streaming.

Edmund Carey's face rose in memory, gaze commending him after the kiln's explosion when Reeves would have seen him blamed. Those faded eyes would look on him otherwise if he learned how he'd wounded Joanna, whose face rose next, banishing her stepfather's. With it came the knowledge that he loved her, and that he was about to die, his last memory of her what he'd read in her gaze there on the doorstep, speaking to him of things neither had the courage to utter. Of need. Longing. Regret.

Would she weep at his perishing? Would she care?

Joanna, Carey, Moon, Marigold, Jemma, Charlotte. Their faces flashed through his mind, and he wondered what would become of them, a thing he'd never know unless . . . Could he climb over the stacked wood that hadn't burned?

Smoke was a wall of gray near the rafters. He'd never make it so far without a clean breath.

Pain seared his back. He slapped at it, thinking the fire had overtaken him. It had been an ember, blown forward by the fire's wind. Flames licked across the ceiling timbers, soon to fall and bury him.

Move. Do something. He was on his knees, head hanging, coughing uncontrollably. Above him timbers cracked.

A voice shouted. Or was it the fire's chuckling roar?

He couldn't reply in any case. Something struck his shoulder a blow, knocking him flat. He tasted dirt.

Mercifully the world went black.

23

Joanna bent over the table where Charlotte painstakingly traced her letters across a sheet of foolscap, evidencing enough engagement that she was about to suggest her sister attempt stitching her letters, when a frantic shout rang up the stairs: "Miss Joanna!"

The quill in Charlotte's ink-stained fingers jerked. "Jemma—in the house?" She thrust back her chair so abruptly the inkwell toppled.

"Charlotte!"

Her sister bolted into the passage. "Here, Jemma!"

Joanna righted the inkwell, snatching up a kerchief to mop the spill before it could soak through the foolscap. Down the passage came the thump of feet on the stairs, her sister's excited voice. "Did you come to play with me and the Annas?"

"No—where Miss Joanna?"

Azuba's voice joined the mix. "Jemma! What you doing inside this house causing a stir?"

In seconds Jemma was in the doorway, gasping for breath. "Miss Joanna—the mill done burned, Jim and Mister Alex inside. They saying *he* the one done it, but it ain't true!"

Joanna let the ink-soaked kerchief tumble to the rug, searching for sense in that jumble of words. The names spoken slammed through her brain. She reached for the bedpost. "Alex."

"He all right." Jemma came into the room. "I raced back once I knew they was blaming him. But they don't know about Demas!"

Joanna lowered herself to the tick, taking in nothing past *he all right.* Azuba and Charlotte were in the room, questioning, exclaiming, while Jemma gasped out half-coherent answers. Their voices filled Joanna's head like frantic bees. She raised a hand, silencing them. "Start from the beginning, Jemma."

In a rush, Jemma spilled the story. "This morning early Mister Alex and Mister 'Lijah was having a row over Mari. It scared me so I run out the smithy, but I didn't go far. Mister Reeves come and say he going downriver to sell that mare and would Mister Alex go to the mill on account they needed his help. Mister Alex went, and since there weren't no work for me, I followed."

Azuba snorted. "Work aplenty in the kitchen," she muttered, but waved at Jemma to go on.

"Mister Alex was riding and me afoot. By time I got there, the mill was burning, the hands and Mister Alex trying to put out the fire. But I seen something whilst they was busy with them pails."

Joanna wanted to put her face in her hands and weep. The mill . . . lost?

Jemma's voice cut through again. "Miss Joanna, you hearing me? I seen *Demas* lurking in the woods. I thought if anyone started the fire, he done it on account he weren't helping stop it. Then he seen Mister Alex go in and not come out, and he run into that burning mill and dragged him out. So I don't know."

Joanna's head felt thick. "Dragged him out? Is Alex injured?" She rose and headed for the stairs.

Jemma trailed her. "He banged up, burned some. He weren't wearing no shirt, but he was sitting up talking, last I saw. The mill hands afraid they get the blame so they passing it on to Mister Alex."

The tap of her shoes on the stairs; the slap of Jemma's bare feet; Azuba and Charlotte's voices buzzing; Jemma's words still coming.

"Two of 'em made it back afore me. I had to sneak into the house so Mari didn't see and snatch me off to the kitchen, but as I come in I hear what they telling Master Carey. Jim's dead and must've been Mister Alex set the fire. I heard Master Carey say *lock him up*."

At the stair's foot Joanna turned. "Lock him up?" The world constricted around her, cutting off her breath. "Come with me, Jemma. Tell Papa all you've said."

"No ma'am. I can't do that." Jemma shrank back. Azuba grabbed for her. The girl twisted away, panic in her gaze. "I can't!"

Did she think she was in for another whipping? Joanna hadn't time to cajole. "All right. Find Alex, see if his wounds are tended. Then come tell me where he is."

The girl nodded. Joanna started for the study. Behind her, still on the stairs, Charlotte called, "Jemma!"

"This is no time for play, Miss Charlotte," Joanna heard Azuba reply.

"But she's different," Charlotte protested. "She looks like Mari."

Halfway down the passage Joanna turned back. Frozen a pace behind her, Jemma glared at Charlotte, poised on the bottom stair. Tiny of stature, amber-hued, dressed in those ragged garments, Jemma bore no resemblance to Marigold.

"Miss Charlotte—hush!" Jemma said in a tone so fierce Joanna jumped.

"Jemma!"

"I gotta find Mister Alex!" The girl ducked past her and made for the door.

Two mill slaves, reeking of smoke, were leaving the study, distracting Joanna. As they left the house on Jemma's heels, she looked in to see Papa, bent over his desk, hands splayed flat, desolation carved into his face.

• • •

The night air was clammy as Joanna made her way down the path behind the kitchen to the row of squared-log smokehouses at the orchard's edge. The smell of curing hams spiced the air. At the last smokehouse, left empty all winter, she stopped and pulled her shawl tighter. Hardly knowing what to say into the darkness between the wooden slats, she drew a breath and released it.

"I hear ye out there," said the voice she craved like water.

She took a step closer, raising a hand to the slatted wall between them. Always there were walls.

"Is it ye, Mari?"

She snatched her hand back. "No."

A space of silence in the dark. "Joanna? What are ye doing here?"

The words felt like a sword's thrust, pushing her away. So many losses, yet the loss of his love, his regard—whatever he'd felt for her—outweighed the rest combined. "Are you all right?"

"Aside from being caged like a dog, d'ye mean?"

Jemma had found her after she'd left the study. Alex's injuries weren't grievous. Minor burns, which Marigold had tended. A chest full of smoke that had left his voice raw.

Her own lungs felt too tight for breath. "I tried

to reason with Papa, but he won't do anything until Mister Reeves returns."

The overseer's name tasted bitter on her tongue.

"MacKinnon is accused of starting the fire," her stepfather had said before she shut the study door. "He was seen coming from the storeroom moments before smoke was spotted. Jim was found, burned almost beyond recognition—in the storeroom."

Those might have been the facts, but she wouldn't believe the conclusion being drawn. "Jemma was there. She saw Demas lurking. Isn't it more believable he started the fire? Or it was Mister Reeves—at his order? Why else didn't he take Demas with him to help with the horse?"

"Phineas?" Apparently she'd lost her mind, to judge by the look on Papa's face. "It's good he didn't. Demas saved MacKinnon's life. Did Jemma omit that detail from her account?"

"No, but she also says Demas hid in the woods and watched the mill burn. He didn't help save it."

"Perhaps the girl wants Demas sold away, or worse." A notion Joanna hadn't been able to refute with certainty. "It makes no sense, Joanna. Why would Demas start the fire, allow Jim to die, but save MacKinnon? Is there a friendship there of which I'm unaware?"

Quite the opposite, she was sure. "Mister Reeves sent Alex to the mill—Elijah will verify

303

that—and we cannot punish Alex unless it's certain he committed a crime."

"I haven't said I will punish MacKinnon. I'll hold him bound until Phineas returns and can give account of his slave—and his reason for sending MacKinnon to the mill."

"Have you spoken to Alex?"

"I've only just had the news." The tremor in her stepfather's voice told Joanna his calm was the result of shock, and it was passing. "I mean to keep MacKinnon safe under lock. And wait for Phineas."

"Why don't you have Demas confined? That would be only fair."

"Do not speak of fair!" her stepfather said, temper exploding. "Life isn't fair, Joanna. I'm minded to have Phineas take MacKinnon back downriver and sell his indenture, and we shall just . . . do without a blacksmith!"

"Papa." She'd held on to the vague hope that given time Alex might change his thinking, soften his heart. The prospect of him removed from Severn was a loss she feared she couldn't weather. "After all you've invested in him?"

"Nothing into which I've invested has proven sound. Should MacKinnon be different?"

Joanna could only stare, cast back to the time of her mother's death, and that dark place Papa had vanished into for nigh a year. Panic at the thought of losing Alex—and her stepfather to that darkness—was a screeching specter in her brain.

"I'm sound, Papa. Charlotte is sound."

"But Severn isn't! Do you think we can continue taking these hulling blows and remain afloat? We're mired in a sinkhole of debt. I'll need to sell the *Charlotte-Ann* to climb halfway out of it, which leaves us one failed crop from ruination and the loss of even this roof."

There had been little to say after that. Or no heart left to say it.

Still shaken by that conversation, she realized why she'd come to the smokehouse. She needed Alex. The strength he'd lent her in months past had been a tenuous thing, but who else did she have? Papa was faltering. Reverend Pauling hadn't replied to her letters. Elijah was lost in his own dark night. Mister Reeves might as well have existed on another continent, for all their sentiments aligned.

"Alex, please." Emotion she couldn't stem thickened her voice, and tears fell. "Tell me what happened at the mill. I want to hear it from you."

Even that he wouldn't give her. "I dinna ken how the fire started. I've my suspicions, but Carey willna want to hear them."

"You need to make Papa listen. I'll stand with you."

The silence this time was long. When Alex finally spoke, his tone was cold. "Why?"

"Because you wouldn't burn down our mill.

Not for any reason. That isn't the kind of man you are."

"What kind of man am I?" She heard a subtle change in his tone, something softer threaded through the chill.

"You're strong—and stubborn—and kind-hearted. I've seen how you encourage Elijah, how you shelter Jemma, the way others look to you. Even Reverend Pauling took to you, and I trust his judgment above all."

It had been the wrong thing to say.

"A glowing endorsement," he said bitterly.

Her next words were the hardest she'd ever had to utter. "I'm not asking you to love me, Alex. Only help me as you've helped others. Help me save what's left of all Papa has built. Maybe together—"

"Joanna . . ." He was laughing, low in the darkness. It made him cough and clear his smoke-ravaged throat. "I'm no more good to ye than were I a side of beef hanging in here. If Severn means all that to ye, that ye'd come to me begging, Reeves is the man to stand beside ye. I canna help ye at all. Unless . . ."

Hope didn't die easily. "Unless?"

"Ye're ready to walk away. Find the life I ken ye long to live."

She leaned her forehead against the rough logs, thinking of her childhood, before her mother died. Simple days. Full days. Afterward, left with a plantation to run, a sister to tend, a step-father sunk in despair, she'd thought they'd taken their worst blow. They need only heal. Happiness would visit them again. It hadn't. Not as she'd hoped. But even those years seemed blissful to what their lives had become, a soulless slog through loss-crippled days, shadowed by an oppressive sense of doom to come. Yet the life she longed for was forever out of reach.

She took a step back, hugging herself.

When Alex spoke again his voice held no hope. "Go back to the house, Joanna. I can do nothing for ye. Ye'll have to help yourself now, if ye have it in ye to do so."

"Miss Joanna? That you out here in the dark?"

She turned with a bitten-off yelp to see Marigold on the path behind her, the bulk of her belly outlined in starlight. She'd something folded under her arm. "I was seeing if Mister MacKinnon had need," Joanna said, then gathered up her shredded dignity and wrapped its scraps about her. "I leave him to you."

She brushed past the woman and made her way along the path to the kitchen. Not quick enough to miss Marigold's next words to Alex, or his to her.

"I couldn't sleep, thinking of you out here. Brought you a blanket. Think we can fit it through the slats?"

"Lass, ye shouldna fret over me. Ye need your rest . . ."

Joanna hurried her steps, not wanting to hear another word.

Compared to what he suffered on the *James & Mary*, his internment in the smokehouse was a light affliction. His wounds were tended, water and food passed through the slatted wall. Fury cut the deeper for it. He had, against his determination to the contrary, allowed himself to grow accepting of a life in this place, linked to these people. Not only through the skill of his hands.

Dinna think of Joanna. Her wounded voice, begging him to be what he couldn't—her knight in shining armor. He was no one's knight. Yet he hadn't been called to account for his actions at the mill. Never charged to his face with a crime. Carey had left him to stew. Joanna's midnight visitation confirmed his speculations as to why— and the identity of Severn's true master. *"Papa won't do anything until Mister Reeves returns."*

When the shift had happened he couldn't say. Before ever he stepped onto Severn's dock? Right under his nose in recent days? Regardless, the master of Severn was no longer Edmund Carey.

Yet it was Demas who'd rescued him from the flames.

Through a second day Alex waited, replaying those moments at the mill before he was overcome with smoke, until in the dark of his second night in the smokehouse, he awoke to the scuff of a man's tread approaching his musty prison. There came the thump of something dropped onto the ground, then the click-and-grate of the lock opening by key.

A low voice spoke through the wooden slats. "Now, MacKinnon. It's all I can do."

He'd sat up, wincing at his burns, forcing his mind to clear. "Who is there?"

Silence answered. The speaker had crept away, or was pretending he had. He'd known the voice in any case. *Reeves.*

Fearing a trap, he approached the smokehouse door, waited, then gave a push. Where before it had held fast, now it yielded to his touch. Outside moonlight spilled, showing plain the knapsack lying at his feet. Still he kept to shadow, gazing along the row of smokehouses, eyes long since dark-accustomed. Not even a breeze stirred.

He knelt and fingered open the sack. Inside he felt the rough weave of his coat, a long, nut-brown garment made by Joanna's hands. His belt, coiled beside it. Bread wrapped in a cloth, a canteen, razor and strop, his eating knife, no bigger than a *sgian-dubh*, the wee blade his clansmen kept tucked in a stocking.

What was Reeves playing at?

As he stood, enlightenment swept the last of sleep's cobwebs from his brain. Reeves had deduced he'd never possess Joanna's affection, much less her hand in marriage, so long as Alex stood in his path. He'd sent Alex to the mill intending him to die in that fire, willing to sacrifice part of his hoped-for inheritance to remove him.

At once his certainty unraveled. Jim, Alex figured, had had the misfortune to be in the wrong place at the wrong time, but if Reeves had set his slave to kindle that fire in hopes of killing him, why did Demas rescue him? Maybe he was ascribing too great a crime to Reeves. Perhaps he'd intended Alex to take the blame for only the fire, inducing Carey to sell his indenture—or have him arrested. Demas had taken things too far. Was Reeves now attempting to get his plan back on a less perilous track?

The more Alex circled the tangle, the more impenetrable it became. Of one thing he was certain: it was to Reeves's advantage that he disappear.

Fully prepared to oblige the man, Alex breathed deeply, tasting freedom on the air. He'd but to snatch up the knapsack and run—as he'd known since waking on the flatboat headed upriver he would do, though for a time he'd lost sight of that goal, allowed attachments to complicate his thinking.

He'd found something more inside the knapsack. A pouch. He fingered the contents through thin leather.

Why would Reeves give him coin?

It didn't matter. He was being offered freedom at the price of a fugitive's life. He'd take it, and more besides. What he had at his fingertips was enough to survive, but he could better the odds.

He reached the smithy unchallenged, where all was silent. Moving softly, each motion measured, he took a hammer from the rack of tools, tongs, iron for nail-making, a few scraps besides, a small tinder box. He took up a hatchet, shoved it through his belt, added a sheathed blade beside it.

They thought him a murderer, an arsonist. Why not add *thief* to the list?

Out in the yard he compiled it all. The pack was preposterously heavy, but he was strong from the forge. Stronger than he'd ever been. As he donned it, regret stabbed deep enough to penetrate the hardening shell around his heart, but he refused to let his gaze linger on the house rising white in the moonlight.

He passed down the lane between stable and shops, the orchard and burying ground, to the creek where it turned upstream toward the ruined mill. There he waded across, moving carefully for fear of snakes, or worse, prowling the brush at night.

Maybe this was all a game to Reeves. Maybe he'd every intention of recapturing Alex and adding *runaway* to his list of crimes. There would be a hunt. Alex hoped he'd be expected to head for Wilmington, to board a ship before they could prevent him. But he wouldn't.

He wasn't friendless in that colony.

On the other side of Severn Creek, he paused. Trees obscured his view of the house. He'd never seen the room Joanna shared with her sister. Never been abovestairs. He imagined her sleeping, long hair in disarray across her pillow . . . then firmly put the vision aside. Even should every accusation against him be swept aside, he wasn't what she needed, an indentured exile long since stripped of the faith she stubbornly—or desperately—clung to. In a kinder world they might have suited one another like hand to glove, however unlikely a pairing.

"Not this world," he whispered.

Still, a weight like an anchor dragged at him as he turned into the darkened forest and took his first steps into freedom—fugitive and thief, foresworn and unrepentant.

24

The smokehouse was empty, Alex vanished. At the end of an exhaustive search and a flurry of interrogations, Joanna was sequestered with Mister Reeves and Papa, no nearer knowing who had aided his escape, if anyone had; the smokehouse key, along with nearly every other to Severn's domestic locks, resided in Joanna's keeping. It was found where it was meant to be, in her room. Suspicion had fallen briefly upon her, but she'd maintained her ignorance of his flight, her distress apparent enough they'd chosen to believe her.

"He's a Jonah, sir—if you take my meaning. That's what I make of MacKinnon."

Staring bleakly at Mister Reeves, Joanna perched at the foot of the bed in Papa's study. "A Jonah? That's a foolish superstition."

Mister Reeves, pacing like a restless panther, halted and cast her a condescending glance. "Do you know what a Jonah signifies, Miss Carey?"

"A person who causes ill luck. But I don't believe it of Alex. Surely you don't, Papa. It's God who ordains . . ." Her own doubt silenced her. *Had* the Almighty ordained the tragic events of the past few days? Months? Or allowed them?

She no longer knew. She was utterly at sea. Storm-swept, like the prophet, Jonah.

"I've seen it in my day," Papa said. "Still, what is to be done but raise a hunt for the man?"

"Yes sir," Reeves agreed, then more tentatively added, "Or we might let him go."

Joanna didn't know which struck her as the more anguished course, hunting Alex like an animal or this suggestion. *Let him go.*

"It's the thing to do with a Jonah," Mister Reeves maintained. "Put him off the ship— or plantation. Let whatever whale awaits him swallow him whole."

The man's unconcern fell across Joanna's senses like a whiplash, yet for once in their acquaintance, she wished she could be more like him, to care so little about Alex as to shrug at his defection and carry on. They'd yet to make sense of what happened at the mill. Upon Mister Reeves's return late the previous night, he'd been told of the fire, Demas's purported actions, and the suspicion fallen upon Alex.

"I can tell you only what was told me," Mister Reeves had said, paled by the catastrophe. "It was brought to my attention there was need at the mill. I relayed the information to MacKinnon— and Moon. As for Demas, should he not be commended for his actions rather than placed under suspicion? Let us hear what he has to say for himself."

Demas, with his cavernous island lilt, had made Papa's study seem small in a way even Alex hadn't. He'd heard about the need of a smith and, lacking Reeves's guidance, went to the mill on his own volition in case his strength could be of use. "When I get there the mill was burning. I found MacKinnon in the storeroom, overcome by smoke. I carry him out."

"What of Jim?" Mister Reeves pressed.

"Him I not see."

"You say you arrived and at once rescued Alex," Joanna interjected. "Yet Jemma saw you lurking in the woods, beforehand."

"I know not of that girl or what she claim," Demas replied.

"No one else claims to have seen Demas until he came forth carrying MacKinnon," Mister Reeves said in his slave's defense.

"Who told you there was need of a smith at the mill?" Joanna asked the overseer, who thrummed with suppressed impatience.

"Do you realize how many slaves I speak to in the course of a single day, Miss Carey? How varied the minutia of their concerns? I was pre-occupied with getting that mare safely downriver and honestly cannot recall. Had I known it would become of issue, I'd have made note."

Frustrated, Joanna had turned to her stepfather. "Isn't it past time to let Alex speak for himself? You listened to Demas."

Looking exhausted, Papa said, "Let us sleep on it, Joanna. MacKinnon will keep another night."

Only he hadn't. Sometime during that second night, Alex had vanished, guilty of desertion, if not arson and the death of a valued slave. But this talk of Jonahs was too much.

On her feet, Joanna demanded, "What proof is there that Alex's presence brought about any of the losses we've suffered? If anyone is a Jonah, I rather think it's you, Mister Reeves."

"Joanna!"

She heard warning in Papa's tone but pressed on regardless. "Think about it, Papa. Our misfortunes began before Alex was brought here. Elijah's accident began it. If you can believe it of Alex, why not Mister Reeves?"

The overseer stared at her, oddly dispassionate. "Pray tell, Miss Carey, are you in love with MacKinnon?"

She was cornered. Not so much by Mister Reeves's scrutiny or Papa's darkening gaze, but by Alex. His desertion had left her vulnerable, all her wounds exposed.

"I did think so. It turns out I didn't really know him." She looked away from Mister Reeves, repelled by the satisfaction flooding his gaze.

"None of us knew the man," Papa said.

"How could we, sir?" Mister Reeves asked. "A rebel, a prisoner of the Crown. A traitor. That is the man I brought among us. I beg your pardon for ever choosing him."

That brought Papa to his feet, looking aged with weariness. Joanna gazed at the two men, one young and vital, the other diminishing before her eyes.

What man wouldn't be diminished after the string of losses they'd suffered this past disastrous year?

She was grasping the folds of her gown, twisting them in her distress. The very gown she'd worn the day she first set eyes on Alex. Gold, as he'd seemed to her in the candle's glow. How subtle it had been, her coming to depend on him, to hope in him, not just for herself but for Elijah. Jemma. Perhaps even Papa. Had she loved an illusion? The man she wanted Alex to be?

Watching Papa and Mister Reeves now, she saw the same dependency mirrored.

"Every indentured man aboard the *Charlotte-Ann* was a Jacobite," Papa said. "If blame is to be laid, let it be at my feet. And MacKinnon's."

Joanna was stunned at how easily Mister Reeves had solidified the notion of Alex's betrayal in her stepfather's mind. The only crime of which they had proof was that he'd escaped his confinement and run.

"Yes sir," Mister Reeves was saying. "I see your point. And please, Miss Carey, do not again defend a man who has so misused you. It's beneath your dignity."

"Misused?"

Mister Reeves looked pained. "I suspect you thought he returned your misplaced sentiments, yet he abandoned you. Are you not as well rid of him as we?" When she couldn't speak for the lump lodged in her throat, Mister Reeves gentled his tone. "I wasn't blind to the striking qualities of the man, how he must have seemed to you, who have so little experience of the world. Your infatuation with MacKinnon may be excused, Miss Carey. I'm willing to overlook it, if you will once again consider *me*. For I am here, still waiting, where MacKinnon is not."

Thunderstruck, Joanna watched the man leave his place beside her stepfather, advance toward her, reach out and take her hand in his.

"How we'll salvage these dire circumstances I cannot see, but there must be a way." His breath enveloped her, scented of stale pipe smoke. "I'm not asking you to love me, only help me save what we both cherish. Help me save Severn—as my helpmeet. My wife."

I'm not asking you to love me, Alex . . .

Joanna caught her breath. Papa was watching, hope written on his face—hope that one thing might go according to his plan, that she, and Charlotte with her, would be covered and protected.

318

Her heart beat heavy, hollow as a gourd.

There came another beating, urgent on the study door. It opened and Azuba peered in. "Master Carey, beg pardon. There's something you need to know."

The door opened wider as Elijah entered.

Joanna pulled free of Mister Reeves. "Elijah? What is it?"

"It would seem tools are gone missing from the smithy. A hammer, tongs. Some scrap iron, I think."

Silence clapped before Papa demanded, "Why didn't you tell me of this sooner?"

Elijah flinched at the accusation in Papa's tone. "I didn't notice sooner, sir. It's not as though I was working the forge." He made no move to hide his crippled arm when all eyes went inevitably to it.

"Something else, Miss Joanna." Azuba drew their attention again. "Jemma either sleeps in Mari's cabin or the smithy. I checked both. Her blanket's gone. She's lit out again."

"With MacKinnon?" A flush darkened Mister Reeves's countenance, suffusing it with anger. "I was hasty in suggesting we allow him to go his way, sir. I'll organize a party to begin the search. If you'll permit?" He swung back to look at Papa.

"Where would you begin? Downriver toward Wilmington?"

Mister Reeves scowled. "It's the world he

knew. That of ships. He'll make for the sea."

Joanna was less certain. She recalled Reverend Pauling's letter, the one she'd shared with Alex, mentioning that fellow Jacobite he'd known aboard the prison ship. Hugh Cameron. What had been the name of the plantation?

Mister Reeves started for the door. She opened her mouth, knowing she must speak of the letter now. But she shut it again, saying nothing.

The FUGITIVE

Spring — Autumn 1748

And His Kingdom shall have no frontier.
—LUKE 1:33 (old Moravian version)

25

April 1748

Not until that morning, the fifth since fleeing Severn, did Alex suspect pursuit. Now, with the sun setting and forest shadows lengthened, he was certain of it; one too many snapping sticks had given it away. With no small bewilderment he wondered who would track him such a distance without attempting capture?

With no intention of being taken, he grabbed the hatchet from beside the knapsack and slipped into the pines. Hunkered low, mosquitos whining about his ears, he watched the clearing where he'd paused to skin a rabbit snared at midday. In minutes a figure stumbled from the wood, small, disheveled, filthier than himself, gaped at the knapsack and rabbit, turned a circle, and burst into sobs.

"Mister Alex! Where you at?"

"Jemma?" He sprang back into the clearing. She stumbled backward at his appearance. He caught her by the shirt and hauled her to her feet. "Ye followed me? What—*how* did ye manage it?"

"Being little and fast, and sneaky with it!" She twisted in his grip. "I ain't letting you leave me behind in that place."

"Your home, ye mean?"

"Severn ain't home. Home's elsewhere. I aim to find it." Tears tracked the grime coating her face. She'd a little bag slung across her shoulder, a blanket tied to its strap. How had she survived all these days?

More to the point, what was he to do with her?

That first night he'd run as far as he could, carrying a pack weighing six stone at least, forced to leave the river and its rough wagon track for stretches to avoid farms, always veering back to it, his only guide. In the stretches of pine barrens, he'd seen deer aplenty. He'd scared a bear up a tree, heard more than one panther's scream, been bitten by every insect known to man, and seen too many snakes to number, one that rattled its tail at him in passing.

On the second day he'd spooked someone's dog into barking and got chased into a tract of swampland where he'd lost himself for a day, emerging muck-covered and ravenous, provisions gone. Yesterday he'd caught a straying chicken. Today the rabbit. Now he was a mile from Cross Creek—he recognized the stretch of river from the time they'd hunted Jemma. On the morrow he planned to risk going among people to get word of Hugh Cameron, or the plantation Pauling wrote of in connection with him.

"What I ought to ask isna *how* but why? Why've ye come after me?"

Jemma thrust out her small chin. "Why you running?"

"Ye ken why. Carey thinks I burnt his mill, killed Jim. Who kens what else they'll lay to my blame?"

She shrugged. "I don't know the minds of white folk. How'd you get free?"

"Ye didna see?"

"I seen you outside the smithy, filling that pack."

"I didna mean to take anyone with me."

The lass's defiance melted. "Please, Mister Alex. Let me come along."

"Have ye the slightest notion where I'm bound?"

"Away from Severn. That's all I care. For now."

"Have ye plans for later?" She looked away. "Spill it, lass, or ye get nothing from me."

Her amber eyes flashed. "I aim to find my people."

"Ye're still fixed on that notion? Running to the Cherokees?"

"Yes! And you my best chance. Reckon my only." Jemma narrowed her eyes. "I can't stay no more at Severn. You neither, else you wouldn't up and leave everyone—leave Miss Joanna."

Jaw clenched, he stared through falling darkness at Jemma. She was the last thing he wanted, a soul dependent upon him to stay alive and whole.

"What have ye been eating all this while?"

She eyed the half-skinned rabbit. "I find my way to the slaves on some farm. They feed me."

That surprised him. Had Severn's slaves aided runaways from other plantations? They'd kept it from his knowledge, if so.

"But you," Jemma went on. "How you going do better than scrawny ol' *rabbit* looking like you do? You too big and white, 'cept where the skeeters got you. But I'm little and brown and—"

"Sneaky with it?" he interjected, scratching at a swelling above an eyebrow.

"That's right. But ain't no hiding *you* in a crowd."

Which was plain truth. He'd stood out for his height even among his MacNeill clansmen, and Cross Creek wasn't a town like Wilmington, where he might have a small hope of going unremarked. It was no more than a trading post with a stretch of docks on the river, a few warehouses smelling of tar and hides. A crude inn served backcountry planters come to sell crops and livestock or transfer them to rivercraft bound for Wilmington. A scattering of cabins for those who made their living thus completed the hamlet. "I've no intention of taking ye to the Cherokees, Jemma. I'm bound for a certain place, can I find it. I aim to go into Cross Creek tomorrow and try."

"This place you want to go," Jemma said. "It in the backcountry?"

"Aye. I dinna ken where exactly."

"It got a name? Let me see can I find out where it is."

"And if someone takes ye for what ye are, and ye're caught?"

"Then you be rid of me. But I find out what you want to know, you take me along?"

He was more than half convinced to let her try but wasn't ready to let her know. "We'll neither of us be doing anything tonight. Settle down for now. I'll cook the rabbit. As for tomorrow, and Cross Creek, let's sleep on it, aye?"

"Ain't gonna make for a comfortable bed," Jemma muttered, but she slipped her bag and blanket off her shoulder.

They slept on it. Or Jemma did. He lay wakeful in the sandy loam thinking of Joanna. He was sore tempted to ask the lass had Joanna spoken of him before the night of their escape, and if so, what she'd said.

Somewhere in the buzzing, croaking, howling night, he decided it was better he didn't know.

In the haggard gray before sunrise, they tidied themselves as best they could. "Ye need to let this mop grow," he'd admonished, giving up fingering her locks into order. "Stop hacking it off so ye can braid it up out of your eyes at least."

"Maybe I mean to now," Jemma said, evasive with her gaze.

They covered the mile to Cross Creek and

reached the settlement as first light showed the figures of slaves moving about scattered buildings, tending ovens and kettles, chopping wood, emptying chamber pots, feeding stock. Armed with the names Hugh Cameron and Mountain Laurel, Jemma crept in among them. Alex settled himself in a vine-entwined copse to wait for what she'd return with. *If not news of Cameron, let it be bread.*

Beyond the scents of earth, water, and pines, he smelled it baking.

"Mister Alex?"

Jemma's whisper jarred him awake, back against a tree. He sat up straighter. Morning had deepened. Sunlight slanted bold through the treetops. "What . . . ?" Then he saw it. Whatever else she may have scavenged, she'd brought bread. A groan escaped him.

Jemma giggled. "Eat some. I already did."

He took a portion of the crusty loaf, still warm from the oven, crammed his mouth full and closed his eyes. When he opened them, Jemma sat watching him. "Had ye trouble?"

"Like I told you—"

"Little and sneaky, aye. Tell me."

Sounding pleased with herself, she related how she'd met the woman doing the baking for the folk in the inn, out back of the place, and spoke of her master looking for a friend. "I say,

'His friend called Hugh Cameron,' and she say as how a man by that name be there now. Right inside."

"What?" Alex nearly choked on his next mouthful. He forced it down. "Cameron's in Cross Creek?"

"Been here two nights. That baker tell me, 'Go fetch your master, girl. Take him my bread, maybe he stay over too. Make *my* master happy.' I took the bread, said thank you kindly, and here I am."

Despite the lass's smug grin, Alex didn't hide his relief. "That's all there was to it?"

"Told you I'm useful. Now you going to take me along or—"

"*Wheest.*" Alex clamped a hand over her mouth. Above his fingers her eyes rounded. She'd heard it, too, footsteps coming through the wood, their owner making no attempt to conceal approach.

Dropping the bread, Alex scrambled to his feet, groping at his belt for his dagger. Jemma darted behind him. He'd drawn the blade but halfway when a pine bough swept aside. Into view stepped a man in a long fringed shirt, whose measure Alex took in the span of a blink. Young, tall—though well shy of Alex's height—hair ablaze as he stepped into sunlight, a coppery shade Alex had last seen on the deck of the *James & Mary*.

The man halted, fixing him with incredulous eyes. "I dinna ken whether to believe what I'm seeing, but it canna be anyone else—Alastair MacKinnon."

Alex shoved the blade into its sheath. "Hugh Cameron." He uttered the name rough with emotion. "Aye, man, it's me. And glad I am to see ye."

Cameron came fully into the open, gaze fixed on Alex's right hand, still resting on the dagger's hilt. "Expecting trouble?"

There was knowledge of him in Cameron's gaze that went beyond the few words exchanged. Reckless or not, he decided on full disclosure. "Aye, Hugh. I've broken my indenture."

Behind him Jemma gasped.

Cameron's gaze dropped to her level. "I was in the necessary out back of the tavern and heard myself named. I followed her back, never thinking 'twas ye she meant. Did ye steal her away, then?"

Jemma stepped out and faced Cameron. "I stole my own self."

Sight of the lass attempting to deflect Cameron's probing brought a swift mix of amusement and warmth. "Ye've naught to fear, *mo nighean*. Hugh's a friend." His gaze swung back to the red-haired man still taking their measure. "Aye?"

"Aye," Cameron agreed. "But ye need beware, MacKinnon. The hunt's up for ye."

"They've been this far upriver?"

"Only word sent of a runaway blacksmith, your rather unmistakable description, what ye stole—what they say ye did." He leveled a look at Alex. "I'll ask ye the once and take your answer for truth. Other than the thieving, did ye do any of it?"

"Burn a mill and kill a man? I did not."

"All right." Cameron crossed his arms, considering. "What mean ye now to do? Where will ye go?"

"I'm going to the Cherokees," Jemma said.

Cameron's mouth quirked. "Are ye now, lass? Is MacKinnon here going with ye?"

Jemma pursed her lips, looking up at Alex. "I hear they take in white folk, sometimes."

Cameron laughed. "Oh, they do. Sometimes. But they're as likely to kill such as him. Ye wouldna want that on your conscience, would ye?"

"No." Jemma hesitated, then asked, "They kill me?"

Cameron regarded her. "Ye've their blood, aye? I can see it."

Alex watched the exchange, willing to let it play out, giving Cameron time to debate his course.

"My grandma was full-blood." Jemma's face lit up so vividly that she actually looked like what she was, a lass. No, a very young woman. He'd thought she must be eleven, twelve at most, puny as she was in stature. Now he was thinking older. Thirteen?

Cameron turned his attention back to Alex, who said, "I mean to make my way in the backcountry if I can. I thought of heading north into Virginia. Out of North Carolina, at any rate. I'd be lying if I said I wouldna covet your help. Or do ye mean to hinder me?"

No doubt there was a reward for his and Jemma's capture.

Hugh Cameron drew his ruddy brows low. "Hinder ye? I'm tempted to take offense ye'd even think it after the *James & Mary*. Of course I'll help ye."

Alex felt a squeeze on his hand, surprised Jemma had taken hold of it, but when Cameron reached toward him, he stepped forward, releasing Jemma to ignore the proffered hand and instead pull the man into his embrace. When they broke apart, Cameron's face was screwed into a grimace.

"Aye," Alex said. "I need a proper washing."

"Never mind stink," Jemma cut in. "Mister Alex, what he meaning to do with us?"

Cameron canted his head toward Alex. "I mean to take *him* off this river afore he's seen and kent for exactly who and what he is."

"Take him where?"

"To the plantation where I'm overseer. Ye as well, if ye're minded."

"Overseer?" She shot Alex an accusing look. "You never say *that*." Jemma swung back to Cameron, wary. "Where it be, this Mountain Laurel Mister Alex tell me about?"

"A fair distance. Near the Yadkin River."

"Where's that?"

"A sight nearer the Cherokees than ye are now," Cameron replied with exasperation. "Dinna be looking a gift horse in the mouth, aye?"

With her face lit at the prospect, Jemma was clutching Alex's shirt. He pried her fingers loose and gave them a gentle squeeze. "What say ye, Jemma? Will ye go with me to Mountain Laurel?"

Jemma freed her hand and clapped it across trembling lips, then uncovered them to say in wonder, "I'm gonna do it. I'm gonna find 'em. Yes, Mister Alex. I'll go with you."

26

On horseback it was a three-day hard journey to Mountain Laurel. Having none but the mount he'd ridden, Hugh Cameron put Jemma in the saddle, along with Alex's knapsack—the weight of which made him grunt and lift a brow.

"I didna steal the lass," Alex said. "Not intentionally. I didna say I took nothing besides."

"Tell me no more." Wearing the fringed hunting frock in the cool of early morning, Cameron took up the lead reins and they started out, leaving behind the copse a mile west of Cross Creek, where they'd arranged to meet. Alex wore the coat Joanna made him. Jemma wrapped herself in her blanket.

Cameron led them through pinewood as the sun rose, streaking beams through the soaring trees. Eventually they joined a road of sorts, a set of ruts carving a northerly route through the vast tracts of forest belonging to the few plantations established so far upriver. Cameron had seen them provisioned, refusing the coin Alex offered. He'd a long gun with a rifled barrel and meant to hunt along the way. They would be a week on the road, afoot, depending on the weather.

With time enough and the safety of distance,

Alex asked to hear Cameron's story. "I ken what happened after, but how came ye to the colony in the first place?"

"I was meant to be transported," Cameron said, settling into the tale. "Same as ye. But the guard bringing us along to be sold like fish at market, maybe he'd some sympathy—for us or for the Stuarts—I dinna ken. Somewhere in the streets of London, he turned his back on us and walked away. Took a moment gawping at each other to grasp we'd been set at liberty. There were three of us. Only me from the *James & Mary*."

"Ye might've gone anywhere," Alex said. "Why not Scotland?"

"I've a wee half-brother there still, and my stepmother, but they've her family nearby. My going back would have put them in jeopardy. I'm exiled like ye, MacKinnon, difference being I've no indenture to serve. Nor do ye, now."

"Aye." Alex gazed ahead to trees stretching on in endless ranks, pushing away a pang at the thought. Not that he wished to be bound for seven years to any man. But he had wished it, briefly, for a woman. *Joanna*.

"Twice I came nigh to being apprehended," Cameron continued, "before I found a ship with a captain willing to take me on. I crewed my passage over, and at first chance, which happened to be Wilmington, I abandoned ship, with less to my name than what ye have now. Days later

I went into a tavern with no means to pay for a swig of cider, much less the meal I was desperate for, when I overheard a fellow attempting to carry on some business in the Gaelic. The men he addressed hadn't a word of the tongue, so I stepped up and presented myself as interpreter. So great was the man's relief, he spent the next two hours feeding me while he scoured his family tree for how we might be related, for surely we must be, both of us Camerons."

"Did he ascertain as much?" Alex asked.

"Some distant connection through a series of marriages. Duncan Cameron's been in the colonies since the Stuart rising of '15. But a clansman who spoke the Gaelic—if ye'll credit it, MacKinnon, the man speaks English fine but has vowed never to let a word of it cross his lips again—was to him like meeting a prodigal son thought lost forever. He took me home with him and killed the fatted calf."

"How long since?" Alex asked.

"Late September last," Cameron said. "And ye? How long in the colony?"

"Since July."

"I've heard it's verra hot then. Guess I'll ken for myself soon." Cameron strode on confidently, rifle at his side, leading the horse. "I was meant to purchase a brood mare in Cross Creek. Duncan and the mare's owner exchanged letters, agreed on the sale. But I reached the place to find the mare a week dead of the colic. He'll not be pleased, will Duncan."

He didn't sound overly concerned. Duncan Cameron, despite his oddities, must be an easy man to serve.

The day passed over them, clouded, cooler than it had been. Not long before darkness fell, they pitched camp near a creek like many such they'd crossed that day. They'd walked nigh thirty miles. Alex was glad for a fire and food in his belly.

"I think it wise ye leave the colony quick as may be," Cameron said after Jemma rolled into her blanket to sleep. "Head north, keep to the backcountry. Find a place in want of a blacksmith. Ye've enough knowledge of the trade to get by?"

"I think so, but there's the lass," Alex said with a nod at Jemma's form. "I'm not keen on the idea of traipsing the wilderness looking for Indians, aye?"

"Nor should ye be," Cameron said. "As you're verra likely to find them. Take her north with ye. Pass her off as your slave. It'll help ye look the man of means."

Alex didn't comment. Such pretense didn't settle comfortably on him. Sure enough Jemma wouldn't fancy it.

The sixth day of their journey, they pushed on after sunset rather than camp again with less than half a day's travel remaining, so it was by starlight Alex first saw Mountain Laurel. Cameron thought it best to conceal their presence from his employer. They were given beds in the tiny cabin, lit by a small fire in a clay chimney, of a slave who left it to sleep on the floor of Cameron's roomier quarters. He laid an exhausted Jemma on a cot, where she was asleep in seconds.

Cameron lingered at the doorway, peering in. "All well?"

"Far as I ken." In the blue after sunset, still on the road, Alex had spied in the distance a set of ridges, what appeared a mountain range in miniature rising from the rolling backcountry. The Carraways, Cameron called them. For days the land had pitched and rolled like sea waves, forested in hardwoods—chestnuts, oaks, beeches, hickory—interspersed with pines, cut by rushing streams, but the road had dipped and climbed more steeply those last starlit miles. Mountain Laurel must be tucked into those higher ridges.

"Right, then," Cameron said. "I'll leave ye to sleep. Come morning dinna leave the cabin till someone comes to ye. There's a chamber pot."

At the door's shutting, Jemma sat bolt upright as if it had been a gunshot, peering wide-eyed at her surroundings. "Where we at?"

"Mountain Laurel. Why are ye awake?"

"Dreamt I was up on that horse. Fell asleep and toppled off. Woke up afore I hit the ground." She gave a shudder. "Why does that always happen? Never hitting ground in dreams?"

"I dinna ken, lass." He lowered himself onto the opposite bedframe, a crude structure with a coarse linen tick. "But ye've seen the last of that horse, I'm thinking."

Wrapped in her tattered blanket, Jemma blinked like a golden-eyed owl. "How near are we to the Cherokees?"

Alex dropped his head to rub his neck. "I've no notion."

Jemma yawned wide. "You think they'll give me a name?"

"A name for what?"

"Me. *Jemma* ain't a Cherokee name. It short for Jemima. If that mean something, I don't know what. A Cherokee name's got to mean something. I tell you my grandma's name?"

"A dozen times." Jemma's talkativeness surprised him. She'd grown sullen since leaving Cross Creek. More than once around their fire at night, he'd caught her studying him sidelong, suspicious. He raised his head to find her expression guarded. "Why must it be Cherokees? I'll take care of ye, lass."

"I knew it! I heard you and Mister Cameron talking that first night on the trail. You thought I was sleeping, but I heard. You gonna tell folk I'm your slave!"

"That was Cameron's notion. Not mine."

"So what? You'll take me to the Cherokees?"

In the hearth the fire hissed, falling in on itself. Alex stared into the gathering shadows. In the crevice between two logs, a spider was spinning its web. "Cameron's of a mind it would be the death of me."

Jemma huffed but said no more, sinking back down onto the tick and turning her face to the wall.

Voices outside the cabin woke him. He lay with eyes closed, recognizing Hugh Cameron's. The other was a stranger's. It was a moment before he realized he was hearing Gaelic spoken. He sat up. Across the narrow space between their cots, Jemma was dead to the world, her mop of hair looking like some small disheveled animal peeking from her rumpled blanket.

"Good, then," Cameron was saying. "I will leave them to your care."

"How long will you be?" came the reply.

"At least until midday. Maybe longer. Let them know where I have gone. I will come to them when I return."

The Gaelic was a feast to starved ears. Alex wanted to catch Hugh Cameron before he went wherever he was going, but hesitated. Was it Duncan Cameron out there too?

He started at a tap at the door.

" 'Mornin' in there. Ye be wanting some

breakfast?" queried a male voice, clearly a native English-speaker though his speech had a faint Scots lilt. Alex rose and in two strides was at the door. He opened it to find a broad-featured African man, older than he but not by much, for his hair and beard showed no white.

The man craned his neck to gaze up at him, dark eyes wide, before bobbing his head in greeting. "Tilly got the porridge warming in the kitchen. Would ye and the lassie come now to eat it? Ye can come," he added, when Alex raised a brow. "Master Duncan and Mister Hugh gone to see about another horse."

"Was that ye talking to Cameron?"

"Aye, sir, it was."

"Cameron said you have the Gaelic," Alex said in that language, feeling a choking in his throat to hear it falling from his lips, astonished to find an African speaking it, no matter he'd been forewarned.

The slave switched nimbly to the tongue. "We all do here. It is required. I am called Malcolm. You are Alex MacKinnon, yes? And the lass is called Jemma?"

From behind Alex a sleep-thick voice murmured, "Mister Alex, who you talking to funny?"

Alex stepped aside to reveal Jemma sitting up in a tumble of hair and blanket. "This is Malcolm," he told her. Switching back to Gaelic, as hungry for it as he was the promised breakfast, he answered the slave. "This lass is called Jemma, yes, and I'm Alex MacKinnon."

Malcolm nodded. "And you have come from nigh the coast, a plantation called Severn?" When Alex hesitated Malcolm said, "Reverend Pauling mentioned the place, the people there."

"I was at a place called Severn."

Malcolm's face lit. "The reverend talked to us of Jesus, as no doubt he did to you at Severn. Master Cameron allowed it."

Jemma joined them at the doorway. "I can tell you talking about Reverend Pauling. Talk so I know what all you saying."

" 'Morning, little miss," Malcolm said. "So ye're acquainted with the reverend too?"

"Probably the best white man I ever known."

"With that I must agree."

"Pauling was here in the autumn?" Alex asked.

"Aye. Then he headed north. Reckon he spent the winter in Pennsylvania with his sister's family."

Alex wondered if he shouldn't try to find the man, his only acquaintance outside North Carolina. Might Pauling help him settle, or would he be of a mind to return him to the Careys?

"What road did he take north?"

"The old Warrior Path—the Wagon Road, some call it." Malcolm stepped back and motioned them from the cabin. "Come get breakfast while it's warm in the kettle."

The morning was overcast but bright. As they walked up from the slave cabins, Alex took in the situation where Hugh Cameron had landed so fortuitously. Fields lay to the northeast of the house, which was starkly white against the hogback ridge rising to the southwest. From the cabins they came up a wagon lane past an apple orchard, a washhouse and stable, to the kitchen. They were greeted by the cook, Tilly, the woman Malcolm called his wife, and their wee daughter, Naomi—six, by the look of her—and an older woman Alex supposed kept house for Duncan Cameron. Other slaves were about the place, field hands and a man for the stable. They'd had their breakfast and gone off to their work.

Seated on a stool at the table, Jemma was still agog over that looming ridge. "That hill yonder. It one of them mountains where the Cherokees live?"

Alex, accepting a bowl of porridge, heard the lassie Naomi laugh and say, "These molehills ain't even the beginning of them mountains."

"We see Indians now and again, but none live nearby," Malcolm told Jemma, who looked so crestfallen not even steaming porridge drizzled with honey brightened her countenance.

Naomi set a plate of corn pone on the table. She stood back, waiting for Alex to sample it.

"Did ye make this yourself, lass?" he asked her.

"I did, sir." She turned to Jemma. "What you like best to cook?"

Jemma made a sour face. "I don't meddle in the kitchen. I work the smithy."

Naomi's small mouth fell open. "You hammer iron? A girl?"

Jemma nodded at Alex. "He do the hammering. I pump the bellows and fetch stuff. But now I'm gonna be a free Cherokee Indian."

Everyone in the kitchen laughed except Alex—and Jemma, who glowered at one and all, then jabbed a spoon into her porridge.

It wasn't until evening Hugh Cameron came to them, shut up in the cabin while a light rain fell. He'd brought supper from the kitchen, which they spread at the foot of Jemma's cot and ate while they talked, conversation circling round the tobacco seedlings soon to be sown, the mare he'd ridden to see, his fortune in landing himself such a position when not long since they were little more than walking skeletons aboard a Crown prison ship.

"Does it not bother ye, though?" Alex ventured. "Being overseer of slaves. I couldna do it, not after what we suffered at the hands of the English."

"Duncan would hire on someone to do it," Cameron replied. "Better a man who kens what it is to lose his freedom than one who's given such matters nary a thought, aye?"

"Maybe," Alex allowed, but the matter troubled him. "D'ye not worry ye'll maybe grow used to it? That it will change ye?"

Not for the better, he was thinking, and saw by the guarded look Cameron shot him that he'd grasped the implication.

"We survive, MacKinnon. Ye and I ken that can mean doing things we thought beyond our scope. For me it's overseeing slaves. For ye it's breaking your oath, taking what that man, Carey, considers his property—the lass, your years of service, whatever else ye may have in that great pack of yours. We do what we must."

Alex couldn't help wondering what Joanna thought of what he'd done. Did she curse his name as her stepfather must? Wish away even the memory of him? Or did she understand his choice?

"And with that in mind," Cameron said, cutting into his thoughts, "what *do* ye mean to do?"

He pushed thoughts of Joanna down deep. "If ye'll grant us provision, we'll be gone before first light, north toward the Wagon Road."

Jemma nearly choked on her supper. "No, Mister Alex. I mean, can't we go west? I got to find—"

"Jemma," he said more harshly than he meant. "Enough about the Cherokees. Even if I kent they wouldna kill me, I dinna ken how to find them."

"Strike the Yadkin," Cameron said. "Follow it far enough, they'll find ye."

Jemma crossed her arms over the loose folds of her shirt. "That don't sound hard."

"I'll set ye on course for the Wagon Road," Cameron said. "Ye'll have a couple of days to decide whether ye mean to follow it, but there's a path intersects it a ways northward, a wilderness path that would head ye westward through the mountains—if that's what ye decide. Ye can always take up fur trapping."

Jemma went on with her supper in brooding silence, but Alex could almost hear the turning of her mind. She hadn't given up her single-minded ambition—dire warnings notwithstanding.

They walked northwest, traveling in cover of woods when possible. The weather turned wet. They met with little traffic on the trail that, according to Hugh Cameron, would lead to the Wagon Road that traversed the middle colonies' western edge. Since Pauling regularly traveled that road, Alex thought it likely they'd meet with folk who knew him.

Cameron had provisioned them, but there had been no firearm to spare. Alex had, as chance occasioned, hunted with a makeshift spear—the smaller of his blades bound to a branch he'd whittled down. Deer roamed thick in the back-country, bounding from copse and thicket, white tails high. He made a dozen failed attempts before, late the second day, he speared a fawn too slow in following its dam. Jemma was still cross with him over it when they camped that evening in the bend of a narrow stream.

"Fetch us water?" he asked as he laid the gutted fawn on the ground, preparing to make a fire.

"I ain't eating that," she muttered, but took the canteen and went upstream to crouch among ferns. He watched her dip her hands to drink, wishing she'd bathe or wash her filthy breeches and that shirt that hung like a tent. She filled the canteen, set it on a rock, then wandered into the bushes. He'd a haunch of venison over the flames, the smell of it filling the little camp, before she returned and hunkered near. Her stink enveloped him briefly before smoke wafted between.

"Smells good."

"Changed your mind, have ye?"

There was bread left. He gave her half. She crammed it into her mouth and around it said, "Maybe."

He cut off a portion already browned and handed it to her. She sniffed it and took a bite.

"It strikes me I'll be needing another name once I find a place to settle. Maybe I'll go by my mother's clan, MacNeill."

Jemma stopped chewing. "Settle where?"

"I dinna ken. Pennsylvania, maybe."

"That ain't where I aim to go!" Before he could say more, she'd shot to her feet and headed back into the brush.

"Jemma!" He half-rose to go after her, but subsided, thinking it best to let her be. She was canny enough not to wander far—from him or the food. He ate his fill of the meat, roasted what remained, set aside a portion for Jemma, then lay down under his blanket, his ears pricked until he heard her creeping back.

Clouds had parted, allowing moonlight. He could see her, hunkered on her blanket.

"Mister Alex?" she hissed, as if afraid he might be sleeping.

He sat up. "Aye, Jemma. Are ye hungry?"

"No. Yes. But . . . I need you to take me *west*."

"I dinna mean to go west, but wherever I do go ye've a home with me—however long ye wish."

"As your slave?"

"No. But a life with me wherever I settle." He sensed in the silence she was thinking it through.

"I'd be free to part ways did I choose?"

"If ye've another place to go, a means to live, aye. I'll not hold ye against your will."

He heard her sniffle. "Let me think on it."

Cautiously relieved, he said, "Let's sleep, aye?"

"Can I eat first?"

"I left ye some venison by the fire." He heard her rummaging as he drifted off to sleep, hoping by morning she'd agree to go north.

But in the gray predawn when he woke, Jemma and most of the venison were gone.

• • •

Along the stream he found the places she'd paused to rest. She followed the waterway no matter how it curved, but always it looped back westward, stubborn in its course as was Jemma.

By midday he'd reached the stream's mouth, where it emptied into a larger watercourse he thought must be the Yadkin, swollen and swift. He doubted she'd have attempted to cross. After scouting the moist bank, he found her prints upstream.

A mile or so on, he pushed through a clump of brush below a stony rise to find a pool at its base and a sheltered beach—and Jemma, crouched with her toes in the mud, dipping a drink.

He lowered the knapsack to the ground. The iron within clanked.

Jemma shot up, spilling water down her front. She made a dash for the trees, leaving behind her blanket and the meat taken in the night.

He snagged her and dragged her back toward the river.

"What d'ye mean by running off like that, after I said I'd take care of ye?"

"I said I'd think on it. This is what I thought!"

She squirmed like a landed fish. He grappled and got her in a hold she couldn't break. "That ye're better off alone in the wilderness?"

"Not alone. With the Cherokees!"

He wrinkled his nose. "What would they think

of ye, turning up smelling ripe as a skunk?"
Inspiration dawned. He hauled her up the stony
rise above the pool, her flailing feet off the
ground. "If ye're to be a Cherokee, then ye'll at
least be a clean one."

"No!" While she bucked and kicked, he looked
over into the water, six feet below. Plenty deep
enough.

"Right, then. In ye go." He swept her high and
tossed her into the pool. She hit with a splash.
He turned to descend the rise to be there when
she came ashore, in case a dunking didn't subdue
her—and froze, taking note at last what the
higher vantage point had revealed.

Mountains. Blue and hazy in the distance, but
unmistakably mountains.

In an instant he was heart-struck, yearning for
cool glens and splashing burns. Steep trails to
craggy peaks. Mist and cloud and the wind forever blowing. And he was shaken with fear that
gusted cold on the heels of yearning. Fear of
what else those mountains held, perils unlike any
found in Scotland.

Wild beasts. Wilder men.

"Mist—Alex—help!"

He'd been half aware of Jemma thrashing in
the pool below. He tore his gaze from that
beguiling rise of blue and realized . . . she
couldn't swim.

He jumped in after her, wrapped an arm around

her, and was nearly to the riverbank before becoming aware of something very odd about her shape. Stunned, he let her go on the bank, and she sprawled on her back, gasping for breath, that voluminous shirt plastered to her form, exposing the shape of her belly poking up round. Even as he gaped at it, it moved.

He stood, his own breath short from shock. "*Jemma.* Who . . . *who* did that to ye?"

Jemma's eyes flew open. She saw him staring and sat up, tenting the wet shirt away from herself. "Don't look at my belly!"

He could look at nothing else.

Jemma's knees came up, as if she could hide what he'd plainly seen. "I been looking, but I ain't found what I need to get rid of 'em."

Them? Was she carrying twins?

"Ye canna just get *rid* of them."

She looked as if he'd grown a second head. "We always do. Miss Joanna see to it."

"Joanna?" He was looming over her, nigh shouting. He squatted, lowering his voice. "Exactly what d'ye think we're talking about?"

"Worms?" she said, sounding miserable and mortified. "Like the little ones get with their bellies all poked out?"

His head was spinning. "Jemma. That isna what's ailing ye. I think ye ken what it is. Ye must ken."

"Like Mari," she said, sounding all of the

eleven years he'd once thought she was. "I got a baby coming, don't I?"

"Aye. Ye do. But ye canna be . . . what? Thirteen at most?"

"Mari says I was born in spring so I could be ten and four now."

She was tiny for fourteen. All but that belly. By the look of her, he guessed she was six months along. What if the bairn was tiny too? Was she nearer her time than that?

"I know I don't look it," Jemma said, as if reading his thoughts, knees drawn up to her round belly. "Wish I did," she added in an undertone dark enough to jar him again.

"Jemma, who have ye lain with?"

"You mean slept beside?"

"No," he said, going cold all over as understanding sank deeper. "What man got ye alone and . . . hurt ye? Another of Carey's slaves?"

Her color drained, but she wagged her head. "No slave ever hurt me, 'cept when Demas caught me in the swamp. Mostly he scared me. You saw."

He had. As evenly as he could he said, "His name, lass."

Jemma looked away. "I ain't ever going back. Can't we forget it?"

"Ye canna forget it. Not with a bairn on the way. Not when . . ."

He clamped his mouth shut, realizing he'd

terrify her if he shared his rising fears. With her clothes clinging wetly, he could see how narrow were her hips. Plenty of small women delivered bairns fine, but he'd never had to midwife them. With a sinking of heart, he knew what they must do.

"We'll go back to Mountain Laurel. I dinna ken what Hugh will say to—"

"Mister Alex, that ain't what we're doing." Jemma got to her feet but made no move to run away. She stood over him, dripping river water, hands fisted against her belly. "Get that notion outta your head."

She'd been bold with him since Cross Creek, but something was different now. Gone was her desperation. What had been merely childish obstinacy had transformed into the iron will of motherhood. It had entered her bones.

"We gonna be Indians, me and my baby, and that's an end to it."

27

May 1748

W hy did you run away, Jemma?"
    Her sister's plaintive question drifted
down the passage, reaching Joanna in the sewing
room where she and Azuba worked while the
morning air was fresh.

Azuba sighed in resignation. "She at it again."

Mister Reeves had returned after a fortnight's
search for Alex and Jemma, not with their fugi-
tives but with the doll he'd promised Charlotte.
Joanna had been thankful he'd remembered, but
gratitude proved short-lived.

"What shall you call this one?" she'd asked, as
her sister hugged the doll with its miniature gown
of pin-striped blue, ruffled cap, and flowing hair
a few shades darker than Charlotte's. "What Anna
name haven't we used? Julianna? Marianna?"

Charlotte had held the amber-haired doll at
arm's length, gazing into its painted wooden face.
"This one's Jemma."

Since then Charlotte had played exclusively
with the new doll.

"Jemma! You're a very bad girl!"

Joanna had bent to her sewing again, but lifted
her head at her sister's scolding tone.

"You cut off your hair!"

She and Azuba rose and crossed to the room she and Charlotte shared. Her sister sat on their bed, holding the new doll out before her. Its ruffled cap lay tossed aside, along with a set of Joanna's sewing shears, and a pile of amber horsehair curls. What hair remained on the doll's head was cropped to ragged hanks.

"Now I can't braid it!" Charlotte burst into tears and threw herself across the bed for what seemed the hundredth time in the month since Jemma had run away. Wishing Mister Reeves had never found that doll, Joanna cast a mute appeal at Azuba, hovering with her in the doorway, and with half-ashamed relief took her leave.

Another need pulled at her. Papa was also abed.

Azuba's soothing tones trailed her down the stairs as she lifted another prayer for Charlotte. Joanna had done her own share of weeping in the silence of the night, holding her misery close, gazing at the corn-husk doll she and Alex had made together, which Charlotte had yet to notice she'd moved to her side of the bed.

Even if Alex was captured and returned, it would change nothing between them. He'd made it clear what he thought of her. She was too weak to follow after what she truly wanted.

Around that memory frustration swirled, relentless as a hurricane. Did following her heart's desire have to mean abandoning those she loved, leaving them in the bondage she longed to escape? Or was Alex the shortsighted one, unable to see beyond that stark choice, or abide in patience until a better way was shown?

Heart-heavy, Joanna knocked on Papa's bedroom door and entered at his bidding. A more private sanctum than the study, the room was spare and masculine, all traces of her mother long since removed.

Papa was abed, the breakfast tray on the rumpled coverlet barely touched. For a week he'd suffered a stomach ailment, though the pain hadn't driven him to his bed until yesterday. The room's chamber pot had been emptied, but the odor of troubled bowels lingered. She opened the curtains and raised the window. The breeze wafting in was already tinged with warmth.

Sunlight showed the thinning of her stepfather's cheeks. "How are you feeling?"

"Better today," he said, contradicting the evidence of that unfinished breakfast. "Phineas was by. I know about Simcoe."

Joanna sighed. Their troublesome neighbor, with his perpetual discontent. "Is it terribly complicated?"

"Apparently it needs my presence in Wilmington."

"Papa, I don't think—"

He waved aside her concern. "Phineas is going with a letter of authority to act on my behalf, should it be needful. He's leaving soon. You haven't seen him?"

"I've been upstairs. Charlotte is having a bad morning, missing Jemma." She clenched her teeth so she wouldn't mention Alex. But Papa caught the welling of her tears.

"And are you?" he asked.

She blinked the tears away and tried to smile.

"You might as well say his name." Papa studied her, blue eyes pained. When she sat on the feather tick beside him, he reached for her hand in a rare show of attentiveness. "You still pine for him, and I don't like seeing you thus."

Of course he didn't. She was the one who held things together.

But that was unfair. He cared about her unhappiness. He simply had a different idea about what would cure it than did she.

"He left without a word."

Her stepfather let go her hand. "Not one word of his intentions?"

"I'd have told you if so. Did Mister Reeves say something to make you suspect I knew what Alex planned to do?"

He looked surprised. "Why should he?"

The man had asked her to marry him, and she'd given her heart to another. Reason enough.

"Few men are accomplished in expressing such sentiments, but I believe Phineas is fond of you."

Mister Reeves was occasionally amused by

357

her. Often frustrated. And in the matter of his proposal of marriage, beyond patient. But fond?

"I know he's fond of Severn," she said. *Ruthlessly so,* she thought, wincing inwardly at memory of a flashing whip.

"That he is," Papa agreed. "Yet despite all MacKinnon has done, it's *him* to whom you would trust your heart?"

"Trust, Papa? No. Though he yet has it in his keeping, I fear." Tears slid down her cheeks despite her willing them away.

"Joanna, I loved your mother, and the loss nigh undid me," her stepfather said wearily. "But love isn't essential for a marriage to succeed. Mutual need or concern will suffice."

Joanna couldn't push words past the ache that swelled in her chest at the bleak prospect.

Papa closed his eyes. "I sometimes wish I'd given Elijah leave to court you. At least there was once true affection between you . . ."

His voice trailed off, and she didn't try to rouse him again. Better to end another conversation destined to go in circles. She took up the tray and left the room, shut the door quietly, and turned.

Standing in the passage behind her was Mister Reeves. By the sharpness of his gaze, she was certain he'd heard Papa's last words. He pretended otherwise, mouth pulling into a stiff smile.

"Miss Carey. I wished to see you before starting downriver."

"You're headed back to Wilmington, Papa said. Something about Mister Simcoe?"

He brushed the matter aside. "Nothing to concern you. However, I do mean to leave Demas behind."

"Again?"

Far from annoyed at her questioning, Mister Reeves looked eager. "I had a notion that Moon might train Demas for the forge. I almost mentioned it to Captain Carey this morning but decided not to trouble him. What do you think? Might it be a workable solution for Severn's loss of a blacksmith?"

She blinked at Mister Reeves, taken aback that he would seek her opinion. She wanted no one at that forge but Alex. Still, they must do something. "I'll speak to Papa about it."

Though clearly the answer he sought, Mister Reeves continued to regard her, hazel eyes piercing. "You wish it could be MacKinnon. You needn't deny it," he added quickly, as she'd been about to do that very thing. "Miss Carey, there's something you should know. I was the one—"

A flurry of knocking had Joanna turning toward the door to the yard. "Papa. He'll be disturbed."

Mister Reeves reached the door first and flung it open. On the threshold Sybil stood. The gaze she darted past Mister Reeves as Joanna joined him was urgent with need. "It's Mari, Miss

Joanna. Her baby coming. She wanting Azuba—and you."

Ten hours later they were still in the thick of things, Joanna, Azuba, and Marigold. The air inside the cabin was muggy with the pans of steaming water Sybil periodically brought, and all were streaming sweat, when Marigold's labor at last progressed to its final stage. Still the baby was long in coming.

"I can't go on to glory without telling you." Grasping Joanna's hand, Marigold pulled her close with a strength that belied talk of impending expiration. "I'm sorry!"

"For what, Mari? No, save your—"

"Listen!" Marigold's fingernails dug into her palm. "Elijah . . . I never meant to take him from you!" The need to push overwhelmed and she strained, then with a whoosh of breath said, "He wanted you! Said Master Carey wouldn't let him ask. That's why he don't claim this baby. He still wants you!"

Joanna wagged her head. "Elijah is like a brother. He doesn't love me in that way. But you and I, weren't we once like sisters?" Her voice broke, and she changed her tone. "Never mind that now. Let's get this baby born. Then we'll talk."

Between the next two pushes, the second of which brought the baby's head to crown,

Marigold nodded, then focused all her being on the job at hand.

Though the sun hadn't finished setting, inside the smithy the air hung dim and stale. Gone was the molten earth-and-fire smell of an active forge. It pained Joanna, yet it couldn't douse the flame ablaze in her heart.

"Elijah?" She paused at the doorway, letting her eyes adjust. As they did, he half-staggered out of the back room, barefoot, unshaven, hair in greasy ropes. She marched across the smithy and halted, smelling the liquor on him. "Elijah Jory Moon, I have never been so ashamed of you."

His head snapped back as though she'd bitten him. "What?"

She recoiled at his breath but stood her ground. "I said ashamed. Mari has spent this day birthing your child, and here you are, drunk on your bed as if you didn't care. As if—"

His hand shot up and gripped her arm. The color drained from his face, leaving his scars harshly outlined. "It's come? She's well?"

"No thanks to you!"

With her tiny, perfect baby nestled in her arms, Marigold had talked of how, in the weeks following Elijah's maiming, she'd been the one to change the dressings to his face and neck, his arm and ruined hand. Then the stump, when the hand couldn't be saved. That much Joanna knew. Then Marigold told how Elijah began to trust her with more than his maimed body. He'd let her see his soul, that devastation of pain and loss.

"One night I didn't go back to my cabin. After I seen to the dressings, we talked like we'd been doing, then did a heap more than talk. I wanted so bad to comfort him. Finally he let me." Marigold traced her baby's cheek with a fingertip while she spoke.

"Then Mister Alex come and it was harder to be together. 'Lijah tried to tell me it couldn't be like before, that we best stop. Then the night we buried Micah, 'Lijah comforted *me*. Guess this one was started then, or just after."

Marigold looked up, exhausted from labor, glowing with motherhood, and afraid. "Now what, Miss Joanna? He won't claim us."

"It's not because of me," Joanna assured her, gazing on the tiny infant cradled to Marigold's chest. "Elijah loves you in a way he never did me. You said it yourself. He let you see his pain, body and soul. Not once did he allow me that. He trusted *you*. I think he's simply afraid."

"He is that." She bowed her head over her baby's scrunched face. "Afraid to take up Master Carey's offer. Afraid even to try."

It shouldn't have to be like this. Joanna wanted to scream it to the cabin, the whole plantation, the world. Maybe she couldn't change their lives

362

in all the ways she wanted, but there was one thing she could do.

"You leave Elijah to me," she'd said, and despite her own exhaustion had gone straight to the smithy.

"How could you?" she demanded now. "You have a woman who loves you, a son born of her love. How could you turn your back on them?"

"A son?" Elijah's stunned gaze filled with things unspoken—joy, longing, fear. Then Joanna glimpsed in his eyes the ghost of the life he'd once thought to share with her. Even as she watched, that ghost broke apart like drifting mist and vanished. "I want to see him."

Joanna wasn't satisfied. "And Mari?"

"And Mari," he said. "I have to see them both. Now."

They named the baby Jory. "After my father," Elijah told her as he held his newborn son in the crook of his undamaged arm. He'd bent and kissed the baby's head, then knelt by Marigold and wept.

Joanna had left them and gone to her room to find Charlotte asleep, clutching her shorn doll. She'd managed to shed her gown and stays before falling into bed herself, where she'd slept the night through for the first time since Alex's leaving.

In the morning she went to see how Marigold

and the baby were faring and found Elijah there again. Perhaps he'd never left.

"Jory," she murmured to the baby she'd been given to hold, wrapped in a scrap of blanket, tiny face peeking out. "He's beautiful, Mari."

Seated side by side on the bed, Marigold and Elijah regarded their son with the absorption of all new parents. She wished she needn't sully the moment. Wished they were what they seemed on the surface, friends celebrating this new life.

The truth was far more complicated. Elijah had no means of providing for Marigold, no way to take up the offer to buy her freedom, and his child's. That he should even have to do so was wrong. All of this was wrong. She'd lived with the conviction niggling at her conscience for years before it finally grew too onerous to push aside.

Reverend Pauling had told her stepfather slavery was an evil.

Alex had known it. *I could never step into a planter's shoes, become an owner of other men.*

The vision that had visited her outside Papa's study hadn't died. It would just take longer to bring to pass than she'd hoped. And Alex MacKinnon wouldn't be a part of it. She might never manumit all her stepfather's slaves, or even many of them. But God willing, this child cradled in her arms would grow to manhood free.

"Elijah, Mari," she said, and waited until they looked up from their son to meet her gaze. "May I sit and tell you something that's been on my mind?"

28

May 1748

She heard them as she entered the house, having spent the morning visiting the kitchen and shops, then a few of her stepfather's slaves fallen ill with spring agues.

"You must have more to relate than it *went well*," Papa was saying. "Tell me everything."

"Sir, I suspect the recent stresses to be the cause of your infirmity. I wouldn't add . . ."

Mister Reeves was returned from Wilmington. Joanna hurried past the study, needing to collect herself, though she'd had a fortnight to think of what she'd say to him—more importantly to Papa—once they were all together again. It had taken nearly that long to convince Elijah of the merits of her plan and his part in it.

The day after Jory's birth, together in their cabin, she'd shared her vision for Severn. They'd gaped at her until Marigold asked, "You want to run Severn after Captain Carey pass, with no husband, then free Jory and me?"

"Not just you and Jory. But there's an issue with that we'll have to face."

"We'd have to leave the colony, Mari and me," Elijah said. "As would everyone ye free. Who'll be left to farm and work the forest? Rebuild the mill? Ye're talking about the ruin of this place, Joanna."

"A scaling back," she countered, "to an economy sustainable without the support of slaves. I'll hire those needed to work with us." What she couldn't afford, she'd do without.

Elijah had remained unconvinced. "What do ye mean . . . *us?*"

"I'm hoping you'll serve as my factor, Elijah, at least for a time. Some issues to contend with will be more expediently handled by a man—but not a husband."

"How do ye mean to talk Captain Carey around to this? He wants ye to marry Reeves."

"I don't yet know," she confessed. "But your support will make it easier."

"Joanna . . . what can I do?" He'd gazed at his knotted shirtsleeve. The shadow of the past year, briefly lifted with Jory's birth, seemed to wrap itself around him again.

It was Marigold who'd risen to battle it back. "You still got a brain in that skull of yours. You a man, you white, you free. Use those things. Help Miss Joanna."

Elijah hadn't agreed to it during that first conversation. Nor the second, nor the third. Then yesterday he'd found her talking with the carpenters and drew her aside to walk with him along the orchard's edge.

"He told me something, did MacKinnon. That day he rode to the mill."

Joanna had lifted her gaze to the peach trees' blossoming boughs. She'd accepted that her life would go on without Alex MacKinnon. She trusted the resignation would sink from her mind to her heart, eventually, that she would cease falling asleep each night imagining herself with him, setting up a forge in some crossroads hamlet, or aboard a ship bound for Scotland.

Free, wherever he was.

"He called me a self-pitying fool," Elijah said. "I expect MacKinnon ought to know self-pity when he sees it, having lost so much himself."

Then a hammer's ring pierced the air, a sharp reminder of her losses. Elijah had agreed to train Demas in the blacksmith's art.

He caught her flinch. "Ye wish it was MacKinnon, don't ye?"

"Elijah . . . I gave Alex more than I should have—my trust, my heart. But he gave me something too."

"What?"

"Courage." She halted and took his hand in hers. "Will you help me?"

To her surprise his mouth quirked.

"What?"

"Oh, something else MacKinnon said, back when Thom Kelly was here and had us forging marlinspikes. He agreed to do the job but said it would take his hands and my brain." He paused, a warring in his eyes. "Mari's right. And Lord knows I long to be of use to someone again."

"You are," she told him, firming her grip. "You will be."

"I'll try." He held her gaze with a flicker of the steadiness she'd long desired to see there. A small flame. A beginning.

Now, with no wish to hear of the latest squabble with Mister Simcoe, she hurried down the passage. She'd nearly reached the stairs when—

"Miss Carey? Might I have a word?" Mister Reeves was striding down the passage.

"Yes?"

"Gone a fortnight and that's all the greeting I get?" He halted and took her hand. Before he could raise it to his lips, she pulled free.

"You're returned with good news?" His eyes were fairly sparkling.

"Very good. That isn't what I wanted to tell you. Our last conversation was cut short, you'll recall."

"By the birth of Mari and Elijah's son. They've named him Jory." He looked at her, brightness dimming with disinterest. "You had something to tell me?"

"Yes. Before you were called away that day, I was about to admit . . ." Mister Reeves dropped his voice as Sybil descended the stairs. "Something I'd rather kept between us. Come into the parlor?"

Swallowing her annoyance, she followed him into that seldom used room. He shut the door and faced her. "It was I," he said. "I stole the key from your room while you slept. I unlocked the smokehouse and released MacKinnon."

Joanna couldn't say which she felt more deeply, violation or astonishment. "You let Alex go? Why?"

"I came to think myself mistaken in accusing him—about the mill. I'm perplexed by the misfortunes we've suffered and find it impossible to believe no human agent is behind *some* of it. But that agent wasn't MacKinnon. Not that I find him innocent of all wrongdoing. I simply felt he didn't deserve the punishment I thought Captain Carey meant to exact—due mainly to my own misguided influence."

"Did you tell him so?" Joanna asked, throat constricting around the words. "Tell him any of this?"

"Of course," Reeves said, gaze locked earnestly with hers. "I gave MacKinnon the one chance I could, then left him to his choice."

And even with Mister Reeves having changed his mind about the most serious of accusations against him, Alex had still chosen to run.

She couldn't give vent to that deep thrust of heartache, not before Mister Reeves. She met his gaze, baffled by the man and his choices. "I don't . . . I don't know what to say."

Mister Reeves shook his head, raising a demurring hand as though she'd praised him. "Let me be completely honest on the matter, lest you think me noble. I set MacKinnon free in large part because of the choice I knew he'd make."

Thoughts darted like hornets through Joanna's mind, angry, wounding with their stings. "You knew he would run? You wanted that?"

"Surely you realize I was jealous of MacKinnon. He had what seemed an instant understanding of you, one that's taken me long to reach."

Her heart gave a thump. "What understanding?"

"That you're merely playing a role here."

Shock held her mute. That he could have gained such insight into her soul made her recoil, as though a snake had uttered speech.

"That may have been a poor choice of words," he said, searching her gaze. "I mean to say . . . I've come to find you far more unhappy with your circumstances than you would have anyone believe. Somehow MacKinnon saw that from the start, though in the end he disregarded the knowledge, whereas I see it now and regard it most highly. I would remedy it, if you'll allow."

Nothing that had passed between them in the months of their acquaintance had prepared Joanna for this, but whatever understanding he'd gleaned, it had come too late.

"Mister Reeves—"

"Please, Miss Carey." Silencing her, he took a knee. "I endured your fascination with MacKinnon, regretted bitterly my choosing him and, yes, set him free that he might go and you forget him. All that is true, but so is this: I still want you for my wife. Will you at last consent?"

She was shaking as she entered the study, where her stepfather sat poring over a ledger, brow furrowed. "Papa?"

He looked up distractedly but nodded her in. She crossed the room and sat on the bed, ran a trembling hand over the coverlet, looked at the conch shell on the desk, then away again quickly. She wished with all her heart Reverend Pauling could be part of the conversation she must now initiate.

"How fares our newest addition this morning?" Papa asked, attention still on the ledger.

"Jory's thriving," she said, smiling briefly as she pictured the two-week-old baby, capped in black curls, skin a lovely deep tan. "As is Mari. And Elijah."

Her stepfather's head lifted briefly. "His training of Demas goes well? Phineas hasn't been to the smithy yet to check."

"That isn't what I was referring to."

His distracted air evaporated. "You're not still wishing MacKinnon was at the forge?"

He and Mister Reeves wished her to forget Alex, but neither seemed willing to let her. "Since you mention him, Papa, should you find Alex, what will you do with him?"

"Sell his indenture. Demas will be our black-smith unless he proves unequal to the task." His gaze dropped to her lap. "Your hands are shaking. What is the matter?"

Joanna swallowed, mouth dry. "Mister Reeves has renewed his proposal of marriage, and I—"

"Left him waiting overlong," Papa finished for her. "Has he not been the model of patience, even while you fancied yourself in love with another? While I've no plans to depart this life soon, I won't live forever. Charlotte isn't likely to marry, or yet desire it. She . . ."

"Is a child," Joanna finished. "And likely always shall be." And this was as fitting an opening as she was likely ever to get.

"That's what I want to talk to you about. Mine and Charlotte's future. My firm and final answer to Mister Reeves was *no*. In fact," she pressed on while Papa's mouth hung open, "I'm asking you to leave Severn to me."

Papa raised a hand, gaunt from the stomach ailment that had abated barely a week ago, and squeezed his temples before he fixed her with a gaze that simmered with impatience. "Whatever it was about MacKinnon that so appealed to you, try to look objectively at the man. He was a rebel and a traitor. Whatever else he might have done, he stole from us, broke his given word, and threw King George's mercy back in his face. Yet Phineas has served me faithfully through all these hardships. He has endured your indifference yet still professes devotion to you!"

His voice had grown heated, bringing tears to Joanna's eyes. "Papa, this isn't about Mister Reeves *or* Alex. I will probably never marry."

"Never? How, then, shall you manage?" Papa challenged, more bewildered now than anything. "You may inherit Severn as an unmarried daughter, but most of those you will need to deal with will shut you out, a woman. How will you manage concerns that lie beyond the pale of the domestic? How will you run our business?"

She'd anticipated this argument at least. "I've convinced Elijah to act as my factor, for when I need the voice and presence of a man."

The sigh that came from Papa was as deep as years. "Joanna, while I applaud your talking Elijah into doing anything besides fathering offspring on my slaves and drinking himself into oblivion, where is this coming from? A broken heart? Or that notion you had months ago about freeing our slaves?"

Joanna stood, praying for the words to come. "Papa, I love you. But my heart's desire is to live a different life than the one you've built.

Here, if I can manage it. I think I can. I think *we* can."

He was standing now as well, arms crossed over a waistcoat that hung too loosely on his frame. "You don't know what you're saying."

"But I do. And I know Reverend Pauling would agree with me. I heard him that night he first fell ill, when Alex carried him to the house. I was coming to check on him and heard your conversation, or part of it."

"You eavesdropped?"

Her face warmed, but she didn't back down. "I heard you speak of me, of Severn. The right man for each of us. I'm telling you, Elijah can be that man. Not as husband, but friend. And Papa, I will manumit our slaves, in time. If it takes me the rest of my life."

He was doing his best to contain it, but she saw she'd angered him. Worse, disappointed him. Even after all their losses, the deaths, every word Reverend Pauling had spoken of the ills of slave-owning, he wasn't ready to lay down his idol of earthly accomplishments.

"And you expect me to name you my heir, knowing what you mean to do with Severn?"

"I hope you will." When he made no reply, she asked, "Will you instead force me to marry Mister Reeves?"

"Joanna," he said, aggrieved and agitated. "I would never force you to marry. But I expect

375

your better sense to prevail . . . in time," he added, echoing her words.

"I've presented you an alternative I can live with, Papa. Please consider it. That's all I'm asking."

29

June 1748

The river had drawn them onward, toward the rising mountains, Alex torn between their siren call and fear of encountering their inhabitants—especially on those mornings when mist wreathed their wooded flanks, settling low in the hollows, and the stillness wrapped him in its cool, moist cloak. Had he been alone he'd have been content to press on westward, risking scalp and life to see what lay beyond the next ridge, a hunger that grew with the feeding. He was keeping them in meat with spear and snare. Jemma kept them in whatever was ripe and edible.

"My grandma taught my mama and other slaves at Severn," she told him when he asked how she knew to tell them apart. "Some got passed to me. Not from Mama. She died having me."

He'd blanched at that, yet it hadn't caused Jemma unease. She hardly ceased talking of the bairn, or the Cherokees. Only one subject shut her up tight as a drum. Her mute, haunted look when he pressed for who fathered the bairn finally curtailed his asking.

His most recent snare had yielded a rabbit,

which he skinned to roast before they set off on a morning he thought must now be June. While the meat cooked, Jemma went to forage in the brush that edged the clearing where they'd slept. All was quiet but for birdsong and the river's rushing until Jemma let out a yelp.

"Mister Alex!"

On his feet at her cry, fearing she'd been snake-bit, he found her squatting in the brush, the trailing hem of her shirt soaked through.

"I wet myself . . ." She clutched her belly, groaning.

Kneeling beside her, he braced her with an arm as she leaned into him. His gut hollowed. "How long has it pained ye?"

"Half the night. Thought my belly was griping over something I ate." The pang passed. She got to her feet.

Alex rose shakily with her. "Your time's come, lass. We'll need water. I'll fetch it. Lie ye down." They hadn't rolled their blankets. He spread his atop hers at the base of the oak under which they'd slept.

She was in the grip of another pain when he returned from filling the canteen. Standing over her, drenched in dread, he gazed at the morning light falling in lush beams across the ridge he'd meant to climb that day.

The breathtaking prospect afforded no comfort, or aid.

The day passed in agony. By the sun's setting Jemma was screaming with each pain. He'd given her a stick to bite down on, but she'd said something rude to that and screamed the louder.

He roasted the rabbit but ate none. Ripped his spare shirt to rags that he soaked to bathe Jemma's face. Kept back enough to wrap the bairn. And waited.

He was kneeling beside her as dusk descended, sick in his gut with uselessness, when an arrow thumped into the tree, inches above his head. With no more warning, the figures spilled from the darkening forest.

Bolting to his feet, Alex stood between Jemma and the painted warriors who formed a half-circle around them. He looked swiftly for the hatchet. It lay on the other side of the fire.

One of the warriors lunged for it himself.

*Her*self. It was a woman, the only one with hair flowing to her waist. Painted like the rest in loops and whorls of red and black, brown legs bared in a breechclout, she came forward into the firelight, halting a few paces from him. One hand gripped a spear, the other his hatchet. Dark eyes menaced in a face strikingly feminine despite the garish paint. She spoke words he couldn't comprehend while the men held back, two with arrows nocked, one with a musket leveled, the rest with spears or tomahawks clenched. Six in all, not counting the woman, whom he wasn't fool enough to discount.

Behind him on the ground, Jemma started another moan.

The men stepped back a pace, leaving Alex and the woman facing each other.

"Ye willna touch her," he said. "Save ye kill me first."

The woman's gaze shifted to Jemma. "Child come."

Stunned by the English words, Alex sought for a coherent reply. "Aye. No—the bairn willna come."

He locked gazes with the woman. Reaching some decision, she tossed aside the hatchet—well beyond his reach—and turned to address the men. She handed her spear to the youngest, then gestured at the fire, saying to Alex, "Go."

When he hesitated, she tapped her chest with a fist. "Help mother."

More weak-kneed with relief than fear, he obeyed. The warriors made a path for him to the fire, where he stood, too wary to sit among them. To a man they were well-built, though he was nearly a head taller than the tallest, a lithe warrior with small eyes deep-set, hair plucked to a scalp-lock above a hatchet-blade face painted black across its upper half. Feathers stood up like a crest from the back of his head. Two bloody scalps, long and black, hung from his belt sash.

Jemma screamed. Alex whirled to find her clutching one of the woman's hands, face contorted. The woman's other hand moved over the mound of Jemma's belly, sure as a midwife's.

Exhaustion shuddered through him. He had to sit down, never mind he was surrounded by warriors who looked as if they'd gut him should the woman give them leave. Two of their number, the oldest and Hatchet-Face, took up station, one to either side of him. Alex ignored them, his gaze on Jemma, but looked away when the examination became more intimate.

The warriors put their backs to the ongoing drama, except the youngest, a lad with the lankiness of one in his teens, who alone seemed interested in the birthing. The rest watched Alex with looks ranging from mistrust to hostility. He'd expected to be bound, but they'd refrained, as if they knew the only binding needed was Jemma, whose screams went on as the night deepened, growing hoarse and weak despite the woman's efforts.

The youngest warrior looked frequently over his shoulder at Jemma, face gleaming in the light of a fire that now and again he fed with sticks. The lad had stiffened more than once, looking ready to leap to his feet. At last he spoke, addressing the oldest warrior standing at Alex's shoulder, who gave a gruff reply. The young one shook his head, features set in determination.

The warriors followed the conversation, faces disapproving, but before any who reached to stop him could do so, the young one was on his feet and crossing the clearing to the oak tree where Jemma labored. The woman looked up, painted face grim. The lad spoke. The woman hesitated, then nodded.

"What's he doing?" Alex started to rise. Firm hands held him down.

He struggled briefly before resigning himself to watching as the youth crouched beside Jemma, placed his hands flat against her belly, and muttered, "*Fah-der-in-heh-ven. Fah-der-in-heh-ven. Fah-der-in-heh-ven.*"

The lad repeated the phrase, rocking and praying—surely what he was doing—until Jemma gave a cry and sat up, grasping the woman's hand and one of the lad's. The woman spoke. Jemma nodded violently. Together they pulled her to her knees. At an order from the woman, the young warrior, looking no longer determined but terrified, got behind Jemma to support her. By the evident strain on her face, she was bearing down.

"Father in heaven?" Alex muttered, drawing the gazes of the warriors nearest him, now talking excitedly among themselves.

The woman was speaking, too, terse and urgent. Alex didn't want to look again but did, to see Jemma fallen back into the lad's arms and the woman with a slick and squalling bairn in her hands.

Alex was too stunned to rise.

The woman washed the bairn and wrapped it in a skin. She laid it beside Jemma, then came to stand before him. She pointed at mother and child. "You?"

Did they think he'd fathered the bairn?

"The child isna mine." Whether she understood or not, he'd had enough of their restraint. Ignoring grasping hands, he rose. At a word from the woman, they let him go.

He squatted beside Jemma. "*Mo nighean?*"

"Mister Alex." Her voice was a thread. "Got me a boy."

"Aye, he's bonny," he said, though he'd barely glimpsed the bairn in the oak's shadow. The young warrior still knelt beside Jemma, protective as a new father. Alex eyed him warily. "Jemma, d'ye ken whether these people are Cherokees?"

Her eyes drifted shut. "I hope so . . ."

He lifted the bairn from her unresisting arms. "Jemma?"

She was fast asleep. He eased her onto her side and lay the bairn beside her, then rose to face the woman and her warriors, all now on their feet.

"His name's Runs-Far," Jemma told him, nodding at the youngest of the warriors, all of whom were still asleep or quiet at the fire. "He knows some

English. See that one with the gray in his hair? That his daddy. He ain't their leader, though. It's the woman!"

"I'd worked out that much." Alex knelt in matted oak leaves beside Jemma, who was propped against the tree, cradling her son. "D'ye ken what they're doing hereabouts, all painted?"

Or they had been. Most had washed their faces and bodies. It was morning, gray and overcast. The warriors had stayed with them through the night, always a few awake and watchful. Though the men ignored Jemma—save for Runs-Far—they'd given Alex little rest. Without apparent provocation, now and again one would feign to attack him. The hatchet-faced warrior started it, with a silent rush he'd made no attempt to conceal. Alex had leapt up to meet it. Those awake watched with interest as they grappled, struggling for mastery of Hatchet-Face's knife— until a word from the woman broke them apart and the warrior swaggered back to his place by the fire, leaving Alex tensed, blood singing but unspilled.

Through the night, others followed Hatchet-Face's lead, leaving Alex bruised and scraped. He'd given back the same. Once he'd turned a blade and drew a bloody score down a warrior's arm. He'd expected swift—and deadly—retaliation, but the warrior merely withdrew to tend the wound.

The woman watched it all, gaze keen with speculation.

Near dawn he'd been allowed to sleep at Jemma's side, but roused when she woke in need of tending her son, who was making urgent noises of hunger. With a confidence—and immodesty— Alex found disconcerting, Jemma pulled down the neck of her shirt and put the infant to a breast.

After a moment she giggled. "Look at him. *She* showed me how to do it." Jemma canted her head at the woman, asleep nearby.

"What do they mean to do with us?" he asked. "That lad give ye any notion?"

Jemma watched her baby nurse. "Reckon they'd have killed us by now if they meant to?"

In no wise certain, he stayed near Jemma, keeping the fire in view. "How do they ken the English they do? From traders, d'ye think?"

"I tried asking. Runs-Far pointed at himself, said something like *tee-muh-tee*."

"What's that mean?"

"Mister Alex, I got no idea. Maybe we 'bout to find out."

The woman had sat up, wide awake. Ignoring Alex, she appraised Jemma in the graying light. "You walk?"

Jemma nodded. The woman moved to the fire. Alex glared after her. "She means for ye to walk? Where?"

"Wherever they going, I reckon."

"*Can* ye walk?"

"I'm sore as kingdom come, but reckon I better try."

Alex crouched on the balls of his feet. "No, Jemma. I willna let them take ye."

Jemma reared back her head. "Don't cause trouble, Mister Alex. Just go along. I want to."

"I canna let—" He broke off his words as the woman returned. She'd brought them each a strip of jerked meat to gnaw.

"*S'gi*," Jemma said with a smile the woman returned.

"*Hawa*," she said.

Hoping Jemma's word meant *thanks,* Alex echoed it. "Ye're learning their words already?" he asked once the woman drew off again.

"Just what I said. I think she said *you're welcome.* I mean to get Runs-Far to tell me more."

As soon as Alex helped Jemma up, two warriors flanked him. He swept the clearing with an assessing gaze. Before he could decide whether to take down the nearest or make a lunge for the one who'd left his hunting knife lying, Hatchet-Face took up his knapsack, then lowered it quickly, looking at Alex with surprise.

Mouth set in determination, the warrior hefted the pack again.

Everyone was watching, Alex noted. He could take Hatchet-Face now, if he could get free of the two gripping his arms. He shot a glance at

Jemma. She was glaring back at him, shaking her head in warning.

Iron clanked as Hatchet-Face dropped the knapsack, neck veins standing out from the strain.

The oldest warrior was next to give it a go. His brows shot high when he tested the knapsack's weight. He gave it a half-hearted try before setting it down. After that all the warriors had a turn. It evolved into a congenial competition, with hooting and shoving, until at last the woman, sounding very like an exasperated mother, said something that made them desist.

Hatchet-Face rummaged through the knapsack and removed the hammer and other implements. Alex thought he meant to parcel them out, but the older warrior stopped him. Looking displeased, Hatchet-Face replaced the tools, motioned Alex over, and gestured for him to don it.

He did so, well used to the weight. A few of the warriors made noises of appreciation.

They let him carry the pack, his hands tied before him. Jemma's son was bound against her in a sling the woman fashioned.

The lass came up beside him as the warriors filed out of camp, headed westward along the river's course. The woman waited until Runs-Far started after the warriors, then gestured for Alex and Jemma to follow. Runs-Far glanced back as they started off through a stretch of woods.

"Yon laddie seems taken with ye," Alex said

to Jemma's crown of tousled hair. "Why do the other men keep their distance?"

The reply came from behind him. "Woman bleed. Luck bad—for man."

Alex glanced back at the woman, who wore no face paint now. She was older than he by a decade, he guessed, though vigorous and strong, with thick hair smoothly plaited.

"Blood and bad luck *gang* together, do they?"

She didn't reply.

Jemma said, "I don't know. The others seem vexed with Runs-Far this morning."

Recognizing his name, the lad glanced back again.

"Anything else ye talk of I should ken?"

"I asked Runs-Far were they Cherokees. He nodded yes, then called them all something sounded like *Ani-un-wiya*."

If they *were* Cherokees, then the lass had got her wish. She'd found her people, and all signs pointed to their meaning to keep her. Judging by the looks of those glancing back to see he came along docilely, his own fate seemed less certain. They'd been testing him in the night, but for what purpose he'd no notion.

30

July 1748

Despite the uncertainty awaiting at journey's end, with each day they traveled deeper into the mountains, Alex regretted the situation less. The rounded, sometimes craggy peaks were somehow both akin to Scotland's windswept heights, yet not at all like them. Here were slopes so thickly wooded no sunlight penetrated, until they emerged along a high ridgeline or bald. Then the prospect of layer upon layer of ridges and coves, unfolding before his eyes like ribbons tossed by giant hands, would make him catch his breath and marvel.

"You good feeling here?"

He'd been standing with his face lifted to the sun, wind caressing his skin, the air in his lungs pure intoxication, but looked down to see the woman come to stand beside him on a promontory overlooking one of those many-layered views. Jemma, picking up their language with studied resolve, had told Runs-Far about her grandmother, Looks-At-The-Sun. He'd relayed the information to the woman—called Black-bird—who thought she recalled a woman by that name. Jemma was beside herself.

"Runs-Far's calling me their word for *walnut*," she'd said their third day out. "On account I'm colored like one."

A nut-brown maid if ever he'd seen one, she'd taken to motherhood as she'd done the Cherokees. The furtive shadow of slavery was slipping from her as they moved westward. Not surprisingly. The very air of that place tasted of freedom. Blackbird had ordered him left unbound that morning.

"Aye," he told her now. "A verra good feeling." He tried to read her gaze, keen to discover what she meant to do with them, but she moved away to speak to the warriors who'd paused to share the water skins among them.

Jemma appeared beside him, the bairn snug in his sling. "Wish some folk at Severn could see this."

Thinking of one in particular, Alex looked westward where ridge and valley dipped and broke like the cresting of rough seas.

"You thinking of Miss Joanna?" When he looked sharply down at her, Jemma made a *tsk*ing sound. "I saw how you was with her."

"I'll tell ye something of Joanna," he said, "then I dinna mean again to speak of her. I wanted to take her away from Severn. She wouldna think of leaving it."

"That surprised you? Then you don't know her like you think."

Leaving him gazing after her, Jemma went to Blackbird and asked for water, which she was readily given.

Alex had lost track of how far they'd traveled. Summer had deepened, likely nearing a year since the *Charlotte-Ann* dropped anchor in Wilmington, with him thinking seven years at sea would be his lot—unless he escaped back to Barra and his life before the Rising, a life that now seemed as substantial as a dream. Even the months at Severn seemed a lifetime ago. Still, the image of Joanna remained vivid in his mind. Ought he to have stayed, given Carey a chance to realize his innocence, found a way to help Joanna? That notion she'd had of a different sort of life there, had it been so impossible?

He shook off the nagging questions. Whatever had existed between them, there'd been no place to take it, no way for it to flourish. Not at Severn.

The reverend didna ask ye to marry her, only protect her.

"*Wheest,*" he said aloud, drawing a curious look from Runs-Far's father, Fishing Hawk.

They'd struck a well-worn trail and followed it for two days before, halted for the night, Jemma informed Alex they'd be arriving in the Cherokees' town the following day. "There's other towns, bigger, but I've a notion Blackbird's someone important in theirs."

The next morning the warriors' spirits were markedly lifted.

"You seen them scalps hanging on their sashes?" Jemma had asked him their first night on the trail. "Blackbird led this band against some other Indians that killed her brother. I think it was her brother." Not until that final morning did Jemma tell him different. "I found out more about him that was killed. He weren't Blackbird's brother. He was her husband."

Alex turned to look at the woman, sitting some distance away plaiting her hair. She wore a scalp at her belt. Who had killed her husband? And why?

Jemma didn't have those answers.

That morning Runs-Far walked beside her, the two chatting in a hodgepodge of Cherokee and English. Alex payed them little heed. Around every bend in the trail, he expected to see whatever passed for a town for these people.

When at last they reached it, spread out below the descending trail they traversed, he wasn't prepared for its size—a riverside sprawl of log-built structures, dozens of them, some covered in reddish clay, with smoking fires outside hide-covered doors shaded by pole awnings. In the town's center rose a large, round-sided, thatched building surrounded by cleared ground, while out toward the town's edges cultivated acres of corn spread, interspersed with groves of fruit trees.

Men, women, children, and dogs moved about town and fields.

The place looked busy as a beehive. One about to be overturned.

His heart gave a thump, but he masked his apprehension. If his experience of them told him anything, these people prized stoicism. Though fear coiled within, he determined to show none.

Beside him, Jemma bounced on her toes, scanning the scene as if someone might spot her and come running with arms spread. None did, but many stopped their activity to stare.

Steeling himself, Alex raised his gaze to the sweeping bend of the river that cradled the town, cutting through a narrow valley. At its widest the river rivaled the Yadkin, which they'd followed to its mountain headwaters days ago and left behind. Beyond the river's curving banks, more mountains rose, lower than those they'd crossed.

"*Tanasi*." Blackbird had come up beside him, looking with pride at her home, though a shadow of grief crossed her eyes.

Tanasi. Did she mean river or town? The land itself?

He'd no time to ask. Blackbird took him by the arm and marched him to the front of her warriors, Jemma trotting to keep near. They wound down the trail and entered the town's outskirts, Alex front and center, conspicuous as an egret among corbies.

A flock of corbies was called a *murder.*

The untimely thought struck as the first yelps and ululations rose from Blackbird and her band, answered by those gathering to welcome their return. The warriors had tied their hair trophies to poles, lofting them high as he and Jemma were paraded around the open center of the town once, twice, before halting outside the big thatched structure.

Cowed at last by the press of so many strange Indians, Jemma clung to him. He gripped her shoulder. Beneath his hand she trembled.

While some of Blackbird's warriors were pulled away by those in the crowd, Runs-Far shrugged off the hands reaching for him, remaining in the space broadening between them and the circle of brown faces moving back a pace, and another, until they stood alone. At a word from Blackbird, he retreated to the crowd's inner edge. She hadn't released Alex. Was this her staking some sort of claim on him? Jemma and the bairn as well? Or protecting them?

Throughout their progression through the town, Alex had been keenly aware of the Indians' reactions to him—wariness, suspicion, fear—yet no hand but Blackbird's had touched him. Having expected to be met with taunts, even blows, it left him bewildered, every nerve on edge.

As the hum of voices settled, a disturbance arose behind Alex. Turning, he saw Hatchet-

Face—whose actual name, he'd learned, was Cane-Splitter—shouldering into the inner ring. Those nearby made way, gazing on the tall warrior with admiration and respect.

Ignoring them, Cane-Splitter halted and glared at Blackbird's back, a gaze so intense Alex couldn't imagine the woman wasn't scorched.

If she felt it, she gave no sign.

Following her lead, Alex faced the direction Blackbird gazed—toward the thatched building, as from its entrance a man emerged, appearing almost magically from its shadow. His long hair showed more white than black, though his back was straight and his gait fluid. Dressed in plain moccasins, deerskin leggings, and breechclout, his only mark of distinction was the fine blanket trimmed in red draping his shoulders.

The man came out of the structure's shade and halted to speak with Blackbird. Then his gaze shifted, appraising first Alex, then Jemma. The bairn jerked in his sling, emitting a hungry mewl. Noting the child, the blanketed man asked a question. Whatever Blackbird replied made a smile twitch his lips. She motioned to Runs-Far, who stepped forward and joined the conversation.

Still pressed against Alex's side, Jemma gave a start. "I caught my grandma's name."

The blanketed man spoke a final word, then turned back to the thatched structure.

Blackbird tugged at Alex's arm to follow. He'd

taken but a step when behind them Cane-Splitter called out. Blackbird kept moving but turned an impatient glance over her shoulder and replied. Alex looked back in time to see Cane-Splitter's narrow face blaze with anger before he mastered his features, turned his back, and pushed through the crowd beginning to disperse.

"Duck, Mister Alex!"

He obeyed Jemma's warning in time to miss cracking his skull on the lintel as they entered.

Once his eyes adjusted to the dimness within, he recognized the place for a meeting house, built to hold a great number of people.

Few had gathered now. The warriors of Blackbird's band—minus Cane-Splitter—plus four old men and three women, arranged themselves behind Alex and Jemma, who stood where Blackbird placed them near the structure's center. Openings in the high roof let sunlight through dusty rafters and a double ring of sturdy posts sunk into the earthen floor. Fishing Hawk and Runs-Far, and a woman who was probably Runs-Far's mother, stood nearest. The man in the red-trimmed blanket faced them.

Blackbird released Alex and addressed the assemblage, speaking with ease and dignity. She smiled briefly at Jemma, then looked at Alex. Whatever she said next caused a murmur to ripple through the gathering, whether favorable he couldn't gauge. He dropped his gaze to Jemma, but she was preoccupied with the bairn, fussing now and resisting her attempts to suckle him.

The discussion seemed to have broadened, permitting all present to engage. Fishing Hawk spoke, then one of the older men, two of the women . . .

Through it all Jemma's bairn whimpered. "Why won't he eat?" she muttered, shifting him to her shoulder, patting his back. "Come on, now."

The bairn let out a wail. Discussion paused. Alex felt the stares. Whatever was being decided, he didn't want the bairn's untimely cries affecting it. Jemma must have felt the same. Tears gathered in her eyes.

"Give him here. Maybe it'll help." He'd never held the bairn while he was awake, but Jemma was desperate enough to try. When he got the wee laddie cradled along a forearm, tiny head spanned by a palm, he grinned down at him.

Jemma's son eyed him, clenched his face, and loosed an ear-piercing scream of outrage. With his own cheeks shot through with heat, Alex looked up from the furious little face to see every eye watching. A woman in the back of the gathering spoke loud enough to make herself heard. Cackles of laughter erupted, breaking the tension.

"Give him back," Jemma hissed. Alex complied.

Wincing at the racket, Red-Blanket-Man spoke

briefly, then dismissed them. Looking satisfied, Blackbird shooed them back into sunlight, the bairn's crying drawing stares though no one followed as they trailed Blackbird—save for Runs-Far, who reached Jemma's side and commenced whispering.

"What's he telling ye?" Alex asked.

Jemma jostled her son, starting to quiet at last. "I don't know. I think Blackbird's taking us home."

Relief was sullied by a dozen unanswered questions. "Who was the man with the red-edged blanket?"

"Their chief. You didn't catch that?"

"D'ye ken his name?"

Jemma turned to Runs-Far as they passed between lodges where wide-eyed children stared. She relayed the question, pantomiming one-handed the swirl of a cloak. After Runs-Far spoke she turned back to say, "Best I make it, he called Crooked Branch."

Outside a lodge that looked identical to every other scattered about, Blackbird halted and faced them. "You here. Good maybe. Or no."

Alex wasn't certain he liked the sound of that, but Runs-Far looked pleased. He spoke to Jemma, and the lass's mouth dropped open. She shut it, but her chin trembled.

"What?" he asked, guts tying themselves in knots.

"They letting us stay, Mister Alex," Jemma said, and burst into tears.

So did the bairn.

Blackbird motioned to the shaggy hide across the lodge's door, the biggest hide Alex had ever seen. "Go. See other."

Alex didn't budge. "Other?"

Blackbird spoke again, but with the bairn's crying Alex didn't catch a word. "What's she saying, Jemma?"

Jemma sniffled. "Got someone else living with her, I think."

"Children?"

Blackbird pointed at him. "Slave."

The word was unmistakable. Alex went cold, until he realized Blackbird was pointing *past* him, at two figures approaching along the path between her lodge and its neighbor. One was a lad, about seven years old, the other a man, back stooped under a load of deadwood bound by twisted cords.

Blackbird barked a word the lad ignored, but it brought the man to a halt. He raised his head. A white man.

Alex looked closer at the wood-bearer. A weary face, thinner than he'd last seen, but he recognized those shadowed blue eyes, and when it came, that smile, ablaze with amazement and delight.

"Reverend Pauling!" Startled by Jemma's outcry, the bairn's fussing ceased.

Runs-Far was babbling in evident excitement. When words failed him, he led Jemma to the reverend, who lowered his burden to the ground.

"Timothy. You've brought friends."

"Timothy?" Jemma echoed.

Runs-Far nodded, pointing at himself. *"Tee-muh-tee."*

"My first convert among his people," the reverend explained.

Jemma laughed. "Reverend Pauling, how you come to be here?"

Blackbird had watched this reunion, her surprise unconcealed. When she again motioned to the door-hide and the lad—her son?—held it open, Alex turned to Pauling, the last person he'd expected to encounter in this place. "No doubt ye've a story to tell, Reverend. But I think Blackbird wishes us to go inside now."

Joy wreathed Pauling's features as he reached for the bundled wood. "Then we best do as she bids, and do it heartily as unto the Lord. After all, I am her obedient servant."

31

August 1748

Reverend Pauling had yet to respond to a single letter since departing Severn nearly a year ago. It was unlike him, and concerning. That worry was a constant backdrop to the strain of Joanna's days.

Mister Reeves had taken her refusal little better than had Papa, though there'd been no attempt at dissuasion, save a single question put to her soon after: "Is it Moon? Has he now captured your capricious heart?"

Maintaining her composure, she'd told him he couldn't be farther off the mark. "I've plans to marry no one, Mister Reeves. Severn shall have my heart—a thing you can understand, surely?"

"To remake into your shortsighted image," he'd retorted. "Captain Carey told me of your scheme to bring down Severn around his ears. It won't happen, Joanna. It's foolish to think otherwise."

Since that exchange, the strain between them had grown so pronounced they could hardly abide one another's presence, a forbearance put to infrequent test. It was the height of summer, the crops demanding attention as well as the forest, still being tapped and lightwood gathered, though the need for lumber had ceased with the mill's destruction. She'd overheard Papa and Mister Reeves discussing its rebuilding, but nothing had come of it, for Papa was again taken ill.

"That same ailment back for another go round," Azuba had said.

They were treating it with the careful diet and steeped herbs they'd used before, which had apparently effected a cure. Joanna prayed it would again; Mister Reeves, on a rare occasion he'd addressed more than two words to her, had all but accused her of being the cause. "You've thrown a wrench in his plans. In more ways than one."

Had she contributed to Papa's relapse? It had come close on the heels of her answer to Mister Reeves's proposal, and telling Papa her reasons for it.

Would that she had kept them to herself.

Halfway down the stairs, descending to face the day's demands, she felt the loss of Alex afresh. He would have listened to all she had to say on the matter, then with a few choice words blown away the fog. Mercilessly, if need be.

Thinking of him only made matters worse. He might have helped her find conviction to do as her conscience demanded, but freedom had proved his first love. Why did she pine for a man who stole from them, ran, and never looked back?

A man unjustly accused . . .

Her mind had yet to cease chasing itself in circles.

She'd passed Mister Reeves's door softly but suspected he was long up and gone to the fields. Azuba wasn't in the house, Charlotte still abed. She checked on her stepfather and found him sleeping too. He'd been awake earlier, judging by the breakfast tray beside the bed, its meager contents picked over.

She stood at his bedside, worry tightening its bands.

A profusion of long white hairs shed on his pillow snagged her gaze. More than was normal to lose in a night's sleep.

She prayed for him, then left his room with the tray, but had barely shut the door when Mister Reeves's voice caught her ear—a sound out of place in the house these days. His voice paused, and a childish giggle erupted.

Joanna halted in the study doorway. On the bed that had last been the reverend's, Mister Reeves sat with a book open on his lap. Pressed close, still in her nightshift, was Charlotte.

"What is this?"

Her sister looked up. "Phineas is reading Aesop's Fables but he's doing it silly!" She giggled again, looking adoringly at Mister Reeves.

Unease coiled in Joanna's belly. "Charlotte, you should be dressing. In our room."

"Of course." Mister Reeves rose, leaving Charlotte pouting on the bed. He returned the book to its shelf and crossed the study, gaze fixed on Joanna, unsettling in its intensity. Not a cold look. Or censuring. He looked hungry.

Mister Reeves stopped before her. "How is Captain Carey this morning?" he asked, as if nothing unpleasant had lately passed between them.

"You haven't spoken to him?"

He nodded at the tray gripped between them. "You have?"

"He's sleeping." Since the man deigned to speak to her with some semblance of civility, she added, "I think we should send for a physician."

She told him of the hair shed on Papa's pillow.

"You'd have me leave the fields and ride for a physician over a few shed hairs? Surely he'll recover, Miss Carey, as he has in the past."

"I hope so, but—"

"He's an old man whose hair is thinning; that is all. And I've lingered long enough this morning. We're still topping the tobacco and it's nigh harvesting time." With a last glance at Charlotte, who'd slipped off the bed and hurried to Joanna, he stepped around her and went out the back door.

Charlotte tugged her sleeve. "Will you finish the story?"

Before Joanna could reply, Sybil entered the

house, stopping when she saw the tray. "I come to see did Master Carey eat anything."

"Not much." Joanna drew in a breath. "Sybil, take Charlotte upstairs and see her dressed for the day. I'll take the tray to the kitchen. We'll finish the story this evening, Charlotte."

Sybil reached for Charlotte's hand. "You'll tell Phoebe what I'm doing?"

"Yes. Is Azuba in the kitchen?"

"Yes ma'am. Talking with Mari and Phoebe, last I seen."

Joanna watched the pair retreat down the hallway. "Sybil? Would you remain in the house until I or Azuba return?"

Sybil stopped to face her. "All right, Miss Joanna. I do that."

She wasn't sure why she'd added the request. Finding Charlotte alone with Mister Reeves troubled her, but everything felt oddly shaded these days, like light falling in the wrong direction through a once familiar room, casting shadows where none should be.

Case in point—on the way to the kitchen, a hammer's clanging pierced the air and her mind filled with vivid memories of Alex, shirtsleeves rolled, tanned skin glistening, blue eyes seeing her . . . and she dropped the tray on the path and put a hand to her mouth.

It would never again be Alex.

Papa's uneaten breakfast lay scattered. Swiftly

she gathered up utensils, bowls, as much of their spilled contents as could be scraped up. When she entered the kitchen and set the tray on the worktable, the three women present didn't look her way or break off their conversation.

She cleared her throat. "Phoebe, I'd like to try some broth for Papa's dinner."

Phoebe, Azuba, and Marigold sprang apart, startled as a deer in the woods.

"Miss Joanna. Thought you was Sybil come back." Phoebe came forward, hesitating when she got a look at the tray's disheveled contents.

Marigold crossed to Jory, nestled in a basket, waving tiny hands.

Azuba hadn't moved.

The kitchen's warmth hummed with tension as Phoebe bustled about the hearth. "You want broth for Master Carey?" She reached for a kettle and sent it clattering across the bricks.

Marigold jumped at the noise. Jory squawked.

Joanna fixed her gaze on Azuba. "What were you discussing when I came in? Had it to do with Papa?"

Nodding, Azuba turned to Phoebe. "You keep an eye on Jory whilst Mari and I speak with Miss Joanna?"

Marigold looked up, seeming to know what Azuba intended.

Phoebe made a strangled noise and went after the dropped kettle. Whatever Azuba meant to tell her, Phoebe was afraid for her to know.

"Come out to the orchard," Azuba bid her. "We can talk more free."

Under the leafy boughs of the peach trees, Marigold shared what she'd witnessed that morning. "Sybil took breakfast to Master Carey in his room. After she go I spied a bowl of porridge on the worktable meant to be on his tray. I run it to the house, passing Sybil coming back. She tell me Master Carey sleeping, so go quiet. I did. Doubt he heard me open the door."

"Papa?" Joanna asked.

Marigold shook her head. "Master Carey was sleeping sound. Mister Reeves was in the room. He weren't when Sybil went in—I asked her."

"I suspect he was checking if Papa was awake."

Marigold shook her head more forceful this time. "He weren't looking at Master Carey. He was bent over the breakfast tray. I couldn't see what he was doing."

"Looking to see if Papa had eaten?"

"Seconds after the food was left and him sleeping?" Azuba asked. "Go on, Mari. Tell the rest."

"My foot creaked a floorboard," Mari said. "Mister Reeves spun round. He snatched the porridge away and told me to get out. So I got out."

"When Phoebe heard what happened," Azuba

said, "she told us this ain't the only time Mister Reeves either took Master Carey's food to serve or else was hovering once it was set out."

Joanna scrambled to rearrange the details of Marigold's account into a more innocent pattern than they portended. And couldn't. She felt a pit open beneath her, and the horrible sensation of falling.

In that moment an infant's hungry cry erupted. Phoebe came around the side of the kitchen, Jory screaming in her arms. At Joanna's nod, Marigold hastened to her child, leaving her and Azuba at the orchard's edge.

"Azuba, what do we do?"

"When Master Carey's food's served," Azuba said, clearly having thought on the matter, "do your best to be there until he's eaten it or says he wants no more. If not you, I'll be. Give it time, and we'll see what happens. That's all I'm saying, but I know you understand me."

Though his back was turned and he was making a din at the anvil, Demas seemed to sense her in the smithy doorway.

"Is Elijah in back?" Joanna asked when the hammer stilled and he turned.

Demas held her gaze.

"Mister 'Lijah at the stable, last I know." That well-bottom voice rumbled through Joanna like thunder. "Master Reeves at the house?"

"He's gone to the tobacco fields. If I see him, do you—"

"Where your sister at? Someone with her?"

This time that thunder-growl trailed lightning in its wake, striking Joanna's nerves. "Why would you—"

Footsteps scuffed to a halt behind her. "Joanna?"

Off-footed by Demas's interest in Charlotte, she turned to Elijah, recalling the conversation in the orchard, and its precedence. "Here you are. Good. I need to speak to you."

Elijah nodded her toward the pasture beyond the smithy yard. Joanna followed him to the railed fence. Demas's hammer rang again.

"How is he getting on?"

"He doesn't balk at the work, but he's not happy away from Reeves." Elijah scrutinized her. "Speaking of . . . has Reeves done something amiss?"

"You know about it?" Joanna asked, startled.

"Do *ye?*"

She'd the sudden suspicion they were speaking of different things. "Elijah, did something happen between you and Mister Reeves?"

"I thought ye must have heard of it, from Mari."

"I haven't—not about you." She crossed her arms, waiting, and listened while he told her how Mister Reeves had come to the smithy soon after she'd refused his proposal and asked Elijah if he was the reason behind it.

"And to warn me away from ye, whether I was or wasn't, that your plans for Severn were . . . I'll not repeat the words he used, but he made it clear that if I helped ye further them, I'd be sorry for it."

"He threatened you?"

"Not in so many words, but I got the message."

Her heart was pounding, her hands gone chill. And she hadn't even told him *her* suspicions. "Does Papa know?"

"Not from me. Mari does. And Demas, as he was there in the smithy pretending like he couldn't hear a word."

"Why didn't you tell me?"

He looked at her, scarred in so many ways beyond the physical, but feeling again like the brother she'd thought of him before the accident. "Ye've enough weighing on ye, Joanna, and what difference would it have made?"

"I don't know. But now I'm going to tell you something, and I need you to listen until I'm through before you question."

Elijah's brows plunged low. "Go on."

She related the conversation in the orchard and judged by his expression he'd been told nothing of the matter as yet.

"Joanna, I'll tell ye what I think, but ye won't like it."

Had she ever thought she might?

"I don't believe Reeves has had our best interests in mind. Not from the beginning."

She grasped for understanding. "Severn owns his devotion, you mean? Not Papa?"

"Devotion?" Elijah barked a laugh. "No. The very opposite."

"What are you saying? He hates the place?"

"Aye. And ye. Me. Even Captain Carey."

Joanna blanched, even as she shook her head in denial—of that last assertion, at least. "What has Papa ever done Mister Reeves but good?"

Elijah's stare was bleak. "That I cannot answer, but I think he does hate us all, Joanna."

"Elijah . . ." She reached for him, as if the ground she stood upon would topple her for its shaking. But Elijah wasn't done speaking upheaval to her soul.

"Another thing. I've no way to prove it . . ." He raised the arm that ended short of a hand, running the stump of his wrist down the scarred side of his face. "But I'm fair certain it was Reeves did this to me."

32

August 1748

That Pauling was Blackbird's slave was undoubted. That Jemma and her bairn were not was equally clear. Murkier in that regard was Alex's status.

The three were out beyond the edge of Crooked Branch's town, in the cornfield belonging to Blackbird's Longhair Clan. For the past two days Pauling had been sent to gather in the ripening corn. Jemma lent a hand when not tending the bairn, though no one asked it of her. Blackbird had asked Alex to help the reverend but in such a way he might have refused had he wished. Though Pauling remained cheerful no matter how he was treated, the ordeal of his capture had taken a toll, and Alex felt compelled to help the man whenever he could.

Pauling had accounted for his presence there that first night together in Blackbird's lodge.

"I left Mountain Laurel in early November and was nigh the Wagon Road when that old thorn in my side overtook me. A band of Cherokees found me as I was rather feebly attempting to saddle the horse you shoed for me—which is no longer in my possession, alas. My apologies to Edmund for the loss," Pauling had added with a glance at Alex.

A glance too rife with questions for Alex to hold.

Pauling had later learned from Runs-Far that the warriors who captured him had intended him for torture, a fate Pauling had suspected. Too weak to escape, he'd determined to make the most of what time he had.

"I set myself to learn their speech, and as we journeyed and the fever lessened its grip, I began to tell them of a God who walked the rocky trails of this earth." But it was Pauling's willingness to obey their menial commands despite his suffering that won respect from the warriors—enough that by the time they'd reached Crooked Branch's town, they'd changed their minds about him. "I was given to Blackbird, whose husband wasn't long deceased."

"We know," Jemma said. "But not how."

"He died on a hunting foray near the end of the previous winter, killed by Tuscaroras. Cane-Splitter led the hunt. He's Wolf Clan, as was Blackbird's husband."

Alex had seen little of Cane-Splitter since their arrival. Those few times, he'd sensed the man's dislike of him simmering. "So Blackbird took ye. Why a slave, though?"

"She'd hardly see me as a replacement for a husband. She needed someone to help with chores, and for the boy," he added with a fond look at her son, Little Thunder, asleep on a bench built into the lodge's wall, under which belongings and provisions were stored in an array of baskets woven of canes. "She's to be made *ghigau*. Soon, I believe."

It was a word Alex didn't know. "*Ghigau*?"

"It means Beloved Woman. Blackbird will become the head of the women's council, have a seat with the chiefs, and a voice on any matter of importance. It's the highest honor a Cherokee woman can attain."

Alex was suitably impressed, but as he'd listened to the reverend, it had struck him—the strength he'd seen Blackbird display from their first encounter wasn't so different from what he'd glimpsed in Joanna Carey. Though if Joanna was a fledgling tottering on the edge of her nest, wary of trying her wings, Blackbird was an eagle soaring high. But give Joanna time and freedom to spread those wings . . .

Not verra likely among the folk on the Cape Fear.

"So here ye've been since," he had said, attempting to banish thoughts of Joanna, "serving Blackbird and trying to convert the Cherokees into proper Christians while ye do? Did ye never attempt escape?"

"I'm fed and clothed," Pauling had replied. "I've work to do and souls to love. Although it burdens me, missing those I've left behind. My sister. The churches I meant to visit on my journey. The Careys."

"I know *they* wishing you was there." Needing no prompting, Jemma had spilled every woe befallen the Careys since Pauling's visit. Hearing it poured out in a troubling stream, Alex felt the losses they'd suffered as he hadn't since the Cherokees found them, distracting him from his warring sense of relief and guilt.

"Then the mill caught fire," Jemma said, gasping in a breath, "and killed poor Jim, and Mister Alex got blamed, never mind it weren't his fault. They shut him in the smokehouse, and I don't know what would've come next if he hadn't got away. When I seen Mister Alex set on running, I took my chance and hightailed it after him. He let me come along once he caught me. We went to that place you know, Mountain Laurel, then moved on, and I'd about talked Mister Alex into taking me to the Cherokees when they found us, like that Mister Cameron said they would."

It was a tale of many plans in shambles, Jemma's the sole exception, to hear her tell it.

Pauling had cut troubled eyes toward her bairn, the same question in his gaze that had been in Alex's mind for weeks. But instead he asked, "What of Joanna? Did she believe you set the fire?"

"He don't like talking 'bout her," Jemma supplied when Alex remained tight-lipped.

"We must," Pauling insisted. "Setting aside that you broke your indenture, you made a promise to me concerning her."

"I said I'd bear your concerns mind," Alex said, bristling. "Ye kent as well as I how little I could do for her."

"Was friendship beyond that pale?"

"Did ye not hear Jemma tell the tale? They locked me in the smokehouse—bound for worse. I'd become another weight upon Joanna's shoulders, a stumbling in her path. So I removed myself."

Little Thunder had stirred on his bed, disturbed by their voices. Alex lowered his. "I'd have taken her far from Severn and its miseries, but she wouldna come."

"Joanna is committed to those entrusted to her care, Charlotte first among them. Would you have taken both Edmund's daughters from him? Broken his heart as well as his trust?"

"Told you," Jemma said when Alex merely glared. "He don't like talking 'bout Miss Joanna."

"Then tell me of Edmund," Pauling pressed.

"What of him?"

Pauling briefly reminded him of Carey's struggle after the death of Joanna's mother and their son, Jemma nodding all the while. "In the end his faith in the Almighty sustained him. Does he hold to it still?"

Alex was struck by a memory of the man, detaining him in his study after the tar kiln's explosion and the death of the old slave, Grandpa Jo. Carey had offered a tentative trust, or the beginnings of it, allowing Alex to glimpse his inner battle. The man had seemed determined then to conquer that shadow.

That was before the mill fire and his internment in the smokehouse. Who could say what Carey or Joanna or any of them had endured since?

"I dinna ken the workings of the man's mind," Alex said, stabbed by a sense of guilt he'd no wish to feel, "much less his spirit. I ken ye care about him . . ."

"But you do not?"

Alex had had no chance to reply, for the door-hide—a buffalo's—had swept aside. Blackbird entered the lodge, curtailing the conversation.

Now, hearing the reverend's voice raised in near-fluent Cherokee, Alex left his capacious basket half-filled with corn and moved through the stalks to see the man conversing with Crooked Branch. Also a Longhair Clan member, the peace chief was in the fields harvesting corn. While fieldwork was ordinarily left to the women's tending, during the busiest times all but those off hunting or making war lent a hand. Even some too aged to stoop in a field found ways to be of use.

Atop a scaffold erected near the field's center, an old woman perched, her task to screech at birds, deer, and other woodland foragers bent on ravaging the crop with their nibbling. A basket of stones rested beside her, should screeching prove ineffectual.

Perhaps sensing Alex's scrutiny, she opened eyes nearly lost in wrinkled folds and peered down. She still had most of her teeth, he saw when she bared them in a grin. She called down words to him in a voice reedy and cracked, a few of which Alex recognized.

Big. White. Grub. He returned a smile, hoping that wasn't a name they were calling him now.

After three weeks among the Cherokees, few he encountered in the fields or near Blackbird's lodge held him in fear, though some still went wary of him. Fewer went wary of Pauling. Among those who did were Runs-Far's parents. Fishing Hawk and Squash Blossom were none too pleased their son had become a follower of Pauling's God. The raid during which Blackbird's band found them had been Runs-Far's first, and according to Jemma, his reluctance to join it had disappointed Fishing Hawk, as had his refusal to kill their enemies. His flaunting of the blood taboo during Jemma's travail, when he'd prayed for her, had been one more strike against Pauling in their minds.

Leaving off trading grins with the old woman

on the scaffold, Alex went back to picking corn beneath the westering sun. Pauling must have done so as well. Alex no longer heard his voice. He soon heard others he recognized. Jemma and Blackbird, chattering in Cherokee.

Blackbird had brought an empty basket, capacious and half her height. She eyed the one he was filling. "You make full another?"

At his nod she set down the empty basket and took up the full one, settling the tumpline across her brow, surprising him with her strength. The basket was as large as the empty one, heavy with its bounty.

Jemma had the bairn in his sling. Alex cast the rounded bundle a soft glance. "Have ye settled on a name, *mo nighean*?"

"I'm waiting for Runs-Far to come back."

The lad had been gone a fortnight, having taken it upon himself to search out a woman Blackbird thought might better remember the Looks-At-The-Sun she vaguely recalled.

"Little girl memory, long ago," she'd said and cautioned Jemma not to raise her hopes that the woman still lived, or that Runs-Far could locate her if she did.

"Bid the wind cease blowing while ye're at it," Alex had muttered.

Jemma meant to leave the naming of her bairn to kin, if any could be found. Someone of her clan, whichever that was. She was hoping it didn't turn out to be Runs-Far's Longhair Clan. Apparently members of a clan never married one another no matter how distant the blood relation. That the Cherokees divided themselves into clans felt familiar to Alex, though with the Cherokees—*Aniyunwiya*, they called themselves, the Real People—clan affiliation came through the mother, not the father.

Blackbird left them to their work, but toward sunset returned and took up the reverend's corn basket, gave him an empty one, and sent him off to the forest for firewood. He went, stooped with fatigue. Leaving his basket nigh full, Alex started after Pauling, intending to aid what he hoped would be the man's last task for the day.

"Wait you," came Blackbird's voice behind him. He paused as she approached. "You help good," she said.

Uncertain whether she commended the quality of his work or the fact of it, he nodded. "Ye've given me a roof, let me eat at your fire. The least I can do is make myself of use."

He and Blackbird had fallen into a tacit rhythm with each other. He'd the sense she was satisfied with the arrangement despite his uncertainties as to its nature or her expectations. Had she some notion of adopting him, as Jemma hoped to be adopted?

The idea of it begged the question. Did he want to stay with these people?

He couldn't push his thoughts past that point without Joanna's face rising up, as if to plead against it.

Even such imagined pleading was in vain. He could never return to Severn. Having stolen his bound years of service, to say nothing of Jemma and the tools, Carey would demand reprisal, legal or otherwise. But was he free to leave the Cherokees and continue his journey northward? He was no slave, probably not even a prisoner, not in the manner he'd been among the English. He knew what that felt like, and it wasn't this.

"Blackbird," he began, wanting to address the question, but got no further before an outcry from the forest intruded. One of startlement and pain.

He was running in that direction, dodging cornstalks and pumpkin vines, Blackbird a pace behind him, before the exclamation registered as Pauling's.

He reached the man as he was shaking off the snake that had sunk its fangs into the fleshy heel of his right hand—a snake fat and patterned, with the twin rows of knobs at its tail tip that proclaimed it a canebrake. It flew into the brush to coil upon itself and shiver the air with its angry rattling before sliding away through the undergrowth.

Alex grasped Pauling's bitten hand and raised it. Puncture marks showed clear and red, the callused skin around them pink, a little swollen.

"Reverend," he said, seized with horror; he'd been warned of the canebrake's deadly venom. "I've carried ye to your bed once before. By your leave I'll do it again."

The Cherokees had their healers, some who knew the forest herbs. Perhaps there was hope.

Alex was ready to hoist the man over his shoulder as he'd done in the smithy yard at Severn, but Pauling shook his head.

"There's no need. It will be well."

He bent for the stick he must have been reaching for when the snake struck. Alex stopped him. "Reverend, be sensible. The more ye move about, the faster the venom spreads, aye?"

Around them arose chattering, as those who'd been in the field nearby gathered. Blackbird stepped forward and took her slave by the wrist. Alex expected the wounds to be worsened, the hand more noticeably swollen. If anything the fang marks appeared cleaner than before, as if some harmless snake had bitten him days ago.

Drawing the same conclusion, Blackbird looked at Alex. "You see snake?" Unable to find the word in English, she made a sound through her teeth so like the snake's rattle several within hearing gave a yelp.

"A canebrake, aye. It had him fast by the hand."

Blackbird questioned the women gathered, then turned back. "They say he die. Or lose hand."

422

She looked hard at Pauling, into his untroubled eyes. "Sick?"

"He will be," Alex said.

Pauling put his bitten hand to Alex's arm, a grip reassuringly strong. "I don't think so. I'll finish gathering wood for the night and see you back at the lodge."

Blackbird let Pauling go about his chore, but no one returned to the fields. They followed the man as he foraged for downed sticks, pinecones, anything that might fuel his mistress's cook fire.

Alex fell in with the task, watching him for signs of the venom's effect. Whenever he glanced their way in the gathering twilight, he saw the number of Pauling's followers had grown until a veritable crowd trailed them through the woods.

When not another stick could be crammed into the basket, Alex took it and nodded for the reverend to make his way unburdened back to the town.

Blackbird followed, taking up the corn basket, Little Thunder now at her side. What had begun as a death watch was turning into a processional with a cautiously festive air. Those they passed called out inquiries, answered by the witnesses of the encounter with the canebrake.

Pauling was stooped with fatigue, but otherwise appeared as he had when he left the cornfield at Blackbird's command. Alex stayed by his side, unwilling to give over concern, unable to explain its apparent needlessness.

At their lodge Little Thunder pulled aside the buffalo hide. In the firelight spilling out, Blackbird took up Pauling's hand, assured herself the snakebite remained as innocuous as it had appeared earlier, then motioned him inside. She turned to shoo away the people, telling them her slave was well.

Someone in the crowd gave a whoop, answered by a few more such. They drifted off, buzzing with excitement. Little Thunder went into the lodge, leaving Alex and Blackbird alone in the dark.

"Have ye ever seen such a thing? Someone bitten by a canebrake taking no ill at all?"

She'd understood his English. "No. His God do this?"

Alex could only shrug. "I dinna ken."

Blackbird didn't share his doubt. "He favored by his God." She gave a shudder, as though in fear. "No more slave. He must go."

33

With the tobacco harvest underway, Joanna saw little of Mister Reeves for the next fortnight, though twice he'd entered Papa's room at meal times to find Joanna ensconced at his bedside, reading aloud while he ate. Both times he'd asked her stepfather some innocuous question and retreated.

Papa's health had marginally improved. He was rising from bed for short periods, keeping down his food, in less pain and better color. Azuba and Phoebe had taken stock of their herbs. Neither were missing anything that, if slipped into his food, might cause such symptoms as Papa had suffered. It had to be something Mister Reeves procured in Wilmington.

She was beyond any hope of calling it a coincidence.

What about Elijah's belief that Mister Reeves caused his injuries? What of Micah, found dead on the border of Mister Simcoe's land? And the mill? The tar kiln that had claimed Grandpa Jo? Had Phineas Reeves orchestrated all of it?

Joanna couldn't wrap her mind around such dreadful calculation. Nor the reason for it.

"You the one got to find it out, Miss Joanna," Azuba said. "Unless you mean to bring Master Carey into it now?"

The last time she'd brought an accusation against Mister Reeves, Papa had been deaf to it. The man was his blind spot. She needed proof. But she'd alienated the overseer, refusing his proposal.

"True, and ye've locked horns with him over Severn's future," Elijah said. "What if ye made like ye'd changed your mind about that much, that ye're coming round to his way of thinking? Maybe he'll let down his guard with ye."

Pretend with a pretender. She was out of her depth.

Marigold must have thought likewise. "How she meant to catch a rattling snake and not get bit?" she asked Elijah before turning back to her. "You best be careful, Miss Joanna."

Careful was the least of it. "Pray for me," she'd said, and shut herself in her room to do the same, longing for that cup to pass. When it didn't, she rose and went out to drink it.

With a mouth gone dry and appetite fled, Joanna presided at a candlelit supper she'd helped prepare, having sent an invitation out to the fields. She'd half-expected Mister Reeves to ignore it, but he appeared at the appointed time, washed and attired, looking less than pleased.

"Miss Carey? What is the meaning of this?"

"I've barely seen you these weeks past." She took a seat and motioned him to do so. "I've wanted to speak to you."

He complied, sitting across from her. "I've much to do. I haven't time for formal meals."

"Still, you must eat." She decided to let him do so for several minutes before broaching her intended subject. Phoebe had made his favorites—veal in a wine sauce, roasted butternut squash, boiled garden kale, drop biscuits with melting butter and honey. Even strawberry jam tarts.

"What is so important as to warrant such effort?" he asked at length, indicating the unusually elaborate supper.

"I wish to know how the harvest is proceeding—and anything else of matter."

He held her gaze across the table. "Why should you?"

"I've thought on what you and Papa have said and . . ." She swallowed, dry-mouthed, hoping he would take her apprehension for sheepishness. "Perhaps my vision for Severn does have its flaws."

Which was true enough.

"Really?" Mister Reeves seemed mildly taken aback but proved compliant. He spoke for a time about the harvest, then launched into a lengthy explanation of why he felt it unwise to rebuild the mill, despite its being a staggering loss of income for Severn. Rather they should sell the slaves that had worked it.

Distracted by the perilous subject she still meant to launch, Joanna sipped the wine in her glass and waited with banging heart for the pause that must eventually come . . . and plunged in when it did.

"Papa asked to join us this evening. I didn't think him quite up to it."

Mister Reeves cast her a look over the glass he'd raised to his lips. "I did tell you he would improve."

"Yes. You did." Joanna clenched the linen napkin on her lap. "You're certain you don't know the cause of his illness?"

She'd caught him mid-swallow. He coughed, face reddening, then demanded, "Did you go to all this trouble merely to accuse *me* of having to do with Captain Carey's illness?"

Joanna felt the blood drain to her toes. "Of course not. Papa *is* improving, but he's had relapses before. I only wished to ascertain whatever you might know of such matters. Surely more than I. You've been places, seen things, I haven't." Inspiration, or desperation, cleared a path in her mind. "It's plain I know little about you, much less than I'd like to know."

Mister Reeves's mouth tightened in a misdoubting smile. "Do you? That is interesting. I don't see how it can be of aid, but what do you wish to know?"

Her mind raced. "Did you encounter an ailment such as Papa's before you came to Severn? Perhaps while under his command?"

Mister Reeves sat back in his chair, regarding her. His stare, as probing as it was veiled, prickled the hairs on her arms, but to her relief he began to speak of places seen and people known.

Gradually she unclenched her hands and focused on his words, only to realize he was rattling off a litany of his past much like the story he told when they first met. Practically word for word. As he'd done then, he glossed over the years he'd remained aboard the *Severn* after her stepfather left the Royal Navy. He was about to launch into his capture by the Kingston pirates when she raised a hand to forestall him.

"Tell me more of those years, Mister Reeves. Before Kingston. You mentioned to Thom Kelly something I hadn't known, that the man who replaced Papa as captain wasn't his equal. You never speak of that time. Did he allow his crew to fall into ill health?"

That last meal with Captain Kelly, before he went back downriver to his death, flooded Joanna's memory, as did the puzzling enmity she'd sensed simmering between him and Mister Reeves, who smiled at her now across the table, an expression bearing no relation to the coldness in his eyes.

"That was the least of it. Those years left aboard the *Severn* were the darkest of my life, their recounting not at all appropriate for your ears."

"Worse than the pirates?"

"Worse in every way."

Her courage to continue nearly faltered when his smile did. "But the *Severn* was your home."

"Not after . . ." He paused, visibly swallowed.

"After Papa left?"

"With Moon. Yes."

Elijah. Papa. She sensed she'd found the thread in all this tangle that needed pulling. "Mister Reeves, should it help you to talk about that time, I'm willing to listen."

"You are." It was said flatly, with no indication of suspicion or pleasure. "Very well, but bear in mind you pressed me to it." There was barely time for her heart to thump at his warning before his voice hardened and he went on. "When Captain Carey left the *Severn*, he'd have done better to hand her over to pirates than leave her in the hands of Captain Potts."

As he'd once before implied. "But why?"

"Potts allowed . . . *abuses* to occur. He cared not how his officers kept discipline. What measures they took. Openly or in secret."

The smell of the food on the table, the wine in

the glasses, thickened in Joanna's nose until she feared she might vomit. She wanted to hear no more. "Things done in secret?"

"Unspeakable things. And those who ought to have put a stop to it turned a blind eye. Not just Potts."

Did he mean Thom Kelly, who'd continued, unhappily, as first lieutenant aboard the *Severn* under Potts's command? She held Mister Reeves's gaze in the candlelight, saw in his eyes a swallowing darkness. Instinct screamed at her to flee from it.

"Mister Reeves . . . Phineas," she said, his given name foreign on her tongue. "I'm so sorry."

The candle flickered with his breath. Wax dripped onto the cloth beneath it. His gaze sharpened with intrigue, and calculation, as though she were an opponent in a game of chess, one proving slightly more worthy than he'd anticipated. "Why?"

It wasn't a question she'd expected. "Why . . . what?"

"Why are you sorry? Why do you wish to know these things? Why have you suddenly changed your thinking about Severn's management? Or have you? Are you rather attempting to undermine me in some manner, in hopes your step-father will dismiss me?"

The darkness pooled toward her, a suffocating thing. She sat back in her chair, certain he'd seen what she was fishing for—reason compelling enough to insinuate himself into their lives, manipulate their sympathies, lull them into trust. And destroy them.

Did he realize he'd revealed it?

"I . . ." A pinched squeak had emerged in place of her voice. She swallowed and forced out, "Of course not. Who wouldn't be affected by what you've just shared? I only hoped my listening might help."

Mister Reeves pushed back his chair and stood. He looked down at her, a hawk eyeing a rabbit from its perch. "Help me . . . or you?" he asked, and left the table.

Joanna found Elijah with Jory, who'd suffered a summer ague since the night but seemed to be improving late in the afternoon. "His cough isn't so hard as it was," she said, entering the cabin to the sound.

Marigold scooped him off the bed and brought him, freshly clouted, into the doorway's light. "Fever done broke. You right, Miss Joanna, cough's sounding better too." Exhaustion threaded her voice.

Joanna took the baby in her arms, filled with yearning at the warm, solid weight of him. Even with a fretful pucker to his brows, he was a beautiful child, skin like dark honey, wisps of black hair curling over a shapely skull.

"Well met, wee bairn," she said, brushing a kiss across his wrinkled brow before realizing she'd mimicked Alex's speech.

She caught Elijah watching from the cabin's chair. He rose and came into the light. "He kept us wakeful the night long, and I look forward to my bed. For the present I must get me back to the forge."

"I'll go with you." Joanna handed Jory back to Marigold.

Stepping from the cabin, she cut her gaze at Elijah and was heartened by what she saw. Despite the present fatigue, he looked in better health and spirits than she'd seen since his accident.

Which mightn't have been an accident at all.

She grit her teeth in fury at the mere possibility Mister Reeves had caused Elijah's crippling. As they came up the lane toward the nearest shops, she related their conversation at table.

"So that's it, then," Elijah said. "He blames Captain Carey for what happened to him aboard the *Severn* under Potts's command. And me, I suppose, for escaping it." He halted and faced her while still out of earshot of the slaves working in the shops. "I'm sorry, Joanna."

"Why are you sorry?" she asked, minding those same words flung at her across the candlelit remains of last night's supper.

"For taking so long to climb out of the pit I was

in—still climbing, if I'm honest. He was right, MacKinnon, what he said when last we spoke. As was Reverend Pauling, so much he said to me."

"I'm glad," she said, "that you and Alex were friends enough he could say such a thing to you. You were, weren't you?"

"For my part. MacKinnon has a heart wider and deeper than he can admit. I think he needed us." Elijah frowned, weighing the words. "Or needed us to need him."

Joanna was gratified to hear it—and all the more furious with Mister Reeves for seeking to turn Papa against Alex. If he were there now, would he be her ally? A warrior to help her fight this battle? But he'd chosen another path. Perhaps the only one that seemed open to him at the time.

Acknowledging that made her feel no less abandoned.

"When Alex first came, I overheard the two of you talking." She recounted the conversation she'd nearly walked in on, that day she came to the smithy to present Alex his first set of clothes. "You were discussing whether the Almighty controls the events of our lives. I hadn't heard as many words out of you in months. I stood there in the smithy yard, praying with all my heart that if I couldn't reach you, Alex might." Her face warmed as she met his gaze. "I never intended to confess that."

Elijah looked at her with tenderness. "I wish he'd never left us, but I understand why he did. There was a time I'd have left, was I in possession of two hands to break free of my prison. But the want of a hand was my prison."

Was. "You no longer feel so imprisoned?"

"There's always a way forward for a man, no matter what's been lost, if he's strong of will, or of hope."

Joanna remembered those words, or some very like them, overheard that day. "And faith," she hastened to add. "If the Almighty has seen fit for you to go on living, there's a reason. A purpose. Alex didn't believe that."

"Nor did I, for a time." Elijah paused, then asked, "Do ye pray for him, Joanna?"

"Morning, night, and sundry times between."

They continued to the smithy, where the hammer's clang rang in the heat. Demas was at the anvil when they walked in. Wrapped in the leather apron Alex once wore, he paused the hammer. Elijah demanded his attention, coming to inspect his work.

Joanna turned to go.

"Miss Carey."

Demas had uttered her name. Speared by it, she turned back. "Yes?"

"You be knowing where is Master Reeves now?"

"Away to the fields, last I knew." It was the final day of harvesting. "Why?"

The crunch of boots outside the smithy reached her ears an instant before Mister Reeves himself entered, stride swift with purpose, jaw set.

Joanna flinched as he drew abreast of her, but he strode past as if he hadn't registered her presence. She looked with alarm at Elijah, fearing he was the target of this advance, but the overseer ignored him as well. He thrust out a small leather pouch at Demas.

"What is the meaning of this?" Mister Reeves yanked open the pouch's drawstring and tipped its contents onto the brick counter. Dried bits of leaf and bark fell, wafted by the forge's heat. "Oleander," he proclaimed, burning gaze fixed on Demas. "Found in your cabin."

"Oleander?" Joanna echoed. It was poisonous—leaf, bark, flower, and root. They didn't keep it at Severn.

Demas stood at the anvil, hammer in one hand, in the other the tongs gripping a length of iron, tip cooling from its cherry-red. He was braced, still as a shadow, as if he awaited enlightenment as well. Or needed none.

Mister Reeves turned on Joanna. "After you all but accused me of poisoning Captain Carey, I decided to discover the truth for myself. I'm aware you've noticed my checking his food— which I grant is the likely cause of your suspicion *and* why you set yourself and Azuba as guards at Captain Carey's beside. I'd no proof to refute your suspicions until now. There it is," he said, pointing at the oleander. "Your proof."

"What are ye saying?" Elijah cut in, stepping nearer Joanna. "That Demas poisoned Captain Carey? With that?" He jerked his head toward the counter.

"Yes, Moon. That's exactly what's happened. What I want to know is why?" Mister Reeves swung to face his slave, features riven with betrayal. "What have you to say?"

Joanna expected a denial, but when Demas spoke it sounded more like warning.

"Phineas. Don't do this." His big hand clenched the hammer.

The specter of violence had arisen, wrapping them in unseen bands. Mister Reeves glanced at her, in his eyes something she'd never seen there. Fear. Then they hardened with a reckless gleam.

"Moses! Billy!" At his bark the head groom and one of the stable hands stepped into the doorway, obviously having lingered out of sight. "Take Demas to the smokehouse. The one where we kept MacKinnon. Miss Carey, your key, please."

While Joanna gaped, the two slaves took one stride into the smithy but halted when Demas leveled a look at them.

"Help them, Moon," Mister Reeves said.

Elijah ignored the command.

With a growl of frustration, the overseer lunged for his slave. Only then did Demas move, dropping hammer, tongs, and heated iron to the earthen floor. With startling swiftness, he stepped from behind the anvil into Mister Reeves's path and swung a massive fist, catching him full in the face.

Mister Reeves dropped without a sound.

Demas put his head down and charged the slaves in the doorway. They leapt aside, then looked at Mister Reeves lying prone.

Elijah had gathered his wits. To the two in the doorway he said, "Best ye do make a show of it."

They shared a look, then took off after Demas.

"Ye'll see to him?" Elijah asked her, bending a nod at Mister Reeves, stirring with a faint moan.

She nodded and he left. She stood, shaken, staring down at her stepfather's overseer as he made an abortive attempt to rise.

Dared she believe what just happened?

She forced herself to offer the support of an arm. Once on his feet, nose bloodied, he brushed her off. "Demas. Where is he?"

"He ran. Do you truly think he poisoned Papa?"

"I know it." He headed toward the door, wiping at his nose, staggering a little, but there Elijah met him. Mister Reeves grasped his arm when he made to step past. "Did you catch him?"

"I hadn't known that slave of yours could move so fast. He's well away."

"To where?"

"Making for the swamps, I suppose."

For an instant Mister Reeves seemed poised to race after his slave. Instead he whirled toward Joanna, bleeding still. "I hope," he said with cutting calm, "this puts to rest your suspicions of me."

34

August 1748

It was the last meeting Pauling would hold at
Blackbird's lodge. After taking no harm from
the canebrake's venom, Blackbird deemed him
worthy of his own dwelling, with the freedom to
come and go as he wished. Longhair Clan hands
had raised it in the Cherokee style, with a central
fire and platforms built into the walls for storage
and sleeping. Pauling had moved most of his
belongings there—household gifts from those
who heard his preaching.

If *preaching* was even the word for what
Pauling was doing. Seated with his Cherokee
flock beneath the pole awning, he talked for
long stretches but invited question or comment. Though unaccustomed to interrupting a
speaker, over time the Cherokees had grown
easier with Pauling's invitation to discourse,
until the gatherings resembled an informal
meeting of friends. Since the incident with the
snake, twice as many were gathering to hear
what he had to say. Even Runs-Far's parents
lingered at the edge, listening with furrowed
brows.

Runs-Far had yet to return from his journey on

Jemma's behalf. Jemma, sitting now by the door-hide listening to Pauling, the bairn in her arms, was anxious for him.

"I have learned that the sufferings of this present life are hardly worth noticing when compared to the good things we will experience in His kingdom. Look around you at the mountains. The very earth the Almighty created is impatient for the redemption that is coming. It awaits it with longing, groaning in pain like a woman giving birth."

As if to illustrate the scripture Pauling read, translating into *Tsalagi*, the Cherokee language, Jemma's bairn was fussing. She'd fed him, patted his back, held him on her knees and played with his toes, but the instant she stopped, his whimpering resumed.

"And when we grow weary in waiting, the Spirit of the Almighty is with us, helping us to pray. It is all right if we do not know what words to use when our hearts are deeply pained with need. God's knowledge of us goes deeper than our pain. His Spirit prays for us, always for our best, making good words out of our sighs and groans. That is why we rest in this assurance: God is a loving Father working the details of our lives into a good pattern, like a skillful weaver makes her basket."

Pauling smiled, gaze shifting to the lodge's doorway. Alex turned to see Blackbird standing there, observing the scene outside her lodge as Pauling addressed his listeners again.

"Have you—any one of you—felt in your deepest self this groaning for which you cannot find words?"

As the Cherokees looked at one another to see who might speak first, Jemma's bairn loosed a howl. Amid much laughter, she shot to her feet and ducked inside the lodge with her squalling son. Blackbird went in as well.

"What you say is true." Pauling was replying to something one of his flock had said, as the laughter settled down. "We are promised that in this life we will have difficult times that test us. That is because there is a war being waged on this earth between our Father in heaven and our enemy, Satan. We are warriors in that battle! But listen, here is a truth to cling to in the fight: it is a battle already won. Do not lose sight of how our story ends. Or begins, one might say."

Pauling had spoken of these things to Moon during his visits to the smithy. It made Alex remember the crowd gathered on the lawn at Severn, Joanna seated at its edge, drinking in this man's words like a thirsty doe.

He'd asked Pauling why he didn't return to Pennsylvania, once his status as a slave no longer prevented it. "Or to Severn," he'd added, causing Pauling to look at him with speculation.

"To everything its season. A time for returning will come."

"Ye've your wee flock of converts," Alex had persisted. "But d'ye not see those who stand opposed? These people may well force ye to go—or worse—if ye dinna cease trying to change their ways." He'd been thinking of Cane-Splitter, but there were others. Not all welcomed Pauling's religion. "Take your freedom and go. I'll see ye safe."

Pauling had confounded him by proclaiming himself a prisoner still. "Christ's prisoner. Not until I sense His release will I move one inch from this place, and certainly not for fear of my well-being. It's by His mercy we're kept. On that day appointed we'll each pass from this life. Until then nothing may touch those who trust in Him unless He allows it."

"Even a rattler," Jemma had pronounced, convinced of what Pauling preached since the incident with the snake.

Nothing may touch those who trust in Him unless He allows it. What of all that had passed at Severn? Had such losses continued? Had Carey conquered that shadow that haunted him? Had Joanna committed herself to another sort of prison—marriage to Reeves, who had, Alex was all but certain, orchestrated the events that forced him to flee?

Anger washed over him as one of the Cherokees

asked another question of Pauling. He shut out the discussion that ensued, shifting attention inward—and heavenward. *Aye, I acknowledge Ye. I ken what Ye did with Pauling. Ye showed Yourself strong to these people through it, but what of Joanna? Are Ye helping her at all?*

As he waited in brooding silence, a thought pierced. Had the Almighty meant to help Joanna through him? Had that been the prompting behind Pauling's request he look out for her? *I canna think there's anything Ye'd have used the likes of me to do for Edmund Carey, or Joanna, even Moon, but . . . was there?*

The stir of bodies rising recalled his attention. Pauling was on his feet, speaking to Runs-Far's parents. Earlier Fishing Hawk had mentioned a hunt he was planning, extending Alex an invitation. Eager to venture beyond the town and explore the surrounding mountains, he'd accepted.

"Alex?"

He looked up into Little Thunder's gaze. The boy beckoned.

Welcoming the distraction, he let Blackbird's son lead him to the door-hide, knowing Pauling likely to be some time answering questions, praying for needs.

Little Thunder spoke in *Tsalagi*, forcing Alex to translate the words. *Was Alex hungry? Did he want to eat now?*

The Cherokees observed no formal meal times, but each fire had something on hand for whenever anyone wished to eat it.

"Aye," he replied in English, which the child was picking up. "I do."

They entered the smoky lodge. Near the central fire Blackbird sat weaving a basket, surrounded by her materials—river cane split, trimmed, soaked, and dyed in shades of red, black, and brown. She was exceptionally skilled at creating an ingenious sort of nested double basket, the two connected seamlessly at the rim, the outer a complex pattern of dyed canes.

He'd watched her weave before, as Jemma was doing now, keeping one eye on the bairn, who had finally dropped off to sleep. She looked up at his and Little Thunder's entrance, warning in her gaze.

Alex put a hand to the lad's shoulder and, when he looked up, pressed a finger to his lips. Little Thunder nodded. Alex caught the trailing end of Blackbird's smile as he and Little Thunder settled at the fire and ate from a kettle of stewed corn.

"How far he go?" Jemma asked in *Tsalagi*, keeping her voice low as she ruminated about Runs-Far, which she did as frequently as she'd once chattered about finding these people. "Think he find woman who holds memory of my grandmother?"

Pauling entered the lodge in time to hear the

question. "The Almighty is in control of all that concerns you, Walnut. Be content with the day's blessings and wait on His plan to unfold. He will strengthen your heart."

Blackbird looked to Jemma. "Probably he is right," she allowed with a nod at Pauling. "At least in this—it does no good to worry over what cannot be changed. Yes?"

Jemma nodded reluctantly.

Pauling said, "I need only move my bedding and I will have properly set up house."

Blackbird set aside her weaving and rose. "I have gift," she said in English. She didn't dig among her possessions long to find it, a stone pipe, bowl carved with the images of birds. A symbol of peace, though Pauling hadn't brought peace to her life. Alex recalled the tense scene he'd witnessed after Blackbird's decision to free Pauling became known. Though he'd been too distant to hear their words when Cane-Splitter and Blackbird met on the path near the lodge being raised for Pauling, the warrior's gestures and the contentious language of their bodies had needed no interpretation.

"I have gift!" As though inspired by his mother's generosity, Little Thunder darted to his sleeping bench and began pulling out baskets, searching for whatever he meant to give the departing reverend, growing agitated when he couldn't find it.

Alex rose to help. "What is it ye wish to give?"

"Rock," the child said, unhelpfully. Alex decided should he find a rock, the lad would know it for the right one. He reached for a narrow birch-bark container. Even as he saw what lay within, Little Thunder said, "No."

It was another pipe, more ornate than the one Blackbird had given Pauling, the bowl carved with the figures of wolves, long stem wrapped in scarlet thread and hung with the flight feathers of redbird, blue jay, goldfinch, and that green bird abundant in the mountains Pauling called a parakeet. The gaudy feathers were rumpled, the threads frayed with handling.

Alex replaced the lid, noting as he did that Blackbird had seen.

Little Thunder found the stone he sought, half a rough orb with a cluster of purple crystals in its belly. Pauling accepted the gift with such delight it left the lad beaming. The reverend bade them farewell, took up his bedding, and left for his lodge.

As the door-hide swung closed, Little Thunder's smile faded. He turned a wistful gaze on Alex.

"If Runs-Far find woman," Jemma said, returning to her favorite subject, "she know my grandmother's clan, I hope. What are we?"

"Is there a Talks-A-Lot Clan?" Alex asked.

Understanding his English, Little Thunder

laughed. Blackbird hid a grin as she went back to her weaving. Her son went to his sleeping bench. Alex went out to where Blackbird kept firewood and fetched in an armful for the morning. He settled by the fire, at a loss for what to do with Blackbird occupied, Little Thunder dozing off with a full belly, Jemma busy with the bairn.

He missed Pauling, he realized with no little surprise as he watched the flames dance, the shift and whisper of the burning wood unequal to filling the void the reverend's absence left. He was reaching for a stick to poke at the whitened embers when Blackbird looked up from her weaving.

"I could tell you of that pipe. The one beneath where my son sleeps."

"That pipe," he said in his awkward Cherokee. "It is . . ." He searched for the word. "*Uwoduhi*. Beautiful thing."

That pleased her, judging by the softening of her mouth. "I will tell you about the man who used it—that one's father," she added, nodding at her sleeping son, black hair tousled on the furs. "Bring it out. Look at it."

Alex hesitated, surprised by the offer. Jemma widened her eyes, telling him clearly to get up off his haunches and fetch the thing. He did so, then seated himself beside her so she could examine the pipe's carvings, finger the bright feathers dangling from the scarlet-wrapped stem.

"That pipe is all I kept of the man who was my husband," Blackbird said. "I was happy with that man in my lodge, happy to bear his son. I had hoped . . ." Leaving the statement unfinished, she launched into a recounting of a hunt her husband had gone on, in the season when snow lay deep on the high slopes. She named the ones who'd gone with him, including Cane-Splitter. "That warrior is born to the same clan as my husband. Born to sisters, so they were as brothers."

A pucker knit her brows. Alex had thought the tension between Cane-Splitter and Blackbird to do with his presence, and Pauling's. Now he wondered if the true cause was something unrelated to their coming to Crooked Branch's town.

"They went to hunt buffalo." Blackbird gestured at the door-hide. "You have seen buffalo?"

She'd addressed the question to Jemma, who shook her head, rapt as a child hearing a bedtime story. "They big, ain't they?" she asked, lapsing into English.

"Much big," Blackbird replied in kind. "Tall."

"Tall as him?" Jemma nodded at Alex.

Blackbird's gaze ran the length of his legs, stretched out before the fire. "Some maybe—big bulls, at hump behind head."

"They've a hump?" Alex asked. "They're not like cattle, then? That's what I thought they must be, judging from the hair on yon hide."

"Bigger than English cow. Wooly head, horns curved." She put her fists to her temples, fore-fingers crooked, then ducked and made as if to thrust those finger-horns at Jemma. Alex grinned at her rare antics, then gazed at the door-hide, trying to grasp the immensity of the creature it once covered.

The hunters, Blackbird went on to say, had found a trail through the snow with fresh sign of buffalo. Only one, but one would have been plenty. It led them far, over a pass, though from the sign it left, they were drawing nearer as the day waned. But they weren't the only hunters on that mountain looking for meat. Tuscaroras were hunting too. The bands met uneasily, but when the Tuscaroras learned the Cherokees were tracking a buffalo, they asked to join the hunt and divide whatever meat might be clinging to those bones at the end of a long winter.

"That meant less for everyone, but the Tuscaroras had women and children starving. The man who was my husband agreed, though Cane-Splitter says he did not wish the bands to join. In this he was out-voiced."

Together the bands followed the trail, winding down off the high slopes until they came to a slope, steep and stony, and could finally see the beast. The one they followed had joined a small herd. Enough meat for all!

The hunters made a plan and began their stalk,

moving in cover to the left and right of the herd, getting close enough to be sure their musket balls hit their marks. One in the group with Blackbird's husband missed his footing and dislodged a stone, which started a rock slide that made the buffalo run farther down the slope. The hunters gave chase.

"Then a bad thing happened. Cane-Splitter saw it, for the man who was my husband was running ahead of him with a Tuscarora hunter."

Jemma was clenching the pipe, gaze fixed on Blackbird. Alex gently took it from her and set it back into its birch box.

"My husband and that Tuscarora leapt a fallen tree," Blackbird continued. "When they landed the Tuscarora stumbled. He fell against my husband and both went down. Cane-Splitter leapt over them but slid a way in snow before stopping to look back. The Tuscarora was accusing my husband of tripping him so he would not be first to reach the buffalo. My husband said it was not so, but the Tuscarora would not listen. He was very angry, maybe crazed from hunger too, for he drove a knife into my husband's belly, then across his throat. The other hunters were running, shooting at the buffalo, and did not see. The Tuscarora saw Cane-Splitter coming to kill him next and ran into the trees. Cane-Splitter gave chase but did not catch him. That is how he tells it." Blackbird nodded at Jemma, adding, "That is why when we found you with this girl, we had the scalps of some of those Tuscaroras hanging from our belts."

"That is how he tells it," Alex repeated, then in English asked, "D'ye not believe Cane-Splitter's tale?"

"Believe?" Blackbird's eyes glittered in the dying firelight. "On the strength of his telling, I went on the warpath, when my mourning was passed. I had my vengeance."

"Then why d'ye sound . . ." He'd meant to say *unconvinced,* but was startled by a knocking outside the lodge. Thinking it Pauling returned for company, Alex rose. The knocker called out, a male voice, not Pauling's.

"Walnut? You there? Come see!"

Jemma's head whipped up. "That's Runs-Far!"

Alex pushed aside the hide to reveal the lad, teeth agleam in a grin so broad the night couldn't diminish its blazing. The raised voices had awakened the bairn. Jemma scooped him up.

Runs-Far came into the lodge at Blackbird's gesturing. Someone came with him. A child, Alex thought, until firelight revealed a long white braid and deeply lined skin stretched over the bones of a round face. It was an old woman, straight-backed and diminutive.

She stopped inside the lodge, gaze fastening on Jemma. Runs-Far put a hand on her shoulder and said in *Tsalagi,* "I bring you this grandmother called Shelled Corn. She is not the one I went to find. I did find that one, but she told me of *this* one. I had to go another long distance for her, who is also one who remembers your grandmother because . . ."

Runs-Far paused for breath, face shining as he gazed at Jemma. "Because she is the *sister* of the one who was your grandmother."

35

September 1748

Clad in a breechclout, Alex balanced on the end of a rock slanting from the river's flow, bow in hand, and waited for Runs-Far to take his shot. The lad spotted a trout undulating with the current, half-concealed by a shelf of the rock he perched on downstream. Careful not to cast a shadow on that cloudless day, Runs-Far raised his bow and sent an arrow slicing through the water. He crouched, plunged an arm deep, and hoisted the speared trout, rainbow scales glistening. He pulled it off the arrow and tossed it onto the bank beside three others.

Little Thunder, sharing Alex's rock, refrained from shouting so as not to scare off other fish but did a dance in celebration of Runs-Far's latest catch.

Blackbird's son found it hilarious that it had taken Alex days to catch his first fish. Alex had been hunting with Fishing Hawk but had lacked any weapon save a spear. Runs-Far had consented to teach Alex the skill of bow fishing, now he was back and Jemma united with her Cherokee kin.

Shelled Corn, who had no daughters, only

sons long since married into their wives' clans, had become Jemma's mother in an adoption ceremony held the previous day, during the same gathering that saw Blackbird instated as *Ghigau*.

Jemma's bairn finally had a name—Blue Jay, bestowed on him by Shelled Corn.

"Good thing we're Deer Clan," she'd told Alex during the feast in the council house marking Blackbird's elevation to Beloved Woman. "Since I mean to marry Runs-Far and I couldn't if I was Longhair Clan."

Bedecked with silver, beads, and quills— Shelled Corn had brought a horse laden with goods—her amber hair oiled and plaited into short braids, Jemma hardly resembled the girl who'd haunted Severn's smithy.

"D'ye mean to marry him tonight, *mo nighean*?" he'd asked, only half-teasing.

"No," she'd admitted. "It's up to his parents to make the offer to Shelled Corn . . . my mother," she'd added with a note of wonder. "That's how they do."

Jemma had moved into a lodge with Shelled Corn and Blue Jay, leaving Alex all the more certain he must decide what to do with himself. He could survive anywhere far enough removed from Severn, but he needed a purpose beyond survival. He needed what Jemma had found—a people.

Shaking away memory of the ones he'd left

behind, he grasped the purpose of the moment, trying for another fish. He'd caught one to Runs-Far's four, but had another sighted. He steadied his stance on the rock as the river flowed past. The trick was allowing for the water's refraction, knowing where the fish truly was despite appearance. He drew the bow, adjusted his aim, and let fly the arrow—biting back a shout as he drew up a speared trout the length of his forearm.

"One of the grandfathers!" Little Thunder exclaimed, then clapped a hand over his mouth as Runs-Far nodded his *well done.*

When he went to toss the heavy fish onto the bank, Alex saw Blackbird at the riverside, watching. He'd barely seen her since last night's ceremony. She'd given him new clothing in honor of the occasion, a quilled deerskin shirt, leggings, and moccasins. He wasn't certain what she meant by the gift, other than not wishing him to go about in the clothes he'd come to them wearing, admittedly falling to rags. He was determined to repay her in hides, once he got them. He would leave on the morrow with Fishing Hawk's hunters, this time venturing days away in hope of finding buffalo.

For now he had the trout.

Leaving Runs-Far and Little Thunder on the rocks, he donned his shirt as Blackbird came down the trail. She hadn't slept in the lodge last night, but had returned as Runs-Far arrived for the fishing, clearly in need of sleep. She still appeared tired from the night's festivities, but something was on her mind. Straight as an arrow, she shot to the point.

"Walnut has mother now. She has clan. You stay too? Or go?"

She'd spoken English. There was no pretending he hadn't understood. Alex slipped on his moccasins and took up his bow and the fish. "Aye, let's talk."

Blackbird led the way up a worn footpath, returning greetings to those they passed. Some of those greetings were for him, good-natured congratulations for his fishing success. Many of these people, especially those who came to hear Pauling teach, had accepted him as though he'd decided to stay.

Autumn was come, with the first hint of what promised to be a conflagration of color on the slopes. Winter would be hard on its heels. There would be snow, he was told, not the mild rains of the low country. Hard and lasting frosts, not the occasional dusting. Either he left them soon, or he'd be staying the winter.

The buffalo hide fell across the door. Blackbird faced him in the lodge's fire-lit shadows.

"I knew you for a warrior when we found you standing over that one now the daughter of Shelled Corn. She is not your blood, but you were ready to die for her. You are strong, and your heart is good." She spoke *Tsalagi*, forcing him to heed her eyes, her mouth, the language of her body, while his own felt vibrant and warmed by her generous words. "You are not a warrior of The People, but you could be, if you wish it."

Her bluntness set his heart going at a strong rhythm. He put down the fish, then his bow. "Ye'd adopt me, do ye mean?"

He'd spoken English; she blinked at him, needing a few seconds to be certain of his meaning, then shook her head. "I do not want you for a son, Alex MacKinnon."

She hadn't often spoken his name. It sounded strange on her lips. "What, then?"

Blackbird held his gaze. "Little Thunder needs a clan uncle to teach him. I would take you for a brother, if it pleases you."

Not husband. He was relieved and, perversely, faintly disappointed. He kept his voice light. "Little Thunder could well teach me."

Her gaze was sober, searching. "You do not wish to be *Aniyunwiya*?"

It was the question he could no longer dodge. If he could have driven Joanna Carey out of his heart and said an unwavering yes, he'd have done it then.

"Ye do me honor in the asking," he said. "And what ye ask is of worth to me. Truly, it is. But I canna give ye answer yet. I go tomorrow with Fishing Hawk and the warriors. Would ye grant me the days of hunting to think on what I mean to do?"

She didn't answer at once, as though waiting for him to say more. When he didn't, she nodded, but he could read the disappointment in her eyes. "If you are done fishing," she said, "will you go into that part of the field that is mine and bring in the pumpkins, if any are ripe?"

Alex headed for the field, no longer in the mood for fishing, his mind consumed with what had passed between him and Blackbird. Had her proposal of adoption made it impossible to remain unless he accepted? Perhaps he should speak to Pauling . . .

That was his last thought on the matter before the cawing of ravens distracted him. Dozens of the large birds dotted the field ahead, hopping among the drying cornstalks and sprawling vines. Well within the borders of the field a herd of deer grazed.

He looked to the scaffold where an elder should be perched, hurling stones and shouting at the birds and deer. A humped shape was visible, wisps of white hair blowing in the breeze.

The scaffold wasn't much higher than the crown of his head. He grasped its edge and hoisted himself up.

The woman lay on her side, facing away from him, a hand extended toward her basket of stones.

She hadn't stirred despite the shifting of the platform as he'd mounted it.

"Grandmother?" The old woman—the same who'd called him a big white grub—didn't stir. He gave her a gentle shake. Her limp body rolled over, revealing sightless eyes in the wrinkled face. A feathered arrow protruded from her chest.

She was no stranger to him now. He knew her name was Wild Goose and that she was Wolf Clan. He knew she'd outlived three husbands, borne seven children, some who lived in Crooked Branch's town with their children. He also knew she was past helping. He didn't recognize the arrow's fletching. Probably wouldn't unless it was Fishing Hawk's or Runs-Far's. Each warrior fletched his arrows according to his fancy. But something about this one set it apart from those he'd seen.

Her body was still warm.

He'd barely registered the observation when another arrow whirred past his head. Alex flattened and dropped over the platform's side. Hunkered low, he started through the cornstalks, tracing the arrow's path from the woods.

The deer had fled, the ravens risen skyward in a harsh cacophony. He'd left his bow in Blackbird's lodge. He'd no weapon on his person save the hunting blade he drew as he ran. By the time he reached the wood's edge, the shooter of arrows had fled. Alex found where he'd hidden, the disturbance of leaves where feet dug deep to spring away.

A coward's act, killing a helpless old woman from a place of hiding. Alex was neither old nor helpless, and he felt the violation of this death as keenly as if Wild Goose had been his own granny.

Behind him rose a shout. He spared a glance to see Cane-Splitter on the scaffold, having found his dead clanswoman. The warrior spotted Alex at the forest's edge, but there was no time to wait. He tore into the woods after the shooter, following a trail of churned pine needles and leaves. In seconds he no longer needed the trail. He heard his quarry ahead, the crackle and thud of feet, the heave of labored breath.

Alex glimpsed his prey climbing through the forest toward a ridge ahead. Not a large warrior but hard-muscled, lithe, painted for war, a quiver across his back, bow in hand, club thrust through a sash. The warrior glanced back, saw him ascending, coming fast—and tripped on a root. He tumbled down the slope practically into Alex's arms.

The Indian twisted and kicked, catching Alex in the chest with a foot before scrambling away again. Alex grabbed the bole of a tree and clung, using it to heave himself forward. His fingers closed round an ankle. He yanked with all his might.

They both fell downslope, rolling and tumbling,

and landed in a shower of leaves and twigs on a level spot in the terrain.

The Indian was bleeding. Alex's blade had scored the warrior's thigh in the clutching fall. The warrior rolled into a crouch, bow lost, club brandished.

It had a spike embedded in the ball.

Despite the war paint obscuring his features, Alex knew he'd never seen this Indian before. He took in the differences in the warrior's scant clothing, the adornments in his scalp-lock, on a level deeper than conscious thought. A Tuscarora?

Astonishment, perhaps a tinge of fear, twisted the warrior's countenance as he took in Alex's size.

"Aye, try me, then—face to face like a man." No understanding of the challenge lit the Indian's gaze, but he accepted it nonetheless, rushing Alex with a whoop.

The fight was over with startling swiftness. The Indian was no match for Alex's size or the strength he'd gained at Severn's forge, but when he had the warrior disarmed, the spiked club hurled away into the leaves, the Indian wrested a hand free and stabbed his fingers at Alex's eyes. Closing them by reflex, he felt the man, half-pinned beneath him, struggling fiercely to slither out of his hold. He fought those fingers, detached them from his face, the knife still in his grasp as they fought.

How it happened exactly, Alex could never say. As he opened his eyes again, the warrior cried out and blood was spurting from a gash across his neck. Then footsteps came, hard and fast. A shrill cry drowned the dying man's gurgling breaths. Something slammed into the back of Alex's head.

He lay with his face in forest duff. Moccasined feet moved in his vision. He was prodded. Dragged. He saw faces but didn't know them. Then there was firelight and his skull was throbbing as though his brain meant to crack its way through to freedom.

He rolled onto his side and vomited onto a reed mat. Someone uttered a protest when he sat up, reaching as if to push him back down. Other hands came at him. He fended them off, blinking in the firelight of Blackbird's lodge, surrounded by faces he knew.

Jemma. Blackbird. Pauling. Memory rushed in. The cornfield. The arrow. The old woman. The warrior.

"Did you find the woman dead?" Blackbird asked. "That is what Cane-Splitter is saying."

Cane-Splitter. "Aye. He . . . he came after me?"

"He said he reached you as you slew the one who killed his clan elder," Blackbird said. "He is angry. It was his place to do it, not yours. But I am thinking you did not know he was coming to check on her. Is this what happened?"

Alex looked away from her into the worried

gazes of Pauling and Jemma. "Was it him hit me?"

"Cane-Splitter?" Pauling said. "No. He reached you in time to save your life."

"He didna save me. I killed that Tuscarora . . . if it *was* a Tuscarora."

"It was," Blackbird said flatly. "One who hunted with my husband that day. Cane-Splitter knew him. But there were two. It was the second who hit you with his club."

"He'd have finished you," Jemma interjected, round-eyed. "If Cane-Splitter hadn't scairt him off. He wanted to chase after that one but saw you weren't dead, so he brought you back instead. Crooked Branch is talking to him now."

"Was it reprisal, for what your band had done when ye found us?" Alex asked.

Blackbird glanced at the scalp she'd worn that day along the Yadkin, hung now as a trophy, and Alex knew the answer.

"More would have died," she said, "had you not given chase."

He put his head in his hands, fingertips encountering the swollen wound at the back of his skull.

"Best leave it be," Pauling advised. "Your skull isn't cracked, God be praised. But I'm concerned with the brain inside that thick-boned head of yours. What made you do it?"

Despite the humor in the reverend's words, the man was pale with concern. Not just for his physical state, Alex suspected. "Ought I to have let the rascal get away with killing the woman?"

"It was well done. Cane-Splitter will accept this." Blackbird spoke with such finality the rest let the subject drop, focusing instead on Alex, whose head had cleared enough to wish them gone, both so they wouldn't see how the incident had shaken him and how discomfiting he found Blackbird's admiration.

He'd killed men before—in pitched battle. This had been different.

He was glad for the distraction when Little Thunder came running into the lodge, needing to hear the story told. Blackbird did the telling. Before the end of it, Alex had fallen into a doze and must have slept the rest of the day. When he woke, the lodge held its familiar night shadows. The fire was low.

Blackbird lay beside him.

She awoke when he stirred, her hand coming cool around his shoulder. "You are well?"

"Aye," he said, glancing across the lodge to see Little Thunder asleep in his place.

Blackbird took her hand away. "It is not long until dawn. Will you still go on the hunt with Fishing Hawk? He asked this while you slept. I did not know what to tell him."

He didn't feel like going hunting but didn't wish to remain behind. "Aye. I mean to go."

She sat up. "Will you return?"

At first he wondered if this was her way of saying he was liable to get himself killed in his condition. Then he knew that wasn't what she meant. "Aye, I will. I wouldna go without a word to ye and the lad."

She held his gaze a moment more, then turned her face away, eyes catching a glimmer from the fire's embers.

The RETURN

Autumn 1748

Whosoever will lose his life for my sake, the same shall save it.
—JESUS OF NAZARETH
to His disciples, Luke 9:24

36

October 1748

"Will you return?" It was Blackbird's question but not her voice. Squinting into the lodge shadows, he saw it was Joanna, only now it wasn't the lodge. The light was wrong—striped, as though it fell through slats. It was the smokehouse, and Joanna was locked inside with him, wrapped in his arms, her hair fallen loose. His fingers tangled in it. It was as soft and thick as he'd known it would be. He lifted her against him so their faces were level and knew exactly what he'd say to her question if ever he stopped kissing her . . .

Heartbeat slamming, he opened his eyes to ghosting breath and stars banded cold across a sky beginning to gray. He was surrounded by the hunters of Fishing Hawk's band, sleeping in their sheltered ridge camp, save the solitary blanketed figure on watch, staring at him. As dawn edged near, it was light enough to identify Cane-Splitter. The Wolf Clan warrior had arrived in camp last night with no explanation—in Alex's hearing—of why he'd belatedly joined the hunt.

Alex sat up. Behind him Fishing Hawk spoke. Runs-Far replied. The hunters, nine in number since Cane-Splitter's coming, were waking to a second day on the trail. They'd yet to find fresh buffalo sign.

"They are not as plentiful as in the time of my grandfather," Runs-Far had explained, as eager as Alex to see one of the beasts.

Fishing Hawk had added that since white men started wanting skins and furs, some Indians hunted more than was needful. "We want your guns and hatchets." He'd fingered the honed blade of his trade knife. "Our women want your kettles and needles, your cloth and ribbons."

They shared parched corn and jerked venison, rolled their bedding, layered on clothing, checked muskets, which each carried save Runs-Far and Alex, and started out.

As the morning passed, Alex's thoughts fell into a well-worn groove, passing the same trail blazes like a man going in circles. Scotland, the colonies, the Cherokees, Severn. He never wanted to see that plantation again yet ached to know how Joanna fared there. Had the dream been a portent? Did she need him?

"Will you return?"

At the very least he should leave Blackbird's lodge. Probably leave Crooked Branch's town. But what was he to do about Pauling? Or—more immediately—Cane-Splitter, still giving him a baleful eye for avenging Wild Goose in his place.

Like as not for more than that.

By the time the hunters reached the ridgeline above their camp, the rising sun streamed over their shoulders. The peaks to westward were catching fire by light and leaf.

That wilderness of cloud-kissed heights and misted bottomlands, with a stream or a deer or both around every bend, so minded him of the remote glens of Scotland with their tumbling burns and stags rising from the heather, he knew he needn't return across the sea to find what he'd had there. Rory MacNeill was gone, his parents long dead. He'd no close familial ties to draw him back. He could know contentment in this land but for one thing. He wanted it with Joanna Carey, despite reason telling him it could never be.

Still . . . Jemma was settled. He could leave her with a clear conscience. But what of Pauling?

His mind made another loop on its inward track as, bow in hand, he followed the hunters coming down a shoulder of the mountain on a trail they knew.

Pauling had asked him recently to share the details of his leaving Severn. "Why would Phineas Reeves have set you free? Have you never questioned that?"

"I have." They'd been alone at Pauling's fire; he'd spoken freely. "Questioned it from the instant I realized who released me."

A frown troubled Pauling's brow. "I've been

thinking much of Edmund of late. And Joanna. I've spoken with Jemma—Walnut, I mean."

"She tell ye something troubling?"

"It's what she hasn't said that most troubles me."

"Blue Jay." And who'd fathered him, though Alex was certain he knew. "Are ye minded to go back?"

"There's still much for me here, but I'm praying about it now."

Alex hadn't been as annoyed by the answer as he'd once have been, but he ended the conversation by rising to go before it took a turn he didn't want—Pauling asking *him* to return to Severn, against all sense of self-preservation, if not his heart's tugging.

If he did so, and was caught, what would be the penalty? Hanging? Imprisonment?

"Edmund could show mercy," Pauling said before he made his exit, as if he'd read Alex's mind.

Mercy. A thing he'd long since learned to mistrust. Alex had glanced back at the man by the fire. Pauling looked tired, and old. "What d'ye think he'd do?"

"That's part of what troubles me," Pauling had admitted. "You aren't the only one who noticed the influence young Reeves has upon Edmund. Or had. Things may have changed."

"Aye. Maybe." But for better or ill?

Ahead on the trail the hunters halted, gathered around a pile of dung still faintly steaming. More scattered the slope ahead. They'd crossed the path of a buffalo herd, Alex gleaned from the talk around him. Eagerness pushed all thought but the impending hunt to the edges of his mind.

Two hunters went ahead to scout. The rest came along, taking stock of the terrain with which they'd have to deal. Runs-Far was shaking with excitement when the scouts returned, reporting a dozen buffalo sighted. Likely more were hidden among the wind-stunted thickets dotting the grassy slope. They hadn't found a convenient cliff over which to drive the herd, the easiest method since the fall did the killing, but there was a steep-sided draw at the base of the mountain's shoulder toward which the herd was grazing. A stream threaded it. Trees grew thick enough for concealment.

Four of the most experienced hunters, including Fishing Hawk, would drive the herd, a task requiring both a canny sense of the beasts and practiced timing. The remaining five would wait in the draw, the three with muskets on the eastern slope, Alex and Runs-Far on the western, staggered many yards apart to prevent them hitting anything other than a buffalo.

When Runs-Far warned Alex not to aim an arrow too far to his left or right, to be sure he grasped the importance, a few of the hunters grinned. Alex caught a sharper flash in the eyes of Cane-Splitter as the Wolf Clan warrior left to take up his position at the head of the draw on the eastern side. Sent to the head of the draw on the western side, deeper in than Cane-Splitter, Alex was told the wait could be long but he'd know when it was ended. First would come shouts and musket fire, then if all went well the buffalo on the move.

For no reason was he to get himself in the path of that stampede.

"You might be taller than a buffalo," Fishing Hawk said, "but that means little. You will see."

Hunkered behind a stump sprouting a sapling from its rotting remains, Alex waited.

A breeze rustled the trees, scented with leaves taking fire with the season's first frosts. The creek chattered. An occasional hawk or eagle circled high. Morning warmed toward noon. What frost lay at that elevation retreated into shade.

Alex fingered the arrows in a quiver at his hip. Strung his bow. Tested it. Decided to remove his outer shirt.

Before he could do so, a distant whoop came from up the mountain. Another. Then a single musket's firing.

Alex's heart leapt with the sound. Blood hammering, he searched the bend in the draw where the buffalo would appear, waiting for the thud of hooves.

Movement across the draw drew his gaze. At first he thought it a deer bounding through the tree, spooked by the ruckus from above. Then it passed through a break in the foliage.

It was Cane-Splitter.

Alex marked his progress, wondering if the drive had gone amiss and the warrior was headed to tell the others it had failed. The buffalo weren't coming. Heart sinking, he watched the next break in cover, but the Indian didn't pass it. He'd stopped. Directly across the draw.

Then Alex heard what he'd been waiting for, a rumble like a landslide coming down the mountain. As the lead buffalo, a heavy-shouldered bull, came into view around the bend, a musket fired.

The stump Alex hid behind exploded in a shower of wood pulp.

He'd shut his eyes reflexively and leapt aside into the brush. Still gripping his bow, the noise of the stampede swelling in his ears, he scrambled up.

Cane-Splitter's shot—it had to have been his—had sent the herd veering toward Alex and Runs-Far's side of the draw. Massive brown bodies, humped and horned as Blackbird had described, careened in his direction, those at the edge already in among the trees, cracking saplings, tearing loamy ground as they came.

Down the draw Runs-Far shouted, but Alex

couldn't make out his words. He'd seconds before Cane-Splitter reloaded, but now many buffalo were between them, cover enough to do what he'd come to do. Hunt.

The herd was nearly upon him, a wooly-coated wave about to crash. Alex ran to meet it, reaching for his quiver—and found he'd lost his arrows when he dove into the ferns. All but one. He snatched it up and ran along the slope, above and a little ahead of the nearest massive forms, a cow with a trailing calf. His path to the beasts and theirs along the tree line converged like the tip of a spear.

A sight just past that tip chilled his blood. Runs-Far, perhaps confused by Cane-Splitter's premature musket fire, had run out to see what was happening.

Alex bellowed, waving him back into the trees.

The lad stood transfixed, staring at the buffalo cow bearing down. The buffalo saw Runs-Far. Its massive body swerved, not away from the lad but toward him.

Alex, dodging alongside the herd, was fitting arrow to string when another buffalo plunged sideways to avoid a tree too large to trample, looming so close he felt the brush of its coat against his arm.

For an instant, awe and terror blocked all sound. There was nothing but the creature, the hot musk of its hide, the sense of its immensity shuddering up through the ground with each hammer blow of hooves. A blast of breath. The roll of a white-rimmed eye. A presence like thunder incarnate that swallowed his own before the animal swerved away again, a tree came between them, and they were once more distinct. Man and buffalo. Hunter and prey.

No more than a second had passed. Runs-Far was moving now but wasn't going to make it into the trees before the cow overtook him.

"God Almighty, save him!" Alex raised the bow and let the arrow fly, knowing it couldn't stop the creature. It arced wildly, then curved back in its flight. The cow's head dipped and shook.

Still, the massive creature barely slowed before the herd swerved back toward the eastern side of the draw and careened on. Musket fire erupted, along with the shouts of the drivers running at the rear of the herd. Fishing Hawk raced past, never seeing Alex or Runs-Far in the raised dust, but Alex saw his son's crumpled body on the ground. His heart split wide with grief as he reached the lad, who sat up, coughing and coated with dust.

"Where are ye hurt?" Alex threw down his bow and put his hands on Runs-Far—neck, shoulders, arms—looking for injury and finding naught but scrapes. The lad's eyes held wild excitement.

"I thought me dead. That cow . . . You shot?"

"I dinna ken. My arrow went wild."

Runs-Far laughed. "Why else cow turn? I hear you call Heavenly Father."

"Over that commotion?"

"God Almighty, save him." Runs-Far looked him in the eye as he quoted what Alex had shouted. "Maybe this is like the snake," he went on in *Tsalagi*, "the one that did not kill."

Alex stared, dumbstruck, as the last buffalo galloped past. His arrow shouldn't have touched that cow. Pauling shouldn't have survived that canebrake's bite unscathed. Jemma shouldn't have done half the things she had. How many miracles did he need to see before he surrendered to this One who seemed to have a plan in place for his life whether he agreed with it or not? Or understood it.

Must he understand *why* sometimes the snake didn't kill and sometimes it did?

Not if the One behind the plan truly had his good in mind.

"Blessed is he who believes without seeing," Runs-Far said, young face earnest. "Yet you have seen His power and still do not believe?"

Alex stared at Jemma's lad, cut to the quick by the words, and by a flood of understanding. *Joanna.* She'd been granted no miracle, no signs, no great show of power, yet instead of bitterness she professed belief.

"Aye," he said. "All right. If the Almighty wants me that bad, He can have me. Now go!

Kill a buffalo. Give the hide to Shelled Corn, ask for her daughter. Ye've my blessing—not that ye need it."

"I want it!" Runs-Far blazed him a beatific grin, then was gone down the draw where Alex could hear the clatter and bawl of the herd, the muskets firing.

With a frisson of alarm, he remembered Cane-Splitter, but when he looked round at the settling dust, there was no sign of the warrior who'd tried to murder him. Perhaps not for the first time.

Nor the last, if he stayed.

37

Runs-Far's mother met them with news that Reverend Pauling lay ill in his lodge. Shouldering his share of the hunters' meat, Runs-Far hurried toward the Longhair Clan lodges. Leaving his share at Blackbird's lodge, Alex followed, finding Pauling in the grip of fever. He crossed the lodge and knelt beside his sleeping bench.

Jemma hovered near. "Me and Squash Blossom been caring for him with willow bark, but it don't help like that other kind—Jesuit bark—and he outta that. What we gonna do?"

If Alex had needed confirmation, he had it. "I'll be taking him back across the mountains."

He stood, the decision resting like an anvil on his chest.

Runs-Far stood behind Jemma, a hand on her shoulder. "Is he able?"

Alex exchanged a look with the lad. "I have to try. Dinna say anything of it yet. I must go and speak to Blackbird."

"I not like you go," Blackbird said in English once he'd said all he meant to say on the matter. "But you will do what you must."

Alex gazed at the fire warming her lodge on that chill autumn day, then around at its familiar shapes and shadows, wishing briefly there was no claim on his heart to draw him away. No other need. He went to the place where he slept, to the knapsack he'd found outside the smokehouse the night Reeves set him free.

"Already you go?" Blackbird said behind him.

"I'll move my things to Pauling's lodge for the night, help watch over him." He'd have to decide how to transport Pauling if the man wasn't capable of walking. Perhaps he could construct a travois as they'd done with the buffalo butchered in the draw.

"You want horse, carry holy man? I cannot give the one was his. The warrior who took it will keep. I give mine."

Blackbird had only one horse. "I canna take your horse, not after ye've given so much. To me and the lass. The reverend too."

Blackbird tilted her head. "What have I given? Food. Shelter. Clothes." She shrugged. "That is reasonable."

"Maybe so, but that's not all I meant. I speak of your friendship, and that of your people."

She looked at him searchingly. "Not all my people."

Not until that moment had Alex known whether he meant to tell her of the incident in the draw. If he thought Cane-Splitter's attempt to shoot him had merely to do with his presumption in avenging Wild Goose's death, he wouldn't concern her with it. But Cane-Splitter had disliked him from the moment Blackbird showed interest. And something else, a suspicion only, yet if it was true, it concerned Blackbird more than anyone. So he told her.

"I canna prove he meant to murder me," he finished by saying. "But I dinna think he'll give up trying to do me harm if I stay. One of us will kill the other, eventually."

Face darkened, Blackbird replied in *Tsalagi*. "You maybe cannot prove it, but I believe it. That one came to me the day you left for the hunt. He asked to be my husband. I refused him."

About to roll up his bedding, Alex went still, certain he saw that other suspicion in Blackbird's eyes—that there had never been a second Tuscarora skulking in the woods that day, waiting to brain him over the head; more disturbing still, that the story Cane-Splitter told of her husband's murder was a lie.

"I will know the truth," she said. "But Cane-Splitter is not your concern, Alex MacKinnon. You must go from this place. Take the holy man so he might live. And so you will live."

Moments later Little Thunder came in, saw what he was doing, and blurted, "I go with you? I help?"

Alex sighed, closed his eyes, then looked at the

boy, waiting with fragile hope that he must dash. He held out an arm. "Come here."

Little Thunder must have heard the denial in his voice, for he burst into tears as he rushed into Alex's embrace.

"Listen," Alex said in *Tsalagi*, holding him. "I not take you from mother. You man here. Her only." He glanced at Blackbird over her son's head.

She made a sound of affirmation, lips pressed tight.

Little Thunder pulled away, face contorted with unhappiness. "I know you must go. The holy man is sick. Will you come back when he is better?"

He took the lad by the shoulders, holding his gaze. "We see again, you, me. Be strong for mother. Help her."

The lad nodded, fiercely driving away his tears. "Still I go with you."

"Lad, ye canna do both," Alex said in English.

Little Thunder shook his head. "Both."

"I dinna ken what ye mean."

The lad said something earnest in *Tsalagi* that Alex didn't catch. Blackbird gasped. Alex looked to her, questioning.

"My son has new name. That is what he say. No more Little Thunder. He is now Thunder-Going-Away-Across-the-Mountains."

The lad was nodding, gazing solemnly at Alex. "Thunder-Going," he said, enunciating each word with care. "With you. Going *here*," he added, and made a fist above his heart.

As word spread of his departure, the members of Pauling's flock came to say their farewells if he was awake, to pray for him if he wasn't. Some brought provisions for the journey. Only Jemma and Runs-Far watched the night through with Alex, taking it in turns to sleep.

During a lull in visitors, Jemma glanced across the lodge to where Alex sorted through the reverend's belongings, choosing what to add to his own pack in the hope the man could walk come morning if unburdened. Alex caught her scrutiny sidelong, but she dodged a meeting of their gazes.

"Jemma . . . ?" The reverend's voice unraveled like a thread from his nest of blankets. Alex rose as the gaunt face turned in his direction. "Is that Alex returned?"

Though he'd spoken briefly with the reverend, mostly Alex had kept to the shadows, letting the Cherokees have their time with the man. Crouching now beside the bench, he reminded him, "We leave come the morn. Ye'll walk out of Crooked Branch's town if ye can. Else I mean to carry ye."

Pauling's eyes widened. "You told me so . . . I thought it a dream."

"We ain't letting you die, Reverend. You need that bark." Jemma shot a glance at Alex.

"But it's only him going with you. Not me."

Pauling's fevered eyes reflected resignation. "Timothy?"

"He there," Jemma said with a nod toward Runs-Far, asleep on a bench. She fetched a dipper of water from a bowl nearby and handed it to the reverend, who pushed himself up to drink. Then she looked again at Alex, amber gaze guarded. "I stole my own self, remember? You ain't giving me back."

Alex put a hand to her shoulder. "Ye're Shelled Corn's daughter now. Ye decide where ye go. Speaking of . . . ye've talked with Runs-Far, I take it?"

Jemma softened as she took the dipper from Pauling and filled it again. "He said we got your blessing."

"Ye do, *mo nighean*. I'm happy for ye, after all ye've been through."

A shadow of that old haunted look crossed Jemma's face. She opened her mouth to speak, but Runs-Far stirred, rubbing his eyes. She went to the lad, and moments later lay down to sleep beside Blue Jay.

Runs-Far wrapped a blanket around Pauling's shoulders and sat beside him, unhappy over the looming separation. "I am not ready," he said in English. "I am young. Not an elder. Not even a husband . . . yet." He glanced at Jemma, already asleep.

485

Alex drifted back to sorting through what they'd take in a few hours' time, but heard Pauling's labored reply: "Do you recall the words I said when last we spoke of this? *Let no one despise your youth.*"

"They are words. Hard to *do*."

"The Almighty will complete the work begun in you, my Timothy. And the work He will do through you." Pauling paused, then said, "Teach the people as I have you. Respect your elders. Be patient with all. Encourage the weak. Always remember . . . you do nothing in your own strength. Wait on the Lord. He will instruct you . . ."

The man was passing on the mantle of shepherd to Runs-Far, yet the words stirred in Alex like living things, casting him back over the seasons of his life to see the pattern that had emerged time and again, whether or not he embraced it. Others had looked to him, yet his own strength and wisdom to lead had failed him every time. It hadn't been enough. Not at Culloden. Not on the *James & Mary*. Not at Severn. Yet he'd denied the Almighty could be both sovereign and good, not with the proliferation of evil he'd seen. Only in choosing to trust himself, and failing at every turn, was it made clear that in giving men a choice to believe and obey, God must allow an alternative, that the potential for evil must exist for those who wouldn't choose Him.

As he'd once done. But no more.

The choice made by heart in the heat of a miraculous moment, in that mountain draw, he now confirmed by reason, casting his lot with a God he didn't fully understand, rejecting the alternative—trusting in men, whose propensity for greed, weakness, and outright evil he understood all too well.

Including his own.

"You were my first convert among your people," Pauling was saying to Runs-Far. "First to embrace Heavenly Father's mercy, and my friendship. You have nearly mastered the reading of it . . . so I leave my Bible with you."

Runs-Far drew in his breath. "That precious thing. You give it?"

"With all my heart." Pauling slid a hand toward the head of his sleeping bench and drew out his battered copy of the Scriptures. "You will find my scribblings in the margins, if you can decipher them—for what they're worth."

A tear ran down Runs-Far's cheek. "They are worth everything."

Pauling placed the Bible in Runs-Far's hands. "With every thought of you, I'll be thanking the Almighty for your life, my Timothy, and petitioning heaven on your behalf."

"Will you come back to us?"

"If God wills it . . . many times." Runs-Far helped Pauling lie down. Before the man drifted off again to sleep, he caught Alex's gaze. "I will walk in the morning. How far, I cannot say."

Alex was relieved to see him sleep.

Runs-Far stood and looked at Alex, his uncertainty evident. The lad might love the Almighty and have a heart for his people, but he couldn't be more than sixteen.

Alex stood before him. "He chose well," he told Runs-Far, placing a steadying hand to his shoulder. "Trust his choice."

Runs-Far nodded once. "And you keep him alive. I need him."

Hours later, with dawn approaching, Jemma woke to find Runs-Far sleeping. She came to stand next to Alex, crouched and tying shut the flap of the bulging knapsack. "How you going to carry all that? Why won't you take a horse?"

"A horse has to rest and graze. We'll go faster over mountains without one. If I must, I'll leave the tools behind. I dinna think the man weighs much more than my pack as it is."

Jemma didn't reply. A trickle of gray around the door-hide illumed her face enough to show a troubled look.

"Whatever ye're wanting to say to me, Jemma, if ye dinna tell me now, ye may never get the chance."

"I know." She heaved a sigh older than time. "Hard getting the words out, is all."

"Aye, I see. Come here." He led her to a bench.

"You remember asking me how Blue Jay come to be?" she blurted, barely seated. "That day by the river."

"I'm not likely to forget it."

"It was Mister Reeves. And he done it more'n once."

Pain in his jaw; he was grinding his teeth. "I'm sorry, lass. Sorry we didna see it when something might have been done. I mind Joanna was worried about ye, going about as ye were in lad's clothes, hair cropped . . ."

Her hair had grown in the months since. She'd grown too. A little taller, fuller. A mother now. Still so very young.

"It was my hair he liked," she said. "That's why I cut it off."

Alex didn't want to be having this conversation. Didn't want to understand the mind of a man who would abuse a slave, much less one as young as Jemma.

"I think he thought I was younger than I was."

"Younger?" he echoed.

"Uh-huh," Jemma said. Then the floodgates opened, and she was spilling. "He told me he'd do worse things did I ever tell, but one time Demas tried to get me to say whether Mister Reeves ever bothered me. Don't rightly know all he was on about, something 'bout breaking a vow."

"What d'ye mean, a vow?"

Jemma shook her head. "That Demas scairt me nigh as much as Mister Reeves, cornering me that day in the dairy shed. Then Mister Reeves hisself caught us, and I was thinking it was gonna get worse, until Miss Joanna found the lot of us and hauled me out."

He remembered the day, the altercation in the stable yard.

"Then I got away from all that, on account of you," Jemma continued. "Now I got Blue Jay and Runs-Far and Shelled Corn. I got so much."

He wanted to draw her close, kiss the top of her head. Given all she'd just said, he didn't dare, but she leaned her head briefly against his arm and his heart melted, sensing her trust. But when she straightened, a frown pinched her brows.

"Is there more, *mo nighean*?"

Jemma reached up and touched one of her braids. "I said it was my hair he liked. Figured it was on account it's fair. Not as fair as hers . . ."

A faint breeze swayed the door-hide, raising a chill on Alex's calves. A deeper chill gripped his heart.

"Hers?" he asked, already knowing what sort of monster he'd left the Careys to face.

"I don't think it was me he wanted," Jemma said. "Those times he was hurting me, Mister Reeves called me Charlotte."

490

38

October 1748

Alarmed to see Mister Reeves exiting Papa's room, Joanna grasped the door before he could shut it and pushed past him, halting at sight of Papa seated near the window, a ledger open across his lap. His breakfast was nowhere in sight. Aware of her heart's pounding, she stepped back and shut the door.

Mister Reeves stood in the passage, expressionless.

"Forgive me," she hurried to say to cover her too obvious relief. "I bear ill news, but . . . I'll not interrupt now."

Since sharing her hopes for Severn's future, Papa had been holding things back from her, shutting her out of even the smallest matters concerning the plantation. She'd given Phineas Reeves a weapon—the truth—which he was well practiced at using against her. She suspected he'd been busy twisting Papa's rejection of her plans into a barrier of mistrust.

"Perhaps you'll tell *me* your ill news?"

The challenge in those hazel eyes constricted Joanna's throat.

After the incident with Demas and the oleander,

Papa's health had taken a turn for the better. She and Azuba had ceased their close monitoring of his food, thinking that, having lost his scapegoat, Mister Reeves wouldn't dare continue his tampering.

For a time they'd been proved right, until Papa's ailment flared anew a few days past.

So it had begun again—the watching, the pretending.

But today another matter had arisen. "Three field hands are missing this morning. Phoebe and Mari say they ran in the night. Did you know?"

Mister Reeves showed no surprise at the news. "Had you been patient a moment, I'd have allayed your concern. They didn't run. I sold them."

"Sold them? To whom?"

"A fellow on his way downriver to Wilmington. Late last night."

Joanna hadn't known the three missing slaves well, but one had been Sybil's kin. An uncle, she thought. "Papa had no objection to the sale?"

Mister Reeves held her stare. "You seem distressed, Miss Carey. I should have thought the news would please you."

"Why would you think so?"

"You wanted a simpler life, no slaves to serve you. Perhaps you may yet get your wish. I'm doing all I can to see you and Charlotte—and

Captain Carey—keep this roof over your heads, but my options are limited."

"Why didn't you tell me of the sale?"

"It was my and Captain Carey's decision."

"So Papa knew of it beforehand?"

Mister Reeves made a dismissive gesture. "He's finally giving Severn his attention. I'd like to see him continue undistracted."

They faced each other, mistrust all but shimmering on the air. Joanna was first to lower her gaze.

Mister Reeves started for the back door.

"Shall I see you at dinner?" she called, hoping for an idea of where the day might keep him, and how long.

He didn't pause or look back. "I cannot say, Miss Carey. Good day."

In the kitchen, Joanna found Marigold about to carry in Papa's breakfast. "I'll take it, Mari, but first . . . are you sure the missing field hands weren't sold? By Mister Reeves."

"No one been *sold,* Miss Joanna." Marigold drew her to the end of the kitchen, away from Phoebe and her girls, including Sybil, who didn't look like a woman whose kin had been sold downriver, but rather one in possession of a satisfying secret.

"I know Mister Reeves ain't sold 'em," Marigold said, low-voiced, "on account he come last night to 'Lijah, tried to make him say what's going on—where the hands had run to. 'Lijah say, 'How you think I know anything about it?' Mister Reeves say, 'You thick now with the slaves having all but married one.' 'Lijah didn't tell him nothing—if he even knows. I didn't ask."

Joanna wouldn't either. She knew all she needed to know. Did Mister Reeves think her incapable of uncovering the truth, or did he no longer care if she did?

"Miss Joanna," Marigold said, "how long till you tell Master Carey all you know? He *got* to take your word, now Mister Reeves done outright lied."

The truth. Would it set them free at last?

"You're right, Mari." Somehow, she'd make her stepfather hear her and believe the man he'd entrusted to an appalling degree had been all along a serpent, striking at their heels.

Papa, seated still by the window, didn't touch his breakfast once she related her conversation with Mister Reeves that morning in the passage. Face set, he glanced at the ledger on his bedside table, in his eyes frustration—with her. "I know the slaves ran away, Joanna. Phineas told me this morning."

"He told *me* otherwise—stood right outside this room not half an hour ago and said he sold them downriver. Which is the truth?"

Papa reached for the cup on his breakfast tray,

grimaced at its contents, and set it down again. He rubbed his eyes, then fixed a strained gaze on her. "Speaking of truth, why did you never tell me about Demas?"

"That he ran? I told you when it happened."

"That he ran, yes. Phineas told me the entirety of it. Demas is to blame for my infirmities."

She hadn't known Mister Reeves had been so forthcoming about his slave, but they were telling each other so little these days, she and Papa.

She'd been seated on the edge of her step-father's bed, but rose now and paced toward the blue-manteled hearth, its fire lit but dying. She turned and faced Papa. "It's true Mister Reeves brought his so-called evidence—the oleander—to the smithy, but no one saw where he got it."

"From Demas's cabin," Papa said.

"No one *saw* it."

"Demas ran rather than dispute the accusation."

Joanna wanted to scream, but kept her voice level. "No matter how much preference Mister Reeves has shown him, Demas is still a slave. What would have come of it had he stayed? He'd have been locked in that smokehouse like Alex was, given no chance of pleading his case."

"MacKinnon again?" Papa winced, a hand going to his side. "Does everything come down to him with you?"

"Perhaps it should. Did Mister Reeves tell you it was he set Alex at liberty?"

Papa's face went a shade paler than his pain had rendered it. "He did not. Is it true? Or do you wish only to discredit Phineas further?"

"I had it from his own lips. He did it out of jealousy. He wanted to be rid of Alex."

"Then perhaps I ought to thank him."

Joanna swallowed back the words she longed to say, amazed her stepfather could so misjudge the two men. "Alex isn't at issue here, Papa. You are. Demas is long gone, and you're once again ailing. Can you explain that?"

"Phineas said it may take time for the poison to work itself out of my system."

"Phineas said!" Joanna exclaimed, losing her patience. "I'm sick to death of what that man says. Why aren't you?"

"Phineas has had my trust these past two years. He's been faithful in my service when heaven itself seems set against me. Can you explain *that?*"

She could, but even as his face twisted again in pain, she feared he wasn't ready, in any way, to hear it. "Elijah has done the same—as best he can—for much longer than two years."

"Speaking of Elijah," Papa said, "perhaps the reason Phineas lied to you is because he couldn't wring the truth from Elijah—with whom you've become thick as thieves again. Perhaps Phineas no longer knows whom *he* may trust."

Alarm seized Joanna. "Mari told me Elijah knows nothing about—"

"Enough of this hearsay!" Her stepfather sounded more like himself than he had in months, yet as he stood, she saw he trembled. "I want to see the three of you together. Here and now."

Mister Reeves and Elijah were sent for while she waited in the passage, Papa ostensibly eating his breakfast, though when she peeked into the room, he hadn't touched the food.

Elijah came first, Mister Reeves practically on his heels. There was time for Elijah to whisper before he entered Papa's room, "Mari told me what ye meant to do. Ye've told him everything?"

Hardly. But she'd no time to answer before Mister Reeves reached them.

The animosity was thick enough to slice as Papa, the only one seated, questioned Elijah about the three missing slaves.

"I don't know what *he* has told you, sir," Elijah said, his disdain for Mister Reeves evident. "Those men weren't sold. They've run."

"Elijah," Joanna began.

Papa's sharp glance rendered her mute. Sweat beaded his brow, though the hearth fire had gone out and the room was cool. "I'm aware of that."

"You are, sir?" Elijah cast Joanna a bewildered scowl. "Mari said . . . I was told Reeves maintained he sold them."

"He did so—to me," Joanna interjected, then stepped so she could face Mister Reeves.

497

"Why would you lie to me? I don't understand."

"Neither do I understand what's going on between the three of you," Papa said. "Did you sell the slaves, Phineas, or have they run?"

"They've run, sir. As I told you."

"Did you tell Joanna different?"

Joanna stood amazed as color mounted in Mister Reeves's face. Could the man blush on demand?

"I own that I did, sir. I'm not proud of it. So much has gone amiss for you since I've been in your employ. It weighs on me that one of the reasons Miss Carey has refused my suit is because she holds me to blame—in your hearing she labeled me a Jonah. I couldn't bring myself to add one more offense to her list."

"Ye *are* to blame," Elijah forced through clenched teeth, with no attempt to cool his heated tone. "Ye can stand here before the very man you've poisoned all these months and say such to him?"

"Elijah!" Joanna's stepfather pushed to his feet, tumbling his chair backward.

Elijah turned to Joanna, perplexed. "Did ye not tell him?"

"Tell him what?" Mister Reeves cut in. "You saw the proof with your own eyes, saw Demas run upon discovery of his betrayal."

"Your slave," Elijah shot back. "At your command."

"Who struck me down in front of you! Next you'll be blaming me for what? The forge's explosion?" Mister Reeves turned to Papa with the air of one beset. "I begin to see how Miss Carey has formed her ill opinion of me, sir. Moon has been stoking those flames for well over a year—ever since you rejected his suit."

"I've done no such thing, yet I do so blame ye." Scarred face flushed with fury, Elijah lifted the stump of his wrist. "Ye cost me my hand, my service. My *life!*"

"Stand down, the pair of you!" Papa shouted, then doubled over.

"Papa—" Joanna rushed to him.

Mister Reeves blocked her way. "Sir, let me help you to your bed. This is too much. Miss Carey, Moon, please go."

"I will not," Joanna began, furious at his presumption, but with much effort her stepfather straightened.

"No, Phineas. I'm well enough to end this." Papa drew breath and, though wasted and pale, seemed to gather the authority once wielded as master and commander around him like a tattered cloak. "Elijah, gather whatever things are yours. I want you gone. This hour."

The flush of battle drained from Elijah's face, leaving his scars standing out a stark and rippled pink. "Ye're asking me to leave Severn?"

"I am not *asking* it."

Shock had frozen Elijah. "I'll take Mari and Jory with me."

"They aren't yours." Mister Reeves had put his back to Papa; only Joanna and Elijah could see the triumph in his eyes. "They belong to Severn."

Joanna looked to her stepfather, certain he wouldn't be so cruel. "Papa, you cannot separate them. It's—" She broke off when Elijah swung toward her, shaking his head.

Without another word to Papa or Mister Reeves, he made for the door. As he passed her, he spoke for her ears alone. "Kitchen."

She found him there with his son in his arms, Marigold clutching his coat sleeve, silently weeping. From the doorway she watched him bend and kiss Jory's head, then return him to his mother. He kissed Marigold's trembling mouth, whispered a few words, then took up a knapsack from the kitchen floor and, as Phoebe and her girls stood gaping, strode to the doorway, meeting Joanna in its square of morning light.

She looked into his eyes, an ache in her throat.

"I've an idea where the field hands have gone," Elijah said. "I'll find them—and, with God's help, a way to still be of aid ye."

Guilt churned within her. "Whatever I attempt, he's a step ahead of me. This is my fault. I never know when to speak and when to stay silent."

Elijah actually smiled. "Joanna, don't. I've

seen this day coming for months. But will ye do something for me?"

"Anything."

"Watch over Mari and Jory for me. Keep them safe."

"I'll do all I can. I promise." She meant it, but as he went out she wondered, with Papa taking Mister Reeves at his word, despite the cost, and Elijah forced to go, who was left to watch over her?

None but You, Lord. None but You.

She waited two days, pretending she'd been cowed into submission by Elijah's banishment. Then she overheard Mister Reeves telling Papa he meant to ride to a neighbor come morning, some miles south along the river, to try to sell one of Papa's last breeding mares.

Once she'd seen him ride away with the mare in tow, she brought Papa's breakfast to the house and found him in his study, standing before one of the maps that once guided him at sea, looking so shrunken from the man he'd been a year ago, her heart nearly misgave her.

But if she didn't do this now, what would follow? His death; she and Charlotte cast adrift with nothing but their lives, if even those.

She set the tray on the wide desk beside the white conch shell. The sight of it brought back vivid memory of Alex in the candlelit passage, his smile as he held it to his ear, hearing its distant echo of the sea.

Her chest ached, as though her heart had twisted.

"Papa, here is breakfast."

He turned from the map. "Where is Charlotte this morning?"

During his times confined to bed, when he'd felt well enough for company, Charlotte had sometimes spent an hour in his room. Now, however, Joanna required his undivided attention.

"She's with Azuba."

"Just you and me for breakfast?" He glanced at the tray, seemed to notice food enough for one. She'd have no appetite until this was done. Likely not for some time after.

"If you wouldn't mind my company, I'll stay."

He seated himself at the desk. Joanna perched on the bed. She ran a hand across the coverlet, wished with all her heart Reverend Pauling was present, breathed a prayer that he might somehow know her need, and began. "I know you put little stock in my opinion these days, Papa, but I need to tell you something. It's to do with Mister Reeves."

Papa had taken a bite of toast. He swallowed, resistance rising in his gaze. Joanna knew a niggling of doubt but was too desperate to draw back.

"Please, Papa. Let me say this, then you can

ask questions—or remonstrate—whatever you need to do. Will you listen? For Charlotte's sake, if not for me?"

Some of her stepfather's color, wan as it was, bled away. "What is it?"

"I'm going to tell you why I believe Mister Reeves is behind most, if not all, the losses we've suffered this past year and more. Please, just for a moment, conceive that it may be true."

Having thought it through a dozen times over the past two days, how she would present her case, she launched into it succinctly, recounting all that had gone wrong since Phineas Reeves's arrival, starting with the explosion of the forge.

Papa didn't take a second bite of toast, but he remained silent, as he'd agreed. She dropped her gaze only once while she spoke and saw that he was clutching the edge of his desk.

"Bit by bit, since his arrival, you've lost nearly everything that was yours, with Mister Reeves lamenting each loss all the while *he* has been behind it, either directly or through Demas's agency. I believe the only reason he sought my hand was to gain complete control over Severn, as my husband and your heir."

"He'd never have complete control," Papa said. "Not as long as I . . ." But he didn't finish the statement, as something flickered in his gaze, and his brow furrowed.

"As long as you lived? Exactly, Papa. Mister

Reeves has been attempting to make Severn his even as he destroys it piece by piece. And I'm certain that poison is, once again, the cause of your illness."

"Joanna, we've been through this. Demas likely set the mill ablaze—I admit I misjudged MacKinnon on that score. Demas may have even caused the kiln's explosion and for all I know the forge's. But Demas *was* caught with oleander in his cabin."

"So Mister Reeves maintains," she said, keeping her voice reasoning with effort. "I know Elijah's words hold no weight with you now, but he was right. Demas was Mister Reeves's slave. Not ours. And since we've been watching over your food again—"

"Who's been watching?" her stepfather cut in.

"Azuba and I," she said and hurried on. "We've let no one else near your food from kitchen to bedside since you fell sick again. And you're feeling better these last few days, aren't you? It's not the first time we've done this, Papa. It cannot be mere coincidence. Only this time Demas isn't a factor."

"Joanna . . . Phineas said it would take time. I might have a relapse, mightn't I?"

There was a note of pleading in his voice she'd never heard. It was almost a physical pain, causing him further distress, but she couldn't retreat now.

"Think back. How many times did Mister Reeves bring your meals to you right before and during your worst spells?" She watched his expression carefully, saw the denial crumbling. "He's divided you from Elijah, from Alex, from *me*. Only you have the power to stop him before it's too late. I cannot protect you alone. You must stand and protect yourself. Charlotte and me as well. Dismiss that man as you did Elijah."

Her stepfather pushed away the tray on his desk, though she was certain the food wasn't tainted. He looked at her with staring eyes that gradually filled with horror.

"*If* this is true . . . *why?*"

"I believe I know why. Think back to when you knew him aboard the *Severn*."

A sheen of sweat sprang to her stepfather's brow. "Phineas was like a son to me. He and Elijah."

"Yet it was Elijah you took into retirement. Elijah for whom you found a place."

"He was my personal servant. Of the two Phineas seemed better suited to life at sea. I thought he was content to remain."

Joanna leaned forward, hands fisted on her knees. "I don't think he was; at least he quickly came to regret it. He's told me things about the man who took command. Captain Potts allowed others to perpetrate cruelties, and Phineas, it would seem, bore the brunt. I'm convinced he blames you—and Elijah—for leaving him."

"Then why, when we met in Wilmington after all those years, would he have sought my help, agreed to . . . ?" He paused, running a hand over his sweating brow, fingertips squeezing his temples, as though his thoughts as well as his words had scattered.

"Revenge, Papa. I believe it's that simple." Unable to sit still a moment longer, Joanna sprang from the bed and crossed the room. "He's been a viper in our midst, striking out at everything and everyone that might have been of help to us. Elijah, Alex . . ."

Tears came, for fury and grief at all Phineas Reeves had cost them.

"MacKinnon," her stepfather said dully, the sound of the name odd on his lips, slurred as though he'd been drinking. But Joanna was in full spate, finally releasing the pent-up fear and heartbreak of the past months.

"Why did I not stand up for him? Why did I not better fight for him? He asked me to marry him, to walk away from this life I've come to loathe, and though he called me weak because I couldn't leave you, or Charlotte, still I loved him!"

Her stepfather made a strangled sound behind her.

Joanna faced him, tears streaming. He'd half

risen from his chair, struggling to speak through a mouth peculiarly twisted.

"You . . . Mac . . . Kin . . . ?"

Alex's garbled name was the last he said before he fell back into his chair, then toppled to the floor.

39

October 1748

Pauling needed all his breath to put one foot before the other, often leaning on Alex as they traversed the steep paths leading them eastward. The autumn days were shortening; the mountain heights were fiery-leafed but frosted cold at night. Alex woke often to keep a fire going, while Pauling shivered and endured. Fishing Hawk had described well the landmarks to watch for, the quickest paths to take. Alex was reasonably certain of his course, but their progress was distressingly slow.

Late the third day on the trail, Pauling's strength failed, forcing Alex to carry him until he found sufficient shelter from a spattering rain in which to build a fire, beneath a grandfather spruce with boughs vaulted enough that the small blaze wouldn't ignite them. Once he had it going, Alex rummaged in the knapsack for something edible.

"When did it happen?"

Startled by the thread of Pauling's voice, he looked up. The man was eyeing him with fever-bright eyes strained with suffering, and alight with joy. Alex knew at once what he meant. His mouth lifted at the corner. "On the buffalo hunt."

He told briefly of the run through the draw, the arrow, the words exchanged with Runs-Far.

"Timothy," Pauling murmured through fever-cracked lips. "I knew him well chosen."

"Ye've a canny sense of folk," Alex agreed. "I once told ye I could never believe as ye did. As ye've already deduced, I take it back." At the smug look on Pauling's face, he laughed soundlessly. "I dinna think ye're one bit surprised."

Pauling shook his head, moisture sheening his eyes. Gradually, though, a soberness overtook his gaze. "Yet you've been encumbered by more than that monstrous pack—and my dead weight—these past days."

Alex shook off a shudder of foreboding. "Aye, ye're right."

Pauling offered a weak smile. "I cannot bear a pack, but I may yet help you bear other burdens."

Alex unearthed a parcel of jerked meat, of which he was heartily sick. He offered a strip to the reverend. "Ye willna like it—not one bit," he warned. "And I dinna mean just this poor fare."

He related what Jemma told him of Reeves, including that most ominous detail. *Charlotte.*

He'd never seen Pauling look so shaken. "Father in heaven."

"I kent the man wasna what he wished to seem," Alex said. "But put him down to a schemer bent on advancing himself, using Edmund Carey to do so, clearing the likes of me from his path. I'd not have left them to his mercy had I kent Reeves for such a monster."

He held out a canteen. Pauling drank, then sat for a time, eyes closed. When at last he spoke, he said, "I'd have had you try to see me to my sister's house, but in light of what you've just told me . . ."

"D'ye mean now to return to Severn?" Alex doubted the man could make it half so far.

"No. Mountain Laurel is close, though?"

Hugh Cameron. A measure of relief flooded Alex. "I'll get ye there, Reverend. If I must carry ye the distance."

Four days later, Alex was less certain of keeping that promise. Though the weather had favored them, Pauling traveled a shorter distance afoot each day. Yet by Alex's reckoning they ought to have reached the Yadkin's headwaters. Camped that evening beneath an overhang of rock, he decided come morning he'd scout for sign of the river.

With the eastern sky beginning to gray, he left the reverend asleep under both blankets, donned the knapsack, and set out to climb the ridge below which they'd camped. Using roots protruding from the steep-sided ridge, he heaved himself up, scrambling past tangles of rhododendron, hoisting himself over shelves of stone. After a half-hour's climb, the burgeoning light showed him an opening in the pines and chestnut oaks growing thick along the ridge above. A bald, or maybe a meadow. He hoped it wasn't so tightly hemmed by trees as to prevent view of the land round about.

He was sweating by the time he broke through the final scrim, scratched and spotted with leafy debris, and stopped in startled wonder.

Far below, a wide river coiled around the diminishing humps of the dawn-shadowed mountains that blended down into the lower backcountry, thickly treed with the fiery shades of autumn, the whole pocketed in mist still sheltered from the rising sun.

The river had to be the Yadkin, which meant the headwaters were far behind them. They were nearer Mountain Laurel than he'd dared hope.

With relief washing over him, he took in the lay of the land directly before him. While the wood he'd climbed through continued up the mountainside, before him was a treeless stretch that had its apex but an arrow's flight to his left. Not steeply sided, save where the woods began, the open land spread gently down between the mountain's shoulders to his right, broadening until it vanished into low-lying mist, while at its upper reach, issuing in a fall that burst from the trees, a creek of generous proportions carved its way down, doubtless to join the river below.

It was a high cove, wide enough to support a modest spread of fields without felling the first tree.

Once he'd taken in what the eye could see, he began to see what wasn't there, but one day might be. Over on that rise where the creek took a bend away from the wood was a fitting site for a cabin, while that level spot downstream, overspread by a chestnut flushing yellow with the season, there he could envision a blacksmith shop. Higher up, at the fall, a mill.

Turning this way and that to survey the land, he saw other sites for cabins, fields, their ghostly images glimpsed from the corners of his vision, built and thriving.

As the mist crept along the creek's course and kissed the first slant of morning sunlight breaking through clouds, he smelled the clean air and the pines and the autumn leaves, while behind him in the trees birds spoke, and knew . . . he'd found his place.

A place for his people, once he had some. "God willing," he said, the words a prayer.

From his pack he removed the blacksmith tools, wrapped in oilcloth for the journey, carried them to the spot where he'd envisioned a forge, and buried them there beneath the chestnut. From the creek he gathered stones and raised a cairn to mark the place. Not that he needed the reminder.

The stones were a prayer as well.

● ● ●

A slender man with a gray wig dressed in curls, Duncan Cameron had nattered on in the Gaelic since before he'd sat to supper with his overseer and his unexpected guest, who'd been too distracted to enjoy the meal prepared by Cameron's slaves, a feast compared to his recent subsistence.

The elder Cameron had required little explanation for Alex's appearance, so thrilled was he to find a Gaelic-speaking Scotsman at his door, even an unwashed, bearded giant dressed as an Indian, cradling a very sick man to his chest.

Since made as presentable as razor and a borrowed suit—inches short in the sleeve—could make him, Alex reined in his scattered thoughts to focus on his host's latest question as the three removed to the adjacent parlor, glasses in hand.

"So 'tis Barra in the Isles where ye were raised?"

With the crackle of the hearth fire filling the room and worry for Pauling, in the care of the man's slaves, filling his mind, Alex replied, "Aye. My mother was a MacNeill. I was brought up by her brother, my parents having passed. But I was born to the MacKinnons of Skye."

"Skye." Duncan closed his eyes, inhaling fumes from the whisky in his glass as though its smoked-peat scent called up the ghosts of heather and gorse and rocky burns long since left behind.

"I tramped the rugged Cuillins in my own youth. But tell me, in the town of Port Righ, does Angus Og MacNab still keep his inn?"

Alex had never heard of Angus Og and said so.

"I shall wager he does not," Cameron said, grief shadowing his features. "Likely that devil, Cumberland, thrust him through on the field at Culloden."

As the man talked on as if he'd been present that April morn the Highland clans were shattered, Alex caught himself drumming his fingers on the chair's arm. Pauling had received a dose of the Jesuit bark soon after their arrival, but Alex longed to know how the man fared. Forcing his fingers to still, he glanced at Hugh Cameron, drawn near the hearth in a matching chair.

With a sympathetic tilt of his coppery head, Hugh quirked his mouth as if to say, What can ye do but humor the man?

To be sitting in a parlor, whisky in a glass, listening to the old man bemoan the destruction of the clans as though he'd left Scotland's shores but yesterday—the whole of it in the Gaelic—had Alex's head spinning with a sense of unreality. His mind was taken up with different places and people. Pauling, aye, but the Careys as well, the more so after what Hugh told him before their meal.

He grew aware of silence in the room. Cameron had asked another question. He'd no notion what.

514

Hugh leapt to his rescue. "Well, Duncan, as MacKinnon here was stuck in that ship's hold with me until we were separated, I am sure he will have no better notion than I what became of the rest of our number."

"Aye," Alex said, with a vague idea now of what the man had asked. "The king's mercy did not extend so far as letting us choose our path into exile. Hugh, here, being the exception."

"A sorrow to the bones is exile from one's country," Duncan Cameron said. "By whatever path. 'Tis natural to cleave to those one finds of his own people in a strange land, as I have found Hugh here . . ."

As Cameron droned on, Alex nearly growled with impatience, until the thought arose that this man sitting in his parlor talking endlessly of a Scotland that no longer existed might very well be what he would have become had he clung resolutely to the past, refusing to yield to One greater than he and go forward into the unknown. *A sorrow to the bones.*

Scotland was his sorrow as well, but it was also his past. While he mightn't have planned or chosen it, this new land and its people were his future. More importantly, his present.

The last words they'd exchanged while Hugh was seeing him shaved and fitted out with serviceable clothing darted about his mind: the ill-fortune that had plagued Severn hadn't ended with the burning of the mill. It was no more than rumor, filtered the many miles upriver to Cross Creek, reaching Hugh's ears but a fortnight past when last there on Cameron's business.

Rumor was enough to torment. What ill fortune? What of Joanna, and the wee lass, Charlotte?

"Ye will surely ken," Duncan Cameron was saying, leaning forward to pour himself more whisky from a decanter, "that North Carolina's governor is a Scot. Governor Johnston is inclined to be generous with the tax exemptions when it comes to granting land to Scotsmen, and there is land aplenty as yet unclaimed, all around these hills." Cameron went on to say how he would sell Alex a few of his own acres to begin, was he interested.

"I thank ye for the offer," Alex hedged. "But I canna yet say what the future holds for me. There are complications . . ."

Cameron batted the air, as if whatever complications Alex eluded to were midges, but at last the talk wound down as the old man sipped his whisky, growing drowsy. When the glass fell slack in his lap, Hugh, watching with a practiced eye, caught it before the remaining liquid spilled. He set it on the side table and fetched a plaid from a settee, spreading it across Cameron's knees.

Hugh nodded toward the front door. They went

out into the chill October night to talk of Severn, and the journey Alex had still to make.

Sometime later he sat at Pauling's bedside, a candle lit, watching the man sleep. He was grateful they'd a small store of the necessary bark at Mountain Laurel, but it wouldn't be enough. Duncan Cameron knew a neighbor who suffered the same malady. Hugh would ride the miles to that homestead on the morrow to beg more.

At some point Alex dozed, awakened by the candle's guttering. Quickly taking up a spare, he lit it, then set it in the remains of the dying one. The faint light flared, showing him Pauling's opened eyes, sunken, underscored by dark half-moons. His hand groped from the bed coverings.

Alex grasped it. "We made it, Reverend. We're at Mountain Laurel."

"Duncan and Hugh?" Pauling's voice was weaker than Alex had ever heard it.

"Both well." He reached for a pewter cup filled with water and helped the man to drink. Over its rim Pauling studied him.

"Something isn't," he said once he'd lain back again.

"Hugh's been to Cross Creek. He heard . . . rumors. The Careys are all but bankrupt. They've lost nigh everything."

Pauling closed his eyes, brow furrowing. "And here I lie . . . unable to go to them."

Alex leaned forward. "I can go. And will go, if ye're sure ye mean to live."

Pauling breathed a faint laugh. "As much as it lies with me, but it will be some time before I've strength enough to follow you."

Alex studied the man, thinking it must be the dimness of the candle's light that made it seem Pauling had almost instantly made his peace with what amounted to another captivity. "How can ye be so sanguine? Clearly ye wish to go with me."

"Long practice," the reverend said lightly, but more soberly added, "If Christ wishes me in the prison of this flesh, then that is where I'll learn to trust Him more." He paused, then asked, "You're worried still about what will happen if you return?"

"I am," Alex admitted. "I stole from Carey. Not just my years of service. He may well clap me in irons the moment I show my face."

Even if Carey did no such thing, what if Reeves hadn't touched Charlotte, or done anything against the Careys that could be proved? He was canny, that one. There was nothing Alex could do to the man for what he'd done to Jemma. Nothing legal.

He remembered the Tuscarora warrior, dying beneath his hands, and knew he would never take a life thus again, in vengeance, cold or heated. But to protect the innocent?

Aye. He would do what he must.

"What is it your heart desires, Alex?" Pauling asked.

"A second chance," he said, unthinking. His mind flooded with the choices he'd made amiss, the crossroads at which he might have taken a different path. One less self-serving. "To be whatever it was I was meant to be for the Careys. For Joanna most of all," he added, for it was in his heart and the Almighty knew it well. He might as well confess it.

"That sounds a good thing to me," Pauling said. "A thing to bring glory to the Almighty and set right what was done amiss."

"I'll answer for the thievery. But aside from myself, I dinna have what I stole. Jemma would say she wasna mine to return, but the tools were. I buried them back along the Yadkin."

"So you could carry me?"

"In part, aye." He didn't speak of the high cove above the river or what he'd envisioned there. It was too precious. A thing between him and the Almighty, for now.

"Let me think on that." Pauling regarded him. "You know that what you desire isn't against the Almighty's Word or what you know of His nature?"

"I dinna believe so."

"Then go in confidence. As you go, pray. Listen. He'll guide you—deliver you, need be.

Shut every door you aren't meant to pass through. He's practical, our God. But you'll never know what good may come if you don't take the first step of faith."

Pauling's voice had faded to a whisper. He was asleep almost before the last word left his lips, leaving Alex alone in the dark but for the candle's light.

"Aye," he said, breath buffeting the tiny flame. "I'll take that step."

He would take it afoot. Though Duncan Cameron wasn't prepared to lend a horse on such short acquaintance—even to a fellow Scot—he was pleased to provision Alex from his kitchen. Saddling up to go beg Jesuit bark from their neighbor the next morning, Hugh Cameron bid Alex farewell, promising to send Pauling on his way to Severn as soon as he was able. "Take ye care, man," he said, "however it unfolds. But seeing as ye survived the Cherokees with your scalp intact, I reckon ye'll handle whatever ye find at Severn."

"If Severn doesna handle me," he'd murmured, then grasped Hugh's hand. *"Tha mi fada nar comain,"* he said; I am greatly indebted to you. "For your friendship—and your clothes," he added, with a wry glance at his coat sleeves.

Pauling was awake in the bed when Alex came to take his leave. He lowered the knapsack, battered now after its long travels, onto the chair he'd occupied the previous night.

Pauling eyed it. "Has that pack of yours room for a letter?"

"If not there, on my person. A letter to whom?"

"Edmund." Pauling indicated a desk pushed to the wall, where lay a sheet of foolscap, freshly inked.

"Did ye get up from that bed to write a letter? What were ye thinking, man?"

Clearly delighted to be chastised, Pauling grinned. "Only that if I cannot go to Edmund, my words can do so. Kindly seal the letter, see it reaches his hands? It may be of service."

Alex went to the desk and found a stick of sealing wax. He folded the page, tempted to read the words in Pauling's inelegant script. Conquering the urge, he warmed the wax over the candle's flame and dripped a dollop across the letter's seam. He found Pauling's seal, and pressed it to the wax.

"Whether or not Edmund receives you," Pauling said, "this he will receive."

Alex slipped the letter into an inner pocket of his coat. He retrieved his pack, hoisted it to his shoulder, and started to bid Pauling farewell. The man's eyes were closed. With a rush of fondness and a silent prayer for healing, he turned to go.

"Alex MacKinnon . . ."

At the door he turned back. Pauling was sitting

up, blue eyes full of light and hope. He stretched a hand toward Alex, who stepped back into the room and took it in his own. The man's grip was surprisingly firm.

"The Lord goes before you to part the waters. To make the way for you, for those to whom you go. Grace and peace be with you." Pauling subsided back onto the pillow, eyes already closed, on the edge of healing sleep.

Alex squeezed his hand a final time. "And remain with ye, Reverend."

And whatever happens now, he added silently to heaven, *make my path straight.*

40

Charlotte and Azuba had come pounding down the stairs when Joanna shouted for help. There had been no preventing her sister seeing her father in his diminished state—right side bereft of mobility, speech mangled through drooling lips. Perhaps most disturbing, his frightened and defenseless stare. They'd gotten Papa into the bed in the study, where Joanna, Mari, and Azuba cared for him in turns through that day and the night following. Charlotte, despite the fright it caused her, begged to see her father again, but Papa's mortification was only worsened by her witnessing it. One look in his eyes had told Joanna as much. They kept Charlotte away.

Mister Reeves had returned the following day from his ride downriver to sell the mare. "An apoplexy." He'd appeared as stunned as Joanna over this appalling turn as they stood in the passage. "I cannot tell whether he knows what he's trying to say."

"He knows," she said, mouth trembling over the words. "Didn't you look into his eyes?"

"I did. I saw fear." The corner of Mister Reeves's mouth twitched, then he seemed to shake himself as a man coming out of a trance. He narrowed his eyes. "Where is Azuba?"

"I . . . don't know." She'd been about to say Azuba was upstairs with Charlotte, but stopped herself in time. "Why?"

"Surely you see this is poison again. Who else has access to Captain Carey's food? Mari? The cook? Are they here still?"

"Where else would they be?"

"Half your stepfather's slaves have run off to the swamps. Carpenters, coopers, stable hands." Scorn twisted Mister Reeves's face. "Hadn't you noticed?"

She'd not gone beyond the kitchen for days. It hardly mattered now. Papa mattered, and poison wasn't to blame for this. Not directly. She'd pushed too hard; Papa had been too frail. She and Mister Reeves together had done this to him.

"Why do you look guilt ridden?" Mister Reeves asked, scrutinizing her with narrowed eyes. "*You* wouldn't harm your precious papa."

"Whatever is the cause of this, he needs a physician."

"As it happens, I know where one is, or was this morning. Whether he's skilled at his craft or merely a backwoods quack, I couldn't say."

"Where? If you know—"

"A fellow was attending a sick child downriver. Where I sold the mare."

She grasped his sleeve, uncertain if he meant to

524

help Papa or let him languish. "Will you go?"

He drew his arm away. "I've just returned."

"Mister Reeves, someone must."

A muscle in his jaw bulged, as though he ground his teeth. "I'll send two of your garden hands. But a physician will only confirm it was poison."

Was Azuba next in his sights? Marigold? Phoebe?

Mister Reeves turned his back and headed toward the door. As she watched him retreat, Joanna knew a moment of pure rage. Had she been strong enough, and a suitable weapon to hand . . .

She had Azuba, Marigold. Others might help. And then what? If they laid hands on Phineas Reeves, a free white male, subdued and held him prisoner, her own freedom would be in jeopardy, the lives of any slaves involved forfeited. *If they were caught.*

Charlotte and Papa needed her. And she wouldn't risk condemning Azuba or anyone else.

"No, Mister Reeves."

Something in her voice spun him round before he reached the door. "No?"

"You said the slaves are all running away, yet you'd send more after the physician? That's the last we'll see of them. Are you giving up on Severn?"

"Don't speak as a hysterical fool," he said

without heat. "I'll go myself and fetch the man. Does that satisfy you?"

He went out before she replied, leaving her praying he'd hurry for Papa's sake, if the physician even existed. Praying likewise for enough time to do the next hard thing now staring her down.

"No, Miss Joanna. I won't leave you to face that man when he get back and find me gone—and who gonna help tend Master Carey?"

Azuba hadn't mentioned the plantation. They knew Severn was a ship sinking fast, its captain unable to abandon it. Therefore neither would Joanna, but she meant to give as many as she could a chance to survive.

"He means to blame you for this. You, Mari, or Phoebe. Maybe all of you." They were in the passage, hovering in the study doorway where they could watch for Mister Reeves's return as well as Papa's waking.

Azuba shook her head. "Why take me down? I'm nothing to him."

"You're important to me. That's enough. I want you to take Phoebe with you. Mari and Jory too. Find Elijah. Tell him what's happened. Ask him to come." It was the one thing that might persuade.

Sure enough, Azuba's shoulders slumped in resignation. "I'll do it, but only to bring Mari and

Jory safe away—Phoebe too. And send Elijah back."

They went abovestairs, where Charlotte had cried herself to sleep, forbidden to see Papa. Both deemed it best Azuba slip away unremarked. Charlotte couldn't later blurt the truth if she didn't know it. But Azuba lingered in the doorway of their bedroom, gazing at Charlotte's sleeping form. "You want me to take her?" she asked softly.

"He'll come after you for certain if you did. If the rest of you go alone . . ."

"He let us be. Maybe."

While Azuba made ready to flee, Joanna went to the kitchen to speak to Phoebe and Mari. They were waiting when Azuba reached the kitchen.

"Sybil?" Joanna asked.

"Ain't even seen her today," Phoebe said. "Dorcas neither. You want I should find 'em?"

"No," Joanna said, hoping they, too, had run. "I want you gone. Mari, you know where to find Elijah?"

Marigold hoisted Jory to her shoulder. "He told me where he meant to go. I reckon I'll track him down."

They gazed at each other through memories thick as a wall, then Joanna pushed past it and embraced her, Elijah's son nestled between them. Marigold stiffened. Joanna kept her arms around her until she relaxed, then drew back and brushed her fingertips over Jory's silky hair.

"I'm sorry, Mari. For so much."

Marigold nodded, brown eyes filling. "So am I," she said. Then she and Phoebe went out.

Azuba hesitated. "Miss Joanna . . ."

Words Azuba had spoken long ago came back to her. *We all got to do things we don't want to do . . . It's the way things are, Miss Joanna. By and by you'll understand.*

By and by she had, and she'd wanted to change those things—for all of them. Perhaps this was the only way.

She grasped Azuba's big-knuckled hand. There were no words.

Marigold stuck her head around the door, gaze urgent. "Azuba. We got to go if we gonna do this."

"She's right," Joanna said, and wrapped Azuba in a final embrace.

"You sure about this?" Azuba asked.

Joanna breathed in the smell of her, cleaning oils and hearth smoke and her own familiar scent. "Send Elijah. Pray for me."

Joanna lingered in the kitchen, not wanting to see which direction they took. Not wanting to see if others joined. She hoped they would, that they'd all go, save themselves however they could.

"Godspeed," she whispered.

Silence answered. The hearth was cold. No

528

kettle hung from the crane. No skillet sizzled. No hands performed their labor over the table. Already the kitchen felt deserted, save for its ghosts.

Assuming his description widely broadcast, Alex had traveled by night south through the Carolina backcountry, then retraced his flight from Severn along the Cape Fear, cutting through forest when possible. The coat Hugh Cameron had given him was none the better for it. Perhaps it was no matter. He intended to reach Severn and observe the state of things before deciding how to reveal himself. First to Moon, or Marigold, someone he could trust not to shout an immediate alarm. He wanted it to be Joanna, but how was he to reach her without alerting Carey? Or Reeves.

About an hour before daybreak, he'd bedded down on the sandy bank of a stream that meandered into the river's course, put his head on his pack, and slept like one dead.

When rough hands took hold of him and the midday sun smote him in the face, he'd been too disoriented to put up a fight in time. A belated struggle availed him little; there were too many of them, all males and strong. His hands were bound behind him, his face pressed into sand, then he was hauled upright.

The features nearest his own resolved into familiar lines. Not a young man—white showed in his wiry beard and the hairs sprinkled across his brown chest—but hale and strong all the same. Edmund Carey's head groom.

"Moses?" Alex reared back his head as men's voices murmured above him.

"MacKinnon." Moses stood, leaving him in the sand. "What you doing back here?"

When he didn't answer, Moses shared a look with another of the men ringing him—six of them in all, Carey's slaves.

"He'll want to know," the other man said.

"He?" Alex asked. To a man they ignored him.

"Make him tell why he back first," another suggested.

Moses's gaze moved over Alex, taking in clothing, knapsack. "You going to answer?"

Alex bent his face to his shoulder, wiping his mouth of sand, giving himself time to think. He hadn't yet crossed Severn Creek. They weren't on Carey's land. And these men weren't behaving as slaves.

"I came back to see how ye fare."

Every set of eyebrows he could see shot high into gleaming foreheads.

"The Careys?" Moses asked.

"Aye." He'd sand on his tongue still. He spat onto the ground, then said, "And Moon, Marigold. All of ye."

"Huh," half the men muttered under their breath, a dark collective utterance.

"What's happening there?"

Again he was ignored. "Take him," Moses said.

The rest closed in and hauled him to his feet. It was like his capture by Blackbird's band, only these warriors carried no weapons save crudely sharpened sticks. Their clothing was tattered, their beards untrimmed. One took up his knapsack. They put him in their midst, striking off through the forest in file, three ahead, three behind.

Pauling's letter. Had he lost it in the scuffle? He couldn't search his coat with bound hands. Lowering his head and raising his shoulder, pretending to scratch his chin, he felt the stiffness of the folded missive tucked in the breast pocket.

Relieved, he set his mind to deal with whatever was to come next.

For a while that proved little enough. Swampland surrounded, dark with cypress and cedar and the musty tang of rotting things, yet these men picked their way with confidence, a torturous route where the ground was often spongy, or inches thick in mud. He'd passed the point where he'd any hope of finding his way out of the morass when the way ahead began to resemble a path, even to his eyes.

He smelled the smoke of cook fires before he made out the squat structures dotting an area of dry ground, about an acre in size. Some were open-faced shelters, others thatched huts covered in clay, tattered blankets hung across low door-ways. Fire rings clustered in the center of the camp. Battered pots rested on ashy stones, with a scattering of crude trenchers and bowls. Dark-skinned women with their heads covered crouched at the fires. Here and there men loitered. Small children went naked or in the barest of clouts.

When the spear-toting party arrived, Alex in their midst, men shot to their feet. Women froze like deer. Children cowered behind their elders.

Alex recognized some faces. One of Carey's coopers. Coming out of a nearby hut was the carpenter who'd crafted the bedstead for him when he'd arrived at Severn. But these people weren't all from Severn—or they'd been part of the work gangs that lived out among the pines. Maybe thirty in all, that he could see.

A glance around as he was brought into their midst showed him racks of drying fish, the carcass of a wild boar hanging from a tree, a brace of ducks outside a hut, feathers half-plucked. They were living wild, and like wild things with survival in mind, they recovered fast from surprise.

Questions came at Moses, who raised a hand for silence. "He gone out with Billy's gang?"

"He here," a woman said, eyeing Alex warily. "In his place, yonder."

Alex followed shifting gazes to a nearby hut

as the blanket across its doorway moved and the first white man he'd seen for days emerged. He was dressed in shirt and breeches, brown hair drawn back and tailed, beard stubble shadowing his blunt chin.

Elijah Moon saw him and stopped in his tracks, recognition running like ripples across his scarred face.

Outside his hut, Moon motioned Alex to sit. Squatting next to a stone ring where a fire burned, he added wood, poking up the embers with a stick. The action showered sparks, stirring memories of Severn's forge, of hours spent in its molten heat. Though it had been long since Moon swung a hammer, his upper body was little diminished. Unchanged as well that piercing stare, which he aimed at Alex from beneath leveled brows as Moses and two more of Carey's former slaves joined them. They hunkered down, skin showing through the threadbare knees of their breeches.

In the presence of the three ex-slaves, Severn's former smith regarded him. "Moses tells me ye've come back to . . . how did he put it? See how we fare."

"Aye. I heard things went ill with the Careys." He paused, giving Moon a chance to offer specifics on the subject. He didn't. "And I mean to make amends for my leaving. Far as I'm able."

"Ye've left it late. Probably too late."

Dread tightened Alex's gut. "What d'ye mean?"

"It was bad enough by the time I was forced to leave Mari and our son behind."

"Ye've a son, then?"

"He's called Jory." Moon's expression softened briefly. "Never ye mind him now. Where have ye been these months? And Jemma? Is she with ye?"

"Not anymore." Alex gave account of his flight, Jemma's following, and their capture by Blackbird and her warriors as Jemma was giving birth. That detail halted the narrative.

Moon was aghast. "She's a child herself!"

"Who done it?" Moses asked.

"Reeves. Though it took her until our parting to say so."

By the time Alex finished telling of Jemma's adoption by her grandmother's sister and her intent to marry Runs-Far, heads were shaking.

"Good for her," Moses said. "She's a free Indian like she say she gonna be."

"I havena told ye all," Alex said. "We found Reverend Pauling among the Cherokees, a captive."

"Ye left him there too?" Moon asked, startled.

"I brought him away with me, verra ill. I got him to a place we kent near the Yadkin River where he's tended. I've a letter from him," he added, touching his coat where it rode. "Addressed to Carey."

Around them rose the voices of women and children, the clank of a pot, the sizzle of frying meat. In the distance thunder rolled.

Alex thought of Blackbird's son with his new name.

The day was clouding over.

"So that's why he never responded to Joanna's letters," Moon said at last. "Is that where ye heard of Severn? Reverend Pauling?"

Impatient to hear of Joanna, he said, "I had it from our mutual acquaintance, Hugh Cameron, overseer at the place where I left Pauling." Mention of overseer hardened the faces at the fire. "Tell me what Reeves has been about."

By the time Moon was done telling, Alex was seeing the red of rage, much of it directed at himself. Moon was right. He'd left his return far too late—if he'd meant to do the Careys any good.

"So Reeves has the reins of Severn in hand and is running it straight off a cliff." Was Joanna no better than a prisoner in that house? "Have ye been back? Or have these others kept ye informed?"

Moon and Moses shared a look weighted with significance.

"Ye didn't tell him?" Moon asked.

"No, man," Moses said. "Thought you do that."

"Tell me what?" Alex demanded.

"Best I show ye," Moon said and stood. Moses and the others trailing, he led Alex past a gauntlet

535

of gazes and hushed conversations to an open-faced shelter across of the camp. Beneath its slanted thatched roof, curled on a pallet of pine boughs, was Demas, oblivious to the camp bustling around him. Another of Carey's former slaves stepped from a nearby thicket, holding a pistol. Alex looked back at Demas, noting the gleam of sweat on his brow despite the cool of the day.

The guard melted back into the brush.

"This I didna expect," Alex said.

"He was found fevered, wandering the swamp," Moon said. "Maybe seeking us, I don't know. In any case, he was beyond resisting, had to be carried in."

"Time we had of it, man like a bear," Moses muttered. He and the others moved off, called away by a group of women to eat the food they'd fixed.

"How long since ye found him?"

"Day before yesterday." Moon told then of a confrontation in the smithy, Reeves's accusation, Demas's assault and escape. "Where he's been since he ran, I cannot say, but ye're looking at Reeves's scapegoat."

"Reeves blamed *him* for poisoning Carey?" Alex asked.

"I saw it happen."

Moon beckoned Alex back toward his hut, but both men hesitated when beneath the shelter that well-bottom voice rasped, "He not lying."

The shelter's roof was so low Alex had to bend almost double to see beneath it, but he wasn't willing to crouch or come within reach of those massive hands. "Can ye talk, man?"

Demas's eyes blinked. "There things I can say."

"So it's true. To cover his crime Reeves threw his one faithful slave to the wolves."

Teeth gritted, Demas pushed himself upright. He cast a bleary look across the portion of the camp visible from his shelter, and drew a stuttering breath.

"No wolves here," he said, then raised assessing eyes to Alex. "Maybe one now. But I never was that man's slave. Give me water, I tell you what I was."

41

A ye," Alex said. "And while ye're at it, I'd ken what Reeves has against Edmund Carey, why he's wreaked such havoc upon the man."

Demas swayed but caught himself. He laughed low in his throat, a rumble like the thunder rolling in the distance. "Oh, he make a mistake in choosing you, man. But let that bide for now."

Moses rejoined them, bringing a canteen from which Demas drank, then began a tale that started years ago, when Edmund Carey retired from the Royal Navy, taking Moon with him.

"The new captain, Potts, he let things happen on that ship another would have punished with a whip. Man named Smith was the worst—Obadiah Smith. Phineas blame Potts, Smith of course, but also Carey, for leaving him. He blame that one called Kelly for not seeing what going on under his nose." Threatened with worse if he told a soul, Reeves had endured two and a half years of terror and abuse until, in port at Kingston, he'd escaped the *Severn*, his home turned hell.

"Not captured?" Moon asked. "What was all that about the pirate ship, the *Isis*?"

"Never was no pirates," Demas said. "He hide

on the docks in Kingston until he run from there too. That when I find him."

Demas had been a lad himself, already big for his age, when he came across the half-starved Reeves hiding in the sugar cane on his master's plantation in the hills above Kingston. Demas brought him food. When the plantation master discovered Reeves and, the three alone out in the canes, commenced to beat Demas for hiding him, something in the strange white boy had snapped.

"It like seeing a good dog go mad. He attack my master, got away that whip, turn it against him. I never see such joy in a face as I see that day Phineas beat my old master."

"To death?" Alex asked, chilled even as a fresh wave of sweat beaded Demas's brow.

The man's bloodshot gaze met his. "Later we hear so."

Demas and Reeves had escaped deeper into the hills, to the maroons—runaways living much as Severn's ex-slaves were now.

Eventually the two returned to Kingston, where Reeves proved an efficient pickpocket and Demas kept hidden. They waited for the chance to escape that island. It came in the form of a ship's captain, bound for the Colony of Georgia, desperate enough for crew to hire the pair despite their youth. Reeves was a skilled enough seaman. What Demas lacked in knowledge he made up in strength. Best of all, no one laid a hand on Reeves with Demas a protective shadow.

At Savannah they abandoned the ship. Playing on the sympathies of strangers, or thieving, sometimes working for wages, they migrated up the coast. Reeves acquired a decent suit of clothes and began passing himself off as a young man of quality, orphaned, owner of a slave.

"Was me told him to say it," Demas said to their lifted brows. "Made others show respect— and leave me be."

In Philadelphia, Reeves, then fifteen, apprenticed himself to a merchant, proving skilled at keeping accounts. Demas served, doing whatever labor was needed.

"We stay there two years before we have to leave that place. We wander then a long while, in one city or another, living as we could. Always Reeves find something to do—or steal." Some years later they came across none other than Captain Potts, drinking in a tavern in Maryland. "I was outside waiting when Reeves run out, a man on his heels. Reeves led the man down an alley. By time I come on them, that man was dead."

Reeves had taken his vengeance against his former captain and found it to his liking.

Vengeance proved a thirst that deepened with that first swallow. After Maryland, their drift through the colonies had purpose beyond survival, searching for those against whom

Reeves held his grudge, following up every rumor gleaned of the *Severn* or her former crew. Especially the officers.

"He kill four I know of, including that Obadiah Smith." Demas gave a shudder at the speaking of the name; neither Alex nor Moon asked what Reeves had done to his chief tormentor. "Then we find Edmund Carey in Wilmington. It fell into place easy. A little at a time, I watch Reeves do what he come to do—this time more than kill. He meant first to ruin that man, body and soul. Sometimes he ask my help. Mostly I watched."

Alex looked away from Demas's glistening, unrepentant face to find Moon drilling the man with livid rage, maimed arm raised.

"Was it ye did this to me?"

Demas's eyes were mere slits. "No. Not your fault, what happened on that ship. You a boy, too, doing as you bid."

"But ye let him do it?"

Alex caught Moon's seething gaze and shook his head. There would be no peace found in trying to untangle the thinking behind the deeds Demas, as twisted in his way as Reeves, had allowed to go unchallenged. As to what he *had* done . . .

"The mill. Ye set that fire?"

"I did."

"And Jim?"

"He catch me setting it."

"But ye saved MacKinnon," Moon said. "Why?"

Demas shut his eyes. At first Alex thought he wouldn't answer, then the man's tongue licked over his lips. "Best you know the rest, then you know why I did it."

With a sick surging in his gut, Alex said, "Charlotte."

Demas's eyes flared, showing bloodstained whites. "You know?"

"What of Charlotte?" Moon demanded.

Alex nodded, needing Demas to tell it and be done. The impulse to race out of that swamp, run the miles to Severn, and lay hold of Reeves was a screaming in his bones.

"Before Charlotte," Demas said, "there was another like her. That merchant in Philadelphia had a daughter."

The girl, called Amelia, had been nine years old when Reeves came into the merchant's employ. From the beginning Reeves had been besotted by her. Demas hadn't seen it, not at first. "He never hurt that girl, but he wanted to. Once I catch him with a girl he find on the street, someone's slave. I saw what he meant to do and stopped him. He swear up and down he never try it before, but his eyes have that look he had the day he kill my master. Maybe it was a demon had him. Maybe the boy in him fighting back in the worst way. No matter. I got him away from that girl and the madness left him. Left him crying like a baby."

On his knees in a filthy alleyway, Reeves had

begged Demas not to kill him. "He could see I wanted to. But I chose another path. I tell him I go on with him like we been, but unless he vow there on his knees never to touch a child like that again, one weaker than himself, then I *would* kill him."

The blood had drained from Alex's face as Demas spoke. "But the lass, Amelia, ye said he never hurt her?"

"One day I catch him with that girl, touching her yellow hair. Just touching, but it was enough. We were done there."

"And he never tried to get shed of ye?" Moon sounded half-choked.

"Once or twice he try. Now he think he done it." Demas reached for the canteen to drain its contents.

"What happened in Philadelphia, that was years ago," Moon said. "Has he never . . . other girls?"

"Ye ken he has," Alex said, his voice ragged. "Jemma."

Demas's breath came deep. "I never catch him. I tried to make her tell."

And succeeded in frightening her all the more.

"But Charlotte," Moon said. "Ye might have led off with that, aye?"

Alex was feeling every second ticking by like a world of possible torment for the wee lass. And for Joanna.

"You think I left that child to his mercy, all

this time since he run me off?" Demas asked. "No, man. I stay out by the old mill, coming in at night. That girl from the kitchen, Sybil, she tell me what I want to know. Then I get sick and these ones here find me. How many days now?"

"Two, they tell me," Alex said.

"What Reeves done in that time, I cannot say." Fury suffused Moon's face, but Demas met his gaze unflinching. "You knew enough of what he was and you left them. Both of you."

Remorse lanced through Alex's vitals. "Aye. We did."

"We have to go back." Moon was on his feet, determined gaze on Alex. "How far are ye willing to go with this?"

Alex stood and faced him. "I'll do what has to be done to protect them, but no more. I dinna want blood spilled in that house if it can be helped."

Moon's eyes narrowed. "Ye haven't mentioned Joanna since they brought ye into camp. Ye broke her heart, leaving like ye did. She loved you."

"I ken that." He feared to ask if hope of mending that broken heart existed. He touched his coat above Pauling's letter. He risked more in returning to Severn than the consequences of a broken indenture.

Moon went to the guard nearby, who handed over the pistol. Moon thrust it into the waist of his breeches, then stood before Demas. "We're leaving for Severn. It'll be nightfall ere we get there. Are ye strong enough to come?"

With a noise through his teeth like a growl, Demas grasped a pole of the shelter. Ignoring their proffered hands, he pulled himself to his feet. He swayed, nostrils flaring. Alex felt the heat of him a pace away.

"I do what I must."

Moon gave a nod. "Come to the fires. Get some food. We'll let them know." He started in that direction.

Alex waited for Demas to take his first steps, uncertain the man could cross the camp, much less make it to Severn. He reached the cook fires but halted near Moon's hut, well back from where the ex-slaves were gathering. Alarm rippled through the camp until Moon stepped forward to explain where they were going, offering any wishing to accompany them the chance to do so. Above their responses—fearful, angered, remonstrating—Alex heard the labored breathing of the man beside him, felt the fever's heat radiating off his flesh.

Demas leaned close. "You know why he chose you?"

"Reeves? Off the *Charlotte-Ann*, ye mean?"

Demas grunted. "Took me time to work it out. He mean all along to do the one thing I never let him do, so he chose you to take me down before that time come. His mistake, choosing the one man wanted to stay on that ship, who wanted nothing of what he offered. In the end, he lose us both."

Alex frowned, gazing at the men and women arguing over going back to aid the master who'd enslaved them.

"But it isna the end," Alex said. "Not yet."

He got no response. That radiating heat beside him had vanished.

Demas had melted away between the huts without a single eye seeing him go.

It was some moments before a woman nearby made the discovery. A cry was raised. Across the space of dark heads, Moon looked straight at Alex, while around them half the ex-slaves were saying to let Demas go and good riddance, the other clamoring to search him out and drag him back.

Moon knew as well as he there was no time for the latter. "Ye men not going with us can hunt for Demas as ye wish. Those meaning to go with MacKinnon and me, take ye food and—"

A new disturbance arose at the edge of camp. The crowd parted, opening a way between Moon and three women in mud-stained homespun, one with a bairn in her arms, emerging from the swamp.

" 'Lijah! We found you at last."

"Mari?" Moon strode to meet her, wrapping her

in his arms, while Azuba gaped at Alex striding toward them.

"Mister Alex? How you here?"

"It's a tale that can wait. How is it with them?"

Marigold and Moon parted, joining the conversation, though Moon kept his arm around her, a thing that gladdened Alex's heart even as Azuba shook her head, tears coming up in her eyes.

"We left Severn yesterday. Took us all the day and night and then today to find you . . . to tell you . . ." Her lips trembled so hard she couldn't finish.

"Master Carey had him some sort of seizing fit," Marigold said. In her arms the bairn set to fussing. She joggled him tiredly. "Left him bedridden. Can't talk. Miss Joanna bid us go. Said find Elijah. No one knew you was here, Mister Alex, but reckon now the two of you might come?"

It was worse than Alex had thought. Not even Edmund Carey stood between Joanna and whatever final designs Reeves had on her and Charlotte's well-being.

"Not just them two." Moses had approached, behind him three young men armed with stout sticks, faces set. Warriors ready for battle. "Who leads us?"

At first no one spoke, and in that moment Alex sensed the shifting as an unseen mantle of authority was laid across the shoulders of each man in turn. As if it could be followed with the eyes, the ex-slaves looked to Moses, then to Moon. Then before an eye could blink, Moon let it pass and looked to Alex, where it settled last.

"I canna even find my way out of this swamp," Alex said.

"We get you out," Moses said. "After that . . ."

Alex glanced once more at Moon, who nodded. "Aye, all right then."

Moses and his men headed off through the camp. Moon and Marigold embraced around their whimpering son.

Azuba reached for Alex's hand and gripped it hard. "Help Master Carey and my girls," she pleaded, eyes turned up to him, afraid but hopeful. "Save them from that evil."

42

It was the second day since she'd sent Azuba, Marigold, and Phoebe away and Mister Reeves had ridden to fetch the physician he claimed to have encountered. Sybil had stayed, taking over what cooking was needed and helping with Charlotte, freeing Joanna to tend her stepfather.

Yesterday, for the first time since the apoplexy struck, he'd made himself understood; the panic in his eyes had receded, revealing a spark of resolve. More than once she'd caught him struggling to sit up in bed, or straining to move his stricken limbs.

Her remonstrations only made him more determined.

He could sit up now for short spells, long enough to feed himself, clumsily, with his left hand. His right leg, more so than his arm, had responded to his efforts to move it. She was all but certain he would walk again. As for his speech, if he concentrated he could force the simplest words past his lips.

Drink. More. Yes. No.

Questions about Mister Reeves, or anything about Severn's state, were beyond him, though they stirred in his eyes. He wasn't diminished in mind, but the inability to care for his most intimate needs was a mortification to them both. Thankfully he spent more hours sleeping than awake. The bedding was spotted with the food and drink he'd spilled, as was her blue muslin gown, the plainest she owned.

At his bedside, she watched him sleep. Between the poisoning and this new affliction, Joanna guessed he'd lost three stone in weight. His cheekbones were sharp, the orbits of his eyes hollowed, his cheeks pasty and unshaved. She could see his scalp through his thinning hair.

Lord, have mercy. Joanna clamped her lips to keep from keening as she prayed for him. For Charlotte, Azuba, Marigold, and Elijah. Reverend Pauling. Jemma.

She rose, picked up the big conch shell on Papa's desk, put it to her ear, and wept to the distant sough of breakers as she prayed for Alex.

"Miss Joanna?"

She returned the weighty shell to its place, balanced on its spikey protrusions, and crossed the room.

Sybil pretended not to notice her tears. "I best get supper started. Miss Charlotte up there playing with her Jemma doll."

Joanna touched Sybil's arm. "I'll go up soon."

"You think Master Carey would eat something?"

"A pudding perhaps?"

550

Sybil nodded. "I can do a pudding."

How far they'd come from the days of elaborate meals and finely set table and the hours it had taken to plan, prepare, and serve each one.

"He's going to be all right," Joanna said.

"Yes ma'am," Sybil said, dark eyes doubting.

What was taking Mister Reeves so long to bring the physician? Unless he never meant to return. Was he finished with them? The thought pumped a desperate hope through her veins.

As Sybil made for the door, Joanna wondered should she send her for help. The McGinnises? They were ten miles upriver, another five along a tributary creek. Could Sybil paddle a canoe so far?

Why had no one come to them in all these weeks?

Maybe she would send Sybil. Or maybe she would kill Mister Reeves when he walked through the door.

As she returned to the bedside chair, through her petticoat she fingered the kitchen knife she carried in her pocket, where needle, thread, and measure once resided. The weight of it was a comfort. And a cold horror. *Lord, forgive me. What can I do?*

Papa moaned, the crooked sag of his mouth evident even in sleep. His eyes rolled beneath purpled lids, head jerking as though he flinched from something in a dream.

At the back door's opening, she echoed his flinch. She rose and crossed the room swiftly. "Sybil? Did you need—"

His hand clamped her wrist before she realized it was Mister Reeves, returned at last. The candles in their wall sconces bent in the breeze from the open door behind him; the nearest snuffed out. He was alone.

"Sybil is in the kitchen," he said, the words carefully pronounced. She smelled liquor on his breath.

"Did you bring the physician?"

"Be glad I didn't," he said. "I waited all night while the man tended that child I told you about. It died."

"Who? Someone we know?" She hadn't even thought to ask, hadn't realized the child was deathly ill—had hardly believed in the scenario at all.

Had he told the truth for once?

"More than likely." He released her, leaving a faint sting where he'd gripped. With effort she refrained from rubbing it away.

"I returned from your errand exhausted and hungry but found Sybil in the kitchen alone. I had it from her—finally—that Phoebe, Mari, and Elijah's brat are gone. Run off into the swamps."

"Is Sybil all right?" she asked, alarm mounting.

"She will be, as long as she hurries supper. Are

552

you going to pretend you know nothing of their absence?"

"Should I? I've hardly left Papa's side."

He didn't blink as he stared at her, taking in the soiled state of her gown. She caught her breath as he leaned toward her and sniffed. "So I see. Why, though? You've Azuba to help."

Joanna hesitated, too exhausted to recall readily what excuse she'd prepared.

Suspicion chilled his eyes. "Where is Azuba, Miss Carey?"

Without awaiting answer, he lifted his voice and thundered down the passage, "Azuba! You're wanted!"

Dismay seized her. "Mister Reeves, you'll wake Papa." When she turned to go back into the study, he grabbed her arm again.

This time she couldn't stifle a cry.

"No one's coming, Miss Carey. Tell me you don't know where Azuba is. Make me believe it."

"Please, I don't know. I—"

Light footsteps sounded on the stairs. "I heard you calling, Phineas. Has Azuba come back?"

Charlotte was coming down the passage, candlelight making a shimmering halo of her golden hair.

Mister Reeves released Joanna. "Charlotte," he said, his voice bearing no resemblance to the harsh tone he'd used with her.

Shocked by the alteration, Joanna looked at him. He was smiling at Charlotte as though enchanted—a snake charmed by its favorite melody.

Get her away. Now. As far as you can. But Papa. She would have to leave him alone with Mister Reeves. *Do it.*

"No, Charlotte," she said, and somehow sounded as though any of this was normal. "She isn't. Let's you and I go upstairs, all right?"

She walked away from Mister Reeves, who made no move to stop her. She took her sister by the hand.

"Can I see Papa?" Charlotte asked as they turned back toward the stairs.

No footsteps followed. Her heart thumped crazily.

"He's a little better, but not yet." Thus far she'd shielded Charlotte from Papa, hoping his improvement would continue. Azuba's absence had proved impossible to explain without revealing the extent of their danger. What was she to tell her sister, that she'd sent Azuba away to a safe place? Even Charlotte would understand that meant their home was no longer safe.

"Sometimes slaves run away," was all she'd said.

"Like Jemma," Charlotte had sighed.

How Joanna loathed a world where such resignation must reside in the heart of a child. A kingdom constructed by the hearts of men, not the heart of the Almighty. *Lord, have mercy.*

She stayed abovestairs no more than a quarter hour. Leaving Charlotte in their room and praying she would stay, Joanna made for the study. Gloom cloaked the downstairs passage as the day waned. No one had replaced the candles guttered in their sconces.

In the study, an open decanter of brandy sat on the desk next to the conch shell, a glass half-full beside it. Mister Reeves sat at the bedside, leaning over with his face near Papa's.

"What are you doing?"

Mister Reeves straightened and faced her. "Talking to my captain. What does it look like?"

Papa was awake, apparently unharmed. Then Joanna registered his ashen face. His eyes held a stricken horror that exceeded her own.

"Talking of what?" she asked, voice shrill to prevent it shaking.

Mister Reeves rose and replaced the chair at the desk. "Times and seasons, Miss Carey."

"I don't know what you mean."

"Your stepfather understands. Don't you, sir?"

Papa was struggling to sit up in the bed. "Jo . . . ann . . ."

She started toward him. Mister Reeves headed her off, grasping her bruised wrist so hard she yelped. "What are you doing?"

His mouth curled in amusement. "Little mouse. You don't even know you're trapped."

He couldn't be more wrong. "Release me!"

He did, so abruptly she staggered toward the bed, catching herself before she fell.

Papa was pushing back the coverlet. "Uh-up."

"Please, Papa." The fire had nearly gone out while she was abovestairs. No wood remained in the room. "It's too cold."

Mister Reeves leaned against the desk, watching them, arms crossed, in his eyes an unholy light. "Let him stand. I want to see him try. I need to know."

Joanna tried not to shiver. "Know what?"

"That my former captain has strength enough to last through what's going to happen next. I watched his eyes as I detailed my plans for this evening. I'm convinced he understood me perfectly."

Joanna's heart gave a lurch so violent she thought for an instant it had failed her. But it went on beating, her lungs drawing air—in short, tight spasms. "What plans?"

"Out . . ." Papa fought the bed coverings, struggling to rise. "Charl . . ."

"Stop hindering him," Mister Reeves ordered. "I want him to try."

"Then I'll help him." Joanna pulled back the coverlet. Papa wore a banyan over his night-shirt. The garment, stained like her own, was

556

disheveled, baring his legs as he struggled to free them of the bedding.

"If he can walk," Mister Reeves said, "sit him at his desk. That should be a good vantage point."

"No," Joanna protested as Papa grasped her arm and managed to sit, bare feet on the floor. "Let me help him to his room."

"Do as I said or I'll put you out of this house and carry on without you. You're of no consequence to me, Miss Carey."

She was very nearly sickened by that name alone. She forced herself to focus on her step-father, an arm encircling him. Tears of fury and frustration leaked from his eyes. "Can you make it to your chair?"

A groan issued from his lips, but he summoned strength to gain his feet where he swayed precariously, Joanna straining to keep him upright as he clung to her. In short, shuffling steps, she helped him cross the few paces between bed and desk, where he fell out of her arms into the chair, panting hard and drooling uncontrollably. She steadied him, arranged his garments, then snatched a quilt from the bed and wrapped it around his shoulders. With a corner she wiped his mouth. Only then did she look at Mister Reeves. "Are you satisfied?"

His eyes flared. Her fear and anger seemed to excite him.

"Soon. Come with me." Moving swiftly, he

took her by the arm and hauled her across the study. "Go upstairs. Get your sister. Bring her down."

"I don't wish her to see—"

"Now."

Joanna took a step toward the stairs, her body operating somehow without her leave. She fought desperately to think. Now was the time to end this, before Charlotte was within his reach. Could she do it? Stab him with her knife? Could she even get the knife free of her pocket before . . .

She heard the click behind her and turned. Mister Reeves held a pistol, hammer drawn, aimed at her head.

Sight of that dark barrel sent a strange sheet of calm across her roiling thoughts.

"All right," she said. "I'm going."

Could she simply lock them in their room? She had the only key, safe in her pocket alongside the knife. A locked door would hold the man at bay only so long, and Papa would be helpless on its other side. Lock Charlotte in alone?

She ascended the stairs, steps slowing as her brain seized upon and discarded each plan.

"Do not make me come up those stairs, Miss Carey."

Halfway up them Joanna halted, looking down. Mister Reeves had followed her to their foot. "You cannot leave Papa sitting up alone."

"If that worries you, by all means move

quicker." He held the pistol steady on her. His other hand, gripping the banister, was more telling. She could see the bones of his knuckles, pressing white against his tightened skin.

She kept going.

Charlotte was sitting with a book in her room, pretending to read it to her doll, unaware of peril. Joanna quailed, desperate to protect her sister from this unfolding horror.

Charlotte looked up from her book. "Is it time for supper?"

"Not yet." There would be no supper tonight. "But we're wanted belowstairs."

"By Papa?"

Oh, Papa, how did I let it come to this?

"Yes."

"And Phineas?"

Joanna reached for her sister's hand. Charlotte took it trustingly. Joanna lifted the single candle burning in the room. It shook in her grasp.

Charlotte must have noticed. "Joanna, are you crying?"

Her cheeks were wet. "Papa . . ." Her voice caught, failing her.

"He'll be better," Charlotte said, patting the hand she held. "Oh wait. I want Jemma."

Joanna paused while her sister fetched her doll. When they reached the stairs, Mister Reeves still stood at their foot.

"Good girl," he said.

Thinking the approbation for her, Charlotte slipped free of Joanna's grasp and ran down the stairs, reaching Mister Reeves and taking his outstretched hand.

The pistol was nowhere in sight.

"What are we doing, Phineas? Is Papa able to talk?"

"Oh yes," Mister Reeves replied to Charlotte's last question. "He wishes very much to see you. I'm certain he'll have much to say."

As he turned away, leading her sister down the passage toward the study, Joanna saw the pistol tucked into the waist of his breeches. She thought of grabbing it, of shooting the man in front of Charlotte. She thought of running, screaming, into the night. Instead she followed her heart's tethers into the study, where Papa sat hunched in the cold.

Darkness pressed beyond the window. Joanna entered, bearing the one small light still burning.

43

Alex's first glimpse of Severn was much as his last had been. No light showed in the upper rooms, all he could see of the Big House in the gloaming, with the orchard and outbuildings rising between. The air was damp, thickly clinging in a way that made him long for the pure, clean mountain air as he, Moon, Moses, and the three who'd followed them came up from the creek along the track leading past the orchard, shops, and gardens.

With each step forward, his thoughts centered, his mind calmed, while his heart leapt at a quicker pace. His nerves felt sheered of the flesh and sinew that protected them. Every current of air, every sound, every detail of outbuilding and grounds was delineated in the falling dark and magnified to his senses—as it had been on that freezing moor near Inverness two years and more ago, when the starving remnants of Charles Stuart's army marched into the sleety gray of a dawn that would, for most, be their last.

It surprised him that memories of Culloden should press near. Flashes of battle. Uncle Rory, wounded. A corbie's harsh cry. Redcoats spilling from the pines. He'd led men on that field by

561

necessity, until every semblance of a functioning army had unraveled and it had been every man for himself.

As it had been since. As it would be no longer, for him.

Was he leading these men into battle now? He'd no army behind him, but he had the prayers of a God-fearing man, and the Almighty Himself. *Dinna let me lead them into needless harm. Give me wisdom.*

They halted at the slave quarters. One of the men peeled away to go cabin by cabin, seeing who remained, gathering news. "He'll warn us, if need be," Moon said, low-voiced.

"Aye," Alex replied. "Let's go canny, circle the house."

"And if all seems well?"

"We'll fall back, decide what next." Alex looked to Moses, getting a nod of assent. No matter what they found, he couldn't leave without seeing Joanna. He'd risk his freedom, his very life, to speak to her, to let her know she wasn't alone. That she had him, if she wanted him.

He led them toward the hedged walkway that curved around the house, to the break in the tall hedge where the path led from kitchen to back door. He'd barely cleared it when he caught a ribbon of light through a parting in a window curtain. The room on the corner. Carey's study.

He put out a hand to Moon, who signaled the others to pause.

Alex altered his plan, sending Moses and his men on a circuit of the house. "If ye see no light in any other windows, wait near the back terrace, but dinna go inside the house." The back door was just outside Carey's study. There could be no entering the house that way undetected. It must be the front door.

Moses led his men into the dark, footfalls as quiet as Alex could hope for with a litter of unraked leaves blanketing the yard.

"Ye mean to go inside?" Moon asked.

"Let's get a look first." Alex gripped Moon's arm briefly, then felt the pistol pressed into his hand, cold and heavy.

"Ye've two hands," Moon said. "Better it's in your keeping."

He took it. They crept onto the leaf-cluttered terrace outside Carey's study. The window around the corner of the house was curtained, too, but these weren't drawn so close as those facing the kitchen. A wider gap showed Carey seated at his desk, wrapped in a quilt, his body canted oddly sideways. Crouched, Alex edged to the side for a wider view. When he had it, it froze his blood.

Joanna stood in the room's center, the whitened terror of her expression lit by a dozen candles, Charlotte clutched against her side.

Moon crowded close, trying to see as well, as another figure stepped into view: Reeves, holding a pistol, waving it as he spoke.

Alex couldn't make out his words.

Gripping the weapon Moon had given him, he set off around the house, Moon at his heels. They hadn't gone a dozen paces before he halted, sensing a figure coming at them out of the dark.

It was Moses. "Ain't no other lights in the place, upstairs or down," he whispered, leaning close to speak. "Left the lads by the back door like you say. Want me with you or them?"

Alex debated, heart hammering, the need to get inside that house making every second seem a lifetime. "Stay by the front door, let the lads guard the back. First go tell them—Reeves is armed, a pistol. I dinna want any of ye getting shot, so if he makes an escape either way, follow if ye can, keep him in your sights, but dinna try and take him down. I'll be coming after him, if I'm still breathing."

Clinging to Joanna, Charlotte clutched her doll, trust assaulted at last by Papa's distress. From the desk chair he gazed at Joanna in mute rage and helplessness. If anyone was to stop Mister Reeves doing the vile thing he intended, it must be her. What could she do but resist for the seconds it would take the man to render her unconscious, or dead? Then he would do as he willed.

Charlotte still didn't comprehend the magnitude of her danger, though the darkness of the study when they entered had frightened her. She'd dropped her doll, but Joanna, too intent on seeing to Papa's welfare, had told her to leave it.

"No," Charlotte had whined. "Jemma's scared of the dark!"

"Charlotte, please . . ."

Mister Reeves had fetched another candle. He'd approached her with it, lit it calmly from the one that trembled in her grasp, then took that one and placed both on the mantel. They'd all looked at Papa, seated at the desk. Joanna started to speak, to ask if he was all right, but hesitated, not wanting to alarm Charlotte. Not one precious second sooner than need be. How many seconds were left before this final shattering of their world overcame them?

Mister Reeves had lit more candles, poured another glass of brandy, downed it, poured another, then crossed the room and bent to pick up the doll. Kneeling before Charlotte, he'd gazed at its shorn hair, raised a brow, then put the doll into her sister's hands.

"You cut her hair," he said. "Don't you love her?"

"Oh yes," Charlotte said. "But she's Jemma."

565

All trace of expression fled Mister Reeves's face.

Charlotte's pale brows drew together. "Are you angry?"

As though he'd commanded it to do so, Mister Reeves's mouth widened in a smile. He caressed Charlotte's cheek. "The doll is yours, sweet Charlotte, to do with as you will. And you are mine. Shall I prove it to you?"

Hugging her doll, Charlotte brightened. "Yes, please."

Joanna's stomach lurched. She couldn't look away from the doll cradled to her sister's heart, with its painted face and shorn hair, but she was seeing the real Jemma, and Micah, Jim, Grandpa Jo, Azuba, Mari, and Phoebe—all those souls she'd thought she'd done her best for, clothing their bodies in homespun while this monster, this man apparently devoid of conscience, was allowed to prowl among them like a wolf.

Guilt was a snake's coils tightening round her chest as Papa uttered a cracked and wavering, "No-o-o . . ."

Startled, Charlotte peered past Mister Reeves. "Papa?"

The figure slumped in the chair, thin hair undressed, features twisted with paralysis and dismay, barely resembled the man her sister had no doubt expected to see. Bewilderment dimmed her glow.

Joanna's thoughts fired like a hundred pistols, banishing the parade of accusing faces. She couldn't help them now. Could she help her sister? *Play for time.* Would anyone come? *Break a window.* Would someone hear? Was anyone awake beyond that reflecting glass? Sybil? *Say something.*

"How can you do this? Why? She's a child—"

Behind Mister Reeves's back, Papa jerked his head, gazing at her, imploring her not to provoke the man.

Wavering candlelight made shadows leap across Mister Reeves's face, their flames a dozen bright points reflected in his eyes. "I've told Captain Carey my reasons. It's enough he knows."

Papa lurched in his chair. Mister Reeves aimed the pistol at him. Her stepfather stared at it, then looked bleakly at Joanna. A gleam of saliva pooled at the corner of his lips. He swayed and gripped the desk one-handed, spilling a stack of ledgers to the floor.

"Please, sir, be still. You're making a mess." Mister Reeves set the pistol on the desk out of Papa's reach, then proceeded to remove his waistcoat, which he folded neatly and placed alongside the weapon.

Undressed to shirtsleeves and breeches, he took a swallow of brandy and reached again for the gun, which he waved toward the bed. "Over there, both of you."

Joanna's belly heaved again, but she nudged her sister toward the bed. They sat on its edge, Charlotte clinging to her.

Papa tried again to rise from the chair, but only managed to wobble and catch himself before he fell. "Oh-ver . . . muh . . . dead . . ."

"Over your dead body?" Mister Reeves interpreted. "I confess I'd planned for such an eventuality, but I've changed my mind. I don't wish to kill either of you. I want you both to live with this." He turned back to Joanna, who'd tensed with her hand at the slit of her petticoat. "But I cannot have you free to interfere, Miss Carey."

Her hand froze, gripping a fold of muslin, feeling the blade hidden beneath. He studied her in apparent indecision, then set down the pistol and began untying his neckcloth.

"Hands behind you."

Papa made an attempt to reach the pistol across his desk, succeeding only in knocking more of its clutter to the floor. The heavy conch shell landed on the rug with a thump that snagged Mister Reeves's attention long enough for Joanna to plunge her hand through the slit in her gown, fumble her way to the pocket, and grasp the knife. Slicing a finger as she drew it free, she bolted to her feet.

Mister Reeves snatched up the pistol and swung it toward her. His gaze dropped to the knife, clenched in her bleeding hand. "What do you mean to do with that?"

"Kill you, if I must."

"Kill me?" He made a sound that might have been a laugh; Joanna's ears were buzzing too loudly to tell. Ready to wield the weapon in defense of her sister, huddled on the bed, she looked once more to Papa, dreading what she would see in his gaze.

Papa wasn't looking at her now, or at Charlotte, or at Mister Reeves, whose back was to him. He was gazing at the doorway. She saw him nod, almost imperceptibly. Then, with no effort to prevent it, he slid from his chair onto the floor. His head made a sickening thump against the wooden planks before the hearth, having missed the rug.

"Don't!" Mister Reeves warned Joanna when she made to go to him. "Let him lie."

From the corner of her eye, she caught movement at the doorway, but when she looked, thought she must be so far shattered in mind that delirium had overtaken her. A man crouched there—or seemed to in her dreaming—half-hidden in the shadows of the passage.

Not until their gazes met did she realize he was real. Joy burst inside her before his name formed in her mind. Alex.

At last. But how?

Cutting through relief and bewilderment like a

beam of light came the understanding of what he was there to do. And what he needed of her.

"I will not just let him lie!" Ignoring the pistol, Joanna crouched beside her stepfather's crumpled form.

Mister Reeves lunged for her. She sprang up, forcing him to pursue.

As she ran behind the desk, heavy footfalls crossed the room. Joanna turned in time to see Alex MacKinnon dive headlong into Mister Reeves, knocking him to the floor.

She'd done it perfectly. In a span of a blink, she'd come to grips with his presence, read his intention, and done what was needful as though they'd rehearsed it a hundred times. As Joanna rushed to her stepfather, Alex thrust the pistol into Moon's hand—too many in that room for guns—hissed, "Get the lassie out," then hurtled across the room and slammed into Reeves. The pistol flew from the overseer's grip and spun across the floor, missing Edmund Carey's prostrate form.

Alex needed no weapon but his hands; those he needed at once, for Reeves was quick to assess the attack and retaliate. Alex caught a blow in the face but landed more before Reeves scrabbled an arm free, clutched the huge conch shell fallen to the floor, and crashed it against Alex's head, stunning him long enough to scramble away.

Alex lurched to his feet, expecting a counter-attack, but Reeves had seen Moon scooping Charlotte off the bed with one strong arm.

"No!" Reeves started after them.

Joanna barred his way, brandishing a knife. Reeves shoved her from his path before Alex caught him and dragged him back.

Moon shouted to Joanna to follow. Alex saw her shake her head. She wouldn't leave her stepfather. Then he'd no attention to spare anything but Reeves. He got a leg around his knee, and they went down hard. Reeves was trying to crawl, to reach something near the desk.

"My knife!" Joanna shouted. She'd dropped it when Reeves shoved her.

He reached it and whipped around, kicking free of Alex's hold.

Alex grabbed for the only shield to hand, the conch shell that held the memory of the sea, smeared now with his blood. They were back on their feet, Reeves with the knife brandished.

"Dinna make me kill ye," Alex said. "Drop it and—"

With a manic look of bloodlust, Reeves rushed him. Alex deflected the blade, catching Reeves's arm with the shell's spikey protrusion. He plowed his fist into Reeves's ribs, then they were down again, grappling, Reeves in possession of the knife, Alex atop him with his hand around the man's wrist. Their gazes locked.

"Alex!" Joanna cried. "He's going to—"

The blow of a powerful fist, carefully measured, caught Alex aside the head. He lost his hold on Reeves. The room went dark, though he remained conscious, expecting to feel the stab of a blade, the tearing of a pistol's ball.

Instead he heard Reeves's incredulous, "You?"

Head spiking with pain, Alex pushed himself to his knees. Joanna hovered near, but she wasn't looking at him. She gaped at Demas, who'd charged into the room, ablaze still with fever.

Reeves was on his knees as well, clutching the knife, staring up at Demas as if at the sudden manifestation of a massive, glittering-eyed angel.

"You came back," he said.

Demas took the knife from Reeves's unresisting hand. For a terrible instant Alex thought Demas meant to turn on him, Joanna, the helpless Carey lying behind the desk.

Demas hurled the knife across the room. He spoke at last, and though he never took his gaze off Reeves, it was Alex he addressed. "He's mine. You know it."

Reeves's face drained of blood, leaving him starkly white.

"He is," Alex said, and crawled to Edmund Carey, gathered the man, took a second to clear his own battered head, then pushed to his feet with Carey cradled in his arms. He turned to find Joanna staring still, horror stricken at the sight of Demas looming over Reeves. "Joanna. *Go.*"

Shaking herself as if from a nightmare's grip, she fled, racing ahead of him out of the room, out of the house, into the night.

44

"What happened to Phineas?" Charlotte asked between sobs, while Joanna held her on the straw-ticked bedstead in a cabin abandoned by their slaves.

"Don't think of it now. You're safe."

Severn's works had been tried, as if by fire, and proved stubble, but she, Charlotte, and Papa were alive, as those come through the flames. While she regretted the terrible cost to so many souls, she didn't grieve the plantation's loss, for lost it surely was.

Perhaps she was still in shock. She'd reason enough to be.

Alex. She'd seen him, heard him, yet could hardly believe it. The one person she'd wanted above all others, the one she hadn't dared ask the Almighty to send, had come back to them.

How had Elijah found him? Where had he been all this time?

Questions spiraled endlessly as she comforted her sister. Charlotte finally calmed enough to be tucked into the strange bed, but Joanna waited until sleep claimed her before leaving her watched over by an elderly slave, one of the few who hadn't run. She checked briefly on her stepfather, asleep in the neighboring cabin, Moses standing guard between them.

Alex had carried Papa from the house to that borrowed bed. Where was he now?

She headed for the kitchen, stopping short on the threshold at sight of Sybil minding a kettle at the hearth. Sybil looked up, seeming as dazed as Joanna felt, one eye darkened by a bruise.

"Be an awful mess in the study."

Joanna crossed to Sybil and touched her face. "Did he do this?"

Sybil dropped her gaze. "I tried not to tell him anything."

"Oh Sybil. That horrid man . . ."

"He past ever hurting anyone now," Sybil finished.

So Phineas Reeves was dead. Joanna drew a breath clean of the fear of him for the first time in so many months it felt foreign to her lungs.

"Don't worry about the house. Go on to bed if you want."

Sybil shook her head. "I couldn't sleep. You want I should go sit with Miss Charlotte? Maybe fetch one of her dolls?"

"There's someone with her, and Moses guarding, but if she wakes, you'd be a comfort. As would one of her dolls—not the Jemma doll." Joanna gave a small shudder. "Thank you, Sybil. I'll bank the fire."

Sybil went out, leaving her alone for the first time since the nightmare of the past few days began. The water in the kettle simmered. Fragile bubbles broke its surface and popped, hissing onto the fire below.

Gone in an instant. Like so much else.

Joanna clamped her arms across her belly, assaulted by that last glimpse of Mister Reeves, Demas looming over him like some dark avenging angel. Terror had washed the color from his face, until a different expression replaced it. Had it been relief?

She'd fled into the night and gone about the business of caring for Papa and Charlotte, benumbed with shock.

Shock was crumbling now, its pieces scattering, leaving her shaking, wracked with silent sobs.

When footsteps halted on the threshold, she knew without looking who it was.

"Joanna."

Breath catching, tears unabated, she straightened. Before she could turn, he was behind her, hands on her shoulders, warm and encompassing. She drew away and faced him, jaw aching with the effort to cease crying, and looked at him, so tall, so *real,* his beloved features racked with concern.

Alarm seized her. "Is Charlotte all right? Papa?"

Alex reached for her again but aborted the gesture when she flinched. "They're fine. Sleeping. I just looked in on them both."

"Why are you here?"

Firelight showed his wincing at her half-choked words. "I had to find ye, see did ye need me."

"Of course I needed you. But why are you here?" This wasn't coming out right. She couldn't find the words. Her heart was at once flinging wide to him, joyous at his return, and curling tight for fear his presence meant nothing of what she wanted it to mean.

"I heard things werena well with ye here and—"

"How?" She stepped back, felt the fire's heat, heard boiling droplets flinging themselves onto the flames, hissing, spitting. "How did you hear? Where have you been? No, don't answer. I don't want . . . I just . . . You . . . I needed you not to leave me! I needed to go with you—but I couldn't have. Not like that. I . . ."

Everything was in pieces. Her thoughts, her words, her heart.

"Joanna." He reached again for her, guilt twisting his features.

Again she stepped back.

"Joanna!"

He lunged for her, clamping her arm and yanking her toward him. She yelped, half-falling against him as he bent and beat at her petticoat, furiously smacking the folds. She smelled the scorching muslin, realized what she'd done. Stepped too near the fire's edge and caught herself aflame. She hadn't time to panic before he'd extinguished the burning.

He was standing close, clutching her, gazing at her with alarm, tenderness, regret. With her free hand she shoved him hard. He staggered, not expecting it, but caught the edge of the work-table.

"You see? I need you, but I don't want to!"

She hurled herself at him, fists raised, and pounded them against his broad chest.

He didn't defend against her assault. She hit him again, knowing he'd already taken blows for her that night, worse than any she could deliver. But she couldn't stop, nor the sobs rising up, bursting from her lips.

A part of her—that calm, rational part so long in charge of her behavior—had gone mute. It stood back and eyed this unseemly display, shaking a disapproving head. What would any-one who came into that kitchen right now say? What would they think of her?

"I don't care!" she cried. "I loved you!"

She heard those last words out of her mouth clear enough. Betraying words she wished she could take back. What was left to do after their speaking but cling to this man who'd given her a glimpse of what her soul longed for—given her a sip, then abandoned her thirsty—and sob while his arms went around her.

His hand cupped her head, cradling it to his chest. Beneath her cheek his heart beat hard and fast. Against it she wailed.

It was moments before she heard his voice lifted. Not in weeping. Nor in soothing murmurs. Not even addressing her. "Merciful God. Help us. Give us peace. We need it . . . need You."

The words coming out of his mouth, ragged with fervency, hushed her at last. She unclenched her fists, let her hands lie flat against his chest. He no longer wore the filthy coat she'd glimpsed earlier but was in his shirtsleeves.

As she quieted, so did he.

They stood thus for a time before he ventured tentatively, "Joanna?"

Her mouth trembled so hard it took a moment to reply. "You were . . . praying?" The words were thick from weeping.

"Aye. There's a great deal I need to tell ye, but for now, the one thing." His breath flowed warm across the top of her head as he held her. "Listen to me. I willna ever walk away from ye again. I promise. D'ye hear me, lass? I promise."

She was unmoving in his arms, silent so long he began to think she'd fallen asleep on her feet. At one point Moon came to the door, lantern in hand. Alex read the question on the man's scarred face. Had they need?

Aye. Time. Healing—neither of which another man could give.

When he shook his head, Moon looked tenderly at Joanna, oblivious to his presence, nodded, and left them.

Alex waited, savoring the feel of her in his arms, slender, solid, warm, melting away the months apart as if they'd never passed. They had, though, and with them the trials and griefs and triumphs that changed a person. He was changed. She would be too. *"I loved you."*

"Joanna?"

He felt her stir. Her hands slid around his waist. "Mmm?"

"D'ye want to sit down?"

She held him tighter. "Don't move."

If he had his choice, he would never move again. "All right."

"I hit you. I'm sorry."

"Dinna be. Ye didna hurt me."

He felt her sigh. "Not even a little?"

He conquered the urge to laugh, but risked a kiss against her hair. When she didn't take offense or try to extricate herself, he said, "Not in any lasting way. Not as I've hurt ye."

It wasn't a sigh she heaved this time, something nearer a sob. "You did hurt me. Very much."

Hearing a hiss, he glanced at the hearth, but

the fire was dying, the water simmering down.

So was he. The red of battle had faded, leaving him aware of its aftermath on his flesh. Bruises. Throbbing head. Throbbing face. A chunk of his hair stiff with blood.

"Aye, I ken what I did. I'm sorry for it. I want to tell ye everything, and I will. I'm not leaving ye again. Unless ye want me to go?"

The pause was long enough to fear she was considering it. Then she lifted her face, tear streaked, ravaged with the strain of months.

"You're different," she said.

"Aye. I am."

Her brow puckered as she searched his gaze. "You look much the same, browner maybe . . . What? Is it God who changed you?"

"Aye, and Reverend Pauling. And a lad called Runs-Far."

"Runs-Far? Wait . . . You've seen Reverend Pauling?"

"I have." All that had happened over the summer and autumn among the Cherokees pressed in. He'd no notion where to begin. She seemed to understand. Instead of more questions about where he'd been, or why, she asked a question he found he was able to answer with ease.

"Will you kiss me, Alex?"

His heart, calmed from its frantic beating, gave a joyous leap. "Oh, aye, I will."

She lifted her face and he lowered his, letting

their lips touch in the gentlest of meetings, afraid to ask more, forgetting she'd asked him. He wanted to lift her into his arms, to kiss her as he'd dreamed of doing since he walked away from her, but she stepped back, took hold of his hands, and spread them wide as if to get a look at him.

Her eyes in the firelight were the deepest of seas at dawn before the sun crests the horizon to wash the world in gold. As her gaze swept the length of him, those sea-eyes widened, filling with the astonishment he minded well from their first sight of one another, by candlelight in the smithy.

"My goodness," she said.

They shut the kitchen door against the chill and talked into the night, tea brewed and forgotten, the rekindled fire warm on Joanna's back. She hoped Alex felt it, too, seated across the worktable. The hand stretched out between them was big and warm in hers. Firelight illumined his features—broad brow and strong cheekbones, deep-set eyes, that mouth that tilted and tipped when he smiled. She'd cleaned the gash on his scalp, noting that his hair was longer now as well as sun-bleached. It had come down from its binding. He was disheveled, bruised, and beautiful.

They talked of the Cherokees, his time among

them, of Jemma and her son, and she was glad she was already sitting down by that time. Many puzzling pieces of her life were falling into place, those marked Jemma no exception. She wept again, this time for what she should have seen. Better, prevented.

"Jemma's where she wants to be," Alex reassured her. "Protected by her clan. She's loved and valued."

And free. "Thank you. For saving her."

What had remained of the Joanna who had fought so hard to control every aspect of her life had vanished this night, replaced briefly by the frightened, abandoned girl she'd once been. But it was coming clear that she'd never been in control of anything. Was never meant to be. She felt raw, exposed, and unmade, balanced on the fearful, exhilarating verge of becoming something, or someone, new.

They talked of Reverend Pauling, found a captive among the Cherokees, of Hugh Cameron and Mountain Laurel. "Ye mind it was ye told me of Cameron?" Alex asked her. "That's where I've left the reverend. He means to come to ye, soon as he's able."

That dear man, carried into captivity and not only surviving it, thriving in it. She could hardly take it in.

They hadn't spoken of what happened in the house that night. After a time she asked, "Demas?"

"Gone."

"You didn't seem surprised to see him."

"I was, but maybe not as much as ye." Alex laced their fingers across the table as he told her of his encounter with the slaves who'd taken refuge in the swamp. Of finding Elijah with them, and Demas, and all Demas had related of his history with Phineas Reeves. "He did the thing he promised to do should Reeves ever cross that line with a child. He never kent for sure about Jemma until I told him, but no mistaking Reeves had every intention of hurting Charlotte."

Joanna squeezed her eyes shut, willing memory of the past hours away. Perhaps one day she might pity Phineas Reeves, gone into darkness forever, but the destruction he'd wreaked was still a smoking ruin.

"Demas left him lying before the hearth," Alex was saying. "No more blood was spilled than had been—mostly mine. Though by now," he added, "Moon and the others will have carried him out."

Joanna never wanted to lay eyes on the man again, even dead. It would bring no closure, serve no purpose. Alex looked as though he wanted to say more. He caught his bottom lip between his teeth.

"What?" she asked.

"I only wondered, the two of ye . . . Did ye marry the man?"

"No," she said. "I'm undefiled—in that way."

His grip on her hand tightened. "In no way are ye defiled, lass."

She pulled free. "I am. And not just me. The house. This place. I'll have no more of it. I wish I could turn back time and run away with you. I made the wrong choice." Tears spilled as Alex rose from the table and came to stand before her.

"No. Ye stood firm. Ye didna leave the place the Almighty had ye no matter the storm that beat. No matter even I called ye weak. I'm ashamed of it now, calling weak the strongest woman I've ever kent."

"Alex . . ."

He knelt before her. "Will ye forgive me for abandoning ye in the teeth of that storm?" He took up both her hands in his. "For choosing my own freedom, and my pride, over your well-being, over everything?"

Forgive. She could choose to do it, though she might need to make the same choice again. And again. But which of them didn't need an equal measure of mercy? They had it from the Almighty, more than enough. Phineas Reeves had gone beyond receiving it, but dare she withhold it from Alex?

"I do forgive you," she said and saw the wash of relief in his gaze before he lowered his head to her lap and rested it there.

Her tears fell onto his hair.

They might have floated in a bubble, the two of them, suspended amid all that remained of the world that had done its best to keep them apart—until he lifted his face and looked at her, clearly with more on his mind.

"Ye said ye want an end to it? To Severn, d'ye mean? Ye dinna want to be here any longer?"

"I don't know what will happen to us. How I'll care for Papa and Charlotte—much less anyone else who chooses to stay, but I never want to set foot in that house again." She would, of course. Papa and Charlotte had had enough upheaval for the present.

"In every ending," Alex said, "there's also a beginning. That's a thing I've learned."

That drew her thoughts up short. "What do you mean?"

"Dinna worry how ye'll care for them. Let me take that worry, with the Almighty's help." He raised a hand to her face, the hand that had fought for her and carried her heart's treasure out of danger this night. A hand most capable and strong. "Joanna, when your heart is healed—as it will be, one day—will ye give it to me to hold, and have the keeping of mine? Besides my heart, ye'll have the sweat of my brow for as long as I can lift a hammer, or anything else I must needs do to provide for ye, if ye'll have me."

She put her hand over his, turned her lips to his palm, and kissed it. No matter how long she waited, how much she healed, that answer wasn't going to change.

"I won't ask how, then, but *where* will we live?"

At that question his tired features lit. "I've a place in mind," he said, with that crooked smile of his tugging at his mouth. "First I want to do this proper. I need to speak with your stepfather. I saw he's much diminished. In body, though, not in mind?"

The reminder of Papa's crippling, as well as what lay between him and Alex—a broken indenture, theft, abandonment—ought to have dashed her like a bucket of cold water. It didn't.

"He's still there. I don't know what he's thinking. About Severn. You . . . ."

"We'll ken that soon enough, and meet it together. For now I think we both best sleep, if the morning hasna yet come." He rose and opened the door to find the night still dark without.

As if in a dream, Joanna saw him hold out a hand to her. She had no memory of taking it, only that she was floating, suspended as if on the sea's embrace. He carried her, she realized, easily, as if she weighed no more than Charlotte. And there was Charlotte, asleep in the cabin. She was lowered beside her sister, Alex bending over her, brushing her hair from her face. Leaving her with a kiss on her brow.

Joanna woke late in the morning to find the sun risen, Sybil in the kitchen starting breakfast, and Elijah gone to the camp where Severn's runaways were living. He meant to bring back Azuba, Marigold, and Jory—the only three he was certain would return.

"Not that Demas," Sybil told her. "Not after what he done. Ain't no one see him since you all left the house. Reckon he gone for good?"

For good or ill. Joanna shivered in the kitchen's early chill, recalling what Alex had told her in the night about Demas and Phineas Reeves. An appalling bond had linked that pair, but she was thankful it had held.

Alex and Moses had buried Mister Reeves early that morning, Sybil informed her. There was much to distract Joanna from that knowledge, such as wondering who Elijah would bring back, who would vanish into forest or swamp to follow their own path to freedom. She wished she might have sent Elijah with the promise of manumission.

Severn's slaves would weigh the risks and make their choices.

For now, Charlotte needed breakfast. Papa, too,

though he proved to have scant appetite when she delivered it. Joanna reassured him Charlotte was well, still unaware of her peril.

"Phin . . ."

"Gone beyond harming us," she answered before he could get out more than half the name. Such guilt and regret flooded her stepfather's gaze, she was relieved when he closed his eyes.

"Papa," she said, coming to sit on the edge of the cot and grasping his left hand. His fingers curled around hers, cool and dry. He opened his eyes.

There was frustration in his gaze, so much he wanted to say, but couldn't. "Mac-Kinn . . . ?"

Despite everything, Joanna couldn't suppress the joy. "Yes, he's here. He rescued us, he and Elijah. But Mister Reeves didn't die by his hand. It was Demas, Papa. He's gone now as well. We don't know where. I know that needs explaining, and it will be, but Alex and I talked last night of other matters, and that's what I want to tell you about."

She paused. Papa swallowed, tried to speak, then simply nodded.

"This is all I know," she said, marshalling her thoughts. "I still have that vision of a life for us, one very different from what we've had here. A simple life, but a good life—for you and Charlotte, and Azuba, Elijah, Mari, and as many others who want to share it. I believe Alex is the man who will help me build it. I know he betrayed you, Papa, but he's changed. He's been with Reverend Pauling, the two of them made captives of the Cherokees. Alex brought him back over the mountains in need of some care, and he'll come to us soon. But Alex couldn't wait. He's here and he wants to speak with you. I don't know all he means to say, but I'm asking . . . will you give us your blessing to build that life together?"

She'd said all she could and so fell silent, looking down at their clasped hands. Papa squeezed hers once, then turned his face to the wall, where the clay between the logs needed patching.

Alex was waiting on the path outside, in possession of a walking stick that looked newly carved. He leaned it against the cabin and draped the disreputable coat he'd been wearing last night over it. Morning sunlight caught his eyes, intensifying their blue. Joanna caught her breath.

"How is he?" he asked, stepping near, sleeves rolled high, grubby from grave-digging. Not caring, she slipped her arms around him, thrilling at the welcome warmth of his embrace, more so when he pressed a kiss atop her head.

Papa hadn't answered her question, and every heartbeat now was a prayer. She breathed in the scent of the man she wanted to share her life with, the tang of oak leaves, the muskiness of earth, the smell of sun.

"It's hard to say." Reluctantly she stepped back. "How long will Elijah be, do you think?"

"If he brings women and children with him, aside from Mari and Jory, it's hard to say." He smiled, echoing her words. "It's maybe too soon but . . . d'ye ken what your stepfather means to do?"

"I don't know if *he* does. Is that for him?" She nodded at the stick.

"Jo . . . ann . . . ?" Papa's halting voice called before Alex could reply.

She went to the cabin door to peer inside. He'd put the breakfast tray aside, spilling its contents a little, and was sitting on the edge of the straw tick, bare feet planted on the dirt.

"Papa, you shouldn't—"

A garbled growl erupted from his lips, but she took his meaning.

"All right," she said, trying to feel encouraged that he wanted to try to rise. He was still in his nightshirt and banyan, but Sybil had brought a suit of clothes from the house. "Do you want to dress?"

"My . . . self," he said.

Unwilling to fight him, yet certain he'd need her aid, she laid out the garments on the cot within his reach, then stepped out of the cabin, leaving the door ajar.

Alex had donned the coat, brushed and made slightly more presentable. "Where did you come by that?"

He tugged at a too-short sleeve. "Hugh Cameron."

"Your friend at Mountain Laurel. I'm glad you found each other."

He nodded at the cabin and asked softly, "Can he walk?"

"With help, barely." She glanced at the carved stick still propped beside the cabin door. "Did you make that?"

"Aye. I thought maybe, when he's ready and able . . ."

"He's ready now. I don't know about able."

They waited in silence, looking at each other, hearing Charlotte's voice from the kitchen, where she'd wanted to stay and help Sybil prepare whatever would be their next meal. At last she heard the thump of shoes on earth.

"You managed it," she said, looking in to see her stepfather had donned all but coat and neckcloth while seated on the side of the bed. He waved away the neckcloth but would have the coat. She helped him to his feet and held the garment for him. Once a snug fit, it now hung on his frame.

The labor of dressing had tired him, but he wasn't through with his demands. "Smi-thy," he said.

"Papa, it's too far." Ignoring her protest, he took a wobbly step, nearly falling from her grasp. "Wait. Alex fashioned a stick for you." She fetched it from beside the door. He accepted the crude but sturdy cane with flattened mouth and leaned his weight upon it. Again he wobbled and she steadied him. "Why do you wish to go to the smithy?"

Alex's tall frame darkened the doorway. "Is it me ye want, sir? Ye dinna need go anywhere. I'm here."

Papa's gaze drilled him hard. "Smi-thy . . . you."

Alex glanced at her, sought and gained her reluctant permission, then stepped forward. "Aye, sir. We'll get ye there."

He wouldn't be carried, despite Alex offering. It was a laborious process, Joanna walking to one side of Papa, Alex the other, supporting him more than they tried to let on, Papa shuffling, face grimly determined. Behind his back they communicated in glances, certain this had been ill-advised, but Joanna knew better than to try to stop it.

He made it to the smithy.

Though Alex had slept in his old cot for the few hours' rest he'd gotten, the smithy smelled deserted, cold ashes and charcoal dust.

They settled her stepfather on Elijah's stool at the workbench, where he spent some moments catching his breath, Joanna hovering. She gave him a kerchief to mop his sweating brow.

Alex moved about the shop, looking at the forge, the tools on the bench, touching nothing, as though he hadn't the right. Joanna wanted to tell him he'd every right, remind him that choices could be remade. Broken hearts mended.

And broken indentures?

"Jo-ann . . . go."

"Papa? Whatever this is about, I want to know."

"We'll be fine, lass," Alex said. "I've things to say to your stepfather, things he needs to hear before anyone else. Ye'll be next to hear them."

Before she could respond there came a throat's clearing at the smithy door—Moses, who nodded respectfully to Joanna and her stepfather but addressed Alex. "Man put in at the dock. Neighbor from upriver. I mind him from the gathering with the preacher last year."

"Ye get a name?" Alex asked.

"Him with all the chilluns—McGinnis. Got one with him now. Oldest boy, I think."

The ease of their exchange struck Joanna, and she realized a thing she'd noticed from that first conversation overheard between him and Elijah. They were drawn to him, other men, willing for him to lead them.

Her stepfather had been such a man, in his day. Would he find it in him now to let another lead?

Joanna sent Moses ahead of her. "Please see

they're tended in the kitchen. I'm coming." She shared a look with Alex, willing him to know she'd be praying—and beside herself with impatience—then left them to it.

Though Edmund Carey had initiated this, Alex knew he'd be the one doing the lion's share of the talking. The man's diminishment was a shock. It pained Alex, watching him struggle to form the simplest words, remembering that first evening when Severn's master strode into the smithy to assess his new indenture, straight and strong, in command of his domain. Which, he realized, was exactly why Carey had insisted on this pilgrimage. So Alex might bear in mind what he still was—master, commander, patriarch, laird—though outwardly he no longer resembled that vigorous memory.

"Thank . . . you, Mac-Kinn . . ."

Thoughts cut short by the last words he'd expected from the man, Alex said, "Ye're thanking me, sir? For what?"

Carey's recalcitrant lips worked until his half-strangled voice produced, "Them . . ."

His daughters' lives.

"Aye, sir. I had to come back. Reverend Pauling and I learned things werena well with ye here. And Jemma, afore we left the Cherokees, she told me about Reeves and . . ."

At Carey's grunt of protest, Alex halted the

account. It was agitating the man, trying to take it in. "Da-a . . . vid?"

"I left him at Mountain Laurel. He's been ill, but . . ." Seeing the questions swimming in Carey's gaze, he pulled over a block chair and sat. "How about if I start from the beginning, tell ye why I left, where I've been, and why I've come back. The whole tale start to finish. Then I suppose ye'll decide what's to be done with me."

Carey's knuckles tightened on the cane he kept firmly planted. He nodded, expectancy in his eyes. Alex knew the man wouldn't last long ere he needed his bed. He'd have to keep his recounting brief.

First he needed something cleared between them.

"Ye ken, sir, I didna set fire to the mill? And that it was Reeves released me from the smoke-house, in hopes I'd do exactly what I did—run?"

Again Carey nodded. He made a choked sound as he gazed pointedly at the tools hanging in their places, the question clear.

"I stole from ye," Alex admitted. "Tools, iron. The clothes I wore. I'll return it to ye, or repay. All but the one thing I took never meaning to."

"Jem . . . ?"

"The lassie followed me that night, trailed me for days before I caught her. She'd tell ye she stole herself, did ye ask her, but I can say I left her settled, content with a new life." He paused to see if Carey wanted more on the subject of Jemma. He seemed content for the moment.

Alex launched full into the tale then, from his and Jemma's meeting with Hugh Cameron, the brief stay at Mountain Laurel, the sojourn into wilderness, the birth of Jemma's son—that made Carey, swift to draw conclusions, flush with outrage—their capture by Blackbird and her warriors and the trek overmountain.

"We found the reverend a captive of the Cherokees since the autumn." He told of Jemma's adoption, Pauling's preaching, the illness that forced his and the reverend's return. "I got him safe out of the mountains, back to Mountain Laurel. He was looking stronger when I left. I had to leave him, sir. I knew by then what Reeves intended. I'd have come back anyway, but . . ."

He fished in his coat and brought out the letter he'd carried from Mountain Laurel. Through all the misadventures since, the seal hadn't so much as cracked.

"The reverend's written to ye, sir."

Carey's gaze fastened on the letter.

"Before ye read it I want to say . . ." Alex forced himself to look straight into Carey's eyes. "I ask your forgiveness for breaking my word to ye. Not just depriving ye of my service but leaving ye to the malice of a man I suspected even then meant ye no good. I oughtn't to have done it, and I repent me of it with all my heart."

Worn and battered as a storm-swept ship, Carey was still sound of mind. "Re . . . pent?"

"I dinna choose the word lightly. I'm ready to return to ye, serve out my years—or submit to whatever punishment ye deem fitting."

"No," Carey managed, holding his gaze. "I . . . failed . . . you."

"Sir," Alex began, but the man made an adamant noise and he hesitated. Carey dropped his gaze to the letter. Alex relinquished it.

Carey managed the seal one-handed and unfolded the page. He pressed it to a knee and set to reading, continuing in silence until he'd finished. A tear rolled down his gaunt cheek and fell upon a line, marring the ink. "You . . . ?"

"Did I read it? Not a word." He half-hoped Carey might let him read the letter now, but the man made no show of offering it.

"This . . . life," Carey said, concentrating so keenly on forming the words he was sweating again. "Done."

"Sir, no. Your life isna done—"

Again Carey made a noise that halted his protest.

"Se . . . vern . . . was . . . van-ity." Though clearly exhausted, he pressed on. "What . . . to . . . do?"

Alex scrambled to understand. "Ye dinna ken what to do? With me, ye mean?"

Carey shook his head. "Not . . . you."

With a roiling in his gut, Alex made another stab. "Ye dinna ken how ye'll provide, for Joanna and Charlotte, if ye dinna have Severn?"

Relief streamed from the man like the sweat down his temples. He nodded. Though far from relieved, Alex decided it was time to lay every hope on the table.

"I've a notion about that, sir. But I'd like Joanna to hear it, too, and if ye dinna mind my saying, I think ye need to lie down."

Carey was attempting to form a reply when someone else beat him to it.

"I'm here," Joanna said, coming into the smithy bearing a laden tray. "And I want to hear it now, Alex. Please."

They settled Papa on Alex's cot, a cup of cider and a roll warm from the oven on a plate atop his blanketed lap. Joanna handed Alex his own cup and settled herself on Elijah's old cot. Alex stood between, cradling cup and bread. Before he could begin, Papa asked, "Mc-Gin-nis?"

"Oh," Joanna said, recalling the visitors she'd gone to greet. "He's tried more than once in the past weeks to see us, Papa, having heard of our"—she paused, beating back the shadows of their losses—"misfortunes. Mister McGinnis was turned away at the dock every time by one excuse or another, and we never knew it. He and his son plan to stay until tomorrow. He wants to see you, help us, if he can. You were about to address that subject, Alex?"

When Alex set cup and bread aside and extended his hand to her, she took it, rising to stand beside him, her stays suddenly too tight to contain her beating heart.

Papa's gaze fastened on that linking clasp as Alex spoke of his journey out of the mountains with Reverend Pauling, desperate to find the river that would lead them back toward Mountain Laurel.

"There came a morning I left him sleeping and climbed the ridge below which we'd camped. I meant to get a view of the land, maybe spot the river—gain my bearings, ye ken."

He'd crested the ridge and emerged from forest to find himself at the top of a cove, wide and gently sloping, with a broad creek running down to the river he'd sought, visible below. He'd stood at the wood's edge in the light of a rising sun . . .

"I'd never kent such a feeling in a place," he told them, gaze abstracted, as though living again that moment in his mind. "As if I could already see it—a house, a mill, and where stood an old chestnut I thought, right there I'll build a smithy. That's where I buried the tools I took from ye, sir. I kent by midday, maybe sooner, I'd be carrying the reverend and needed to lighten my load. I raised a cairn over the spot, with stones from the creek."

Papa tried to say a word. It came out mangled. They waited, glancing at each other, while he tried again.

"Bib-li-cal . . . of . . . you."

Alex smiled at that, but uncertainty marked his gaze. "I dinna ken whether it sounds a place ye'd fancy seeing, much less settling. But this is what I propose. Let me lead ye to it, and Elijah, Mari, Azuba, any of your people here minded to stay with ye. It's a good place, not too deep into the mountains, nor far off beaten paths. And I've the sense if we settled there, others would come. I'm told the governor, Johnston, is generous when it comes to granting land to fellow Scots. Though, I am still indentured."

"Papa knows the governor," Joanna said when he paused and looked to her. "Alex, what you're describing, it sounds much like the vision I had. Or the beginnings of it."

Of a simple life, with a man who simply loved her. And here stood the man.

"I mind it well, lass." Tenderness and question filled his eyes. "Ye wouldna be afraid of the mountains, or of living rough to start?"

"I don't think I'd be afraid anywhere, so long as you were there too."

Alex appeared to grow taller, if that were possible. She saw it in his eyes, a healing confidence, a restoring strength. But he wasn't the only one present whose life would be changed by what they decided this day.

"Papa? What say you?" She waited while her stepfather gathered his thoughts, knowing her heart on the matter. Praying silently for his. He'd forgotten his bread and cider, his gaze on Alex.

"Marry . . . her . . . Mac-Kinn-on."

Joanna's breath caught, robbing her of speech.

Alex wasn't so afflicted. "Above all things I want to care for ye, sir, and your daughters, and all that's yours for the rest of my life, but . . . d'ye think she'd have me?"

"You could ask!" Joanna exclaimed, finding voice at last.

"To be fair, I all but did last night."

She blushed at the half-teasing remark, remembering her behavior in the kitchen. "And I all but said yes."

"So ye did." He took both her hands in his, holding them tight. "But so there's no misunderstanding here . . . Joanna Carey, will ye marry me?"

You know well that I will, she thought, and opened her mouth to say it, but Elijah's voice cut through the moment. "If ye don't say yes to the man, Joanna, so he can lead us all to this promised land I've just heard described, I might never speak to ye again."

Quite unperturbed, Alex turned to include Elijah, standing in the doorway surveying them.

Joanna didn't mind the interruption either, glad Elijah had returned in time to join the conversation, even if it included a proposal of marriage.

"I suppose we cannot have that," she said.

Such happiness felt as if it belonged to some other life. Some other Joanna. The one she would become.

"Then I'll leave ye to sort this out," Elijah said, smiling with a lightness Joanna hadn't seen in far too long. "Once ye have done, ye'll maybe want to come see who's returned to ye."

"Yes," she said, then there was nothing else in the world but Alex gazing down at her, not even Papa in the cot nearby.

"Ye dinna mean that's the only reason ye'd marry me? To please Elijah?"

He was teasing, but there was an earnestness to the question. He'd once asked her what it was she wanted. Not what Papa wanted for her, or Charlotte needed from her, or anyone else expected of her. She hadn't followed her heart then. Too much had stood in the way. Now all that hindered had been removed, and she could see the path forward.

"No, Alex. It's far down the list of reasons why I mean to marry you." There, in front of Papa, she lifted her hands to his face, drew him down and kissed him, leaving him in no doubt what reasons topped her list.

Papa made no protest.

They drank their cider and ate their bread, a simple meal to mark the ending of a life grown threadbare, ready to be folded away like a worn garment, exchanged for something new. A new life.

Not until Papa had drifted to sleep, though, did they leave him to go out and see who would be sharing it.

Postscriptum

19 October 1748
To Edmund Philip Carey
Severn Plantation

Dear Edmund,

Finding myself again prisoner to my frequent Infirmity, I pen this letter to you, longtime Friend. Also to Joanna, Charlotte, and Elijah. I remember you each in Prayer, that the Almighty would minister to you, His Spirit ever comfort. Even during my captivity in the Wilderness, news of you reached me. While my Heart is deeply burdened for your sore testing, I trust you cling to our unchanging Christ and pray the more fervently that this Faith we hold in common will be manifested in your innermost Being so that those looking on will see Christ in you, and recall during this time of Loss your generosity to the Church that oft met on the grounds of Severn in brighter days.

Not to add to your troubles, but to ease them, I ask of you a kindness. By his own accounting, Alex MacKinnon proved of little use to you in service or in Friendship, but now I venture he has become useful in both. Such has been his Service to me, I should have been content to keep him with me until I am fitted to travel, but I send him back to you now with my blessing because of your Need. Only consider this, that perhaps it was for the best he left you for a season. He returns to you more than your indentured Man, but now a Brother in the Faith, willing to endure whatever punishment his defection may warrant. However, I plead with you to welcome him back. Whatever he owes, charge it to me, bearing in mind your Words to me when last we met: *And you know as well all that I owe you—my very Life.* Therefore grant me this kindness, Friend.

Now, before Alex comes to bid me farewell, be so kind also as to ready a bed for me. With your Prayers and the Almighty's Grace, I expect to come to you. Duncan Cameron, my host, sends his greetings—in the Scots tongue, which I will not attempt to pen—as do his believing slaves, Malcolm and Tilly, and their little daughter, Naomi, already the accomplished cook.

Until I see you, God willing soon, peace to you, Edmund—from our Lord and Savior, Jesus Christ!

David Cornelius Pauling
Mountain Laurel

16 April 1750
To Reverend David Pauling
Crooked Branch's Town

Dear Reverend,

How good that your letter of last autumn reached us before the snows sealed you off, away in the mountains. There being little hope of a reply reaching you until spring, I held off writing, and am glad I did so. You asked how we have settled in our "edge of the wilderness" cove, as you called it. You will recall from your brief visit on your way to Runs-Far, Jemma (I cannot think of her as Walnut), and the rest, that we did not have an altogether smooth time of it, moving our considerable tribe here, though of course Alex, Papa, and I were pleased to welcome our former slaves who chose to remain with us, and how thankful I am for Papa's longtime acquaintance with Governor Johnston, which enabled us to procure a dispensation for those who wished not to seek their fortunes beyond this colony, as the law would otherwise have forced them to do.

The process of divesting ourselves of Severn, then the unfortunate discovery of Mister Reeves's further perfidy while last in Wilmington—bearing that letter of authority to act in Papa's name on a matter with Mister Simcoe; a matter that, as it turned out, was an utter fabrication—took longer than we would have liked. We were blessed in the end by Captain Bingham. Upon learning the outrageously low price he paid to purchase the *Charlotte-Ann* from Mister Reeves had not originated with Papa, that we had no knowledge whatsoever of the sale, the captain did a gracious thing. He named Papa a fair price for the ship he had already bought and has since paid us in full. Alex was more affected by this than anyone. He and Captain Bingham had an unfortunate history, but they parted well this second time, and so on that note of grace, we cut our ties to that old life and left for the mountains to claim the headright grant Papa obtained from Governor Johnston, which includes our beloved cove.

You know all that Demas confessed of Mister Reeves's past, the extent of his crimes against his former shipmates—only Thom Kelly's death, it seems, was not of his agency, though I am certain he was pleased by it—so I shall not mention it in detail. Scripture tells us that all things work together for good for those who love the Lord. I thought that meant the Almighty uses even our tragedies to bring about some good thing, some unforeseen blessing, given time. Now I think there's more to it—that the very thing that causes our pain can become the source of our joy, much as a baby causes agony in its birthing, but once born is cherished, its mother's rejoicing beyond measure. Or perhaps I merely have babies on the brain. More on that shortly.

All my heart, and my hours, are taken up with establishing our new home, and while the work is never ending, the rewards are as ceaseless. It has not been a year since you were here but much has changed. Little Jory runs about now, keeping Marigold on her toes when she isn't tending to her and Elijah's daughter born this winter past. Jory is a feisty one, and it takes us all—Marigold, Azuba, Phoebe, Sybil, and me—to keep him from falling into continual mischief. What may surprise you is the one person Jory never crosses or even tests is dear Papa.

I realize it was a shock, seeing the change in Papa when you joined us at Severn, though you treated him with the dignity and compassion you've always shown. Papa's recovery continues, but slowly. He walks still with a cane and likely always will. His speech is yet labored, but the greatest blessing is that thing which you noted during your visit. His soul is at peace. He no longer frets over the things of this world but wants only now the things of the Lord. He has lost so much of this world's treasure, yet now his aim is to store up treasure in heaven, where no thief can steal. That is what he talks to Jory about, to all the children of our former slaves, anyone with patience to sit and listen. Perhaps the mountains are healing to him as Alex suggests, but I know it owes as much to breaking the chains that bound us at Severn. Papa's soul has been set free along with his slaves. As you always knew it would be.

Charlotte is still her sweet child-self, growing more beautiful with each passing season. While in Edenton another physician examined her, reaching the same conclusion as those before. Perhaps something happened at her birth, or this is merely the way the Almighty chose to knit her in our mother's womb. I am thankful for this: she will never comprehend how near she came to having her soul marked by darkness. Charlotte has friends among our former slaves, one girl in particular who reminds me of Jemma. Nothing hinders their friendship. As long as I have a say in it, nothing shall.

We miss you and your teaching from the Word. But to our surprise, Elijah has recently taken on the mantle of teacher, for all on the Sabbath, daily for the children we have about us. I am grateful, as are we all, to see him finding purpose and joy. Speaking again of joy, when Marigold stood up with me at our wedding, and Elijah with Alex, I wondered whether she did so because she was still Papa's slave and I had asked it of her. Now she is free to choose, and still she chooses me. We are building this life side by side, with Alex and Elijah. And Azuba, Moses and his family, Phoebe and Sybil and their families. We are quite the village on our own, though we are no longer alone.

I have held off mentioning my beloved Alex and his doings until now. As you know he journeyed west into the mountains months ahead of the rest of us, Moses with him, to raise cabins, put in a late crop of corn, and establish our settlement while we waited with Governor Johnston in Edenton for Papa to regain strength enough for the journey. There was little more for you to see here last year than what Moses and Alex accomplished. Now I could write pages about the additional acres ready to be planted in corn, the gardens, the smithy under that big chestnut, the new cabins, and the mill I can hear Alex building as I write. It is to be a grist mill. Down where the creek spills into the Yadkin others have settled, drawn not only by promise of a mill but by the nearness of a blacksmith. Alex has grown in skill with Elijah by to continue his training. "His brain and my hands," Alex is fond of saying.

I do love the man, and am grateful for King George's mercy that brought him to us, and our Great King's mercy that returned him. He is a leader of men, so full of vitality and drive at times he still overwhelms me. Yet where once there was in him a hardness of heart and will, I find now a willingness to yield, to allow that strength to be channeled where he sees God leading. He says he is the blessed one to have someone as patient and steady and forgiving as me for his wife, but I know better.

Moses will be our miller, though his first love will always be the horses, of which we have the beginnings of what we hope to be a respectable herd one day. He and Papa talk often of fillies and colts yet unborn. Azuba looks forward to the next building project we have planned once the mill is finished, what she calls a Proper House. I quite like our snug cabin, though Azuba maintains there is not room enough to cuss a cat—if we had a cat. What we do have is a need for the extra space, and soon, as we anticipate our first child's arrival. She will be a June baby. Or he will. Or they will. Azuba thinks it's twins. Alex is partial to the notion, but I am not sure I want to believe her.

A trader has come up from the river on his way into the mountains. He says he will find you at Crooked Branch's town and put this letter into your hands. Though the high-country snows were deep this year, he expects the trails are passable. If so, you will read this soon.

You are in my prayers daily, as are Jemma and Runs-Far, Blue Jay, Shelled Corn, Blackbird and her son, and many others. All here bid me give you greeting. Alex bids you greet Thunder-Going-Away with these words: "Before the snows come again, little brother, you will see me." He has a hunting trip planned for after our babe is born and our crops sown. I hope soon to see you again, dear friend.

Yours most sincerely,
Joanna Carey MacKinnon
MacKinnon's Cove, North Carolina

AUTHOR'S NOTES AND ACKNOWLEDGMENTS

Toward the end of the New Testament, following several lengthy epistles by the apostle Paul addressed to the early churches, is an epistle Paul penned to a friend, a wealthy Christian man in Colossae called Philemon. In this brief letter, Paul writes concerning another man he encountered while a prisoner in Rome—a runaway slave belonging to Philemon. This encounter changed the life of this slave, Onesimus. In the letter, which Onesimus is bearing back to his master, Paul describes this slave, once unprofitable to Philemon, as having become a fellow laborer and brother profitable to them both. Paul asks Philemon to receive back his runaway—as a personal favor to Paul. The letter is written with an air of confident hope that forgiveness and reconciliation would be its outcome.

I've long been partial to this brief epistle in which Paul seeks mercy for Onesimus. A few years ago, with it stirring around in my mind, it occurred to me that the situation these three men find themselves in might well translate to an eighteenth-century setting. All the necessary elements were present during this time in colonial North American history: masters and slaves, captivity and chains, indentured servitude, itinerate ministers, and more than one Great Awakening of Christian faith. I wondered, could I write an eighteenth-century frontier story of the type readers have come to expect from me but with a twist—a foundation of story elements lifted from Paul's letter to Philemon?

As my mind began firing off possibilities, and characters started popping up, one thing quickly became obvious. This wouldn't be a strict "retelling" of the biblical account; already I felt the story pressing for room to expand. During the writing of *The King's Mercy*, I would eventually graft in quite a few elements the book of Philemon doesn't include. Among these are a number of secondary characters and subplots involving them, a female protagonist with her own story arc, and a central romance involving her, and (to me) the most disturbing antagonist I've yet written. Instead of a retelling, this would be a novel "inspired by" the story of Philemon, Onesimus, and Paul, where the main elements of the apostle's letter to his friend, on behalf of Onesimus, his repentant son in the faith, remain traceable in *The King's Mercy*, if perhaps not at first glance.

As always, I received help and input in researching and writing this story. Much of that input came from books: *Culloden* by John

Prebble and *This Remote Part of the World* by Bradford J. Wood being two most helpful volumes on the decade of the 1740s, the former on the Jacobite Rising in Scotland, the latter Colonial North Carolina—but I must also mention two individuals. My thanks to Iain MacKinnon, talented musician and teacher on the Isle of Lewis, for his aid with the Gaelic that appears in this book (any errors or deviations made over successive edits of the manuscript are mine alone), and for vetting appropriate eighteenth-century Scottish character names with me before I finally settled on Alex. And Betsy Pittman, resident genealogist, Burke County, North Carolina, whom I first met while writing *The Pursuit of Tamsen Littlejohn*. Thank you again, Betsy, for answering in detail my questions on obscure eighteenth-century legal situations!

And as always, thank you, Wendy Lawton, for your unfailing encouragement when my confidence flags; and Shannon Marchese, for your eagle eye across these pages. I still don't know how you do it, taking the story I've managed to produce, finding all its weak points, and nudging it closer to what I always meant it to be. I'm pretty sure by now you are a mind reader.

Jon Courson, mentioned in the dedication to this book, is a gifted and faithful teacher of God's Word. For any reader who, like Joanna Carey, hungers and thirsts for more of God's

Word, taught in a practical, applicable style, you can find Pastor Jon's teachings from the entire Bible, Genesis to Revelation, online at www.joncourson.com.

Let the word of Christ dwell in you richly . . .
—COLOSSIANS 3:16

Lori Benton

READERS GUIDE

1. Joanna Carey bears a burden from which she longs to be free. What is the source, or sources, of this burden? Do you think it's partly self-inflicted? Why? At what point in the story are Joanna's chains broken? What factors lead to her release?

2. After imprisonment and exile, Alex MacKinnon believes he will navigate life best by looking out for himself alone. This causes him both inner and outer conflict. How has this belief changed by the end of the story? Who or what were the greatest influences in this change?

3. A plantation mistress and a warrior-turned-blacksmith seem an unlikely pairing, yet as they grow acquainted, Joanna and Alex each discover strengths in the other they lack and admire. What are these strengths? Do you agree with Joanna that Alex truly understood her, even before his change of heart and return? Why or why not?

4. Alex has the gift of empowering others with a sense of self-worth and purpose. At what point, or points, does he operate in this gifting despite his will to the contrary?

Which characters does he attempt to empower in this way? Does it make a difference in their lives?

5. A number of secondary characters experience their own emotional journeys in *The King's Mercy*. Which of them do you find most engaging? Why does that character resonate with you? What one character might you like to know more about?

6. The relationship between Phineas Reeves and Demas, the slave he helped to freedom, is darkly codependent, complicated, and discomfiting. When did you first suspect Reeves was behind most of the tragedies that befell the Careys? Did Demas's final actions in the story surprise you?

7. While *The King's Mercy* has a clear antagonist, the main setting, Severn Plantation, is also a force set against Joanna's goals. While chattel slavery is a deplorable institution, does the setting of Severn contain any positive aspects? Of the three regions of North Carolina the characters inhabit— low country (Severn), Piedmont (Mountain Laurel), and mountains (Crooked Branch's town)—which is your favorite setting? What in particular about it appeals to you?

8. The theme of mercy is explored in this story. Which characters need mercy? Which characters show it? Which characters deny it

to another or refuse to receive it themselves? How might their stories have played out differently had they chosen otherwise?

9. Suffering, and an individual's response to it, is another theme explored. Each of the story's main characters—Joanna, Alex, Elijah, Edmund Carey, Reverend Pauling, Jemma, Marigold, Demas, and Phineas Reeves—experience suffering, but their responses to it are vastly different. With whose response do you most identify? Why?

10. Miracles play a part in Reverend Pauling's sharing of the gospel among the Cherokees. Alex's faltering belief in the Almighty is restored, in part, through witnessing these miracles, to a place where he is ready to yield his will to God in faith. Joanna holds to her faith despite the apparent lack of miracles during the same season in her life. Which of them do you think had the most difficult path through this story, in terms of their relationship with God?

11. "Thou hast enlarged me when I was in distress" (Psalm 4:1). Joanna's vision for her life looks very different from the one she's living, and she reaches the point of believing it impossible to realize. Through loss and tragedy her vision eventually comes to pass. Have you experienced a new beginning born from the ashes of something ending, or have

you had a prayer answered as a result of difficult circumstances?

12. Readers may have detected a familiar framework to this story (see the author's notes). Do some story elements and characters in *The King's Mercy* strike you as familiar? If so, from where?

GLOSSARY

GAELIC
tapadh leibh—thank you
Cobhair orm! Na gabh air falbh—Help me!
  Don't go.
mo nighean—my girl
Air do shocair . . . Sin thu, a laochain—Take it
  easy . . . Enough, my good fellow/little hero
sgian dubh—a small, single-edged knife
Tha mi fada nar comain—I am greatly indebted
  to you

SCOTS
wheest—hush; be quiet
loundering—a severe beating
bairn—a small child or infant
stramash—a disturbance; a tumult
thrangity—a press of work; the state of being
  busy
wearit—weary
braw—handsome; worthy; excellent
gang—go

CHEROKEE
S'gi—thank you
Hawa—you're welcome

Ghigau—Beloved Woman
Aniyunwiya—The Real People; the Cherokees
Tsalagi—the Cherokee language
Uwoduhi—a thing of beauty

Books are produced in the United States using U.S.-based materials

Books are printed using a revolutionary new process called THINKtech™ that lowers energy usage by 70% and increases overall quality

Books are durable and flexible because of Smyth-sewing

Paper is sourced using environmentally responsible foresting methods and the paper is acid-free

Center Point Large Print
600 Brooks Road / PO Box 1
Thorndike, ME 04986-0001 USA

(207) 568-3717

US & Canada:
1 800 929-9108
www.centerpointlargeprint.com